CHOSEN DESTINY

TWISTED FATE TRILOGY
BOOK 3

JEN L. GREY

CHAPTER ONE

NO MATTER how hard I clung to the present, the world morphed around me as if I were trying to teleport away from Halfway, Oregon. My wolf howled in protest, the sound ringing in my ears as my heart shattered.

I had to get to Bodey.

He was unconscious and surrounded by Queen Kel's wolves. I shouldn't have encouraged him to run to help his sister Jasmine. Now I might pay the ultimate price, losing my fated mate.

A deep, comforting laugh came from behind me, one I didn't remember hearing before but sounded strangely familiar.

My chest expanded as my surroundings took form.

I stood in the backyard of a huge mansion. The house was a deep gray with two levels. The bottom entrance seemed to lead into a basement and the top into the main area of the house. Stone columns supported the top story.

"Caroline," a warm female voice called from behind me. "We're about to play tag with your brother."

My breath caught. Even though my name was Callie

Caroline fit just as well. I spun toward the voice, and my world tilted.

Ten feet away stood my parents.

Mom's light-brown hair was braided down her back like always, and her dark-chocolate eyes sparkled as she watched me.

At her feet, Samuel turned toward me, his too-large toddler head nearly toppling him over. Even as a baby, he looked like our mother, except for his baby-blue eyes, which twinkled in the twilight.

A lump formed in my throat. What the fuck was going on here? I needed to find my mate. Any other time, I'd be happy to relive whatever *this* was, but not when my mate needed me.

"What's wrong, baby girl?" Dad's ice-blue eyes narrowed as he ran a hand through his ash-blond hair. He held out his arms toward me. "Did you think we were going to leave you out? Every wolf likes to play chase even if they haven't shifted yet."

"Something's wrong," I said, but it wasn't my voice. It was the voice of a five-year-old. A shiver ran down my spine. "Where's Uncle Zeke?"

The warmth in Mom's eyes vanished. "He's gathering his things to leave. We had a disagreement, that's all. Nothing you need to worry about."

Something inside me eased, and I glanced at my hands, noting they were small.

I swallowed hard. This was a memory. There had to be a way to wake up and get back to Bodey.

"Okay." I nodded and ran toward my parents. "I'm it first!"

Dad smiled and wiggled his fingers. "You better not get me, or I'll tickle you to death."

I paused and placed a hand on my hip. "Daddy, you can't

tickle someone to death. That's just silly." Then I bolted toward him.

Despite the lightheartedness swirling through me, my fear of what was going on with Bodey took precedence in my adult mind. Each second I stayed here was another second that the scouts had to kill my mate. I needed to get back to him.

As I leaped onto Dad, Samuel laughed, and Dad followed through on his promise, tickling my sides as I squeaked to roll off him. Then he stood up and yelled, "You better watch out. I'm coming for all of you now."

I yelped and ran to Samuel. My childhood happiness and love swirled within me, mixing with my adult heartbreak. What I wouldn't give to have many more nights like this *and* have Bodey here beside me.

The four of us played for what felt like only minutes, but the night sky engulfed us. Samuel yawned, and Dad picked him up in his arms. "I'll get this little one to bed. Care, head up to the study. I want to go over some things with you before you go to bed."

Heart soaring, I nodded eagerly. I wanted to do everything in my power to make Daddy proud. He was counting on me to help find a way to unite the packs, especially with the new queen of the Southwest. Daddy said he knew her and she had lofty goals, and we needed to be united and strong so she would never attempt to take over our lands. Though he made me promise to keep that part to myself. He didn't want to worry the alpha advisors.

"Come on, Caroline." Mom took my hand. "Let's grab you a snack before Daddy steals you away from me."

I loved our late-night snacks. They usually involved ice cream or chocolate, and on the best occasions, chocolate ice cream. She'd sing to me as she made my snack. That had to be why I always focused on music and lyrics now—they often held so much meaning.

I was getting answers about my past, but I desperately tried to pinch myself awake to help Bodey.

When we followed Dad onto the back terrace, an overly musky scent hit my nose.

Zeke.

I'd never understood why Mommy liked him. He stared at her in ways that made me feel uneasy, and then his gaze would turn to me and harden into something that made me want to disappear. My wolf always helped me lift my chin and not cower.

Mommy stiffened, and her hand clutched mine harder. She rasped, "What are you doing here? You're supposed to be gone."

Her speaking out loud caught me off guard, but then I remembered that she'd told Daddy she had to make sure Zeke understood that their relationship had changed. That had to be why.

Zeke's emerald eyes darkened, and his face twisted in agony. Stepping away from the corner of the house, he rolled up the sleeves of his pale-yellow button-down shirt, revealing more of his dark-olive skin. Adult me noticed there was more black than gray in his hair, unlike his salt-and-pepper look of today. "We need to talk," he said softly. "We've been best friends for forty years—you can't just throw us away."

My stomach clenched. Zeke never talked to anyone like that. He seemed genuinely hurt.

"I'm *with* Richard." She tugged me behind her. "We have two kids, and we *love* each other. You need to get that through your head. You and I have always been *friends*. Nothing more."

I froze, my blood turning to ice. Zeke had been in love with my mother.

"But—"

Mom sighed and linked to me, *Care, I need you to go to the study. I'll be there soon with your favorite snack.*

Chocolate ice cream! I replied. Gone was my discomfort about whatever conversation these two adults were having.

Adult me screamed at young me not to go inside, but my little legs propelled me into the house. I guessed it didn't matter since I couldn't change the events of this memory.

As I hurried into the basement rec room, I heard Daddy telling Samuel good night. Without pausing, I took the wooden stairs straight ahead to the main floor. At the top, I turned left, rushed through the kitchen and dining room, and made it to Daddy's study in less than a minute.

I walked past the huge mahogany desk and hurried to the globe that sat in the far-right corner in front of a built-in bookshelf beside the brick fireplace. When Daddy joined me, the first thing he would do was light the fire. Then we'd sit and talk about whatever business he wanted to keep me in the loop about. He always asked for my opinion and listened to what I had to say, even if he didn't take my advice. He said I had a unique way of looking at the world, and he treasured the insight I gave him.

I spun the globe, playing a game my friend Bodey and I often played when our dads met. Bodey would spin the globe, and wherever I was pointing when it stopped would be one of the places we'd visit together when we got older. The idea of traveling with him made my stomach feel funny.

Adult me knew why it did. Bodey and I had been drawn to each other because we were fated mates. That was why I needed to wake up and get to him *now*.

Daddy stepped into the study, smiling warmly. He arched a brow. "No snack this time?"

Turning around, I pouted. "Mommy said she'd bring it in a minute. Zeke stopped her outside."

His smile changed into a deep frown. "She's talking to him." His eyes glowed, indicating he was linking with Mommy.

"Should I have not left her?" My head hung. "I'm sorry—"

"Oh, baby girl." Dad came over and kissed the top of my head. "You didn't do a thing wrong. You listened to your mother."

My bottom lip quivered. "But—"

"She's heading up now." He winked, though adult Callie could see his tension. "Everything's fine. We just might not see Uncle Zeke for a little while."

"That's good with me." I nodded eagerly.

Daddy laughed. I liked the sound of his laughter. It was one of my favorites, besides Bodey's.

Sounds of Zeke and Mommy echoed through the house, and Daddy scowled. He turned and headed back toward the foyer as he linked, *I'll be right back. If you hear Mr. Valor come in, don't be alarmed. I asked him to return to help with Zeke.*

Zeke's, Mommy's, then Daddy's voices grew louder, and I wrung my hands. I didn't like how they were all fighting.

"Why don't you go into your study?" Zeke growled. "This is between Mila and me."

"There's nothing left to discuss," Mommy replied. "You need to leave."

"Come on, Mila," Daddy said. "Follow me."

"Mila, wait," Zeke said. "Just talk to me a little longer. I need you here for a few more minutes."

All three sets of footsteps headed toward me, and the

three of them paused in front of the study doorway. Daddy's face was flushed in a way I'd never seen before. His nostrils flared, and his eyes glowed. "Leave our house. *Now*."

Something powerful laced his voice, and my wolf trembled within me.

Zeke flinched.

"He didn't want to do that." Mommy shook her head. "I think it's time we cut ties. Lynerd will be announced as the new Oregon royal advisor soon. Go back to your wife and son. Spend time with them. Let me go."

Zeke bowed his head as he strained not to walk away. But his feet moved, step by step, away from the study.

I heard the front door open. Mommy stayed put as if to make sure he'd left as Daddy went to the fireplace.

He'd bent down, his finger touching the button to turn the fireplace on, when Mommy spun around, her eyes locking on mine. She raced toward me, yelling, "Richard! Don't!"

Bile churned in my stomach as Daddy's head turned toward us. Mommy's body crashed into me, shoving me against the wall just as the world shook all around us.

Hot air hit every piece of me, and my mother's body sagged against me like dead weight. The stench of burned flesh and the sound of crackling flames were the last things I experienced before blackness engulfed me.

My body was being jostled, and each jerk felt as if I were burned alive. The movement stopped, and I looked up to see Zeke's tortured eyes staring into mine. Tears dripped down his cheeks as he shook his head and glanced back at the house.

I managed to turn my head enough to see flames shooting from the study's window. Zeke hurried to a car parked at the edge of our property and slid me into the back.

"Fuck," he growled. "Fuck. Fuck. Fuck."

"Samuel," I croaked. He'd been downstairs.

"Michael's here." Zeke ran his hands through his hair, his expression strained. "I can't get him, so we'll do the next best thing. You're coming with me." He closed my door and went to the driver's seat.

The car moved, and my chest constricted. "My brother." Even the little girl version of me knew it was pointless to ask about Mommy and Daddy. My current heartbreak blended with hers, and the tears in our eyes and the pain of our loss hurt worse than her burned skin.

Zeke slammed his hands against the steering wheel. "Shut up!" His breaths came out in *whooshes*. "Let me think. This wasn't how it was supposed to happen. I wasn't supposed to lose *her*." His voice broke on that last word.

Even as his words rang in my little-girl ears, my surroundings faded again.

I tried to force my eyes open. Maybe I'd regret it later if this was the way to get all my memories back, but now I knew Zeke was to blame. He'd been behind everything.

"Callie," Samuel's grown-up voice sounded far away, but something inside me stirred.

Whatever I'd done was working. I just had to keep it up.

A hand gently slapped my cheek, barely making it sting. I wanted to smile, knowing Samuel was probably cringing from such a minor thing.

"Everyone, help search for Bodey," Samuel commanded out loud, not having the luxury of being able to link with everyone like Bodey and I could since being marked as king and queen.

My eyes popped open, and the afternoon light startled me. "Bodey," I whimpered, sitting up. I needed to find him. Through our fated-mate bond, I had the best chance of tracking him down.

But as I tried to stand, my head pounded, and I nearly fell over.

Lucas's strong hand gripped my arm and held me upright. My head throbbed as if a hammer had beaten my brain into a bloody pulp. It felt the same as when Sybil had tried to free my memories.

Sybil.

I turned and saw her dead body a mere ten feet away from me. Blood oozed from her ripped-out neck, and her bronze skin was pasty. Zeke stood by her, staring at me warily.

"Don't move too fast," Lucas said as he moved, blocking my view of the dead witch. He squatted, his dark hair messy from the fight and his dark-brown eyes filled with concern. Blood trickled from the scratches down his arm.

Guys, he's gone, Jack linked, and we all felt his trepidation. *There's no sign of him, not even his scent. They must have had a witch here.*

My mate was gone. He'd been taken from me. And this man not even fifteen feet away was the cause. Maybe not directly, but he'd killed my parents and set all of this into motion.

All the wolves have retreated, Miles replied.

Anger boiled within me, and I stood up straight, my mind clear and begging for Zeke's blood. "You," I snarled and lunged at him.

CHAPTER TWO

ZEKE STUMBLED BACK A FEW STEPS, but I countered each move, my wolf surging forward, wanting blood as desperately as I did.

His eyes widened as I barreled into his chest, both hands punching his ribs.

"Get off me!" he spat, but I heard the fear behind his voice.

Good. I wanted him to feel what my mother had felt before the explosion. I wanted him to die the same way —terrified.

I punched him in the face as my arms tingled from my wolf surging forward. He fell backward and landed on his butt, me half on top of him.

A *hmph* escaped him as the impact jarred us. Hoping he was distracted, I snaked my left hand around his waist, trying to pry the knife he had to defend against Kel's wolves away from him as my wolf pushed forward. She wanted to taste his blood as much as my human side wanted to make him bleed. In animal form, I could make both of those things happen.

The sound was damn near intoxicating. I wanted to watch

as his blood pooled under him from my teeth in his neck. I wanted to see him slowly bleed out as the life drained from him.

Who knew I'd ever be like this? But after everything this bastard had done, my humanity faltered.

"Callie!" Samuel shouted, his arms wrapping around my waist and pulling me back.

Oh, fuck no. This bastard was the reason my parents were dead, why I'd lost so much time with my brother, and why his pack had abused me for most of my life. I also suspected he'd been involved in this latest attack, which had resulted in my mate's disappearance. Death was the punishment he deserved.

I elbowed Samuel in the face and clawed Zeke's cheek. My nails dug into his skin, scraping his cheek raw, but it wasn't enough. I needed to hurt him more.

Pain flashed through my connection with Samuel, but hot rage blinded me. All I could see was Zeke's face and the hell he'd put everyone through.

Another pair of arms snaked around my waist just as Zeke loosened his hold on the knife, and I swiped it from him.

What's wrong? Lucas asked as he tried to pull me off Zeke.

I tried to elbow him in the face, but Lucas had anticipated the move, and I missed my mark. I tucked my legs underneath me, striking out and landing a fist in his stomach. Lucas grunted but held firm as I desperately swung the knife at Zeke's chest, aiming for his heart.

For whatever reason, my wolf couldn't surge forward any further, which was okay with me. I could inflict a bad enough injury in my human form. It'd be a slower death this way, anyway. The scent of fresh blood hit my nose, making my wolf eager for more.

"Callie, I hate the guy too, but we need to focus on finding Bodey." Samuel's voice came out more nasally than usual.

I froze.

Bodey.

He was right. The more time I spent on Zeke, the farther away Bodey would be. I stopped fighting, and Lucas lifted me with ease and placed me on my feet.

I stared at Zeke, unable to tear my gaze off him. I'd missed his heart by inches, stabbing him in the upper right chest. I hoped I'd hit a major artery.

"What the *hell* is wrong with you?" Zeke grunted as he sat up and glared at the knife protruding from his body. "That was an unwarranted attack! If that's—"

"Unwarranted?" Rage had my skin boiling uncomfortably. "You *killed* my parents and would have killed me too, if it hadn't been for my mom!"

His face blanched, and his eyes widened.

"You got your memories back?" Samuel moved to my side.

I glanced at him, and bile burned my throat. His nose was slightly crooked, and blood poured from it. I flinched as remorse slammed into me. I'd hurt my baby brother—the last blood family I had left. "Yes, I did. And I'm sorry for doing that." I gestured at his face.

Zeke tried to get up, likely to escape but groaned from his injury.

Wolves dotted the tree line, and Lucas hurried to Bodey's Mercedes SUV and popped the trunk. Luckily, Bodey had left the keys in the car when he'd raced to open it in the hope we could get Sybil away before the wolves learned about our plan and attacked us in the open.

My heart thundered as I searched for the human who'd witnessed the bloodbath. No more humans had driven by yet. Blessedly, Halfway was a small town.

The human lay unconscious on the ground ten feet away from Zeke, which was probably a good thing. We needed to bring a witch here quickly to alter his memory.

Lucas grabbed a black duffel from the back seat of the SUV and raced toward the tree line. Miles, Jack, and Jasmine had to be there, wanting to shift back into human form.

Now that I'd calmed from reliving my memory, logic was catching up to me again. Finding Bodey and getting him back was my priority, even over killing Zeke.

We need more wolves out there, searching for Bodey, I linked with Blake, his twenty pack members, Theo, Lucas, Samuel, Jasmine, Jack, Miles, and the former advisors—Michael, Dan, Phil, and Carl.

Don't worry. The four of us are still searching the area, Michael linked. *They couldn't have taken him too far yet.*

Of course Michael would be almost as frantic as me. Bodey was his son, and of all the former advisors, Michael knew how crucial it was to retrieve him. If Queen Kel had taken my mate captive, I'd do *anything* to get him back.

I connected with my wolf, trying to urge her forward, but pain flared in my head again, and my surroundings shifted as I fell back into the past.

The sky was a faint orange as if the sun were rising. My skin still burned. I opened my eyes to find another man in the car, sitting in the passenger seat.

He glanced back at me. Unlike Zeke, this man's dark eyes were warm with kindness. He scratched at his cinnamon-colored beard and shook his head. "We need to take her to our coven, not meet some random witch near the mansion. She's hurt and needs protection—she's our future queen."

"She's going to be *protected.*" Zeke spat out the word with hatred behind it that was all too familiar to this day. "She's Mila's *daughter,* for gods' sake."

The man's expression softened. "I'm sorry. This has to be a hard night for you too. You lost the love of your life."

Love of your life.

Those words had young me confused but sickened adult me even more. That was Zeke's motivation. He hadn't just been enamored of my mother—he'd truly believed they were meant to be together. My skin crawled, though my body didn't move since I was trapped inside the memory of my five-year-old self.

"You don't know what I'm feeling," Zeke said coldly. "So please be quiet."

The passenger nodded, and I suspected this was the best friend Zeke never spoke of. I tried to remember his name, but it eluded me.

The man turned and stared at me again. "She must look like him. She looks nothing like Mila."

"Believe me." Zeke scoffed. "She does." Bitterness dripped from each word.

"That must be hard—"

"Dammit, Nick. Shut up. I don't want to talk about Mila or Caroline anymore. I need to get her to this witch, and I need you to keep an eye out to make sure no one sees us here."

Silence descended, and my eyes grew heavy as pain engulfed me.

THE CAR JERKED TO A STOP, and my eyes fluttered open. The burning pain was horrible, which meant my body must have taken one hell of a hit despite Mom blocking me from the worst of the blast.

Even though I wanted to turn my head to see my arms, my body remained still.

"Let's get this over with," Zeke bit out as the driver's door swung open.

Nick sighed. "You act as if this is difficult, but it's not. The witch will heal her, that's all. Though I don't understand why we're doing this in secret."

I knew why. He was going to have my memories erased. I wondered if that was why his best friend had died—he'd learned the truth and tried to stop Zeke.

The door by my head opened, and Zeke popped inside, leaning over me. "If the other royal advisors learn about this, they'll try to take her from me. You know alphas always want control over the most powerful."

A laugh bubbled in my throat, but my kid version was frozen in terror. Even then, I'd known I couldn't defend myself and that Zeke was involved in what had happened to my parents.

"No," I murmured, but Zeke already had his arms underneath me, pulling me out. My skin felt as if it were on fire as I was jostled and cradled against his chest.

He murmured in my ear, "Say another word and your parents won't be the only ones you mourn. Samuel is still alive."

I swallowed hard and focused on the connection I knew was Samuel. After Zeke did whatever, I would find my brother and tell Michael about the strange fight between my parents and Zeke moments before the explosion.

My heart panged. That wouldn't happen. Adult me knew the outcome: I'd lose seventeen years with my brother and Bodey.

Bodey.

I needed to snap myself out of this memory so I could find him. But Fate was being a bitch, keeping the very thing I wanted most desperately in life just out of my grasp.

"So where—" Nick started, but the soft sound of approaching feet cut him off.

"Where is he?" a woman's voice asked from behind Zeke.

Zeke turned to her, and the world swirled around me. My body throbbed from every spot he touched, and my skin burned from the chilly breeze that wafted across me. Zeke's chest rumbled as he replied, "He's here. You'll get him once you do what you promised."

The woman took in a shaky breath. "Fine. Bring the girl to me."

"Are you sure about this?" Nick asked from his spot beside the car. "Maybe—"

"Go check on the witch and make sure she doesn't have something that will hurt Caroline," Zeke commanded, but his arms tightened around me and shook faintly.

The hair on the nape of my neck rose.

"Fine." Nick sighed. "I can do that."

I heard Nick walk past us, and Zeke's heartbeat quickened.

Something was about to go down.

As the man approached the witch, the woman said, "On your knees."

The wind picked up, rushing past us toward Nick, and forced him to his knees.

"Zeke!" Nick yelled, but Zeke stood still.

Something wet hit my face, and I opened my eyes to see a tear drip off Zeke's chin and fall on me.

He was crying.

"Take this sacrifice to bind the girl's wolf," the woman chanted. "Bring the girl to me."

Zeke moved forward without hesitation as more tears hit my face. He laid me on the ground, and Nick's eyes were so wide that the whites showed all around.

The witch's dark-blue hair hung in her face, and her dark skin glistened from the magic churning within. She held out a hand. "I need the knife."

"Knife?" Nick's voice quivered. "Zeke, what the fuck is going on? Tell her to let me go." The wind continually whipped around him, causing him to stay frozen on all fours with his head raised, staring at us.

Something sharp lodged in my throat. When she met me, Dina had said I had blood magic all over me. This had to be it.

I watched the witch, who had to be Salem, take the knife from Zeke and yank Nick's head up with her free hand. Her face twisted, and she murmured to Nick, "Please forgive me." Then she slit his throat. "With this sacrifice, lock down the girl's wolf until a mutual exchange of blood occurs between her and her mate." She lifted the knife, the blood dripping off the end onto her fingertips.

Blood trickled from the corners of Nick's mouth, his skin already pale from the knife's direct blow.

Salem walked over to me and rubbed a bloody finger over my forehead. Her bottom lip quivered. "This seals the sacrifice, and the wolf will be bound from now until the exchange of blood happens."

The warmth I now knew was my wolf burrowed deep inside, and something cold covered it like a blanket. I wished I were old enough to shift and pack link with everyone, but all I could do was scream, "No! Please."

But it was done, and I knew it would take me seventeen years to feel her again.

"Now heal her and make her forget everything," Zeke commanded.

My eyes were already closing, the agony of losing my wolf and the pain of my injuries taking me under.

I woke up in the present, inside the real estate office.

Michael, Dan, Phil, and Carl were pacing in front of me, and a woman I didn't know was standing in front of the human, touching her fingers to his forehead.

When I sat up straight in the chair they'd placed me in, Michael turned to me. He looked relieved. "Thank gods you're awake. We were worried." Michael's chestnut hair had a bit of gray coming in on the sides, and his jade eyes were darker than normal from everything that had gone on.

"I remember everything." I stood, wanting to find Zeke. Rage charged through me. "Where's Zeke?"

"He's in the kitchen." Carl gestured toward the door behind me. His blond hair was messier than usual, giving him a younger appearance.

Phil took a few steps closer to me. His dark-bronze skin hid the faint scars of his wounds, which had mostly healed, and he rubbed his ebony beard. "What did Zeke do? For you to beat him up like that—"

Dan lifted a hand. "I'm sure we're about to find out." His spiked brown hair stuck out in every direction, and his tan complexion emphasized the dark circles under his eyes. "My son, Miles, Samuel, and Jack are back there with him. We should join them now that she's okay."

That was fine with me. We needed to come up with a plan. I spun on my heels and headed toward the kitchen as I linked with everyone—the royal advisors, Samuel, Jasmine, and the former advisors. *Did we pick up signs of Bodey?*

No. We found tire marks and his scent before it vanished, Michael replied, tensing beside me.

In the kitchen, Jasmine hovered in one corner with her arms around her waist. Her strawberry-blonde hair was tangled, and her jade-green eyes were cast downward. She looked guilty.

Theo hovered next to her. His caramel-brown hair fell

into his face, and his topaz eyes were locked on her. He stood a little in front of her, ready to defend her if anyone attacked.

Zeke was sitting at the table with Jack, Lucas, Miles, and Samuel around him. Even better, the knife was still protruding from his chest, so obviously, the witch hadn't healed him.

Samuel's shirt had blood on the front, but I was relieved to see his nose was no longer bleeding. At least that had healed.

The former advisors surrounded me as Miles and Jack stood from the table and took a few steps back, making room for me. I moved between them as Jack's cobalt eyes flicked to me before focusing back on Zeke. Miles crossed his arms, emphasizing his thick build, and his dark-green eyes narrowed.

Queen Kel's promise from the night we met rang in my ears. She'd vowed to take everything I loved from me, and I feared Bodey was the first part of her fulfilling that vow. "Are you working with the queen?"

Zeke's brows lifted almost comically. "That wasn't the first question I expected you to ask."

Fury rose inside me once more. "Oh, I'm sure you know what I remember." I pointed at the knife. "To be clear, that was meant for your heart. Be glad Lucas and Samuel were trying to pull me away from you." I leaned forward, getting into his face.

He winced before his mask of indifference slid back into place.

I smirked, enjoying causing him discomfort. "You see, I don't need to ask any questions about my parents' deaths or how my memories got locked. I remember *everything*. What I don't know but suspect is whether you're working with Queen Kel. Tell me the truth, or I'll cut it out of you."

Part of me hoped he didn't tell me. The thought of causing him more pain sent a thrill right through me.

He must have seen it because his Adam's apple bobbed. "Yes. That's who I was texting the entire time."

Though I wanted to hurt him, my desire to get my mate back was stronger. "Good. Then you're going to get Bodey back for us."

"What?" Zeke's mouth dropped open. "You can't be serious."

I punched him in the face, and his head jerked to the side.

Jack snorted. "I think she *is* serious, but if you need to ask her again, I'm here for it."

Normally, Lucas would have smacked Jack in the back of the head and told him this wasn't the time, but everyone wanted to see Zeke get punched again.

"Let me say this again." My wolf surged forward, brushing my mind as power laced my voice. "You will get Bodey back. I don't care what it takes."

"That's what I'm trying to tell you." He blew out a breath, his eyes lowering in submission. "She won't listen to me."

My phone rang in my pocket, and I jolted. I'd forgotten it was there. I pulled it out, and Queen Kel's name scrolled across the screen.

Fuck. Speak of the devil...

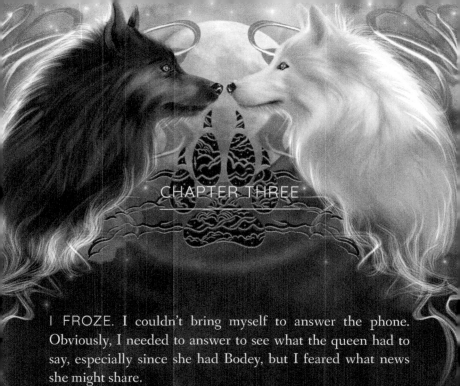

CHAPTER THREE

I FROZE. I couldn't bring myself to answer the phone. Obviously, I needed to answer to see what the queen had to say, especially since she had Bodey, but I feared what news she might share.

I rubbed my chest, still feeling our mate link. He wasn't dead.

The phone rang a third time.

"You should answer that, Callie." Zeke snickered, glancing down at the phone in my hand. "It's probably about your *mate,* after all." The word dripped with disdain.

"It's Caroline to you," I spat as I swiped the answer button on the phone. Michael inhaled as I put the phone to my ear and said, "Hello."

Theo murmured, "Why is she calling herself Caroline?"

"That's her birth name," Miles replied. "She really does have her memories back."

Of course they'd know that. The former advisors and their sons had been around me as a child. Flashes of memories of them coming to our house to meet with my dad while the guys gave me a hard time played in my mind.

"Ah... I was beginning to wonder if you would answer." Kel clicked her tongue. "I'm thinking the king consort doesn't mean as much to you as I thought."

Her insinuation had me growling before I could stop myself. "I will *kill* you and relish each moment."

Jasmine flinched, wrapping her arms tighter around her waist. Her guilt poured into our bond. Even though I hadn't put the call on speakerphone because Zeke was here, everyone could hear what Kel was saying due to their wolf hearing.

"Now Callie—" Kel started.

"It's Queen Caroline to you." That was the name my parents had given me, and I'd be damned if I allowed her to call me anything else.

Samuel went to Jasmine and placed a hand on her shoulder. Theo's jaw tensed, but I didn't have the energy to focus on whatever was brewing between him and my new sister.

"See!" Kel laughed, the sound caressing me like a piece of silk—smooth and comforting and a way to hide the evil within. "You did get my present, and you're still threatening to kill me. Poor form. It's polite to thank someone who helped you out."

I laughed bitterly. "Taking my mate is not a present. If you don't want to make me a real enemy, bring him back to me now."

"Silly girl. My present was killing the witch for you."

I gritted my teeth. "How was that a present?" This woman didn't understand the concept of giving gifts.

"It gave you what you wanted." She chuckled darkly. "Your memories are back."

"Sybil was about to unblock them when you attacked and killed her." I didn't want Kel to think I was indebted to her in *any* way. "If you wanted to gift me something, Zeke should've been your target."

She laughed loudly. I imagined her throwing her head back, her dark, full hair flowing around her. "Zeke said you were weak and didn't have the stomach for such things. I'm glad he was wrong. Tell me, is Zeke still alive, or have you already killed him?"

"He's alive." I couldn't hide the disappointment in my voice.

"Ah... that's unfortunate. He's a weasel, but then again, you'd know better than anyone. Did he mention that he was the real reason we were able to attack the coronation?"

Zeke flinched as every person in the kitchen glared at him.

"Dad?" Theo gasped. "That was you?"

"She's the queen." Zeke gestured to the phone in my hand. "She could be lying about everything!"

"That's not an answer." Samuel marched back to our group and stopped between Lucas and Michael.

"Did he share that he orchestrated getting my prisoner out of his basement?" Her voice was so animated.

I wanted to rip his throat out, but she wanted us to focus on Zeke... to fight among ourselves. That would make it easier for her to take over our territory. I couldn't allow that to happen.

The former advisors closed in around me, blocking Zeke from attempting to leave.

Samuel lifted a hand. "We need to wait."

I nodded and linked to everyone but Zeke, *This is a tactic to turn us against each other. We can't fall for it.* I was thankful that my brother must have come to the same conclusion I had.

Jack huffed, but no one moved closer to Zeke.

This call needed to end before all rational thought left me.

Bodey was way too important to let her distract us from my goal: getting my mate back.

"What do you want?" I asked, cutting through the bull-shit. "You called for a reason, and I doubt it was to out Zeke. None of us trusts him anyway, but my memories justified my reasons."

"Fine." She sighed dramatically. "I was hoping to have more fun and get you to see how much you should appreciate everything I've done for you."

A laugh escaped from deep in my chest, and I nearly coughed. "Everything you've *done* for me? I fail to understand what you're insinuating. Once again, I could've gotten my memories back from Sybil without you *killing* her."

"I'm not so sure. Zeke wasn't going to *allow* you to get them back." She blew out a breath. "It's foolish of you to think you had things handled."

Every fiber in me wanted to reach through the phone and strangle the cocky bitch. "Sybil was releasing my memories when your wolves attacked. Your attack stopped her magic."

"Still so young and naive," she cooed. "Zeke was messaging me, telling me to attack before he took matters into his own hands."

My eyes flicked to Zeke again, and sweat beaded on his brow. He might try to deny it, but his reaction showed the truth. I didn't need to bother questioning him. "How? Killing her made my memories return."

"Who said anything about killing her?" She *tsk*ed. "He could've fallen into her, breaking the spell before it could be completed, or claimed he got some worrisome news and you needed to leave. There are endless possibilities. This is why I need to take charge of your territories. You're too naive to lead. You weren't raised as a royal and trained to lead your people."

I hated that I'd given her the opportunity to say that. I felt inadequate enough without having her throw inexperience in my face. "Don't put yourself out. I'm a fast learner, which is why I'm going to ask what you want one more time before hanging up."

"Please. You won't hang up when you know your *mate* is in my possession." She paused. "Or, rather, will be soon unless you give me a reason to kill him."

"If you hurt so much as a hair on his head, I will rip out your throat." I'd never understood the expression *I saw red* until that moment. Red infused my vision even as my senses strengthened, making it hard to remain logical. I could hear every person's heartbeat. My head began to swim.

"A fight between us is inevitable and may happen sooner than you realize."

We all glanced at one another.

Her words sounded more like a promise than a threat. A shiver coursed down my spine.

"No questions?" A door slammed shut on her end. "How boring. I'll answer what I know you want to ask. I have an offer for you."

My heart hammered. I doubted it was a true offer, but she was right. There was no way I'd hang up. Not with Bodey in her custody.

I forced myself to remain quiet, which took every ounce of willpower I could muster. I wanted her to get on with it so I could focus on getting my mate back. I needed him beside me.

It was like Fate wanted me to lose everyone near and dear to my heart, just as Queen Kel had vowed.

Hatred curdled within me. She didn't give a shit about Zeke; she just wanted to remind me of everything I'd lost to break me.

I'd thought I could never hate someone as much as I hated Zeke, but boy, she was determined to prove me wrong.

Kel remained quiet, dragging out the moment, wanting me to break.

The problem was, if I broke, I would confirm she had complete control over me, and that would further jeopardize Bodey's safety.

I ground my teeth together, and an ache shot through my jaw.

"Even though you're not saying a word, *Caroline*," the queen said, "I can hear your rapid breathing. So I'll still make this kind offer since I know you're *invested*."

Jack and Miles inched closer to me, their arms touching mine, maybe afraid I might snap.

In fairness, I might.

"I'll give Bodey back to you if you submit to me."

The word *done* was right on my lips, but I held it back. I'd seen how her promise not to attack us at the meeting spot had turned out. She'd chosen her words carefully and had instead attacked two of our packs in other locations.

"Not good enough." I wanted to throw the phone, but then I couldn't negotiate. "For all I know, you'll give him back dead or on the brink of death. I'm not falling for your games."

She snickered. "Look at you. You learned something."

"I told you I'm a fast learner." I couldn't falter. Dad had told me during my time with him in the study that, to an adversary, it was the first sign they had you where they wanted you. Worse, he'd been talking about Queen Kel and how, if we didn't stop her, she'd eventually become a dangerous adversary.

And here we were, in the exact situation he'd foreseen.

"What assurance do I have that Bodey will be

unharmed?" I asked, keeping my voice steady, though all I wanted to do was shriek.

You can't be serious. Samuel stared at me, mouth slack. *There's no way you're going to hand yourself over to her. As soon as you submit, she'll kill you. You're the biggest threat to her reign.*

Even though he was right, there was something he didn't realize: I had no intention of submitting to Kel. A lifetime of torture and mistreatment had prepared me for the exchange. As long as Bodey came back in one piece, the risk would be minimal because Samuel had been trained to rule. This option would prevent Queen Kel from following through on her promise to take everyone I loved away from me. I would save my family and my people. x

"Since capturing your mate, it sounds like you've come to your senses." She chuckled.

"That doesn't answer my question." All of this ended now. "Before we make the exchange, I need to link with my mate and make sure he's well."

Absolutely not. Michael shook his head. *This isn't happening.*

My head jerked back. I hadn't expected him to discourage the exchange—this was his son we were talking about.

"Deal." Queen Kel laughed. "I'll call you in two days."

"What?" I gasped. "No. We do it now."

"Nope. That's not how this works. I need to make sure you don't do anything foolish. After two days, you should be willing to do anything to get your mate back since you refuse to sacrifice him."

Pulse galloping, I didn't know what to do. Two days without Bodey would be torture, but if I truly handed myself over to her, I would be without him for a lot longer than two days. "There's no need—"

"I'll call you when it's time to meet. Don't do anything stupid. I'd hate for your mate to get injured." She hung up, but I kept the phone to my ear as if that would make her come back on.

Call— Miles flinched before clearing his throat. *Caroline, did she hang up?*

I nodded. I looked at the screen to make sure she'd disconnected. "She's gone."

"There's no way you're handing yourself over to her." Jack shook his head. "I admit I have some pretty dumb ideas, but you just surpassed *me.*" He knocked his hand against his chest, emphasizing the point.

"I have no intention of submitting to the queen if that's what you're worried about." I looked at Zeke and wrinkled my nose. "Someone here taught me to endure pain and hatred."

Zeke straightened his shoulders and winced when the knife in his chest shifted.

"You're the rightful queen," Phil said from behind me. He placed a hand on my shoulder, urging me to turn around. "If you become weak, so do the rest of us. Don't you see? Even if you don't submit, if you're weaker than she is, she could take over our territory. Our power is only as strong as our alpha's."

I barely managed to swallow around the lump in my throat. I remembered another thing my father had told me: *Our people are at their strongest when we're at ours. A weak king or queen makes a pack vulnerable to a takeover. It's better for a royal to submit than to allow her people to be weakened. By submitting, the wolves in our territory can still fight against the new queen and try to break free.*

My wolf surged forward, refusing to let me seem weak. That had to be what she'd been doing inside me while she'd been locked down. She'd had just enough influence to make me refuse to cower.

The truth was that I might remember things, but I still wasn't fit to lead. I'd thought I could do the right thing by handing myself over, but again, I would be playing right into Queen Kel's hands. Worse, if I submitted and she killed me, she'd turn her focus on Samuel. He would be as big of a threat as me.

But leaving Bodey with her wasn't an option. "What do we do?" I asked, needing their help. I had no clue where to go from here. "We've got to bring Bodey home."

Jasmine cleared her throat. "I have an idea."

CHAPTER FOUR

EVERY HEAD TURNED TOWARD JASMINE, and she wrung her hands as if she didn't like the attention. To her credit, she stood taller and said, "Remember what I told you, Samuel, and Bodey in the car on the way to Lynerd's?"

I stared at her. Between regaining old memories that somehow felt like new ones, the fight, and the deep ache from losing Bodey, my head was foggy.

"Can you just tell us?" Samuel rubbed his temples. "It's been a long day, and I don't feel like guessing."

She lifted her hands. "Yeah, sorry. My best friend back at university is a wolf shifter from the Midwest pack. I've met her dad, and he's one of the strongest alphas in that region. He holds a position similar to the royal advisors here. They might be willing to help."

That dangerous feeling of hope spread through my chest, anchoring me in the present. Bodey had brushed her off, but I had been planning on talking to her about it later. Now was the perfect time.

Miles steepled his hands. "Why would they consider helping us? It would put them on Queen Kel's radar."

"They already are." She stepped closer to us. "That's what I was trying to tell you, but you were all more focused on Lynerd, and rightfully so. When Queen Kel visited them a year ago, she made it clear they should follow her. They told her no."

My brows rose. "Then why is she attacking us?" The Midwest would be easier to take down—they had smaller numbers than we did.

"Because we're closer." Carl took a few steps back and leaned against the counter. "Even though we're larger than her packs, we're spread out farther, and she can easily retreat into her own territory to regroup."

The Midwest was almost half our size, and the wolves did live close to one another. Their supreme alpha, King Sutton, lived outside of Minneapolis, Minnesota.

Dan pursed his lips. "Not only that, but their cities are larger, so there are more humans around."

I didn't care why we'd been attacked first. One thing was more important than hearing any more theories from Jasmine or anyone else. "There's something we need to address." I pointed at Zeke. "We need to execute him."

Zeke tensed and glanced down at the knife protruding from his chest.

Theo gasped. "Callie, you can't be—"

"Serious?" I cut him off, glaring at him. "Oh, I'm *deadly* serious."

Jack snorted. "I know now isn't the time, but damn, I'm so glad we protected her."

"Man." Lucas shook his head yet still didn't smack his friend.

"Listen to my son—he has my pack's best interests at heart," Zeke practically croaked.

"Your pack's best *interests* at heart?" I wrinkled my nose.

"Killing the king *and* the queen, then kidnapping the princess to block her wolf and hide her memories, were only in *your* best interest. Don't act like you're the victim here."

Forehead wrinkling, Theo blinked. "Dad, you did all that? Working with Queen Kel was shitty, but this..."

"None of us are fans of Zeke." Michael patted my back. "I know we're reeling from Bodey's capture, but killing Zeke won't fix it."

I cut my eyes to the man I now saw as a father figure. Not even my adoptive dad had shown me much affection, saving most for Pearl and Stevie. "It might make us feel better."

"It might, but we'd regret it soon enough."

"Fine." They were right. Death was too much of a blessing for Zeke. He should stay alive and suffer for what he'd done to my parents, which meant stripping him of every inch of power, beginning *now*. "He needs to go somewhere he can't hear our conversation. I don't trust him. For all we know, this could be an act he set up with the queen."

"It's not." Zeke laughed dryly, then groaned. "Believe me. I wish that wasn't the case, but the Southwest queen and I are no longer working together in any capacity."

There was no stench of a lie, but that wasn't enough proof for me. "Remove his cell phone and take him away. Also, get the witch to heal him enough so he doesn't die, but I want him to feel the pain of his injury and heal on his own." I smiled sweetly and batted my eyes. "That was what he did for me."

Evil woman, Jack linked to Lucas, Miles, and me as he beamed. *It's going to kill him to be excluded from talks.*

Hopefully, I replied. "Carl, Phil, and Dan, will you please take Zeke to the witch? Make sure the human's ready to be released, and let's deal with Zeke. The witch needs to do whatever she can to ensure Zeke doesn't hear a damn word. I don't care if she knocks him out or busts his eardrums."

Zeke's face turned scarlet. "You need my—"

I shoved past Miles and Jack, knocking them both to the side. I got in Zeke's face, allowing my wolf to surge forward. "I don't need, nor do I want, *anything* from you. I blame you for *everything* that's happened since the moment you killed my parents."

His bottom lip quivered. "She wasn't supposed to die! Only *him*. We were supposed to be together, but you had to be in the study. She went to save you. *You* killed her."

I punched him in the face so hard that my knuckles throbbed, but seeing his head snap back and his face contort in anguish was worth possibly breaking my hand.

"She didn't *want* you." I sneered. "And I'm not the one who cut the gas line to the fireplace."

Zeke flinched as if I'd struck him again.

"I still don't understand how you all didn't smell it." Samuel shook his head, his face twisted in pain.

Phil wrinkled his nose. "Because the house was originally built before gas companies had to add the smell. Even wolf shifters couldn't smell gas leaks before then."

Call—Caroline, I know you're upset, but we need to focus on Queen Kel and saving Bodey, Michael linked, again grounding me.

I was letting my emotions take control, and Bodey would pay for my mistake. "Take him out of here. Samuel and I need time to calm down and decide how to handle Zeke. We all need to focus on saving my mate."

The three older men nodded, walking past their sons and forcing Zeke to his feet. Zeke didn't fight, but that could've been because of the knife lodged in his chest.

I moved next to the chair he'd been sitting in and leaned against the wall where I could see everyone.

Losing Bodey had taken a toll on Michael. Dark circles

lined his eyes, and his face was taut. Despite that, he was still focused on the goal while I was allowing my pain and anger to take over. I had to rein in my emotions.

My gaze landed on Jasmine, and my heart broke. Guilt wafted off her through our regular pack link. I wanted to say something but now wasn't the time. Not in front of everyone.

Theo's eyes were narrowed. "I'm so sorry. If I'd known about *any* of that..." He rubbed a hand through his hair, making it even shaggier.

"Don't." I lifted a hand. "You were just a child. There's nothing you need to apologize for." I was glad to see him taking it this hard. If he had been involved in my parents' deaths, I would have questioned everything.

When the three men returned, Carl said, "The witch put him to sleep. He can't hear anything, and she's leading the human outside."

Good. Now we could focus on what mattered most. My gaze landed back on Jasmine. "Do you think your friend's pack might be willing to help?"

She mashed her lips together. "I don't know, but I can call them and ask. What's the worst they can say?"

"The worst isn't what they could say." Samuel tilted his head as he took the spot next to me. "They could attack us while we're focused on Queen Kel."

My chest tightened. They both had a point.

"They're not like that." Jasmine placed a hand on her chest. "Katelin is a great person, and when she took me home with her for a long weekend, I met her dad, Russell, and her other pack members. They're just like us—they support and care about each other. They wouldn't take advantage of us."

Michael sighed and ran his hands over his jeans. "Russell might not, but what if King Sutton does? None of us have met with him since King Richard's, Queen Mila's, and Princess..."

He trailed off, his gaze landing on me. He coughed and continued, "Since the king and queen's memorial."

A chill ran through me. I hadn't considered that I'd been given a memorial, and for some reason, that didn't sit well with me. All those people saying goodbye, only for me to be alive and hidden from them. Fury bubbled up again, but I tamped it down. "What type of person was he then?"

Phil bit his bottom lip. "He'd only been ruling for about seven years then, but he seemed confident and steady."

"King Richard had hoped you and he could bridge the gap between the territories in a few years," Dan added, a small smile on his face. "King Sutton's mate had just gotten pregnant, and he thought that children might be another way to bring us closer, as the royal families could relate to each other in more ways than just running a kingdom."

An alpha is as strong as the family and friends they surround themselves with. My dad's voice replayed in my head. *And King Sutton seems to have good people around him.* Dad had been right regarding his concerns about Kel, so I had no reason to doubt his judgment now.

Samuel waved a hand. "Which never happened, so I'm not sure we should trust a stranger none of us has seen in seventeen years." Unease flowed off him in waves.

I understood his trepidation. I'd changed significantly in the last few weeks, so there was no doubt someone could change over many years. "Okay, what do you suggest? As I see it, we have three options. Two involve me handing myself over to the queen, and one is asking the Midwest pack for assistance. I'm open to any and all other ideas."

The room fell silent as Jasmine bounced on her feet.

After several long seconds, I made eye contact with each person. "Anyone?"

Lucas shrugged. "I've got nothing."

"Handing you over isn't an option." Miles arched a brow while meeting my gaze head-on.

My wolf surged forward, feeling threatened, and a low growl came from my chest. Though I knew he wasn't challenging my position, I didn't like him telling me I couldn't do something.

His bottom lip quivered, but he kept his attention on me. I had no doubt I was stronger than him, and I forced my wolf down. Forcing people to bend to my will because they thought differently from me was the exact thing I'd vowed I wouldn't do. Besides, Miles and I knew if I alpha-willed him to let me go, he wouldn't have any option but to obey.

My wolf didn't completely recede until Miles had looked away.

"We only have one good option." I looked at Bodey's sister. "Jasmine, make the call."

"What?" Samuel's head snapped toward me. "I don't think that's the right decision."

I crossed my arms and nodded. "So you want me to hand myself over?"

He shook his head. "Absolutely not."

My heart dropped. "Are you saying you want us to *allow* her to keep Bodey?"

Samuel's cheeks reddened. "We'll get him back. I'm not saying—"

"Not happening." I karate-chopped the air and filled my lungs, trying to calm down. "She's agreed to meet us. This is a way to get her out into the open instead of storming her home. I won't give up this opportunity even if it requires handing myself over. Do you understand?" I couldn't risk her killing Bodey. I'd already lost too many people I loved, and I wouldn't add him or anyone else in this room to that list.

His nostrils flared. "Your life means more than his."

I fisted my hands. "No, it doesn't. If anything happened to him, I would change. Hell, I'm barely hanging on to who I am, knowing he's with them."

"I'll make the call." Jasmine removed her phone from her back pocket.

"Wait." I begrudgingly turned my attention away from Samuel and asked her, "Are you sure about this?"

She hit her chest. "I swear to you, I trust them. I wouldn't put the rest of my family in danger." Jasmine's eyes glistened with sincerity.

"Fine. Make the call, but do it here." I gestured to the door that led outside. "I don't want to risk anyone overhearing you besides the people in this room."

She grabbed the phone and dialed as she paced in the corner. Nerves wafted off her, and the former advisors, Jack, Lucas, and Miles, formed a tight circle around me.

In the corner, Theo fidgeted uncomfortably. "I'll check on Dad while you work on this." He winced. "Not that I agree with him, but…"

That was for the best. I'd rather Theo not know everything. Zeke was his dad, and it was nearly impossible to break the familial bond. I smiled sadly. "I get it."

He blew out a breath. "Thanks. I'll be back shortly." He hurried past us and out the door.

"There's something else we all need to discuss," I murmured to the eight men around me. "Before my parents died, they made it clear to each other in front of me that they were about to strip Zeke as the royal advisor and put Lynerd in his place."

Michael's eyebrows shot up. "King Richard asked me to come see him because something was going on with Zeke. I didn't know it was that."

Jasmine mumbled quietly, but I heard a young woman's voice reply to her.

"I don't think he knew." I licked my lips. "I think he was trying to get Mom to be with him. She kept saying she was with Dad. I wasn't around for whatever caused the disagreement, but since Lynerd was cleared of working with Queen Kel, we need to hand Oregon over to him."

"Fuck yeah," Jack agreed. "There's no reason not to now that your memories are back."

He was right. Before, we had no real proof to force Zeke to step down, but now I knew what he'd done, and he'd confessed in front of everyone here. "We'll do it as soon as we get back to Lynerd's." My chest constricted. We'd have to tell him what had happened to Sybil, and it wouldn't go well.

"What about Theo?" Lucas scratched his scruff. "How is he going to take the demotion?"

Samuel snorted. "How can it be a demotion when he never took the role? It's more of a transfer of power back to the rightful owner."

That was one way to look at it, but Theo had been so happy when he'd thought his father was handing him the reins. Still, Lynerd made the most sense as the Oregon alpha council member, and his position had been taken from him. I was sure my parents had realized their mistake once Zeke had revealed his true intentions.

"Okay." Jasmine put her phone back into her pocket and came over to us. "She got her dad on the call, and he's linking with King Sutton. They'll call me back soon, but they hope to offer their pack's help at a minimum. Russell just wants to talk to the king before committing to it."

So there was a chance they could turn us down.

The largest connection in my chest warmed, indicating that Bodey was stirring. Though I hated for him to wake up in

Kel's custody, my heart fluttered with the hope of talking to him. My breath caught as I linked, *Bodey?*

Babe? He replied groggily. *What's going on?*

Before I could respond, pain sliced through our connection.

CHAPTER FIVE

THE SHOOTING PAIN stole my breath, and I sagged against the wall. I gripped my chest, wishing there was a way I could take his suffering away.

"Callie!" Samuel placed his hands on my shoulders. He hunched over so he could stare into my eyes. "What's wrong?"

I couldn't speak, not with all the emotions and sensations bombarding me. I linked with everyone, *It's Bodey. He's hurting.*

A tear dripped onto my hand as I took a shaky breath. *Bodey, I'm here.* I tugged at our connection, trying to figure out a way to help him. *I wish it was me instead of you.*

I'm fucking glad it's me and not you, he replied, his sincerity pushing through to me. *They kicked me to see if I was awake. I managed to fool them into thinking I was still asleep.*

Under normal circumstances, those words would have warmed me, but not now and not like this. At least they might leave him alone if they thought he was unconscious. It wasn't fun to hurt an unconscious person.

"How badly is he hurt?" Jasmine's brows furrowed. "I

don't want to link and interrupt your conversation." Her shoulders sagged.

I wasn't sure how to answer that without making her feel worse, but I did the best I could. "They think he's unconscious, so they're leaving him alone." I managed to straighten for her sake and linked with Bodey, *Do you have any idea where you are?* If they were close by, maybe we could save him and not have to worry about the Midwest pack—if they agreed to help us.

I'm pretty sure I'm in a van. I'm lying down with two wolf shifters sitting on either side of me. The floor is metal, like a work van or something. We're moving, and based on the speed, I'm assuming we're on an interstate.

They must be heading back to California. I repeated the information to the others. *Bodey, we're working on getting you back.*

Leave me with Queen Kel if that keeps you safe. I'd rather endure whatever she has planned than risk you getting captured. Promise me.

Even though I could lie and he wouldn't know since he wasn't near me, I refused to pollute our relationship that way. *Bodey.*

Promise me, Callie, he insisted, his fear nearly strangling me. *I need to hear you say it.*

I can't. She took you to get to me. Don't you realize that losing you would destroy me? My chest constricted at the thought of never seeing him again, let alone the queen torturing him to the brink of death. *I would be more sane if I were in your place, knowing you were safe.*

What about me? He nearly growled, even through our connection. *You think I'd be better off if you were here? I'm only the king consort—you're the actual monarch.*

We could argue all day, but we were wasting our energy.

If you aren't careful, your heart rate will pick up, and they'll know you're awake.

Sorry if the thought of you getting beaten or killed upsets me. His frustration enveloped our bond.

I feel the same way. I didn't want to waste our time fighting. There was no telling what they had planned and how long we could communicate before they knocked him out or something worse happened. *We can agree on one thing: Neither of us wants the other to be in your situation, so let's focus on a way to free you without me getting captured.*

If it hadn't been for his bond remaining warm, I would've thought he'd gone back to sleep.

You're right, he finally replied. *I can't look out to see where we are, but even if I could get up, I don't think there are windows back here.*

Not wanting to repeat everything, I pulled Jack, Miles, and Lucas into the conversation. They were the royal advisors I trusted, and I needed the five of us to be on the same page with any decisions made. *I'll link with the alphas in Oregon and Idaho and spread the word to keep a lookout for a van that might seem suspicious.*

We can help out since Zeke's gone, Jack linked.

Lucas smacked him on the back of the head and murmured, "Dude. Bodey doesn't know anything about that."

The damage was already done. Bodey's dread flowed into me as he asked, *What did Zeke do now?*

Before I could answer, agony shot through Bodey into me. The pain receded before more slammed through him, making me sick.

If she won't tell you, I will, because it's that fucked up, Jack started, unaware of what was happening to my mate.

"Stop," I rasped. "They realized he's awake." I closed my eyes and clenched my hands so tight that my nails bit into my palms. They were hurting him, and I had no fucking way of getting to him. How could I expect to protect all my people when I couldn't protect my mate?

"Are they hurting him again?" Michael's face twisted in agony.

I nodded, unable to say anything more.

Something buzzed. My eyes fluttered open to find Jasmine looking at her phone. Her face was pale, but she whispered, "It's them, but I can call them back."

"Take it now." I needed to know their answer. If they weren't going to help, I had to determine a way to pretend to hand myself over to Queen Kel.

Each new jolt of pain made me more desperate to save him.

That had to be Queen Kel's goal.

Jasmine nodded, swiped her phone, and placed it to her ear.

The connection between Bodey and me cooled again. The discomfort lingered, but he wasn't conscious to feel it. That didn't make me feel any better. I raised a shaking hand to my mouth.

Miles placed a hand on my shoulder. "We will save him. We'll figure out a way without you sacrificing yourself."

"You can't make that promise." Samuel crossed his arms. "There's no way she can sacrifice herself, so she may—"

"With all due respect." Miles's normal, quiet demeanor slid into that of someone who'd be heard. "You don't have a mate. You don't understand the emotions she's going through, and though I have an inkling, they probably aren't half as strong as what she's experiencing because, fortunately, I've never experienced this situation with Stella. If we don't find a way to get him back, she *will* make the trade, and there's not a damn thing we can do to stop her."

Even though Miles was the quietest of the advisors, I'd never doubted his fierceness. He reserved his words and actions for when they were warranted, and I appreciated him for standing in my corner.

"That's why we need to stop her." Samuel nodded, his nose wrinkling. "We can tie her up or put her in a room."

Jack snorted. "I think you're forgetting she's our *queen* and you aren't our king. We do anything to her, and we'll be alpha-willed so hard she'll have us lying on our backs, wanting belly rubs as she skips past us."

A strangled laugh escaped me, sounding more like a croak than anything. Leave it to Jack to get me to laugh even while I was losing my sanity.

"Enough." Michael stepped between Miles and Samuel, breaking up whatever stare-down the two younger men were having. "Fighting among ourselves isn't the solution, and Samuel, I know we groomed you to lead, but you aren't the leader. Instead of arguing, we need to work together. Like Caroline, I'm all about getting my entire family home safe and sound, which includes her."

Being called Caroline sounded weird. Even though the name was mine, it didn't embody the person I'd become. "Everyone here, please keep calling me Callie."

"Whew." Jack wiped his brow. "Good. Because I was getting nervous about the new name."

Lucas raised a hand to smack him, but Jack shuffled away while pointing his finger.

"Thank you, Katelin," Jasmine said. "I know you did everything you could. Give me a call when things are settled."

That didn't sound good, and that blasted feeling I'd tried all my life not to feel vanished, deflating me like a balloon.

Damn hope.

While living in Zeke's pack, I'd learned how dangerous

hope was, but the thought of having allies to rescue Bodey had caused that emotion to surge within me, and here I was, devastated again. I should've known they'd say no. It wasn't their fight.

She hung up and placed the phone into her back pocket.

Michael asked what I already knew. "What did they say?"

That was the thing about this group—they'd never had the odds consistently stacked against them, so they needed confirmation.

Jasmine smiled sadly. "Russell had hoped to bring a hundred wolves here to help us get Bodey back, but King Sutton didn't approve."

There it was, the answer I'd heard in her voice.

"He said he didn't want to get involved until he could see that our region had a chance to win." She rubbed her hands together. "If Queen Kel manages to take over this region, the last thing he wants is for her to attack them in retribution."

I couldn't blame him.

"Yeah, but she'll pivot to the Midwest territory eventually. She'll take them over too, if her goal is world domination." Lucas shook his head.

Jack rolled his eyes. "And he acts like I'm the dramatic one."

"At least they considered helping." I needed to give them credit for that.

"Great." Samuel sighed. "We need to figure out something. I refuse to be like Miles and let Callie hand herself over."

"Man, that's not what I said." Miles glowered, and his neck corded. "You can't stop her from doing that if she decides that's her only option."

Great, we were fighting among ourselves again, which was

probably part of Kel's plan. She had us right where she wanted us, and I hated her for it.

"Stop arguing and let me finish," Jasmine snapped. "I got my brother into this, and I'm with Dad. We'll find a way to get Bodey back without Callie handing herself over, and if you'd stop bickering for a second, we wouldn't keep having the same conversation over and over again." Her eyes glowed as her wolf surged forward.

Her wolf was the weakest in this room, but that didn't mean she wouldn't take a stand. Guilt was clearly driving both her and her wolf.

Silence descended, and I could feel the shock coursing through the royal advisors. Michael smiled proudly.

Samuel waved a hand. "Please, continue. I wasn't trying to be rude. I thought you were done."

Her gaze met mine. "Though King Sutton didn't agree to send his region's one hundred strongest shifters, he said he wouldn't stop Russell from bringing people from his territory here if the alpha decided he should help."

My heart lurched. The king was smart. He didn't want a ton of shifters coming from all over the Midwest and sparking rumors that they were allying with us, but he wouldn't prevent us from getting aid he hadn't directly authorized. It was a strategic decision. If Queen Kel confronted him, he could tell her without lying that he hadn't sent his shifters to help us. It was plausible deniability while helping us.

Hope expanded again in my chest, causing discomfort. They had to be bringing people here, or Jasmine wouldn't have been so forceful with Samuel. "What did Russell say?"

"It's not a huge number, but he's coordinating fifty of his strongest fighters to come here." Jasmine blew out a breath. "It's not a lot—"

My body felt as light as a feather. "It's more than I could

have expected or hoped for." My dad had been right. King Sutton was a smart leader who had compassion for more than his own shifters. If he wasn't concerned about our well-being, he would've told Russell he couldn't help. But I wasn't foolish. There was also self-interest in his decision. "He knows if we're overtaken, he'll be her next target."

Michael nodded. "I suspect the same thing, but if the roles were reversed, I'd recommend the same strategy."

That was fair. His people were his priority. "When are they coming? The queen said she'll want to meet in two days." The thought of being away from Bodey for that long and knowing he'd endure more pain damn near had me falling apart, but I had to be strong for both of us. Maybe there was a chance we could come out of this together. Now that we had help coming, I couldn't stop hope from spreading through every thought.

"They're contacting the shifters through the evening and plan on leaving sometime tomorrow." Jasmine wrung her hands again. "We also need a strategy. They don't want Queen Kel to see a bunch of cars with Minnesota license plates coming in, so they might stay off-site. I'm thinking I'll stay with them so I can link with you, Samuel, and Dad."

"That's an excellent plan." I smiled at her. If Jasmine hadn't ignored her parents' wishes and come home, we wouldn't have extra people coming to our aid. Even if they only brought twenty-five, it would give us a fighting edge. I'd take anyone they had to offer.

"In the meantime, we need to settle things here." Carl winced. "Like informing Lynerd of Sybil's death."

My heart sank. "You're right." I bit my bottom lip. "We need to take Sybil's body back to her coven, and Zeke needs to travel there with us."

Dan's brows rose. "Why take Zeke with us? I thought you wanted him dead or imprisoned."

"Oh, I do." There was one more important thing I had to do, not only for Oregon but to right the wrongs of my parents. I needed to talk to Lynerd and make things right. "He'll be locked up before long. But I want to get back to Lynerd's territory before it gets dark. And I'm hoping everyone will go with me."

Eyes twinkling, Jack grinned. "You know I'm down. I can't wait to see what you have planned."

"It's a three-hour drive, and it's getting late." Miles glanced at the entryway. "Let's get out of here."

Everyone was eager to leave. We wrapped Sybil's body in a white sheet, and the Halfway pack kept a lookout for oncoming cars as we placed her in the trunk of Bodey's Mercedes SUV.

Heart aching, I climbed into the passenger seat, unable to take his place in the driver's seat. Samuel slid into that spot, giving me a sad smile as Jasmine and Theo climbed into the back seat. I hadn't expected Theo to come, but he'd asked to stay close to his dad.

What I had to do would affect him, but I didn't want to notify him about my plan, afraid of how he would react.

Once Zeke was in the back seat of Jack's vehicle, next to Miles, everyone else climbed into the cars, and we took off.

———

DURING THE CAR RIDE, Jasmine filled me in on what had happened during the fight while Bodey and I were split up. He, Jack, and Miles had reached her and helped her and Theo. Then Bodey had left to rush back to me and got cornered.

Somehow, my heart broke further.

Callie, we'll get him back, Samuel linked, reaching over. *I know I wasn't supportive earlier, but now that things have calmed down, I can see how much this is affecting you. It's no one's fault but Queen Kel's.*

Samuel was right. And the bitch would pay for everything she'd done.

A LITTLE OVER three hours later, just as the sun slipped below the horizon, we pulled into Lynerd's neighborhood. Unlike last time, the pack wasn't blocking our way, but Lynerd stood outside his house with his arms crossed and two male shifters behind him. A group of five women in long dresses also stood in the yard. They had to be witches from Sybil's coven.

I climbed out of the car, lifting my chin. I needed to address Sybil's death first—that was what she deserved.

The others followed suit, exiting their vehicles.

Lynerd scanned our group, his gaze landing on Zeke. He scowled, "What is *he* doing here?"

"We'll get to that in a minute." I pointed at Zeke. "But know that stab wound you see was done by my hands."

He arched a brow and observed me once more. "At least he got some sort of punishment."

Zeke had no clue what sort of punishment I was about to inflict.

"Where's Sybil?" A pale-skinned woman with long ebony hair stepped forward. The scent of herbs hit my nose, confirming they were witches.

I tensed, fearing how they would take the news. "She's here, but I need to tell you something." I placed a hand over my heart, trying like hell to feel Bodey as best I could. What I wouldn't give to have him near. I needed his strength and his support more than I even realized.

Jaw twitching, Lynerd waited, staring me down.

"Sybil is dead," I whispered, but there was no doubt everyone heard.

CHAPTER SIX

THE EBONY-HAIRED WITCH'S upper body sagged, and I was surprised she didn't crumple to the grass. The other four witches' faces twisted in agony, but their gazes remained on me as they lifted their hands.

Eyes glowing, Lynerd clenched his hands and rasped, "You killed her."

The witches took a step forward in unison, ready to chant a spell together.

My head jerked back, and I pressed my hand to my chest even harder. "No!" Here I was, trying to handle the situation as delicately as possible, but instead, I'd insinuated I'd killed their priestess. "It was Queen Kel."

"What do you mean?" Lynerd asked, brows furrowed. "She was with Zeke."

"She was—just like you were with your pack when the queen attacked here," Samuel countered, moving around the hood of the car to stand by me. "There was an incident. Sybil was killed, and Bodey was kidnapped."

My heart constricted further. The more people who knew about Bodey's abduction, the weaker I would appear, but that wasn't the real problem. I needed him by my side. With each passing moment, functioning became harder.

Samuel's words hit their mark, and Lynerd's face switched from anger to concern.

The man I recognized as Lynerd's beta stepped forward. His hair was shaggier than the last time I saw him, and a shade darker than his copper beard. His eyes narrowed, and he laughed bitterly. "This is fucking great. We might as well hand ourselves over to her with a twat like him"—he pointed at Zeke—"in charge and our community half as strong without Sybil."

I looked behind me at Zeke, who scowled deeply. Theo glanced at his father and cleared his throat. "Dad's injured, so maybe it's time for him to hand off the pack and royal advisor responsibilities."

My throat closed. This was *not* how I'd wanted to have this conversation. I'd hoped to talk to Theo and Lynerd alone before making anything official. Theo was showing initiative at the worst possible time.

"Are you fucking serious?" Zeke snarled at Theo, his upper lip curling. "Now isn't the time to take the position from me. Things are too volatile."

Theo flinched, which further strengthened my decision, but I wanted to handle the change of advisor positions respectfully. Lynerd and Theo deserved that. I opened my mouth to take control of the conversation again and stay focused on Sybil's death.

Jack snickered. "Didn't you promise Theo you'd relinquish the position after the crowning, and then you said that, since Theo was *injured,* you should remain in charge?"

Leave it to Jack not to let it go, especially when I needed him to with what I had planned.

Zeke spat, "That is none of your business," drawing their attention away.

"That's the thing." Lucas placed his hands on his hips and glared at Zeke. "It's *all* of our business, and after—"

We didn't need to argue among ourselves, especially not when the coven needed to pay their respects to Sybil. There was only one way to handle this.

I'm sorry, Theo. I meant to talk to you before this in private, I linked to him. *Please know this has nothing to do with you.* Then I spoke out loud, "Zeke will no longer be the royal advisor or in charge of his pack," I said, mustering as much authority as I could my voice. "After kidnapping me and colluding with the queen, he's lucky to be breathing. None of us can trust him to continue in *any* sort of alpha or advisory role."

Zeke's jaw clenched, but he remained silent.

That's a wise decision, Michael linked, and I was surprised by how much I needed to hear that. *Instead of hiding everything so there is less turmoil, you're taking the more challenging path. Your father would be proud.*

With Bodey not here, Michael's words were a lifeline for me. Though having his support wasn't the same as having Bodey at my side, it was enough to keep me going.

Chest puffing, Theo smiled sadly at me and nodded. "I agree wholeheartedly." He then linked, *I understand that you don't want him to serve. I get it.*

My heart clenched. *That's not what I had been referring to when I'd said this had nothing to do with you. It's the next part I was referencing.*

Zeke's jaw clenched. "You need me. Just wait. You'll come begging."

I'd rather die than take any advice from him. The next words would hurt to say. Theo had been one of my few friends over the past seventeen years, but my memories had revealed that friendship had a way of persuading a person to make horrible decisions, ones that could result in death... maybe even my own. *And I'm sorry.*

"You're dumber than I realized, thinking you'd still hold any position with influence"—Jack lifted his hands and stared at Zeke as if he had two heads—"after betraying us."

"What do you mean, betraying us?" Lynerd asked through gritted teeth.

Jack, be quiet, Miles linked, his frustration bleeding through. *Let Callie handle this.*

I straightened, wanting to look as strong as possible since I didn't feel that way. "He was working with Queen Kel, which led to Sybil's death and my fated mate's capture." I wanted to put Bodey first because his absence felt like the most important piece in everything that had happened, but Lynerd wouldn't see it that way, and I was trying to relate to him. He would take Sybil's loss hardest. "Which is why I'm replacing Zeke with you as the royal advisor of Oregon. Theo will still be the alpha of his pack."

"What?" Theo rasped, his voice full of hurt, while Lynerd's jaw dropped.

I didn't trust Zeke, and Theo was too influenced by his father. Hell, he'd even assumed we would keep Zeke in an advisory role.

"You want *me* to be the Oregon royal advisor?" Lynerd's pupils dilated.

"It was what my parents were going to do before their untimely death." I glanced at Zeke, who had the intelligence to avert his eyes. "You and your pack are strong—the strongest in Oregon, from what I can tell. It makes sense to offer the position to you."

And to screw me, Theo replied, his hurt surging between

us. *You know I grew up expecting to step into this position. Is this your way of getting back at me for not helping you sooner?*

A lump formed in my throat, and I tried to swallow around it. I hadn't meant to hurt him. *Theo, it isn't personal. Your father killed my parents, and your pack mistreated me until a few weeks ago when I was crowned queen. That history and your dad's imprisonment won't go over well. It's not an insult, I swear, and I'll find a way to make this right for you too.*

He didn't say anything, but I saw the way Jasmine was looking at him. Her heart broke for him, but I needed Lynerd to say *something*.

Lynerd scratched his head. I'd expected him to jump on the offer, but his hesitation had my lungs seizing. I'd offered him the role in front of everyone without considering that he might not want it.

I hated to think of giving the royal advisor role back to Theo after embarrassing him like this.

We're going to have a problem if he doesn't accept, Miles linked. At least he didn't lecture me.

"It should be me," Theo said and glared at me. "He doesn't want it."

Lynerd growled. "Don't speak on my behalf when you don't know what I'm thinking."

Heart pounding, I wanted him to answer instead of jerking us around. "Which is?"

"All the sacrifices it'll take to make sure I can protect my people." Lynerd ran a hand down his face. "All this time, I was angry, knowing the responsibility should've been mine, but now that you've offered it..."

He was thinking the decision through. Though it was painful for me to bear, I had to respect that. It would've been nice if Fate had found a way to restore my memories and give me a chance to think through the royal responsibilities before marking me as queen. Yet, here we were. I refused to pressure someone into taking a role they might not want.

"Take a little time. We need to bury Sybil anyway." I looked at the witches and forced another small smile. "She deserves to be returned to nature."

All five witches nodded, and the ebony-haired woman came closer. "Yes, we need to relinquish her power back into the earth. The sooner, the better."

Jack, Lucas, and Miles headed to the trunk of the SUV while the witches came over. Then, the former advisors walked toward me. There were various questions and concerns on the former advisors' faces, and I had no doubt they were thinking similarly to Samuel.

Maybe I'd messed up by following my gut, but Theo didn't feel like the right option.

"May we visit some of your pack and check on them?" Phil leveled his gaze on Lynerd.

That way, you can talk to Lynerd without all of us here, and we can see how his pack's doing after Queen Kel's attack, Michael linked.

"Go ahead." Lynerd glanced over his shoulder at his beta. "You and Frank go with them and introduce them to everyone. They'll be jumpy around unfamiliar wolves so soon after the attack."

"On it." The beta strolled past me, motioning for the others to follow him.

Samuel stayed put and crossed his arms. "I'm staying with Callie."

He was probably afraid to leave me alone after I'd made a decision he didn't approve of, but having him here might be for the best. Lynerd might not accept the new role, and I might have created more of a mess than I'd intended.

"Uh." Dan glanced at me with concern. "If—"

"It's fine." I nodded. "Samuel can stay with me."

Dan paused, but Carl wrapped an arm around his shoulders and guided him to follow the betas with everyone else while Jack, Lucas, and Miles followed the witches, carrying Sybil to wherever they wanted her.

Samuel, Lynerd, and I stood outside Lynerd's house while Jasmine and Theo climbed back into Jack's vehicle with Zeke.

After an extended moment of silence, I couldn't take it anymore. The world seemed to be closing in on me, so I said, "I hate that we couldn't come here right after the attack. We were trying to get my childhood memories back."

Lynerd arched a brow. "Then why did you come here this morning?"

"Because Salem, Sybil's mother, was the witch who locked them away." I wanted to be truthful and mend some of what was broken between us. "Zeke ran off with her because he knew Sybil could return my memories. Apparently, Queen Kel was supposed to get Sybil from him before we arrived, but instead, she killed her. Sybil was the last surviving person of her bloodline. Her death ended the spell."

Lynerd pinched the bridge of his nose. "Six years after becoming alpha at sixteen, I had to deal with losing our strongest witch. I remember finding her and her husband dead a few miles from here. Are you telling me Zeke was responsible?"

I blew out a breath. "Yes, he was. I remember seeing her and the spell she performed. Zeke sacrificed his best friend to block my memories."

"He's going to be punished, right?" Lynerd locked gazes with me. "For everything he's done."

"I plan on locking him up and never allowing him to see the light of day again." I never thought I could have more anger for that man than I'd had growing up, but knowing everything made me despise him. "When I got my memories back, right after Bodey was taken, I wanted to kill him. But I realized something. Zeke living without control or influence over anyone is a worse punishment than death."

I still don't understand how I made it out alive and with Michael, Samuel said.

I winced. I should've made telling him the story of what happened during the explosion a priority. *You were in bed downstairs when the fireplace exploded. Dad had called Michael back because of how Zeke was acting, and he got to you before Zeke could. It happened not long after the four of us came in from playing chase outside.*

Our parents played with us? Longing wafted from him.

Eyes burning, I blinked to hold back tears. *They did.*

Tapping his fingers on his lips, Lynerd tilted his head. "I suppose you're right, but I won't lie. I'm shocked you asked me to take the role and not Theo."

"It's what my parents wanted." I stared into his eyes, hoping he would find whatever reassurance he needed there. "But you don't have to take it."

He exhaled loudly. "Being a good royal advisor takes sacrifice."

I laughed bitterly, the harshness grating my throat. "Believe me, I get that. Having Bodey taken from me isn't a price I'd ever want to pay."

"Are you trying to talk me into rejecting your offer?" Lynerd tilted his head, but there was something kind in his face.

I shook my head. "I want to be honest. Yes, you rejecting my offer will put me in a bind, but it's better than you taking on a responsibility you don't want."

Callie. Samuel frowned. *I think we should rethink this whole thing. We're giving him too much power—*

"I'll do it." Lynerd bowed his head, showing me respect. "If you're this transparent, you're someone I'm willing to fight next to." He smiled wryly. "Besides, the first time I met you and you kept Theo in line even when you didn't seem to have a strong wolf, you intrigued me. There was something about you I liked."

My face flamed, but I held his gaze. "Thanks." I bit the inside of my cheek, trying to channel my embarrassment. "Now we need to make it official." I cleared my throat as I tried to remember what it took to make someone an advisor. Nothing came to me, so I linked with Samuel, *What do we do to make it official?*

Zeke has to submit to him, Samuel replied easily.

My heart lurched. *He won't do that.*

If Lynerd is stronger than him, it's inevitable. Samuel shrugged. *Or you can alpha-will him to stand down.*

I flinched. Zeke would fight this, but if I alpha-willed him to stand down, he'd use that to say I had something to hide. It wasn't a big deal, but with Kel breathing down my neck, I needed to avoid as much turmoil as possible. The lesser of the two evils was allowing Lynerd to force Zeke to submit and hope that I wasn't wrong in assuming he was the stronger wolf.

"There's no time like the present." I gestured to Jack's SUV and went to Jasmine's passenger-side back door, not wanting to make things worse for Theo. I linked to Jasmine and Zeke, *I need you two to get out of the vehicle.* I opened the door and forced myself not to avoid Theo's gaze.

His eyes darkened, and he glanced away. All his life, he'd thought his dad would never step down, and here that day was, and I was taking away the future he'd always wanted. My chest ached, but I had to do what was best for my people.

Are you sure this is the right call? Jasmine asked and gnawed on a fingernail. *Theo—*

Jasmine, you know better than to challenge our queen, Samuel scolded.

I glanced at him and raised a brow. *You asked me something similar not ten minutes ago.*

But as your brother... not— He stopped.

Jasmine was my sister now, and he caught the error before I pointed it out. I squeezed her arm and forced a tight smile. *I promise I'll make it up to him. He and Stevie are two of the only people I had growing up.*

She scowled but nodded, moving out of my way.

I turned my attention to Zeke and allowed alpha will to coat my words. "Get out of the car *now*."

His wolf obeyed, forcing his human body to scoot across the seat and stand. Each movement had him wincing in pain from his injury.

At least now he knew what I'd felt all those times he'd punished me when I was injured.

When he got out, I turned to Lynerd. If he wanted this role, it was time he took action.

Lynerd stepped toward Zeke, and their gazes locked.

They stared at each other, eyes glowing as their wolves surged forward. I knew Zeke wouldn't give up without a fight, so I kept watch as I turned my attention internally to my connection with Bodey.

It was still lukewarm, indicating he was unconscious. I wished I'd had the opportunity to talk to him about what I'd done. I wasn't sure this was the right call, and everyone else seemed uncertain about whether Lynerd should lead.

Maybe my gut was wrong.

Sweat beaded on Zeke's and Lynerd's foreheads as they continued their stare-down. Theo kept his face turned away as if refusing to acknowledge what was happening.

Both of their bottom lips quivered, and for the hundredth time today, fear strangled me. What if Zeke won?

CHAPTER SEVEN

ZEKE SNEERED, his hands shaking at his sides. "I will not lose to *you* or *anyone*." He didn't have to glance at me for me to know I was included in that equation.

At least we had no doubt that Samuel, the other royal advisors, and I were stronger than him. I wasn't worried about him taking over, but I feared I'd overestimated Lynerd's strength and this move was going to crash around me. If Zeke was strong enough not to submit to Lynerd, I'd do what I had to, including making him rogue. Locking him up in the basement would prevent him from causing any more havoc. If he slowly lost his mind too, that might be satisfying after everything he'd done.

If I couldn't tell which wolf was stronger, what did that say about me and my leadership skills?

"Please." Lynerd snickered. Despite the sweat coating his forehead and the quiver in his bottom lip, he wasn't struggling as hard as Zeke. "The only reason you've lasted this long is through your last-ditch effort to prove you're strong, but there's no doubt my wolf is stronger." His eyes glowed as he stepped forward, and his voice lowered as power radiated through him. "Stop wasting our time and submit *now*."

Zeke closed his eyes, his chest heaving. Whether his human side wanted to admit it or not, his wolf side was succumbing to Lynerd's command, and it wouldn't be long until he submitted.

Samuel placed a hand on my shoulder and linked, *What will you do if Zeke pulls through?*

I nearly flinched. He still thought I'd decided wrong, but there wasn't a damn thing I could do about it. The change in leadership had already occurred.

If he loses, I'll do what needs to be done, even if it's casting Zeke out. I winced and hoped I'd hidden it from Samuel. I wasn't sure what other options I had.

Zeke would not be triumphant.

After what felt like hours but was mere minutes, Zeke averted his eyes to the driveway, breaking contact with Lynerd.

My lungs filled with air, and my body sagged. Thank gods Lynerd had taken control.

In my chest, one of the large warm spots and a slightly smaller one pulsed, and the two spots switched in size. I assumed that was Zeke and Lynerd switching roles. I wondered what it felt like for all the packs affected by the transition.

Hot anger and hate darkened Zeke's eyes as he stared at Lynerd and me. He snarled, "You two will pay. I don't care—"

My wolf surged forward. She and I were sick of all his threats and games. "Shut the *fuck* up."

His lips slammed shut, which was almost comical, and he went quiet.

I brushed past Lynerd, clutched Zeke's shirt, and lifted him slightly. He groaned, likely from the pain of his knife injury, but I held strong. I wouldn't tolerate anyone, especially *him*, talking down to me. This prick had taken everything he could from me.

I bared my teeth. "If you so much as threaten anyone or say something that doesn't give us insight into *Kel's* plans, I will knock your ass out and injure you again. Do you *understand*?"

He nodded, but his nose wrinkled as if *he* were disgusted with *me*.

The nerve.

I spat, "Get in the car, and keep your mouth shut."

Zeke's nostrils flared as his body obeyed.

Jasmine frowned as she opened the door to let Zeke into the back seat. Luckily, she didn't say anything, but she didn't need to. Even though she knew everything Zeke had done, I suspected Theo's feelings were influencing her.

I hated that I'd hurt Theo, so I understood her displeasure.

Not wanting to dawdle, I turned to Lynerd and linked, *We need to put Theo in charge of the Oxbow pack.* Even though I was more than able to do that, allowing Lynerd to handle it would reinforce his new role, and that was what I needed: a united front and for Kel to think she could continue to create discord in my leadership team.

Something akin to pride floated from Lynerd to me, and he replied, *I can do that.*

Good. I wanted to get away from everyone and have a moment to myself. Ever since I'd woken up with my memories and remembered that Bodey had been taken, I'd been around at least three other people at all times. I needed to process everything that had happened during the past few hours to ensure it wasn't affecting my judgment, especially since Samuel wasn't thrilled with my decisions. I linked with

Lynerd and Samuel, *I'm going to check on a few of your people.*

I rubbed Bodey's spot in my chest, wishing he were here with me. The fact that his bond was cool was a blessing. If he had been awake, he probably would've been enduring torture. But I missed his touch and hearing his opinions more than I'd thought possible.

Samuel's hand dropped as he replied only to me, *I'll stay here to make sure nothing gets out of hand.*

I nodded. My absence might calm the volatile situation, so I headed in the opposite direction of the neighborhood, ready to perform my job and find some solitude.

By TEN AT NIGHT, Sybil had been buried, and the former advisors and I had dropped by every pack house for a few minutes to check on them. Jack, Lucas, Miles, and Samuel had joined us for the last hour, and we'd just finished updating Lynerd on everything, including our plan.

Now it was time to get Theo back to the Oxbow pack neighborhood as the official alpha leader. With Zeke out of commission, they were down one strong wolf.

As I passed Jack's vehicle to slide into the passenger seat of the SUV, in which Zeke was pouting comically in the back seat, Lynerd grabbed my arm.

My breath caught. "Everything okay?" I tried not to wince, but having a man outside of Bodey and my newfound family touch me didn't feel right.

He dropped his hand as his brows furrowed. *I feel like I should be going with you like the other three royal advisors, but I need to stay here tonight. I'll meet up with you all tomorrow instead. Between the coven mourning and my needing to prepare for my absence tomorrow and the next night, I don't feel comfortable leaving at the last minute.*

I mashed my lips together, but when I opened my mouth, he lifted a hand.

I get that all of Oregon is my responsibility, but my pack isn't used to not having me here. He blew out his cheeks.

He didn't want to abandon his people. I understood and respected that. *Stay. Get things settled. You just took the position a couple of hours ago, so of course you need time to organize things. Besides, you're already a step ahead.* I forced a smile, wanting him to know I understood. *Normally, the Oregon royal advisor fights me on everything, so the fact that you want to support me and help to make decisions is leaps and bounds better.*

Taking a step back, he sighed. *I can't believe I'm the royal advisor now. Thank you for making it possible, and I'm determined to do a far better job than Zeke ever did.*

In fairness, it wouldn't take much to make that possible.

I have no doubt you will. I fought back a yawn. *But we need to get Theo back to his pack so he can take on his role and get Zeke situated before we leave tomorrow. I'll link with you in the morning to tell you where to meet us.*

Sounds like a plan. He held the door open.

As I slid into the seat, Samuel cut his eyes to me and started the car. He glanced to the back seat where Jasmine and Theo sat.

Without saying a word, I already knew what he was implying. The ride to Oxbow was going to be a doozy.

Soon, all three of our vehicles had backed out of the driveway, and I leaned my head against the headrest. I was happy that Bodey wasn't in any additional pain, but I couldn't help but worry. It had been a while since he'd woken up. My only solace was our connection. At least he wasn't dead.

I wrapped my arms around my waist and exhaled. That wasn't as comforting a thought as I'd hoped.

As we pulled onto the main road, I wished I could fall asleep, but the tension in the car was palpable, and my worry for my mate made sleep impossible.

When we'd been on the road for a while in complete silence, I began hoping Theo would let it go. He usually avoided confrontation, but as some of the worry wafted away, he cleared his throat.

"Why did you take that position away from me?" he asked, his voice low.

Great. We were going to have this conversation out loud. I guessed I deserved that. "It wasn't about taking it from *you*. It was about honoring my parents' wishes from seventeen years ago. They didn't believe he was fit to lead anymore."

"You don't trust me to do that?"

Samuel shook his head. *You can't allow him to challenge you like this. You made a decision, and we must respect that. Fate chose you to lead us.*

True, but he just wants to talk to me about it. Every person who asked me to explain my logic wasn't necessarily trying to undermine me. I'd hurt him, and we were friends. He needed a chance to process. I was just thankful he was willing to hear me out.

"Theo, this isn't about you as a person." I turned in my seat to look him in the eye. He and Jasmine were holding hands, and I hid a grimace. Bodey wouldn't handle that well, but Jasmine was an adult who could make her own decisions.

Theo hung his head. "How else am I supposed to take it?"

This was one of those times when it would have been amazing to know how to lead. If my parents had raised me, I'd be able to think of the perfect words to make him understand. But I only had myself to go by, the former omega of the

Oxbow pack whose existence most hadn't acknowledged unless they needed me to clean or do yard work. "You might think of it as... you're off the hook." Something I would never be, especially with the queen's mark on my collarbone and chest.

He huffed and glanced at Jasmine. "See, I told you talking to her was pointless. She can't even give me a real answer."

"You shouldn't speak to her like that." Samuel frowned, his hands tightening on the steering wheel. "I get that you two grew up together." His lips curved downward. "She and I didn't have that privilege, but you can't talk to her like she's in your pack anymore. She's your queen."

Theo snorted. "Oh, believe me, I know. I see her tattoo every time I look at her, and she just yanked my future out from under me."

He was taking it personally, proving he shouldn't be in charge. My decision hadn't been an act of retribution.

Jasmine squeezed his hand and glanced at me. "Can you give him more context?" She then linked to me, *He's really hurting, and I don't know how to help him. Only you can do that. Imagine how Bodey would react if his title was taken from him.*

That wasn't the same thing, and I was surprised she didn't see that, but she hadn't been around Theo long enough to know how he'd acted around Zeke. Not wanting to make an enemy out of him, I kept hold of my calm. "Theo, your attention needs to be on your pack." I lifted my hands. "Your father allowed people to treat each other like crap, and people were afraid to bring their concerns to him the way you're doing with me. To do this job correctly, you need to heal and transform the pack. You can't do that if you're focused on all of Oregon. It's not a demotion but a way to help you be a successful and strong alpha."

His forehead lined. "I have authority over one pack and not all of them. How is that not a demotion?"

"How fair would it be for me to ask you to not only fix and make your pack stronger but take on all the other packs as well?" I shrugged, wanting him to understand. Maybe that wasn't the whole reason, but it was a strong one that would hopefully make sense to him. "I'd be setting you up for failure. Besides, once things are going better with Oxbow, I'm sure Lynerd and I could give you more responsibilities."

He tapped his fingers on his legs and frowned. I wasn't sure how else I could justify my decision without destroying our relationship.

When I was about to give up hope, he said, "Yeah, okay." He bobbed his head. "That makes sense. Dad did make a mess of things."

Thank you, Jasmine linked just as Samuel replied, *Good job with the spin. I don't think I could've done that half as well.*

I nodded at Jasmine and Theo and turned around as I replied to Samuel, *It wasn't all spin. Just enough truth for him not to feel hurt.* The last thing I wanted to do was to call his wolf weaker than his father's and Lynerd's, especially in front of Jasmine.

My link with Bodey blazed. I rubbed my chest, both relieved and terrified that our connection was strong again.

Bodey? I linked, closing my eyes to focus on the warmth. *Are you okay?*

I'm... He grew groggy. *Fine. But the queen is with me.*

My heart raced, and I prepared for the inevitable pain. The longer it took to come, the more worried I became. *What's going on?*

She's trying to get information out of me by promising me food and water, he replied.

Throat drying, I couldn't believe what I was hearing. *Tell her something. You need to eat and drink.* As long as the information kept him alive, I didn't give a shit how bad it hurt us. I just needed a chance to bring him back to me.

Like hell I'm telling her anything, he rasped. *Anything she learns about us, she'll use against you, and that's not happening.*

He was just as stubborn about protecting me as I was about protecting him. *I can't—*

Agony surged through the bond, slamming into me.

She'd told me that having my fated mate taken away would weaken me, but I'd never believed her until now. Not having him near me had my heart in tatters.

And she was right. I'd gladly hand myself over to her to protect him. What kind of queen was I? I grunted from the shock of anguish that shot into me again.

"Callie, what's wrong?" Samuel asked, the car swerving.

"Bodey," I groaned and hunched over, clutching my chest. "He's awake, and the queen's hurting him." My vision blurred as tears dripped down my cheeks. I needed Bodey to know that I would always be with him.

Babe, I'm going to get you out of there. I promise. I tugged on the pain, trying to bring more into me. Anything to give him some relief.

The throbbing in my body increased tenfold.

After a long moment of torment, he finally replied. *No.* His fear mixed with mine. *You can't take my place.*

I didn't want to tell him too much. Not because I didn't trust him—I did. But I didn't want to tell him anything that he'd have to hide from the queen. *Listen to me. We're going to be together again. I promise. I love you, and I won't let that bitch keep us apart.*

"Callie, I can't link with him," Jasmine gasped. "I wanted to check on him, but it's like there's a block."

"It has to be because he's latching on to Callie and their fated-mate bond," Samuel growled. "I can't either."

"I'm taking on some of his pain." I kept pulling to give him relief. I was so glad Dina had mentioned that fated mates could share things like this. When this was over, I would have time to eat, drink, and heal. My mate wouldn't.

I wasn't sure how long it went on, but Bodey's link cooled back to lukewarm as he linked, *Your parents...* before fading completely.

Growling in frustration, I wondered what else I didn't know about my parents. I reined it in. At least Bodey wasn't aware of his pain anymore, but... damn. Every time I believed I was getting a handle on things, something else popped up.

I didn't get a break because Mom linked to me and said, *Unfamiliar wolves are approaching us. Pearl saw them during a run, and they're on their way here.*

Shit. Maybe he'd meant my adoptive parents.

CHAPTER EIGHT

I PLACED one hand on the center console and the other on the door armrest. The queen was relentless, and every time I thought we had a moment to gather our wits, she attacked us again, catching us off guard.

At what point would we not be taken by surprise?

What do you mean, 'unfamiliar wolves'? I couldn't react irrationally, but then I spoke out loud to Samuel, "Go faster. Oxbow might be under attack soon."

Wolves we've never seen before are five miles out, she said hastily, which wasn't like her.

"What?" Theo croaked and leaned forward, placing his head between the two seats to stare into my eyes. "You can't leave me in the dark. I'm the alpha now."

I winced. "I'm sorry. Mom linked to me. I'll include you in the conversation." With that, I tugged his link into the connection.

Samuel pressed the gas, going faster, as I focused on Mom.

The base of my skull throbbed from an oncoming headache. Everything was catching up to me, and I felt helpless and useless. I was certain any of the advisors would be doing a better job than me.

We've been mostly isolated from the other Oregon packs. Are you sure it's not one of them on a run? I didn't want to jump to the worst conclusion and give Queen Kel more power over us than she already had.

I'll have Lynerd reach out to all the other packs to see if anyone is outside their territory, Theo added.

That was an excellent suggestion and one I should've thought of myself. Damn, even Theo was better at this than me.

Someone else joined our link, and my breath caught.

Pearl.

Her joining our link startled me since she'd never liked to speak to me in person, let alone now that I could finally pack link.

We need help. Pearl's words were rushed. *They found our scent, and five of them are chasing us.*

Aren't you heading back to the pack? When Mom had mentioned that Pearl had seen the wolves, I'd assumed she'd be running straight home. Staying in the woods was dangerous. At least, in the houses, she would have a chance at hiding.

We were running in the opposite direction from the wolves, she replied.

Why weren't you heading back to the house? Mom asked.

I already knew the answer. Charles, the leader of their friend group of five, and Pearl had many things in common. They wanted to appear stronger than they were, thought their poop didn't stink, and were completely self-absorbed. They were probably running away, hoping they wouldn't get caught up in an attack. A sour taste filled my mouth.

Because... She trailed off, confirming my assumption when she couldn't come up with a reason.

Listen, if these are Queen Kel's wolves, that likely means they're attacking this pack because it's where I was raised and they know my adoptive parents are there. That comment alone solidified my fear. Now I was on the same page as Mom— these wolves had to be Kel's. She wanted to take everything I loved away from me. What better way to start than with my fated mate and the people who'd raised me? How was I supposed to fight someone so cruel and vindictive? *Mom—you and Dad need to go to someone else's house so they can't find you right away.*

What about me? Pearl exclaimed.

If they're chasing you, I doubt you can get back there before the rest of the attackers do. Part of me was glad that her whole saving-herself plan had gone wrong, but even though she hated me, I still had to protect her. *The best thing you can do is put as much distance between you and them as you can, and find water and swim. Let the water hide your scent. Go as far from your current location as you can.*

Theo rejoined the conversation and brought Trevor into the loop. *Lynerd is meeting with the Halfway and Joseph packs to send more people over. Halfway can get there in thirty minutes.*

Good, we'll need all the help we can get. I wished we were already there. I hated to think that another attack would happen and we wouldn't be there to provide support. *How many wolves are they sending?*

Half their pack, Theo answered. *They're afraid to bring more in case someone attacks them at home. They'll already be at a deficit.*

I clenched my hands. *Move the weaker pack members to the center of the neighborhood and grab all the guns we have.* One good thing about living in such an isolated area—we had guns at our disposal. A few of the men liked to hunt in human form during hunting season.

"What's going on?" Samuel glanced at me.

I rolled my head in his direction. Then I linked with him, the former advisors, Jack, Miles, Lucas, and Lynerd, and both Lynerd and I provided an update on the situation.

With everything settled the best possible way, we focused on getting there before Queen Kel hurt any more of our people.

Thirty minutes later, Trevor linked to Theo, Lynerd, and me, *They're here.*

I swallowed hard and straightened. We had another forty-five minutes before we'd arrive. "Samuel, go faster."

He nodded, his face flushed as he drove faster than any human could've safely done. I hoped no cops were out here to give us a ticket.

What's going on? Lynerd asked.

They've circled the houses and are moving in. Trevor sounded stressed even through the mental link. *They're organizing an attack.*

How many guns did you find? I knew there wouldn't be a lot, but the enemy wouldn't know how many if we were smart.

Five, he answered.

That wasn't surprising. Only a few pack members enjoyed hunting that way, most preferring to stick to animal form. *Did you distribute them among the houses?*

I hated that we weren't there. We'd left the pack in the hands of a sexist male who was just an older version of Charles.

Yes, but it won't do much good. How far away are Halfway and Joseph?

Halfway is arriving now in wolf form, Lynerd linked. *They should be there in five minutes.*

Trusting Lynerd and Theo to handle this part of the conversation, I linked to Mom and Pearl. I hadn't heard from either of them in the past few minutes, so I tried to keep calm. *Where are you two?*

The wolves are still on our heels, Pearl answered, her fear evident through the connection. *No matter how fast we run, they're gaining on us. Charles thinks we should split up.*

Knowing him, he'd injure one of them to save his own ass. *I'd stay together. If a fight happens, you'll have people to fight alongside you.*

Pearl, where are you? Mom asked, giving me pause.

Close to where I told you a few minutes ago, Pearl replied, and my blood ran cold.

Mom, please tell me that you and Dad aren't—

She's our daughter, Mom interrupted. *We won't hide in a house while the enemy is hunting Pearl.*

I'd assumed they'd listen to me, but that was foolish. Now, not only was Pearl at risk, but also the two people who'd sheltered me for the past seventeen years. Worse, they were pretty much handing themselves over to Kel for her to use against me.

I gritted my teeth. That was the real reason none of them had continued to communicate with me.

Where are you and Dad? I asked.

We left, heading in the other direction from where they're coming, Mom tried to reassure me, but it didn't work.

If they'd gone the opposite direction, the enemy would be picking up their scents about now. Even in wolf form, Mom and Dad couldn't move much faster than in human form due to their weak wolves. If strong wolves went after them, it'd take about half the time to catch up.

At least most of the pack wouldn't be fighting every enemy wolf that came, but Mom, Dad, Pearl, and the other idiot four were in danger.

I shivered. The restlessness of being locked in the car while they were under attack made me want to crawl out of my skin.

Samuel glanced at me. "What's wrong?"

I closed my eyes and focused on breathing steadily. Getting flustered wouldn't accomplish anything but me biting others' heads off. I had to calm down and not let fear overtake me. "Mom and Dad snuck out to search for Pearl."

"Have the wolves captured them?" Jasmine murmured.

"Not yet." That was one small blessing. I updated them on what my parents had done.

Samuel leaned over and squeezed my hand. "We should be there in twenty minutes. I'm going double the speed limit."

I pulled Dad into the conversation. He still wasn't thrilled about my having locked Stevie up after I'd learned she'd been working with Kel, and he'd become more distant with me. But this was life or death, and he had to get over it. *They're going to pick up your scent soon if they haven't already.*

We'll be fine, Dad linked. *Don't worry about us.*

I laughed, and Samuel's forehead creased.

Yeah, in fairness, I must have sounded crazy. Whether they liked it or not, I would always worry about them. Maybe they hadn't treated me the same as Stevie and Pearl, but they'd protected me the best they could, even if it had been for their own good. For seventeen years, they'd been the closest thing I had to a family.

Where is everyone? I needed to know where to go once we got there. The familiar sights of the road to Oxbow came into view.

We're in Hells Canyon, nearing the Snake River, Mom

answered. *Pearl is down there somewhere with Charles and their friends.*

I knew the route Mom and Dad would have taken to Hells Canyon. If I could pick up their trail, I could find them within ten minutes. *I'll be there soon.*

I turned to Theo. "What's going on in town?"

"The wolves are attacking." Theo rubbed a hand through his hair. "Two of our own are dead, and the Halfway pack just arrived. Joseph is thirty minutes out."

Fuck. "How many do they think there are?"

Theo flinched. "Easily one hundred."

With how fast Samuel had been driving, we were beating the Joseph pack. I nodded and linked with everyone in the three vehicles. *When we get there, I need the former advisors, Theo, Jasmine, Jack, and Samuel, to help the pack in the neighborhood. I'd like Miles and Lucas to come with me to track down Mom, Dad, Pearl, and the four others.* Though I'd protect them out of duty, that didn't mean I had to name them as if they were as important as my family.

I hated taking the two royal advisors from the rest, but if Kel's wolves suspected it was my family that had run, the strongest would go after them. I needed good backup.

That's fine with us, Michael answered.

Jack scoffed. *Why am I not going with the three of you?*

As we approached thick trees that led into Hells Canyon, I lifted a hand. "Samuel, stop the car." Then I answered Jack's question. *You're driving your car with Zeke in the back. I need you to, you know, drive and keep an eye on him.*

Slowing down, Samuel arched a brow. "What's going on?"

Miles, Lucas, and I are getting out here, I linked with everyone as I opened my door. Time was of the essence, and I was going to save my family.

I hopped out and slammed the door as Miles and Lucas

followed suit. I ran off the gravel road toward the trees, and my wolf brushed my mind. She didn't hesitate, surging forward as my skin tingled, and I ran between two firs and up the incline that would take me toward the river.

Light-blonde fur sprouted across my body, the same shade as my hair, and my clothes ripped away and my spine cracked, causing me to drop to all fours. I ran awkwardly for a few steps until I was completely in wolf form.

With my senses heightened, my vision was crisper in the darkness and my sense of smell was so much better. I could hear the sound of a goat running two miles away in the canyon. I ran fast—but a little slower than I normally would so Lucas and Miles could keep up with me. They didn't know the area as well as I did.

They flanked me, and the three of us moved in tandem. Our paws hit the mulch, helping keep our steps quiet.

A piercing howl rang in my ears.

They found us, Pearl linked.

Shit, we were still five miles away. I linked to Lucas and Miles, *They found Pearl and the others. Can you run faster?* I hated to push them, but there was no time to spare.

Don't worry about us, Miles linked. *Just go. We won't lose pace.*

Holding them to that, I took off toward my family.

My paws pounded against the ground, and bits of dirt flew up behind me with each step. My tongue rolled out of my mouth as I panted, trying to keep up the pace. *We'll be there soon.*

Two miles away, just as I locked on the scents of Mom and Dad, I heard snarls and whimpers. They must all be together, and I wondered if Kel's wolves had coordinated it that way.

How many enemy wolves are there? I asked.

Fifteen, Dad replied, confirming my worst fear.

They were outnumbered.

Tapping into my wolf, I allowed her to take control. Each step took what felt like a lifetime as whimpers and yelps sounded. I had no idea which side they were coming from, but I was certain it wasn't only the enemy.

After what felt like forever, the ground curved downward and gravity propelled us faster. A few minutes later, the fight scene came into view.

It was the same location where Bodey and the other three advisors had taken me after Charles, Pearl, and their friends had attacked me when I was alone in Hells Canyon. The irony of the situation wasn't lost on me.

A brown-and-gray wolf was on top of Pearl, biting her shoulder. I hunkered down and jumped, ignoring the stench of blood that assaulted my nose, then slammed into the brown-and-gray enemy.

I knocked him onto his side and into the Snake River with a loud *splash.* Pearl blinked at me, blood running down her sides from the wolf's teeth marks. She had a bite mark on one leg.

They had taken a beating, and I wasn't sure if we would make things much better. I probably should've brought more wolves, but I didn't want to risk the main pack since we had no idea how many wolves had been sent there.

Get up, I linked, running around her head. If she stayed down, another wolf would be on her in seconds.

As I ran into the water toward the enemy, he got back to his feet. I threw my weight forward, splashing river water in the wolf's face, then sank my teeth into his neck and ripped. The metallic taste coated my mouth, and I forced myself not to think about it as I spun around to assess the next threat.

Along with my kill, two other enemy wolves lay dead on

the ground, leaving us with twelve. When my gaze settled on Josh's beige wolf, vomit burned my throat.

The enemy clawed into his stomach, splitting it open. Blood poured out.

No wolf could survive that without a witch.

His eyes widened, and he stumbled, and I glanced elsewhere, only to find Fred's charcoal wolf cornered by three of our enemies.

Without a thought, I raced toward him, sick over not even trying to help Josh. But Josh was as good as gone. Fred wasn't.

I snarled, and two of the wolves turned their attention to me. Their eyes focused on my chest, where I'd learned that, even in wolf form, my tattoo was visible.

They knew who I was.

The two of them left Fred and charged at me.

CHAPTER NINE

I HUNKERED DOWN, ready for the fight.

The two enemy wolves, one with copper fur and the other with gunmetal-gray fur split apart, running at either side of me.

Tongue hanging out, the copper one bounced as he charged toward me like this was a game he enjoyed, while the gunmetal wolf was more cautious in her approach, keeping her pale-brown eyes locked on me.

I snarled and forced myself to be still and patient. If I reacted too soon, they would have enough time to counter my move.

When they were within five feet, I jumped as high as I could backward, clearing six feet. The gunmetal wolf tried to correct herself, but the copper wolf slammed right into her, knocking her to the rocky ground.

I landed on them, my claws digging into their backs. The gunmetal wolf whimpered and went down, but the copper wolf rolled away, causing my legs to spread and ruining my

I landed on my stomach hard, and the copper wolf swiped at my side. His claws sank into my fur and skin, the sharp sting of the damage stealing my breath. I yelped, unable to keep the noise in, and stood. My blood added to the metallic stench around me, but I snaked my head to the side and caught one of the copper wolf's paws in my mouth.

As he jerked his leg back, I sank my teeth clean through it. He squealed, and I ground my jaw, inflicting as much damage as possible.

The gunmetal wolf steamrolled into me, and I slammed into the copper wolf. My jaw went slack, and the copper wolf yanked his paw from my mouth. He stumbled and dropped, unable to put weight on the leg. I tripped over him, my legs knocked out from under me.

I landed on my uninjured side, a rock bruising my body. Using the momentum, I turned in the opposite direction from the copper wolf and stood. The gunmetal wolf was already there, jaw open and aimed for my right shoulder.

That was a common theme with Kel's wolves—if they weren't going for the kill, they went for the shoulders. I jerked my shoulder back enough for the tips of her teeth to graze me and sank my teeth into her neck.

Her body jerked, and she swiped at my chest. Her nails ripped my skin, but I kept my jaws locked in place, ignoring the burn of yet another wound in less than two minutes.

A snarl came from my side, and I thrashed my teeth through the gunmetal wolf's neck before pivoting toward the copper wolf.

Warm blood dripped down the fur of my chest, and I tried not to dwell on yet another death being added to my ever-growing list.

The copper wolf limped toward me, dark eyes wide with

rage. Not wanting to waste more time, I met him halfway, readying to take the fatal blow. Then my fated-mate connection blazed back to life.

Callie, Bodey linked, his worry soaring into me. *You're hurt. What's going on?*

I froze. If he was awake, something had to be wrong. *Are you okay?*

That moment of hesitation was all it took for the copper wolf to bite into my shoulder.

A searing throb of pain seized my lungs as I scraped a paw under his belly, slitting him open like his friends had done to Josh. He released me and stumbled back, falling onto his butt.

Dammit, Callie, Bodey linked, his fear strangling me. *I need to be there. Kel told me you're at your parents' pack.*

I had to get my head back in the game and reassure him so I could block our connection until this was over. *We are, and as much as I love hearing you in my head, I need to focus. My injuries aren't fatal. I swear.* I scanned the area to determine who needed help next. Lucas and Miles had each killed a wolf, leaving us with eight enemy wolves to fight.

Fred, Charles, Dad, and Bryson were each fighting a wolf while the rest of the enemy had split into pairs to attack Lucas and Miles.

Mom and Pearl were missing.

I could still feel the warmth of their pack links. I linked to them, *Are you two okay?* I searched the trees for them.

We're fine, Mom replied. *Pearl ran off, and I chased after her in case more wolves arrived. We should be back soon.*

Get into the water and hide, I replied. They'd be safer away from here. *We've got it handled.* At least, I hoped we did.

The graphite-gray wolf fighting my dad stood on its hind

legs and scratched Dad's face and snout. Dad ducked his head to his chest and attempted to back away, but there was a large rock behind him.

He needed help the most.

I raced toward him, and my chest tightened as Dad fell onto his back. The graphite wolf was on him in seconds, slashing Dad's neck open.

Acid burned my throat, and I pushed it down as I shoved the wolf off Dad. I linked to Jack, Samuel, and the former advisors, *If there are any witches nearby, I need them to come to me* now.

Snarling, the graphite wolf steadied himself and faced me, chest heaving. Dad's blood covered his snout.

There aren't any witches, Samuel answered.

Hot rage blasted through me, and something inside me snapped. Power rolled through my body, my magic sizzled, and I moved faster than ever before. I slammed into the enemy wolf, who flew backward into the nearest larch tree. His body thudded into it, his head cracking against the trunk, and he crumpled to the ground. I waited to make sure he didn't get up.

When he didn't move, I hurried to Dad, making sure to face the fighting so no one could attack my back.

Blood poured from Dad's neck, and his eyes were wide. He tried to use his paws to put pressure on his neck, but they weren't like hands. Hell, even if they had been hands, they wouldn't have done any good.

How bad is it? Dad linked as he kept trying to apply pressure to the wound.

This would have been a good fucking time to be able to lie, but the stench would give me away. *Not good.* I lowered my head, my eyes burning. Even though he'd always been more indifferent toward me than my mom had, at least he'd been there. He'd tried to do right by me, going so far as to punish Pearl when she treated me horribly. We'd just never had a true father-daughter connection, not like he had with Stevie and Pearl.

He nodded, dropping his paws in acceptance.

My eyes flicked toward the others. Lucas and Miles had taken down another two wolves. Now there were five to our seven. Charles and Bryson had gaping wounds, and I needed to help them, but I didn't want to leave Dad.

Not like this.

Go to the others. Dad rolled his head to the side. *Charles and Bryson—they need you. They won't ask for your help.*

But—

Help them, but Callie. Dad made a noise between a gargle and a whimper. *I'm sorry. I should've done more, but when you were pushed on us and our family was treated worse because of it...*

Even though he was a weaker wolf, he still was driven by his animal to be seen as stronger. Every wolf wanted respect, and I understood that. *Don't. I get it. You gave me food and clothes and tended to my wounds. You did more for me than I could have ever asked for.*

It wasn't enough. Dad's breathing slowed. *And I'm sorry. Just please... watch out for your sisters and Julie. They'll need you.*

A steel-gray enemy wolf bit into Charles's neck, way too close to his main artery.

I swear I'll protect them, I vowed as I stood.

Go now, Dad linked.

That was it. The enemy had gone too far. I linked to Mom, Pearl, and Stevie, *Dad's dying.*

What? Stevie gasped. *Is there a way to help him?*

I could only imagine how helpless she must feel, being hours away from us at the Valors' house in Grangeville.

The steel-gray wolf unlatched from Charles's throat, and I raced toward him. As he repositioned himself for the killing blow, I slashed his face, digging my claws into his gums right above his teeth. His head snapped back.

No, there's not, I answered Stevie as I shoved the steel-gray wolf back several feet. He caught his balance and didn't fall down as I'd hoped. *Mom and Pearl need to come back. He won't be alive much longer.*

And we won't be either if we come back now, Pearl snapped.

I'd always thought Pearl was selfish, but she'd been good at hiding it until now.

It's no use all three of us dying, she finished.

The steel-gray wolf bared his teeth, blood pouring from his gums. He wasn't showing weakness, which was fine with me. I was tired of waiting for the enemy to make the first move. That ended now.

I dug my paws into the muddy ground and pushed off for speed. The wolf rose onto his hind legs, ready to claw me, so I pivoted to the side and attacked at an angle. He tried to turn, but I was faster than him, and I bit the spot under his front leg right where a human's armpit would be.

He groaned and lifted higher, trying to break free, so I bit into his lower chest. This time, he lowered his front legs, trying to box me in, and I rolled under him and dug all four paws into his body as I continued to bite down on his chest.

I didn't know what my strategy was, but I wanted to inflict pain until he couldn't hurt anyone else again. His body sagged against mine, and I used my legs to toss him off. He landed beside me, grunting as he closed his eyes. His underside was gashed, and blood streamed from the sizable wound I'd bitten into his chest.

Fur matted with his blood, I rolled over and searched for whoever needed help next.

Miles was ripping the throat out of the final enemy wolf. I took a ragged breath and glanced at Charles and Bryson. Charles was worse off and bleeding profusely, but he'd be okay, thanks to shifter healing. Bryson had a few bites on his body, but they looked superficial. Luckily, those two were the strongest wolves in Theo's pack after Theo, Trevor, and Zeke.

Charles didn't look at me. Instead, he stared at the Snake River as if it were the most interesting thing in the world.

Prick.

I hurried back to Dad just as Mom ran into the clearing. She dropped to his side and nuzzled him. His chest barely moved. His link to me was cooling, and sorrow pierced me. I hated that I hadn't been able to protect him enough to save him.

Mom whined, the heartbreaking sound tugging at my soul. I wished there was something more I could do.

But there were so many more people I needed to worry about as well, so I linked back to Samuel and the others, *We've lost one, and a second is fading quickly. The enemy wolves are dead or severely injured, so Lucas, Miles, and I are heading back your way.*

Now that the imminent threat was over, my adrenaline started to wear off, allowing the pain in my shoulder and sides to filter through. Fucking lovely.

Be careful on your way back, Michael replied. *We haven't been able to accurately gauge their numbers.*

Of course not. Kel was all about keeping us in the dark. I had to find a way to take back control. *Miles and Lucas, can you come with me to the neighborhood to help fight?*

Lucas nodded, but he examined me and huffed. *Bodey will kill us for letting you get injured again.*

I stared at him intently. *You didn't allow me to do anything. I make my own choices, and believe me, I wouldn't choose to get hurt like this or lose my dad.*

My attention flicked back to Dad, whose chest had stopped moving. His pack connection cooled in my chest, and my throat tightened, nearly choking me. Mom threw her head back and howled, breaking another piece of my heart. My eyes burned, and I linked to Pearl, *Get your ass here now. The threat is gone, and Dad just died. Mom needs you.*

But— Pearl started.

Enough. I laced my thought with alpha will. If she was going to be selfish, I'd force her to be there for Mom. *Say goodbye to Dad and come here to support Mom. I'm going back to the neighborhood to help the rest of the pack.* I then linked to Bryson and Charles, *You two stay here and alert us if any enemy wolves find you.* I couldn't leave Mom and Pearl completely unprotected, not after what I'd promised Dad.

Lucas, Miles, and I ran toward the neighborhood, my sides and shoulder throbbing with every step. I pushed through the agony and connected to Bodey, *My dad just died.*

Dammit, Callie. His pain and frustration merged with mine. *I'm so sorry. If I'd been there instead of trapped here—*

Don't. This is all Kel's fault. You have nothing to feel bad about.

If I'd stayed with you instead of chasing after Jasmine, maybe... He trailed off.

I would've done the same if it had been Stevie, I replied, pushing my determination toward him. *You did nothing wrong. Kel has been several steps ahead of us all this time.*

If anyone can defeat her, it's you, he said lovingly.

I wasn't sure about that, but with Bodey now mostly inaccessible, I realized how much I'd come to rely on him saying things like that. *Is she with you again?* He wasn't in pain, but given how unpredictable Kel was, I wasn't sure if that was a good thing.

I'm locked in a basement that reeks like urine, complete with rats. I keep thinking I hear someone else in here with me, but it might be my imagination. As far as Kel goes, I don't think she knows I'm awake or cares that I am. It's another form of torture.

You won't be locked up for long. I had to believe that Russell would come through. *We're coming up with a plan.*

One that doesn't involve you sacrificing yourself, right?

I'll do whatever it takes to save you.

Callie— he started.

I can't tell you anything, Bodey, not while you're her prisoner. I need to protect you the best I can, and I need you to trust me.

Always, he replied with no hesitation.

Miles, Lucas, and I crested the highest ridge of the canyon and ran down toward the neighborhood. Snarls and growls from the fight echoed up to us, punctuated every so often by a random shot from our limited guns.

We pressed on through the trees, and I wondered if we might be able to sneak up on some of Kel's wolves and get some insight into their numbers and their plan.

The first houses appeared in front of us through the trees, and I saw five enemy wolves and one in human form shrouded in darkness at the back door of the first house. I sensed several pack members inside.

We slowed and circled to the side of the house, where I could see the front and the back. Twenty wolves were attacking the front door, creating a huge ruckus, and I realized that every shifter inside was probably focused on that immediate threat.

I watched the back in horror as the human jimmied the lock, slowly opened the door, then slipped inside, followed by the five wolves.

Shit. I had to let them know before it was too late.

CHAPTER TEN

I TUGGED at the connection of the Oxford wolves closest to me. I wasn't sure who was in the house, which belonged to Trevor, Charles's father, so I linked with everyone. *Whoever is in Trevor's house, there are five wolves and one shifter in human form coming in through the back. Everyone be on alert. This won't be the only house they try this on.*

Miles, Lucas, and I increased our speed. Each time my front paws hit the ground, my shoulder ached, but the pain was easing, indicating that the injury had begun healing.

Zeke, Trevor, Jack, and I are in here, Jasmine linked. *We had Zeke tied up, but we let him go to help us, so he and Trevor are firing the guns to hold off the wolves outside.*

I hated that Zeke was involved, but the damage was done, and he and Trevor were the best shots in the pack.

It'd be up to Jack and Jasmine to take down the six intruders without risking the twenty out front, forcing their way in. I wondered why the hell so few of them were in the house. It would've been safer to have twenty pack members together, but we needed to get in there to protect them.

Theo's pack contained two hundred members total.

including children, split between the sixty houses that made up the neighborhood.

We reached the door, and I stood on my hind legs and used my mouth to turn the doorknob and let us in. Someone inside screamed. My blood ran cold. It sounded like Jasmine.

As I walked back a few steps, I dropped to all fours. Then the three of us ran into the kitchen. Since all the houses here had the same floor plan, I knew to barrel out of the kitchen and turn left to run straight into the living room.

I took in the chaos. Zeke and Trevor were at the windows. Each had a gun aimed out of a small opening they'd created by raising the pane a couple of inches. I despised that Zeke had a gun, but I didn't have time to challenge that decision. Jack and Jasmine were in wolf form and taking on the five animals while the human charged Zeke with a knife.

Only one wolf challenged Jasmine, swatting at her sides, while the other four ganged up on Jack close to the kitchen.

Help Jack, I commanded, and Miles and Lucas sprang into action, obeying my command, while I focused on reaching Jasmine.

Zeke, behind you, I warned, needing him alive to help hold off the enemy in the front yard.

The black wolf hit Jasmine in the side, staining her strawberry-blonde fur with blood. They were in the center of the room on the other side of the couch and the love seat.

I hopped onto the arm of the couch and pushed off, then landed on the black wolf's back. Without pausing, I sank my claws into his side and bit the back of his neck.

He tried to buck me off, but I clung on and didn't budge. He stumbled into the glass coffee table and tipped it over. The glass fell from the top and shattered, shards and chunks of glass scattering across the wooden floor.

The black wolf turned and rammed my side into the

closest table leg. It hit the side where I'd been scratched, and I lost my breath.

A gunshot cracked, and I jerked my head up. Jack yelped, and I turned to see that the bullet had hit him in the butt, right next to his tail. An alabaster wolf and a muddy-brown wolf sprang on Jack together.

There was no way we were going to survive.

Kicking up his back legs, the black wolf dumped me on the upside-down table frame. My back landed hard on a table leg, splintering the wood and crushing it to the floor. My body jolted, and Bodey's panic trickled inside me.

Moving slower than I would've liked, I desperately tried to roll over before the black wolf could attack again. He spun, ready to strike, when Jasmine surged forward and bit into his neck. The black wolf moved to the right to get out of her grip, but she held on tight.

Help Jack, she linked. *I can take it from here.*

Another shot was fired as I finally spun to see Zeke hit the enemy human coming for him with a knife.

An enemy wolf from outside leaped into the window-pane, cracking the glass. With Zeke distracted, the wolf had advanced on that side of the house.

"Zeke, get your ass back in position," Trevor snarled, and I was glad I wasn't the one to chastise him.

Back on all fours, I moved toward Jack. The alabaster and muddy-brown wolves launched simultaneous attacks on him. Miles and Lucas were still engaged in battle, and the enemy wolves could now take several good blows at Jack, thanks to his injury.

The alabaster wolf was the strongest, so I targeted him first. I ran to the corner of the room just as the lighter wolf lowered his head to charge, and I decided to do the same. I crouched, gathering all my strength, and leaped into his side a moment before he could ram into Jack.

A strangled whimper came from him as I shoved him past Miles and into the wall, his head hitting it so hard it dented the drywall.

Thank you, ass-kicker, Jack linked, and out of the corner of my eye, I saw him handling the battle with the muddy-brown wolf better now that they were one on one.

You haven't called me that in a while. I tried to sound annoyed, but I'd take the nickname he'd given me after the first time I met Samuel. I'd attacked my brother with a lamp, thinking he was a threat.

The alabaster wolf's head bobbled like he was seeing stars. Good. I needed to finish him.

I went for the kill shot and leaped at his throat.

You deserve it after saving me, Jack replied. *I'm not sure how much longer I could've hung on.*

My teeth sank into soft flesh, and the copper taste of blood filled my mouth. *Your ass did get shot.*

As the alabaster wolf stopped fighting. I released my hold, allowing his body to sag against the wall, and turned to see who needed help next. Miles and Lucas each had a dead wolf at his feet, and Jack had ripped into the muddy-brown wolf's stomach, making the kill. I spun to check on Jasmine, who was rushing to the windows as more wolves descended.

More could come around the back. I linked to everyone nearby, *How is everyone holding up?* With the guns on hand here, I could leave to help another outnumbered house.

Theo replied, *I've lost five pack links. I'm not sure about the other packs that came to help.*

Dan and I are at Zeke's house with fifteen other shifters, and we're okay, but the enemy is almost through the door. We won't be okay much longer, Michael interjected.

Then the Halfway pack alpha chimed in, *We're almost there.*

So far, we hadn't lost many shifters, but that would change. We were at a complete disadvantage.

The faint hum of engines sounded.

My legs almost gave out. Had Kel sent more reinforcements to tear us down? I'd already lost Dad. What else did that bitch want to take from me?

A wolf howled as the engines became louder. The world blurred around me, and I tried to determine a way to get the hell out of this.

Incoming, Samuel linked. He must have just heard the noise; my ears were stronger than anyone else's. *We need to stop them before it's too late.*

I wanted to snap at him, but that wouldn't accomplish anything. We needed to work together and not waste energy fighting among ourselves. *We need a diversion.* The problem was that I had no clue what.

I knew one thing for certain—Kel didn't want me dead. Maybe I could use that to my advantage.

Tugging at my wolf, I let her know I wanted to become human. I could feel her surprise, but she receded, trusting my judgment. At least one of us did. I shifted into human form and tried to forget I was naked. Modesty wasn't important right now.

What are you doing? Lucas asked.

I blew out a breath. "I'm getting as many wolves as I can out of here."

Zeke and Trevor were still shooting from the window, not paying attention to what was going on behind them. I jogged over to Zeke and grabbed bullets from the floor next to him.

I held out my hand. "Give me your gun."

His head jerked toward me, and his eyes bulged. "Go put on clothes and let the men handle this."

Even though I was his queen, he still disregarded me, and I had to put an end to it. I allowed alpha will to creep into my voice. "Give me the gun. I won't ask again. You shot Jack. You can't be trusted with a firearm. Now, stay put and only do what I or the royal advisors tell you to."

Jaw tensing, he snarled as his wolf forced him to hand me the gun. The cool metal felt foreign in my hands, but I had to trust I could do enough damage with the weapon. I'd seen Dad load his gun often, so I added more bullets as I moved to the front door.

Callie, what the hell are you doing? Miles growled.

Protecting my people. I opened the door, raised the gun, and stepped outside. I fired round after round, certain I wasn't hitting anything, but the enemy wolves scattered.

Everyone, leave through your back doors and run toward Hells Canyon as fast as you can. I hadn't sensed any enemy wolves there when we'd left.

No one responded, so I wasn't sure if they'd listen. Running toward the enemy wolves, I fired shots a few seconds apart. The wolves backed up, and another howl came from the far end of the neighborhood where my childhood home was located.

All the enemy wolves around me took off in that direction, and I noticed a few of my people running through their back-yards, obeying my command. For a moment, I couldn't believe it, but then reality set in. *Run past Zeke's house to the canyon. Head to the Snake River, and swim across to the Idaho side, then run as far as you can.*

I stayed in the middle of the road, firing at the enemy wolves who were brave enough to get close to me. I wasn't sure why they were running that way, but it was giving my people a chance to get out of here.

Callie, come on. Lucas appeared a few feet in front of me, bouncing on his paws.

Miles appeared beside him, his dark eyes locking on mine.

"Not everyone is gone." I couldn't leave people behind. I watched more of my people run toward the woods as I'd directed. I had to make sure everyone made it out of there.

You're the queen, Miles linked. *You have to go.*

Shit. He was right. If I got caught, it would be worse for everyone.

Headlights shone between the neighborhood trees, and my heart thudded harder. At least five cars were coming.

True, the queen didn't want to kill me, but she wanted to take me captive. She'd taken Bodey to ensure that happened, so I couldn't hang around here and hand myself over.

I'd stayed too long.

"Fine." I nodded and spun on my heels, then ran for the canyon. I linked, *Get out now.* The cold air rushed over my naked body, but with the threat breathing down my neck, not even that could cool me off. I continued to fire the gun at the enemy as they hauled ass past me. One yelped and stumbled to the ground.

Holy shit. I'd actually hit someone. Maybe I could get this down pat. It would've been helpful if I'd gotten some practice before now.

A vehicle roared in nearly on top of us, and I glanced over my shoulder to see a cherry red MINI Cooper racing toward me. I picked up my pace, and my wolf brushed my mind, wanting to take control again. *I'm shifting,* I informed Lucas and Miles.

My skin tingled as she exploded and forced the shift

quickly. I sensed a wolf coming at me from my right, and I could tell by my pack links that it wasn't one of my people.

I'll get the one running toward us, Miles linked. *Get Callie out of here.*

As I landed on four legs, wind stirred around me.

The breeze grew stronger, whipping my fur around me, and my paws inched off the grass. Blood rushed through my ears as a sickening sensation unfurled in my chest. There wasn't any rain, and we rarely got tornadoes. This had to be a spell.

I hovered in the air, slowly circling. *I'm sorry, Bodey.* I couldn't believe how stupid I'd been. I shouldn't have run out in front of the house, but I'd needed to protect my people. That decision might wind up hurting not just everyone here but the entire Northwest Territory.

My mate's worry crashed over me. *Baby, what's going on?*

Between that and the spinning, acid burned my throat. *Kel's witches have captured me. I was just trying to protect everyone ...*

Bodey added in the former advisors, Jack, Samuel, Miles, and Lucas to our connection and said, *Everyone, get your ass out there and protect Callie.*

Miles and I are already here, man, Lucas answered. *We're trying to get her down.*

We're turning back to help, Michael linked. *We aren't far.*

An older man's voice linked to us, *The Joseph pack is here. We're coming in near the neighborhood entrance.*

Thank gods we had reinforcements. *I'm captured and need help, as does anyone who hasn't made it into the woods yet.*

Then the air disappeared, and I dropped to the ground.

CHAPTER ELEVEN

I INHALED SHARPLY, bracing for the pain, but when my body hit the lawn of the front yard two houses down from Trevor's, it hardly jarred me.

Maybe I hadn't been as high in the air as I'd thought.

I spun around, snarling at the red car, ready to attack. Yes, the witches had magic, but I wouldn't lie down and take a beating. It wasn't ingrained in me. If it had been, I would've given up years ago.

Four more MINI Cooper electric cars followed the first. I blinked. I'd never seen so many electric cars together in one place.

The passenger door of the front car opened, and a young witch close to my age stepped out and threw her hands toward me. "Blast them out of the way," she chanted.

I dug my paws into the grass, racing toward her. The blast would hit me before I could reach her, but at least I'd be closer to her once I came around, hopefully. I braced myself, waiting for the pain, but a flash of wind breezed past me.

A yelp from beside me caught my attention, and I glanced over to see an enemy wolf slam into the house.

My legs faltered, and I looked back at the witch, who was lowering her hands.

She beamed, her cognac eyes warm. "We got you, Your Majesty."

I tilted my head, wondering if this was a dream. The witch had lifted me inside a tornado, and now she was vowing to protect me. Her actions were at odds.

Oh, by the way, our witches may get there before us, the older man who had to be the alpha linked again. *They decided to drive instead of trying to keep up with us while we're in animal form.*

I almost laughed. *That would've been good to know five minutes ago. We thought they were Queen Kel's backup.* Some of the tension rolled off me, and I linked with all of our wolf shifters, informing them of what was going on.

With fresh eyes, I turned from the five cars and noted that I no longer saw enemy wolves running past.

Sorry, I didn't think they'd get there that fast, and I was talking with Lynerd. The alpha sounded regretful. *But you're right. I should've notified you immediately. He recommended that I tell you we were on our way.*

That was enough to cool my annoyance. I couldn't fault someone for making a mistake while under pressure—gods knew I'd been making them left and right, and unlike some alphas, he'd apologized without sounding sarcastic.

We're all under stress, but that's not a good excuse. Next time, talk to both Lynerd and me. I didn't want to discount Lynerd right after putting him in power. I needed the Oregon advisor with me, not working against me like Zeke had been.

You got it, Your Majesty.

I didn't like that title, but I didn't want to correct him. I was new to the position and needed as much authority as I could muster, which included using the honorific.

Dad's death came to the forefront of my mind. Mom needed help, especially if Pearl was giving her shit, not wanting to be there.

With the witches here, I didn't feel right leaving, so I linked with Jack, Lucas, Samuel, Miles, Theo, Jasmine, and the former advisors, *Can two of you split off and help my mom bring my dad's body here? She's there with Pearl, James, and Bryson, and I don't trust them.* My throat constricted as my vision blurred. Even in wolf form, I couldn't hide from the loss of the man who'd been the closest thing I'd had to a father.

I'll go, Jack linked. *He's Stevie's dad too. It seems right that I should be there.*

I'll join Jack, Theo said. *Your father was from my pack, and I should help bring him in and get everything ready for the burial.*

Theo stepping up as alpha eased some of my concerns. I was afraid he wouldn't be assertive enough to lead, and I hoped he continued to prove me wrong.

Jasmine and Lucas, can you two please keep an eye on Zeke? He needs constant supervision. Miles and the former advisors, can you get everyone back here and account for injuries and deaths? I hated to say the last word, but I could feel the cold spots in my chest from the loss of life. *And Samuel, could you shift back into human form and join me? There are five cars full of witches here, and I'd like for you to address them with me. I'll take them to my old house so I can find a change of clothes.*

On my way, Samuel said.

Shaking my wolf head, I huffed, trying like hell to communicate with the witch. I nodded toward my old house. I'd taken all my favorite clothes to my new home with Bodey, but I had left some behind.

The witch tossed her long caramel-colored hair over her shoulder. "We'll follow you."

Taking off through the neighborhood, I noted Theo's pack returning to their homes. Several of them were moving slowly, but most didn't seem injured. Pearl, running across Kel's wolves and warning our parents, had given the pack time to prepare and bought us time to arrive.

As members of my former pack trotted past me, a few of the stronger members Zeke had favored made a point of looking everywhere but at me. Most of the women in the pack stared at me with what I thought might be hope—hope that I could make a difference?

I wasn't sure I could. So far, during my week as queen, we'd been attacked, my dad had been killed, and I'd lost my fated mate to my adversary. If that wasn't the worst first week any new leader had experienced, I felt sorry for them.

The cars followed me as I trotted to my parents' house. Though my side and shoulder were healing, each time my front paw hit the ground, my body twinged with pain.

Hey, Bodey linked.

My heart pounded against my rib cage. How I wished he could be here beside me. *Hey, sorry. It's been crazy here.*

I could tell, and I was trying not to distract you, but I was scared there for a while. And I can tell you're injured.

His unhappiness wafted between us as my parents' house came into view. I replied, *It's fine. It's mostly healed.* Then I updated him on everything.

Baby, I'm so sorry. I'd give anything to be there with you.

Me too, but for now, this had to be enough. At least he wasn't being tortured, and we could talk with each other. *You're still aching too.* He didn't get to act like I was the only one hurting.

I'll be fine, he replied. *Don't worry about me.*

I snorted, unable to help it. A few of the wolves trotting past me to get home glanced at me. Everyone had shifted to get out of the neighborhood as fast as possible.

As I reached the house, reality slammed into me. Dad would never walk through this door again. I pawed at the handle, opening the door. With tears in my eyes, I ran through the living room and into the bedroom Stevie and I used to share. I linked with Bodey, *I don't know what I'm supposed to say to Mom, Pearl, and Stevie.*

What do you mean?

I shut the door and pulled my wolf from my mind. Within seconds, I was human and walking past the stripped bed that had been mine to the closet. *Kel attacked here because of my family. Why else would she have mentioned my parents before knocking you out? It's my fault Dad died.*

Bodey's heartbreak pushed into me, and the ache inside me doubled. He said with venom, *It isn't your fault, baby. Yes, Kel meant to capture them to hold them over you along with me, but that's no reflection on you.*

I slipped on one of Stevie's black shirts and a pair of jeans that had more holes than cloth, but at least my privates were covered. The deep pain in my chest made breathing hard. *That doesn't make me feel any better. Everyone I love is in danger because of me.*

No. Everyone is in danger, not just the people you love, because of Queen Kel. You aren't the person causing this.

He was right. Part of me *knew* that, but something inside me couldn't grasp it. *If I wasn't queen—*

Then everyone Samuel was close to would be in danger. You aren't the problem. Kel is after whoever the ruler is, and whether it was you or Samuel, she would've targeted me.

Bodey's capture and my dad's death had me questioning my ability to lead. *I feel like my decisions keep giving her the advantage.* I blew out a breath. He was the one person I could share anything with, but I hated to lean on him when he was in danger.

Babe, I love you, and you're doing your best. He paused, and my stomach knotted.

But?

But nothing. You need to trust your gut and realize a lot of this is out of everyone's control, and I promise I'll be there for you more when I get out of here.

What do you mean? I looked at Stevie's unmade bed. Her black comforter was tossed to one side, and I realized it was probably from the morning she'd rushed to reach the coronation site. I shook my head, though Bodey couldn't see me. *You've been there for me the entire time.*

I know, but being away and seeing the bigger picture, I'm realizing some things. Things I want to talk to you about... if I ever get out of here. You should trust your gut if it screams at you that something's off, even if Samuel disagrees. You two aren't the same people, so if he thinks something is right and you disagree, that doesn't mean your thoughts are wrong.

I hadn't thought of it that way. *I grew up being treated as worthless, and I've only ever had to make decisions for myself. Now I'm deciding on behalf of thousands of people, and I need help to gain confidence. I appointed Lynerd to Zeke's role, and Samuel wasn't happy with the decision.*

Samuel is your brother and loves you no matter what he thinks. Bodey pushed comfort toward me. *You're amazing and strong, and I don't want you to discredit yourself.*

My heart skipped a beat. Even when he was far away and kidnapped by my nemesis, he had a way of making me feel completely loved. *I love you.* I didn't know how else to convey everything inside me. He was the lyrics to the perfect song, one I would never tire of listening to.

Samuel linked, *Callie? Is everything okay? The witches and I are outside waiting, and we're starting to worry.*

I exhaled, not wanting my time with Bodey to end. But I needed to get out there. I connected with Bodey, *I've gotta go talk to the witches.*

Okay. I'm tired anyway, Bodey replied. *I'll try to get some sleep on this wet, cold floor.*

My chest throbbed. *I love you, and I will get you out of there.* That was one promise I was damn sure going to keep.

Focus on keeping yourself safe. Losing you is the one thing I could never endure.

As I walked through the living room to the front door, the house seemed eerie, like Dad's essence was lingering. The sense of loss was overwhelming. The reality that I'd never again see him in the kitchen watching Mom cook or sitting on the couch watching hockey slammed into me with its finality.

Outside with Samuel, I found twenty witches in our yard. The one who had cast the spell stood in front of the group, flanked by two older witches. The other seventeen were searching the area for threats.

Like every other witch I'd seen, they all wore long, flowy dresses in earth tones, emphasizing their frames while looking boho-chic.

I strolled over, trying not to panic as Bodey's link cooled. He'd told me he was going to sleep but to do so that quickly, he must be exhausted.

"Samuel informed us that you thought you were under attack when I lifted you in that tornado." The cognac-eyed witch frowned. "I'm sorry about that. I didn't realize Nate hadn't informed you we'd arrived."

I rolled my shoulders to relieve some tension. Shifting back hadn't been painful, and with the burst of magic, my wound had healed. But the tightness from stress remained. "Okay, but why was that necessary?"

"Two wolves tried to attack you from behind." She shrugged. "We were worried you might not sense them, and lifting you out of the way was the simplest choice." She held out her hand. "I should introduce myself. My name is Iris, the high priestess of the Joseph pack's coven, and these two ladies are my right hands." She pointed at the woman with dark-bronze skin and dark curly hair to her left. "This is Louise, and this"—she pointed at the witch with pale skin, ash-blonde, almost white hair, and ice-blue eyes on her right—"is Bonnie."

I shook her hand and nodded to the other two women. "I'm Cal—" I paused, knowing I should use my birth name to reinforce my position. "Caroline, and thank you for the help."

"We know who you are." Louise beamed. "It's an honor to meet you and work beside you."

Bonnie lowered her head. "How can we help you?"

That was a hard answer, but I had one, nonetheless. "We need to make sure the enemy doesn't come back while we bury our dead." I rubbed my chest. "We've lost five of our own, and we're lucky it wasn't more."

"And we need someone to help one of the wounded advisors." Samuel pressed his lips together to keep his smile away.

I arched a brow. "What do you mean?" Then I remembered Jack had gotten shot. "Is he not okay?"

"Let's just say he couldn't help us more because he can't shift out of animal form." Samuel rubbed his temples. "The bullet is in his muscle and causing damage."

"But my dad—" I flinched, thinking of Charles or Bryson touching him. I didn't trust either of them, especially with their dislike of me.

"Miles went with them." Samuel touched my arm.

"Let's get to work."

THREE HOURS LATER, we were honoring the five fallen in the graveyard a mile away from the pack neighborhood. The witches had spelled the perimeter and healed Jack while Theo, Miles, Lucas, Samuel, and I, along with the families of the dead, had dug the graves. The former advisors had offered to help, but I'd sent them to check on everyone, hoping our assistance would help eliminate the distrust between this pack and the rest of the advisors.

Stella had driven Stevie here, and once they arrived, it was time to bury the dead.

Tears fell down Pearl's cheeks while Mom completely broke down, and Stevie clung to Jack. I was damn thankful that Stevie had found her mate, even if they hadn't completed their bond.

When Zeke had tried to lead the memorial, Theo had shut him down. I'd thought I might have to intervene, but when Zeke saw me step toward him, he backed off. I assumed he didn't want everyone to see me alpha-will him.

I stayed strong until it came time to cover the dead, and then something inside me snapped. Samuel wrapped his arms around me, giving me the support I needed while I sobbed and watched them bury my dad.

When it was all done, the Joseph and Halfway packs left five of their strongest wolves, and five of Iris's witches stayed as well. Until we knew my family was safe, we were adding extra protection. Stevie, Jack, Miles, Stella, Lucas, Samuel, Jasmine, and the former advisors decided to stay in town and get some rest.

Pearl and Stevie crawled into bed with Mom while Samuel and I slept in Stevie's and my old room. Jasmine, Lucas, Stella, and Miles stayed with Theo, while the former advisors elected to stay in Zeke's house and secure him in his own basement. They would take turns keeping watch to ensure Tina didn't try to let him out, and tomorrow, Stevie, Stella, and Dan would escort him back to Grangeville to keep him there until we decided what to do with him.

Somehow, I got a few hours of sleep.

I WRUNG my hands in the front passenger seat of Bodey's Mercedes. As usual, Samuel was driving. We were on our way to meet Russell and his pack members, following directions to the address he'd sent Jasmine earlier today.

The over eight-hour drive to Cold Springs, Nevada, had made me restless. Bodey had been hurt twice already, and I wanted to pull out my hair. I hated that I was safe while Kel was doing whatever the hell she wanted to him.

Between that and losing Dad, my emotions were swinging like a yo-yo. I'd tried to play music, but inevitably, a sad song had come on, the lyrics pulling at my heartstrings, and I'd had to turn it off.

As we drove into the neighborhood, my heartbeat quickened. Russell hadn't said how many wolves he'd brought, but at least he'd come.

When we pulled up to the house, three people stood out front, including one who shouldn't have been there.

My heart dropped.

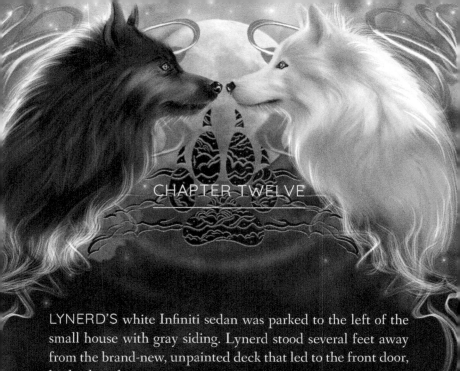

CHAPTER TWELVE

LYNERD'S white Infiniti sedan was parked to the left of the small house with gray siding. Lynerd stood several feet away from the brand-new, unpainted deck that led to the front door, his back to the street.

A man I suspected was Russell blocked the steps, arms crossed. He appeared to be in his fifties, which, in shifter years, likely put him in his eighties.

Behind him stood a young woman whose lips were mashed together. She twirled a piece of her chestnut-brown hair around one finger.

Jasmine gasped. "I didn't think Katelin would come with him. Russell is very protective of her—if you can't tell."

I exhaled. These were the shifters Jasmine knew. I'd been fearful this might be a trap.

But something had gone wrong. I linked to Lynerd, *What's going on? You were supposed to wait for us before getting out of the car.*

He glanced over his shoulder at us and frowned. *I wanted to scope out the area, and I parked here to walk around. The brown-haired girl came outside, and we were talking until this man came barging out.*

We had to calm the situation before things escalated further. "Jasmine, come on. They'll want to see your face."

"I agree." Samuel put the car into park. "Seeing you should de-escalate the situation."

Jasmine and I got out, and I linked with everyone, *Stay put. Russell is already uncomfortable with Lynerd. Let's not overwhelm him.* I didn't want him to feel as if we were teaming up on him, especially if he hadn't brought many people. This place looked small.

I tried not to show my disappointment. They'd brought whoever was willing and able. Even a handful was more than we'd had moments ago.

"Hey, Russell and Katelin," Jasmine said as we moved around the front of the Mercedes. "Is everything all right?"

Russell's russet-brown eyes focused on her, and he straightened. "Depends. Do you know this man?" He nodded at Lynerd.

"He's the Oregon royal advisor who came to meet us here." I needed to be the one to answer since I was the queen. "Is there a problem?"

"He was snooping around and asking my daughter questions." Russell's eyes narrowed on Lynerd. "So I didn't know if Queen Kel had learned about us coming and was trying to gather the proof to justify attacking everyone back home."

I understood that. The queen had a way of gathering knowledge. "I don't blame you, but he came here to make sure you were an ally."

Russell's jaw twitched. "If you don't trust us, then none of this will work."

"The same way you didn't trust him?" I had to think of something fast. Saving Bodey hinged on this plan, and we needed them. If they walked away, I'd be back to two options —sacrificing my mate, which wasn't an option, or handing myself over.

Katelin snorted, startling me.

She tossed her hair over her shoulder and leaned against the white wooden door. "She's got you there, Dad."

He growled. "Maybe, but what else am I supposed to think when some random man starts sniffing around and then flirts with my daughter?"

I tensed. There had been more going on.

"Dad..." Katelin's turquoise eyes bulged. "He wasn't flirting."

Russell huffed. "I'm a man. I know exactly what he was doing." His nose wrinkled as he observed Lynerd.

What did you do? I linked, surprised.

Nothing, I swear. Lynerd didn't even look at me and instead continued to stare at Russell, fueling the conflict even more.

I stepped between Russell and Lynerd, cutting off their view of each other. I extended my hand, wanting to pull Russell's focus elsewhere. "We appreciate you coming to aid us. I know that wasn't an easy decision."

Russell exhaled, his face smoothing as he shook my hand. "Well, it's Jasmine's brother that Queen Kel took hostage, and if we help you, I'm hoping you'll return the favor someday."

"Of course." I was willing to do almost anything as long as it got Bodey home to me. "Jasmine has only good things to say about you and Katelin."

"The girls have become close friends, and Jasmine spent some weekends with us, so the feeling is mutual." Russell's attention went to my neck.

I swallowed and fidgeted, uncomfortable with the intensity of his stare.

"Sorry." He flinched. "It's just, well, King Sutton's tattoo doesn't move. I didn't expect that. It's damn near mesmerizing."

"You better not let Mom overhear that." Katelin stepped down and laid her chin on her father's shoulder. "But damn, you're right. That's sick."

All the attention on me had the hair on my neck rising. I pulled my fuchsia sweater a little higher on my collarbone to hide the moving portion of the tattoo. "Sorry, I'm still getting used to it."

Russell cleared his throat and glanced at the three vehicles. "Who did you bring with you?"

I introduced everyone, pointing to them in each vehicle. "I told them to stay put until you felt comfortable with everyone getting out."

"Why?" Russell's brows rose. "You don't think Katelin, my men, and I could take you?"

"Your men?" I didn't see any other vehicles here. If he'd considered Lynerd a real threat, I expected he would have called his men out here.

He laughed. "You think Katelin and I are it?"

"Why wouldn't I think that?" My wolf growled in my head, inching forward. She didn't like what Russell was insinuating. "You thought Lynerd was a threat."

"A threat I could handle." His eyes glowed, indicating he was using his alpha link. "Come on, bring your people in."

Katelin and Jasmine hugged as our group got out of the cars and headed over. When we stepped inside, I realized the house was actually huge. It was built longways, and the den was massive. The back porch ran the length of the house and overlooked a dock on the lake.

Walking past a tan cloth couch and sectional, I moved to the glass door that led out back. I could smell twenty different shifter scents, but they were fading, suggesting the shifters hadn't been in here for the last thirty minutes. The trip here had taken most of the day, but I wasn't tired, more like worried and wired since tomorrow was the day.

The sun was setting, and smoke rose from below, along with the smell of cooking meat. My mouth watered.

As if the queen knew we were up to something, Bodey's link warmed in my chest. This was the fourth time today, and I knew what would follow.

Immense pain.

Callie, Bodey linked, tugging on our connection. I could feel him clinging to me to get through the pain. He'd fought against using our connection for relief at first, but the beatings had gotten so bad today that I didn't think he realized he was doing it. I'd gladly embrace his agony if it gave him a reprieve. At least I could do that for him.

A sharp jolt sliced through our bond, and I sank to my knees. I reached out and grasped the back of the couch to keep myself upright.

Samuel and Jasmine appeared on either side of me, their scents informing me who they were, but I couldn't lift my head as I focused on the agony swirling inside me.

"What's going on?" Russell asked with concern. "Is she spelled or something?"

I wanted to reply and assure him that wasn't the case, but hell, what Kel was doing to me was far worse than any curse.

"Queen Kel has her fated mate, my son." Michael's voice shook with his own pain. "The queen has been beating him to break Callie."

"That's *horrible,*" Katelin murmured. "She's more of a monster than we realized. To torture someone like that... it's unthinkable."

Lynerd scoffed. "It's an effective strategy. Kel wants

Callie to trade herself for him, so the best way to ensure she's willing to do that is to torture her mate. She'll do just about anything to give him peace."

"Yeah, your ass *would* find it effective," Russell growled.

As I was about to intervene, another blow pounded through our bond, stealing my breath. I crumpled over the couch just as my phone rang from my back pocket. Gritting my teeth, I reached for it.

"Here." Samuel removed the phone and handed it to me. He tensed as he relayed, "It's the queen."

Why wasn't I surprised? Her calling after a day full of agony made sense. She wanted me desperate to end Bodey's trauma. I swiped the phone and forced myself to stand so I didn't sound as bad off as I was. "Hello?" I managed to say in a clear voice.

"Ah... *Caroline*. How are you doing today, my dear?" Kel chuckled maliciously.

I turned to face the others, knowing they could hear everything. Phil, Carl, and Michael stood on the other side of the room, which was part of the kitchen, while Jack, Lucas, and Miles watched from the doorway to the open room. Russell, Katelin, and Lynerd were by the glass wall overlooking the deck at the threshold of the kitchen and living room.

"I've been better." She knew exactly how I was, so there was no point in pretending. I was certain that would bring Bodey more harm. But I wouldn't grovel if that was what she was hoping for.

"So has your mate." She *tsk*ed. "Which I'm sure you know."

My jaw popped from how hard I clenched. "Why are you calling me?"

"To talk about our meeting." She clucked her tongue. "Why? Is this not a good time?"

Another wave of anguish crashed into me. My blood boiled. "Stop torturing him."

"I can't." She paused. "I have to make sure you don't do something foolish, like attempt to attack me or not hand yourself over. I have to make my point so you understand what's at stake."

A deep groan came through the phone, the sound completely Bodey. "Like hell she will!"

The queen laughed maniacally, and Jasmine winced beside me.

"Aw, love. It's so stupid." The queen huffed. "I tried to warn you, Callie—er, Caroline." She snickered at her *mistake*. "I told you it's best if you cut your losses with your mate. Loving people is a weakness. Even against my better judgment, I tried to help you prepare for this day... but you didn't listen."

Jack's nostrils flared, and he took a few steps toward me. Miles and Lucas grabbed his shoulders, holding him back.

What the fuck? Jack linked.

Losing your cool won't help. Miles squeezed his hand tighter. *Let Callie handle it.*

Lucas nodded. *Queen Kel doesn't give a shit about you and your threats. You'll only make things worse for Callie and Bodey.*

We were all on edge, which I assumed was the point.

Pain blasted again, and my breath caught as Bodey whimpered. A sob lodged in my throat, and I tried to swallow it, but a faint yelp escaped.

"Oh, you're still there. That's good," Kel said. "I was wondering if you'd hung up when you didn't say thank you for how I've tried to help, even to my own detriment."

A noise between a laugh and a cry choked me. "You took my mate and had my dad killed yesterday. There's no way in *hell* I'll be thanking you for *anything*. But I will show you exactly how I feel the moment I stab you through the heart and watch you die." This woman had uncovered something far darker and more sinister in me than I had ever imagined. I craved her death.

"Your dad was a miscalculation." She sighed. "I didn't mean for him to die, but eh, things happen. Besides, you killed many of my wolves in return, so we're even."

I blinked, processing what she'd said. "You attacked my childhood pack. We protected our own, so that doesn't make us *even*."

"Unfortunately for you, you aren't in control, so it doesn't matter what you think." She yawned as if the entire conversation were boring her. "Anyway, I'm calling about our meeting tomorrow."

Make sure you mention the trade, Michael linked with me. *She has to think you're following through on the offer.*

My attention landed on the former advisor as I asked, "When and where do we make the trade?"

She chuckled as if already victorious. "Humboldt-Toiyabe National Forest. It's in northern Nevada, so neutral ground, though it'll take you over nine hours to get there from Grangeville or eight hours from Oxbow. Either way, I'd like to meet at four in the morning before the humans are out and about."

Samuel punched buttons on his phone, which revealed we were only twenty-five minutes from the location. My stomach dropped. How had Russell known to stay here? That couldn't be a coincidence.

I glanced at the time on his phone. It was six thirty. If we'd been in Grangeville, we'd have to leave immediately to get there in time. "We need it to be later." That was the last thing I wanted to do, but I didn't want to give her any insight into where we were.

Nodding, Carl gave me a smile. He knew what I was doing.

"That's all the time you have," Kel replied. "Make it work, or your mate dies." The last word lifted as if she hoped it happened.

I couldn't shake the cold that engulfed me. What sort of monster was she? "Fine, then I'd better get going."

"Take the Horse Meadow trail and stop a mile in where the trees are thick to ensure no one sees us. We'll be there. I'll have only ten people with me, so don't bring more than that yourself. I promise, as long as you don't do anything foolish, no harm will come to any of you."

Samuel typed in the location. It was a trail in the park that was recommended to visit between April and October. It was also classified as a day hike, so at this time of year, we should be the only people out there. That was her plan, and it was one I could support. We didn't need any additional people getting injured. "Fine. See you at four." Just as I removed the phone from my ear to hang up, Kel called out, "Oh, Caroline."

I winced but placed the phone back to my ear. "Yes?"

"Don't do anything rash." She snorted. "Because I won't hesitate to kill your mate." This time, she hung up.

You can't meet her, Bodey linked desperately. *You need to let me go.*

I shook my head and pressed my hand over my heart.

"What's wrong?" Jasmine asked.

"He wants me to let him d-die." My voice cracked on the last word.

Phil lifted a hand. "We won't let that happen, but you have to make Bodey believe you're handing yourself over.

Otherwise, Queen Kel will know we have something in the works."

My heart ached. I didn't want to lie, but if this was the cost of getting us back together, I'd do it. I nodded and linked back with Bodey, *I love you too much. I can't let it happen.* It was the truth; I hadn't lied. I'd just misled him.

Jack crossed his arms and stared at Russell. "How did you know she'd want to meet close by?"

"I guessed." He blew out a breath. "She lives near Valyermo, California, and this area is near the California border, close to northern Nevada, with the best forest. I assumed she'd want to meet us within eight or so miles of here. I got lucky."

Russell, knowing where the queen lived when I didn't, proved how much I didn't know.

No, you can't, Bodey sounded broken.

Before I could respond to my mate, the attacks began on him again. There was not much I could do, so I lay on the couch and took as much of the pain from him as possible.

AFTER THE CALL, the seriousness of the situation sank in. Lynerd and Russell stopped fighting, and Russell informed us that he'd brought twenty-five men, plus himself and Katelin.

Lynerd had insisted that five of his pack members come down with us. His pack was the closest to this location, so I didn't fight him, not that I would've anyway. The attacks on Bodey were near constant. Kel was making her point, and it was very effective. I'd hand myself over to her now if she'd let me.

The rest of Russell's guys had been grilling, and they brought up hamburgers, steaks, and hot dogs, but I couldn't eat much. Everyone was on edge, me worst of all, with Jasmine and Michael right behind me.

We pulled into the parking lot at two a.m. to prepare. Russell and his pack were parking several miles away. We'd researched everything we could about the trail and had a grasp on the area where Kel wanted to meet us. Jasmine had gone with Russell so we could link with her to tell her when to attack.

The attacks on Bodey had stopped, and his link had cooled. I assumed he'd passed out. That was better than the alternative, but I feared the state he was in.

Remember to secure your knives, I linked as I reached down and checked my own around my ankle. After the last meeting with Kel, none of us would risk meeting her unarmed. We'd been foolish last time, and this time, she might hurt one of our own.

As we climbed from our vehicles, no one spoke. The cool breeze brushed past us, and when I reached the pine and aspen trees where the trail began, I could already smell shifters.

And two familiar scents.

Queen Kel was here... and so was Bodey. My heart pounded against my ribs as my gut clenched. Why couldn't I feel more warmth through our connection?

Something was wrong—and I was going to find out what it was.

CHAPTER THIRTEEN

MY WOLF SURGED FORWARD, forcing my legs to move. She was desperate to get to our mate, but a hand grabbed my arm, tugging me backward.

Kel's wolves were several miles out, both a blessing and a curse. They wouldn't know we were here because they couldn't hear us from that far away.

A snarl vibrated from my chest, and I spun, getting in Samuel's face. Between him stopping me from reaching my mate and the way he'd grabbed me, my blood boiled.

"Listen to me," he snarled. "If you charge in there, you'll get Bodey killed. I realize I don't understand what you're going through, but Callie, for *his* sake, you need to keep your head on straight."

That was just the slap in the face I needed. Knowing Bodey was so close and not being able to feel him properly tore me up inside. He was either bad off enough that he was still unconscious, or a witch was involved. Neither option was good.

Michael hurried over and placed a hand on my shoulder.

"His link's cool to me as well. It's not just your bond that's affected."

That didn't provide much comfort. "What if a witch is blocking him from us?"

"He's alive. That's what we need to hold on to." He squeezed me comfortingly. "We'd know if that changed because Samuel would take his spot. A pack can't be without an alpha."

Bodey was alive, and that was all that mattered. I took a deep breath and turned to Samuel, whose brows were furrowed. "What's wrong?"

He scratched his neck. "Why would I be the alpha that replaces Bodey?"

Michael arched a brow. "You're part of our pack and the strongest wolf in the region. You could've taken over Bodey's position if you wanted, but we always assumed..." He dropped his hand from my shoulder. "You know how that story ends since Callie was crowned."

"Let's talk about it later." My voice cracked, emotions flooding through. "I don't want to think about that." Losing Bodey would break me, which was what Kel wanted. But surely she knew that if she killed him, there was no way in hell I'd hand myself over or submit to her. I had to hope she was as determined to capture me without incident as I was to save my mate.

Jack marched over to me and turned me toward him. His cobalt eyes glowed as he vowed, "This will work. Bodey is like a brother to me, and I'll be damned if we don't save him. If nothing else, you need to believe that."

Following a few steps behind, Lucas came up beside him. "You need to trust we're all going to come through but don't be afraid to let her see your pain. She needs to believe you're turning yourself in to save your mate, so the anguish should be visible."

"It will be." Miles frowned. "She's already struggling, and she hasn't even seen him."

Some of the pressure eased. I wasn't expected to act strong. I feared I wouldn't be able to hide my emotions even if they needed that from me.

My wolf whined in my head, and I couldn't stand there any longer. I needed to get to Bodey. "Let's go."

Carl, Phil, and Lynerd were near, so we were all together and ready to move. I followed the musky shifter scents. Kel hadn't lied—I smelled a total of twelve scents: ten of her people, her overly sweet smell, and Bodey's cinnamon and sandalwood.

With each step I took, the scent grew stronger, and my heart yearned harder. My mate was close, and I hadn't realized the magnitude of what our separation had done to me. I hadn't been myself, and getting closer to him had me feeling more whole than I had since his capture.

The terrain was easy to navigate. A moderately challenging path for humans was easy for us. The rustle of elk roaming in the distance sounded normal.

If a ton of magic was being used, the animals wouldn't stay so close.

The trees crowded in, and a stream trickled nearby. As the scents became stronger, my legs wanted to move faster.

Lynerd broke through the group and came to my side. He glanced at me. *Hey, we're going to get Bodey back. I promise.*

I almost missed a step, but my wolf surged forward, helping me to catch my balance. *I'm not sure you can promise that.*

He winked. *It's going to happen, and I want you to remember you owe me.*

I snorted, the sound surprising me. His confidence made it seem as if he knew something I didn't. *If you can get Bodey back to me, I'll have no problem remembering that.*

The hairs stood on my neck. Were we being watched? We had to be getting close. If she'd brought ten men and one of them was watching me, he wouldn't stray far.

Just know it means a lot to me that you gave me this position. Lynerd rubbed his hands. *Not many people would've done that. It would have been easier to hand things over to Theo, but you're clearly like your father and don't mind taking the hard road. I always respected him for that, even when it worked against me. I strive to be the same type of leader he was.*

Even though I appreciated Lynerd wanting to chat and form a relationship with me, this was not the time or place. All I could reply with was, *I'm glad.*

I stepped through the next set of thick trees, and the stream came into view, as did the enemy standing beside it.

My gaze first went to Kel, who, despite her vileness, was more gorgeous than I remembered. Pieces of her dark hair fell artfully from the bun on top of her head, framing her face, and even though the moon wasn't high, her tan skin glistened as her haunting gray eyes focused on me. She pursed her blood-red-stained lips. "You're early and without a certain royal advisor. Where's Zeke?"

Stomach hardening, I searched desperately for my mate, but he was nowhere in sight. Eight men stood behind Kel, blending in with the trees. I could feel their gazes on me.

"Not here. Where's Bodey?" My voice came out rough, but I didn't give a damn. I needed to see him *now*.

"That's not how this works." Kel smoothed a hand down her beige silk dress, which draped her body and wrapped low in the front, revealing her ink—a simple small moon right under her collarbone. Like the last time we met, her feet were bare. They were submerged in the water, but I could see the crimson paint on her toes. It matched the nail of the finger she pointed at me. "You're early. You were to come later. How did you get here so quickly?"

"We knew you'd want to meet in Nevada, so we were already traveling in this direction." I shrugged. "Is that a problem? You're here, and I want my mate *now*."

She chuckled. "You aren't in a position to make demands."

I felt the others step closer behind me.

"Actually, isn't that why we're meeting?" Jack strolled to my left side and rolled his shoulders. "You demanded that we come here, and we obliged. It's your turn to keep the peace."

Sneering, she tilted her head, observing him. "This isn't about peace. This is about domination. You don't have any leverage over me, and I have the one thing your little *queen* wants more than anything in this world—her mate."

"Eh." Jack scrunched his face. "I'm pretty sure her desire to kill you is just as strong. You know, with you being a narcissistic bitch and all. I know it might be hard to understand, but nobody here likes you. You choking right now and floundering like a fish out of water would make us happier than a buffet of tacos, which is really saying something. I love me some tacos."

Lucas linked, *Man, shut up. Don't make me smack you in front of her.*

I didn't know why, but having Jack act like his normal jovial self helped me control my panic. My breathing was still fast, but it wasn't as harsh. Although, no matter how many times I searched the woods, I couldn't catch a glimpse of my mate, which was *super* problematic.

The queen smiled and almost purred, "I really like him. Maybe I should include him in the swap? He and I could have a lot of fun."

Jack's nose wrinkled and he took a step back. "Imma have to pass."

My patience snapped. "Where's Bodey?"

Kel's brows lifted, but she nodded. "Fine. But they can't take him back until you hand yourself over to me."

Callie— Samuel started.

I didn't have the patience to listen to him. "After last time, I don't trust you."

"Why not?" She smirked, knowing the answer. "I vowed I wouldn't hurt anyone there that day, and I kept my word."

I crossed my arms, ignoring the cold. "You attacked two of my packs before everyone who was with me got back to our vehicles. So, although you technically followed through on your word, you implied something different. To me, that's lying."

She grabbed her skirt and swirled it around her, allowing the end pieces to trail in the water and darken. "That was an error on your part. But I promise that today, there's no play on words. No one in your territory or here will be injured today as long as you hand yourself over."

"And Bodey?" I asked, listening to her words.

"He'll be allowed to go home and recover." She nodded.

Miles stiffened, flanking me on my other side. "You know none of us approve of Caroline handing herself over, but if she does, then we're going to do an even trade with no funny business. You will hand Bodey over to us at the same time Caroline surrenders. It's not happening any other way."

"You aren't the leader, so I don't need your blessing," Kel snarled.

"Maybe not." I tried to keep my voice steady, but I was searching the tree line for my mate again. "But I agree with Miles. It happens simultaneously or not at all. You just promised nothing would happen while we were here, so unless you want your people and mine to learn they can't trust you, that's how this will go."

Her nostrils flared, but she nodded. "Fine." Her gray eyes glowed eerily as she linked with her pack.

Someone from the middle of the group moved, and I watched as the person bent down. He lifted a body and threw it over his arm.

That has to be Bodey, Michael linked, his breath ragged. He wanted his son back almost as badly as I needed my mate.

Make sure Michael doesn't do anything rash, Phil linked to Miles and me. *He's been more worried about Bodey than he's let on.*

I couldn't focus on his words. Every cell was urging me to race toward my mate, but that would only cause problems.

Carl connected with Jack and me, *Callie, you need to inform Jasmine that the trade's about to go down.*

That was enough to ground me. If I wanted to go home with Bodey, I needed Russell's group ready to attack. Lynerd's men were to hold back and keep an eye on Russell. They weren't part of the attack. With the tense relationship between Lynerd and Russell, Lynerd wanted his men to keep an eye on things.

Jasmine, if there aren't any signs of wolves nearby, come closer. The exchange is about to happen. They're bringing Bodey to us. My legs moved of their own accord, and I stepped into the water, getting my socks wet.

"Nu-uh." Kel waved a finger at me. "You stay put." She grinned victoriously.

She knew she had me.

After what felt like hours, the tall and hairy wolf shifter she'd introduced before as Hank, her right-hand man, stepped out of the coverage. He smirked as he stomped over, jostling Bodey.

I growled, unable to keep my displeasure inside. "You said you wouldn't harm anyone here, yet Hank is hurting my mate."

She rolled her eyes. "Please. Mates are oversensitive. Bodey's unconscious, so Hank's not hurting him. He's *fine*... if you keep your heads on straight. You did come early, which I already don't approve of."

This is good, Samuel linked. *She didn't have the time to take all the precautions she wanted.*

Some of that damn hope sprang up in my chest. I tried to squash it, but I felt lighter. Maybe we would pull this off after all.

Hank reached the edge of the trail behind Kel, inches from the water. He dropped Bodey to the ground.

Acid inched up my throat, burning. Bodey was almost unrecognizable. His usual messy chestnut hair lay plastered against his face, and his eyes were bruised purple and green from where they'd punched him. His skin was pale with no hint of his sun-kissed complexion, and his usual scruff had grown into a dark-brown beard. The only thing familiar about him was his lean, muscular form from his wolf keeping up his strength.

A sob startled me until my chest heaved. The noise had come from me.

I stepped toward him, but an arm wrapped around my waist. I almost fought it, but Jack tightened his hold and linked, *Not yet. Remember, we're doing this to save him* and *you. He won't forgive any of us if she takes you.*

He was right. If I swapped myself for him, Bodey would come to save me, even if it meant getting captured all over again.

Kel beamed. "Good. This is what I need to see. I need to

make sure you won't do anything foolish. You're not going to, are you, *Caroline?*"

I clenched my hands. "I'm going to *kill* you."

She threw her head back and laughed. "Thank you. I needed that." She tilted her head down, and her eyes glistened with unshed tears. "I haven't laughed like that in quite a while."

"Enjoy it while you can." Jack sneered. "When we slit your throat, that sound will never happen again."

Kel grinned and scanned him.

He shivered beside me. *Gross.*

At the last meeting, you said she was hot, Lucas reminded him.

That was before I found my fated mate, Jack retorted. *Now I want to get away from her so I can get back to Stevie.*

Removing myself from their banter, I linked with Jasmine, *Are the guys in place?*

Yes. Just tell us when to move, she replied.

"Let's do this," I rasped, fighting like hell to stay still. She had to be purposely dragging this out to make me do something rash, and I hated her more for it.

"Fine." She lifted her chin. "Do you have any plans to attack us?"

I let out a haughty breath. "None of my people would dare attack you with my mate in your possession. They know if their actions bring him harm, I would make them all pay." The words chilled me because they were filled with raw honesty. I hadn't realized I'd be willing to harm any of my people, but Bodey was the one person who changed all my rules.

She smirked. "Let's make the trade." She snapped her fingers. "Hank, pick him up and take him over to the sexy blond one with the big mouth."

Other than the sexy part, that description pegged Jack.

Hank arched a brow at Kel, but she nodded, reinforcing what she'd said.

The trade is happening, I linked. This was when they needed to attack.

When Hank stepped past Kel, I took a step closer to her, giving the illusion the trade would happen simultaneously.

Each step I took closer to Kel was torture, and when Bodey was next to me, I tried to touch his arm, needing to feel him. It had been so long... but Hank smacked my hand away and moved forward.

I spun around, and Kel grabbed my arm. She snarled, "You're not going anywhere."

I've got him, Jack linked, which was the only reason I didn't shove her off and run back.

Lynerd shouted, "Queen Kel, you're about to be attacked."

The queen's grip tightened on me, and she went rigid. "That's impossible. She said—"

My body turned to lead, and the world spun. Lynerd had betrayed us, and I wasn't sure how the hell we were going to get out of here. No wonder he'd wanted five of his men to join us.

I'd been so wrong.

CHAPTER FOURTEEN

WHAT ARE YOU DOING? I linked, prying my hand from Kel's grasp and spinning around.

Lynerd's jaw was set. *I'm doing what's necessary for my people and not taking the easy way out.* His eyes remained on Kel as he continued, "It's not *Callie's* wolves. The wolves are from the Midwest pack."

The freezing water sloshed all over my shoes and the bottom of my jeans, soaking them as I marched toward Lynerd. I was going to kick his ass. He better hope nothing more happened to my mate.

My wolf surged forward, ready to alpha-will his ass, and Lynerd snarled. His wolf surged forward too, his eyes glowing, reading my intent. Suddenly, his warm spot was gone.

Two thousand others vanished too.

He'd left my pack and taken all of Oregon with him.

Cold fear and hot rage swirled inside me, the two emotions at war. He'd betrayed me and left us at Kel's mercy.

Lynerd just left the Northwest Territory, I linked with everyone. I was still trying to understand the repercussions

Fuck him, Jack replied.

"Bring her to me," Kel snarled, followed by a *slosh* as if she had kicked the water. "Everyone else, *attack!* Take Caroline and her worthless mate!"

Branches snapped as the men she had stationed in the woods rushed toward us.

Hank spun and raced toward me, and I linked with everyone in my territory, *Get yourselves and Bodey out of here.* There was no way in hell I would allow Kel to take him back into her custody, kill him, or hurt anyone else here.

I'm taking him to the car, Jack replied.

Jasmine linked, *Lynerd's men just left me. They're chasing after Russell.*

Shit. We had no way to warn Russell since Jasmine had stayed behind to ready the cars for when the time came to leave.

Out of the corner of my eye, I watched Lucas jump on Lynerd's back as Miles and the former advisors rushed toward me. The former advisors had knives in their hands, ready to fight.

That's not leaving! I exclaimed as Hank reached me. I punched him in the jaw.

His eyes widened, surprised that I'd fought back, so I spun around and kicked him in the balls. Cheap shot or not, I had to get out of here.

I reached down to remove the knife from my ankle as he grunted, hunching forward to clutch his nonexistent jewels, and I turned to face the incoming threat.

Samuel replied, *We're not leaving you. Don't alpha-will us either. If she gets you, we might as well all be dead. She won't let your advisors live. She'll want to neutralize all potential threats.*

Damn them and their logic.

As soon as I touched my knife, someone grabbed my arm and yanked my hand away.

Kel.

She dragged me forward, and my feet slipped on the rocks. Even my wolf couldn't keep me upright, and my bottom hit the riverbed. Freezing water rushed over my jeans and the bottom half of my sweater.

Miles flashed past me and jumped on the queen, causing her to release me. Her back hit the dirty path as Miles wrapped his hand around her neck and squeezed.

Running past me, Samuel lifted his knife high.

I couldn't see his or Miles's face, but I could see the hatred and rage in Kel's eyes as she curled her legs underneath him and pushed him off.

A hand grabbed my ankle to swipe my feet out from under me. I glanced over to find Hank there, his nostrils flared, just as Michael appeared and stabbed Hank in the arm. Hank grunted and rolled over to fight Michael.

Kel yelled, and I climbed to my feet, ready for war. I reached down, finally removed the knife from my ankle, and gripped it in my hand.

Samuel had just clutched Kel's arm and dragged her toward him when someone fired a gun. I watched in horror as Samuel whimpered and dropped his knife.

Knife in hand, Miles raced back to Kel and Samuel.

I ran toward them, needing to help protect my people.

A slender guard in the center raised a gun, pointing it right at Miles.

My heart dropped. How many of them had guns?

The slender guard fired, and Miles stumbled back as the seven other enemy wolves turned their attention to me, Samuel, and the former advisors. The sounds of battle rang out behind me, and I glimpsed Lucas still fighting Lynerd.

Howls pierced the silence as Russell and his men approached. I needed their asses here. We must have underestimated the distance they'd have to travel since the queen had been here when we'd arrived.

One of the queen's wolves found me, Jasmine linked, her fear coming through. *I'm on the run, but he's chasing me.*

Four of Kel's men focused on me, and I jumped out of the water, ready to take them head-on. I replied, *Why you? Are you alone?*

Yeah. Lynerd's men took off after Russell's. This wolf found me alone, heading to the vehicles. I had to shift to outrun him. And luckily, he isn't gaining fast.

This wasn't going according to plan in any way. If we didn't get out of here, they'd overtake us.

The queen coughed, recovering from being strangled. She stood several feet away from me, her focus on my brother, who was clutching his arm.

"Do *not* touch him," I snarled as I wrapped my arm around her neck, placing the knife at her throat.

She snarled and turned her head in my direction. "Breaking you will be more painful than I planned." She jerked her head back, hitting my nose.

There was a sickening crack, and I let her go as warm blood flowed down my face and onto my shirt. Dammit, I hadn't thought that through.

Gunfire pelted through the darkness, and I watched as Phil and Carl got hit. Miles was back on his feet, just in time to get shot again in the other side of his chest, and Samuel was bent over, holding his arm.

We had to retreat.

I couldn't allow my people to die because of me. *It's not up for debate. Everyone, head back to the vehicles and leave.*

Trying not to focus on my injury, I straightened to find the queen smirking in front of me.

"You'll never beat me." She laughed as more howls rose from the opposite direction of Russell. "I thought you might do something foolish, you *stupid girl.*"

My heart dropped. I'd been counting on her keeping her word and not having any backup, but I'd been wrong... again.

I swung my hand, my knife cutting her cheek. Her gray eyes glowed as another shot rang out, and something hot sliced through the upper arm of the hand holding the knife. Blinding hot agony tore through me, adding to the throbbing pain of my nose.

She sneered, and my vision narrowed. All my senses focused on her. I'd never understood tunnel vision until now.

The sounds of battle surrounded me as my people stayed beside me despite my order to leave.

She touched the blood trickling down her face and caressed it like it was a gift I'd bestowed upon her. My hand shook hard, and I dropped the knife.

"Remember, *this* is your fault and will make it oh so much easier to break you."

That snapped me out of my haze, and I glanced around. My nose was barely bleeding, evidence that my shifter healing was kicking into gear. But that was the only good news.

Michael was crumpled on the ground to my left, and to the right, Carl's and Phil's shirts were covered in blood. Miles was a few feet past Michael, his body slumped in agony next to Samuel. They'd practically beaten us to bloody pulps. The only person I couldn't see was Lucas, and I glanced behind me to find him and Lynerd still fighting. Lynerd was holding him off, and Lucas was still going strong. Kel didn't seem eager to help Lynerd, even though he'd ratted us out.

I had to appeal to her. "Please, leave them alone. They don't want to be a part of this. This is between you and me."

We were losing, and there was no telling if Lynerd's men were attacking Russell's men, so we might not have the other twenty-five shifters heading to us.

"Too late." Kel smiled, her gray eyes lightening in delight. "I gave you a chance." She walked over to me and ran the finger, still wet with her blood, across my cheek, marking me. "But this is the perfect ending. Every threat eliminated, and all because one of your own betrayed you." She scoffed. "I might keep you alive after it's all done, just for you to suffer the rest of your days in prison."

"If you harm them in any way—"

A howl interrupted me, and the sound of paws hitting water had us looking to the right.

Russell's wolves ran around the curve of the spring. It wasn't the direction I'd expected them to come from, but they'd known we were meeting near the water and had followed it here.

Kel's backup hadn't arrived, so I could only hope we could make a big enough dent in her defenses to get away before gods knew how many reinforcements appeared.

I was certain they'd heard the gunfire, but I didn't want any of them to be taken by surprise. "They *all* have guns!" I yelled, and Kel slapped me across the face.

The sting had me sucking in a breath. I gritted my teeth, refusing to break as Kel kept her focus on me.

She yelled, "Kill them. Kill them *all*. King Sutton needs to be sent a message."

A lump formed in my throat. I hated that Lynerd had told her where they were from.

The guards pivoted their attention to the newcomers, raising their weapons, but I lifted my chin high, ready to fight to the death.

This is our last chance, Samuel linked with conviction.

Attack now.

My brows furrowed, but I was the only one who missed a beat.

Samuel swiped his knife from the ground with his uninjured hand, and he and Miles charged the two guards closest to them. Samuel stabbed one enemy in the chest, and Miles slit the throat of the one closest to him. Kel gasped.

If I'd thought chaos had descended before, it was nothing compared to this.

Three of the enemy guards pivoted toward my brother and Miles, and my instincts kicked in. As the guards pointed their weapons at them, I tapped into my wolf, hoping to the gods she guided my knife and threw it at the one in the center.

The knife sailed across the opening and embedded into his arm. He flinched as he pulled the trigger, jerking the gun toward me.

I braced myself, but Kel was the one who groaned. She reached down, grasping her leg, and I realized he'd hit her.

The other two fired, hitting Miles and Samuel in their chests.

The other three fired at the incoming wolves. We had to find a way to end this. I could hear Kel's wolves approaching, and it sounded like there were just as many as, if not more than, we had.

Kel limped toward the trees. She was abandoning her people while they fought on her behalf. Part of me wanted to go after her, my wolf desperate to taste her blood, but we didn't have time for that. I cared more about getting my people and Russell's out alive.

I turned toward a guard who was firing at the wolves and jumped on his back. The man lowered his gun and grabbed me by the hair, pulling hard and making my eyes water.

"Callie!" Michael exclaimed, but the deed was already

done.

I didn't have my knife anymore, but hell, I was half wolf, so I bit into his neck. My teeth didn't slice through the skin like my wolf teeth would have, so I clamped my jaws harder.

"Shit," he groaned and threw his right elbow back.

The taste of copper filled my mouth, and I gagged.

Tell the former advisors to step back, Samuel linked.

Unable to see what was going on, I obliged. Then gunfire went off behind me. My heart pounded. Miles and Samuel were well enough to use their guns. I wouldn't be upset about that.

My enemy bent forward and tried to flip me over his head, but I tightened my legs around him, hanging on for dear life.

Vomit crept up my throat, and I hurled all over the enemy.

"Get off me," he snarled.

More than happily, I rolled off him, and as I did, three wolves jumped on him.

But Kel's wolves had arrived too. I spun around and saw close to thirty racing toward us.

Shit. My people were too weak to keep fighting.

The former advisors grabbed guns from the dead guards, and our group turned toward the incoming threat.

You've got to get out of here, Samuel linked.

I must have misunderstood him. *Not happening.*

I ran to the guard I'd vomited on—who was now ripped to shreds, thanks to the three wolves—and grabbed his gun, then pivoted toward the arriving wolves.

My throat closed. Russell's wolves were fighting Kel's, and I couldn't tell which was friend or foe from here, except for Lynerd and his pack. But I couldn't fire at them without potentially hurting one of our allies.

Samuel ran to me and linked, *Russell told us to go.*

My brows furrowed. *How could he—*

He walked over to me and nodded toward the cars. Samuel grabbed my hand, dragging me that way. *Let's go. We're all injured, and Russell is winning.*

It didn't feel right to abandon them, but Samuel was in agony. My attention flicked to the others who made up my party, and I realized they were all in worse shape than me. Staying here would put them at greater risk. *Everyone, let's go.* We'd taken all the guns from the guards so they couldn't use them against Russell and the others.

Samuel sighed with relief, and the others turned to leave. We moved as quickly as possible back in the direction we'd come from.

As we reached the tree line, we found Lucas. He lay on his side, beaten up but with his chest still moving.

Thank gods, he was breathing.

I ran to him and squatted, and he opened his eyes.

Is it time to go? he asked, and I nodded and tried to help him up.

That was why I hadn't felt his injuries—he'd never lost consciousness, so the link had stayed warm. He groaned, but soon, we were all moving again, albeit at a far slower pace.

What happened with Lynerd? I asked, encouraging him to lean the brunt of his weight on me.

He and I beat the shit out of each other, and then he shifted and ran off. He whimpered with each step he took.

Something must have happened, but that wasn't my concern right now. We needed to find a place to rest, give everyone time to heal, and then figure out how to handle losing Oregon.

I could easily vomit again.

Jack linked, *Uh... how much longer will you be? Jasmine, Bodey, and I have a real problem on our hands.*

CHAPTER FIFTEEN

THE GROUND SHIFTED UNDER ME, but I righted myself a moment before Lucas and I could fall. Lucas moaned in agony, and I winced.

Sorry, I linked to Lucas before connecting with all the advisors. *We're about a mile and a half out now, but we're moving slowly.* My chest ached. *What's going on?* I hoped they could wait for us, but if they couldn't, they had to get him out of there.

Ten wolves are surrounding the vehicle. It won't be long until they knock us over, Jack replied, turning my blood to ice. *All I have are two knives, which won't do much good with us this outnumbered.*

He didn't have to say that. Even with Jasmine, there was technically only one fighter. Jasmine hadn't trained like the others. The only saving grace was that she had a strong wolf.

I slowed to a stop, trying not to jerk Lucas again, and turned toward the others. I murmured quickly, knowing not everyone here could link, "I need someone to take over for me with Lucas. Our cars are under attack."

Michael nodded, looking unsurprised. Jasmine must have

discussed it with him while Jack had informed me and the other advisors.

"I'll take him," Miles said, his face covered in sweat.

Are you sure? I asked him, still heading toward him. I didn't want to question him out loud. Miles was strong, but he'd taken a beating on top of getting shot. He wasn't much better off than Lucas.

He nodded. *It'll be best if I help him rather than try to run and help Jack fight.*

I handed Lucas over and took Miles's gun. If the ten of them hadn't been in battle, none of us would be up to the challenge. Our best bet was to use their weapons against them.

Michael, Samuel, and Carl rushed toward me. Each of them clutched a gun. That left Miles, Lucas, and Phil behind.

Are you sure all four of us should go? I linked with Samuel and Michael as I turned and ran. One thing that wasn't up for debate—my ass was heading to my mate. But I hated to leave Phil as the only protector.

He'll be fine, Michael replied. *There's no one close to them for miles. Worst case, we can come back and help them if someone gets close.*

The three of them ran behind me even though I could run faster. I was hurt the least, proof that the queen wanted me alive, and my wolf was the strongest. I tapped into her, needing to reach Bodey. He'd gone through enough, and I refused to lose him again.

My wolf howled in my head as I linked with Jack and Jasmine, *We're on our way.*

Good, Jack linked. *Because I'm about to get out of the car. They just had us on the edge, and I don't know how we didn't fucking roll over. I need to distract them since Bodey is out.*

That was enough to make my legs move faster. I ran damn

near as quickly as I would have in animal form, the trees blurring past as I expertly navigated the terrain. With each step, the other three fell farther behind, but I didn't give a damn.

I had to save my mate, as well as Jack and Jasmine.

Callie, wait for us, Samuel linked. *This could be a trap.*

My gut said it wasn't. This was about Queen Kel trying to punish me for not making the trade. I had no doubt those wolves had been instructed to kill my mate, and that wasn't something I would let happen. If it was a trap, I'd gladly run right into it as long as it protected my mate, his sister, and Jack.

"Dammit," Samuel huffed from behind me, but I didn't waver.

I heard the sound of a door opening and knew it had to be Jack getting out. The enemy wolves' growls grew louder, and I heard the scurrying of paws.

A sour taste filled my mouth, but I didn't slow. I kept pushing on.

Everything became louder. I had to be only half a mile away with how hard I was pushing myself. Sweat dripped down my face and into my eyes, but I refused to slow down even when the gun kept knocking against my leg.

I need help, Jack linked, and though I couldn't feel him physically like Bodey, I could sense his terror and pain. Gritting my teeth, I surged forward, tapping into my wolf like never before. *I'm almost there.*

My human body wasn't used to running this fast, especially for this long, but I didn't slow even when a stitch pierced my side. Soon, I ran through more trees and saw the Mercedes.

Five wolves were readying to topple it over, and five more were crowded on top of somebody.

Jack.

Acid burned my throat, and I stopped short. I lifted the gun and tried to ignore how uncomfortable it was to fight with it. I'd taken a few shooting lessons with Theo since Zeke was an avid hunter and had made Theo into one as well, but I'd never fired something like this.

I aimed at the center of the wolves on top of Jack and pulled the trigger.

My heart stopped, and time slowed. Within a millisecond, the bullet hit the back of a light-gray wolf at the end of the pileup. The enemy yelped and turned in my direction.

Not exactly where I'd been aiming, but hell, at least I'd hit one of them.

The attack on Jack and the Mercedes halted as the ten of them locked on me.

Great. If I missed, they'd know I was a piss-poor shot, but I couldn't stand here and not fire at them again.

The five who'd been attacking the Mercedes ran toward me. The other five stayed close to Jack and the injured pack member.

I swallowed and aimed again. Even though I pretty much knew Fate hated me, I still prayed to her. *Please, please, let me save the person you chose for me and my people.* Then I fired.

The bullet missed a dark-gray wolf racing toward me. The enemy stumbled out of the way. The other four slowed warily.

I blew out a breath and steadied my hand.

I aimed at the wolves on Jack. I needed to split my time between both groups so they didn't think they weren't at risk.

Michael, Samuel, and Carl were getting close. I had to make do until they joined me, inflicting enough damage so the enemy wolves feared my shooting.

After a few more shots, I ran out of bullets.

A wolf made a sound like it was choking, which was how

we sounded when we laughed in animal form. They knew I was no longer a threat.

The edges of my vision darkened.

As the ten got into position, Michael, Samuel, and Carl appeared through the trees. All three of them lifted their weapons and fired. Of course, they were all better shots than me, each hitting a mark.

The enemy backed up, realizing they were now in danger.

That wasn't good enough. I needed each and every one of them dead to keep my loved ones from getting injured and dying. I was so sick and tired of Kel attacking us. But I couldn't run toward them without risking getting shot.

When the wolves scattered into the trees, the three of them stopped firing. I ran toward the Mercedes just as Jasmine's head popped up from the front passenger-side door. Her gaze landed on us, and relief filtered through me.

Are you okay? I linked as I ran to the back door and glanced at Jack.

He had bite marks all over his chest and face, but when his cobalt eyes found me, he linked, *It's about damn time you got here.*

That was when I knew he'd be all right, but our entire group had taken a beating. *You said it was always Bodey and me taking the brunt of things—you sorta asked for it.* I shrugged, but I couldn't help but feel grateful. I yanked open the car door as I said, *Thank you for protecting him.*

My eyes focused on my mate, and my heart felt sick all over again. Kel had beaten him senseless, and he needed healing, like most of the people in our party. First, we had to get out of there. I touched his face, the comforting buzz of our connection bringing tears to my eyes.

I'd almost believed I would never touch him again. A tear dripped off my chin before I realized I was crying.

"He'll be okay, right?" Jasmine's voice broke. "He hasn't stirred. Not even when the wolves almost knocked us over."

A lump lodged in my throat, and I wasn't sure how to respond, so I said the only thing I could. "He's a fighter. He'll hang on, but we need to get him and several others to a healer. We're all pretty bad off."

I looked out the back window. Carl and Samuel were racing toward Jack just as Michael hurried to the front passenger door and opened it. He pulled Jasmine into his arms and glanced into the back seat to examine his son, then frowned, which almost broke me.

He normally emanated a sense of calm, but worry was written all over his face, and it rattled me. Fear coiled tightly in my chest.

"Jasmine, can you drive?" Michael asked.

"Uh..." She pulled back and glanced at me. "I can, but Bodey doesn't like me driving his car."

I snorted. That sounded like my mate, and thinking of him like that seemed important... especially in this moment.

I could have offered to drive, but the thought of not touching Bodey made my skin crawl and my wolf snarl. I *had* to be near him.

"Jasmine." Michael cupped his daughter's face. "Callie can't leave Bodey after being apart for so long and with him this injured. Her wolf will lose it. You have to drive. You're the least injured of the three of us."

My wolf settled, realizing Michael understood I couldn't part from my mate. There was no way anyone could pry me away from him unless it was the only way to save him.

"Okay." She inhaled sharply. "I can do that."

"Good." He released her and took a few steps back. "I'll help Jack." He shut the door.

Jasmine climbed over the center console and turned on

the car, blasting the heat. I hadn't realized how cold it was, but now I shivered at the realization. I lifted Bodey's head and slid under his front half, then closed the door. Even though I was worried, being next to him gave me peace. He was safe from the enemy.

With my mind clearing, I linked with Lucas and Miles, *Are you three okay?*

Yes, we're at the curve. Did you fight off Kel's wolves? Miles asked.

For now. They could come back. I rolled down the window despite the chill, needing to listen in case they did.

I looked at Jack's Navigator and found Samuel leaning against the back with the rifle in his hands.

He was prepared in case the wolves came back. Thank gods for him because I'd been totally focused on my mate.

I kept waiting for something else to happen, but Miles, Lucas, and Phil soon joined us. Samuel jumped into the passenger seat of the Mercedes, and once the rest got into the other vehicles, we pulled away. Jasmine drove fast as the sun rose, marking the sky with swirls of pinks, oranges, and blues. The sunrise was gorgeous, and if Bodey had been healthy beside me with "Perfect" by Ed Sheeran playing on the radio, this would've been one hell of a romantic moment, the sort I'd love to share with my mate. But all we'd managed so far were stolen moments between chaos, and our relationship deserved better than that. I had to believe things would calm down and we would eventually spend time together without danger hovering over us.

One day.

When we were half a mile from the main road, Jasmine tossed Samuel her phone.

"Uh... thanks?" Samuel arched a brow.

I ran my fingers through Bodey's hair, hating the grease

that clung to my fingers. With the dirt caked under his nails and all over his body, I feared I didn't want to know where she'd kept him. My heart ached as I thought about the hell he'd endured just for being my mate.

"It's unlocked." Jasmine pulled onto the main road. "Put in the address to the house Russell rented. We're supposed to meet him there."

Her words were like a kick to the gut. I hated that we'd left Russell and his pack behind, but we'd had to. We would've made things more difficult for them if we'd stayed, given how beaten up we all were.

I laid my head back and tipped it down to stare at my mate. I'd give anything for him to open his eyes, but he was still out cold. My salvation was the fact that he'd turned his head to nestle into my lap and stomach, the jolt between us increasing. Even in his sleep, he recognized my touch and was leaning into it. My chest expanded to the point of hurting.

Thirty minutes later, Jasmine drove up to the house. She didn't turn the car off, just nodded. "The code to get in is 9-0-8-1-2-4."

My hand paused on the door handle. "Are you not coming with us?"

She shook her head. "I'm going to dump the car somewhere and head back."

My brows furrowed. "Why?"

"The wolves around our vehicles could've gotten our tag numbers. They could locate us if we park here." Samuel sighed. "Good catch. I'll go with you."

Shit. I hadn't thought of that. "We need to do the same thing with the former alphas, Jack, Lucas, and Miles."

"I'll take Jack's car since all three of them are injured, and I'll talk with Michael." Samuel opened the door and jogged to the vehicle behind us.

I sighed and looked back at my mate. Even though I was strong, I wasn't sure how to get Bodey out of the vehicle alone, but I'd be damned if I didn't figure it out.

Opening my door, I climbed out and placed my arms under Bodey's armpits and around his chest. His cinnamon and sandalwood scent was mixed with sour body odor. I didn't focus on that but rather on carefully dragging his body out of the back seat and allowing his feet to land gently on the asphalt.

Michael came over and lifted Bodey's feet off the ground so they wouldn't drag. I exhaled and smiled at him, thankful for the help.

The two of us worked together to get Bodey to the front door, and inside, we settled him on the couch.

"Whoa!" Katelin's jaw dropped as she gazed at Bodey's blood-crusted body. "Wait. Let me grab some towels and blow-up mattresses."

"Towels first, please." A mattress could wait. We needed to lay Bodey down.

She raced off and returned, then covered the couch. When he was settled, I leaned over him and kissed his forehead.

Our mate bond warmed slightly, and his eyes opened. The gorgeous indigo color was darker than normal, but that didn't matter. He was awake.

He lifted one hand and cupped my face as he smiled. "Best dream ever," he murmured before falling back asleep.

I swallowed a sob. "I love you."

But he'd already begun snoring.

Turning around, I noticed that Lucas and Jack were still standing. We were all injured, but they were the worst off after Bodey.

"I'm contacting Dina." I hated to ask the priestess to help us again, but we needed a witch.

There was no doubt Kel would retaliate.

I sent Dina a text message.

Me: We took a beating. We need a healer. Can you help us find one?

I already knew she wouldn't leave her coven, and I respected that. With Bodey, Samuel, and me gone, we'd left the Grangeville pack exposed, and she'd want to protect the wolves and her coven.

Carl and Katelin left to get more towels for the others to sit on, not wanting to chance leaving blood evidence behind for humans to find.

A few minutes later, the witch replied.

Dina: There's a coven in south Idaho I can send your way. I just need your address.

Good enough. I trusted her, so I shot off the address. Once we'd rested, we'd determine how to fight back. But we weren't in a state to even discuss strategy.

The front door opened, and I expected to see Jasmine, Samuel, and Phil.

Instead, I found what could only be described as death.

CHAPTER SIXTEEN

HEART LURCHING INTO MY THROAT, I was almost sick. Russell stood at the door, a few fading scratch marks on his neck and bare chest and a shirt tied around his waist. His skin was pale, and he was clutching his side.

Between that and the fact I didn't see any other wolves with him, my every limb shook, and I thought I might crumple under the pressure.

My wolf surged forward, keeping me standing. Even though she couldn't speak, the message was clear—we would *not* look weak.

"Dad," Katelin gasped as she stumbled over to him. "What's going on?"

If Katelin didn't know, that was a bad sign.

When she reached for him, he brushed her off. Her expression twisted into hurt, but he held up a hand.

That was when I noticed the blood on his right side. It dripped from the shirt onto the wooden floor. He was hurt, and he'd been in wolf form. He'd shifted from one form to the

"Please tell me you got the bullet out before you shifted." If the bullet remained inside, it could've torn through muscles.

"No, but there are more pressing matters." Russell swayed on his feet. I feared it was from blood loss. The fact he was here without his pack spoke volumes.

Samuel placed a hand on his back. "Where are your pack members?" he asked, his voice lower than normal.

He feared the answer to that question, the same as I did.

"Five are dead. The rest are hurt but alive," Russell gritted out. "I need four people to ride with me and get them. They're hiding in the woods because they couldn't shift back, and I couldn't take all five vehicles back here, let alone have a group of wolves running here. They're moving down the mountain slowly, but the queen could attack."

Now I was conflicted. The last thing I wanted to do was leave my mate's side, but Russell and his pack were the *only* reason all of us had gotten out of there alive. If they hadn't run interference, Kel would've killed a few of us, if not all.

I stood, knowing I couldn't sit here and do *nothing*. "Tell me where they are. I'll go."

Jack shook his head. "Fuck that. Your ass isn't going anywhere."

"Son!" Carl's jaw dropped. "She's the queen."

"Yeah, which reinforces my point." Jack strolled over, his bite marks already scabbing over. "The point of what we just went through was to prevent you from handing your ass over to the queen. The last thing we need is for you to go near her again. Then everyone's help would be for *nothing*."

Lucas sighed. "Man—"

Miles cleared his throat and winced. "I'm not one to agree with Jack often, but Callie, he's right." He rolled his shoulders. "Everything we did was to protect you and get Bodey back. The three of us are loyal to you. We would never defect to Kel or anyone else. Besides, if you leave Bodey, you'll be distracted. Jack, Lucas, Samuel, and I can help Russell."

"Damn straight." Jack nodded. "That thought would never cross my mind, and even if it did for a fleeting second, I have no doubt Stevie would cut off my nutsack."

"Man, just say you agree." Lucas huffed. "But yeah, Callie, you're stuck with the three of us forever."

Some of my tension faded, which then made me feel awful. "I trust you three. I'm worried because you've been shot."

"We're hurting, but we're fine to do this," Miles assured me. "We'll remove the bullets when we get back." He smiled sadly. "Trust us about this, too."

Damn him, but he had me. He understood the fated-mate bond since he was the only one who had completed one with Stella. And he was also right. I would be rushing to get back here to Bodey, which could make me reckless. Besides, he'd named the four strongest wolves besides Bodey and me, which would prove to Russell that we were willing to risk those important to our territory for them as well. "If any of you don't want to go, I can—"

Samuel waved a hand, cutting me off. "We're all good with going. Right?" He glanced at Lucas.

"Of course." Lucas huffed. "Anything to keep her safe. I just didn't want Jack telling her what to do."

Crossing his arms over his chest and grimacing from pain, Jack arched a brow. "Look, I'd rather piss her off than Stevie. She may seem weak, but man, get her mad and you'll see another side of her. A sexy-ass one, but scary all the same."

"Okay, now I wanna see that." Lucas smirked.

Jack scowled. "She's my mate."

"You haven't sealed the deal, my man." Lucas smiled so wide his teeth showed.

A threatening growl emanated from Jack just as Russell's nostrils flared.

Samuel noticed Russell's expression, and he and Miles moved toward the front door.

I understood they needed to blow off steam, but not with Russell's people in danger. *Bicker on the way there so you can help the people who kept us from dying.*

They had enough sense to flinch, and they followed Samuel and Miles. As four of my crew walked past Russell and out the door, Katelin moved to follow, but Russell shook his head.

"You need to stay here." Russell pressed a hand over his wound, causing a bigger trickle of blood to drip onto the floor.

If his body didn't start healing soon, he'd bleed out. I wanted to tell him that, but I suspected he was well aware. If I were him, that wouldn't matter to me, and I'd bet he felt the same way.

Katelin mashed her lips into a line. "Dad, those are my pack members too. I want to help."

His face softened. "I know, honey. I do. But I need you to help your friends, and that way, I'll have someone here I can link to if something goes wrong."

"But—"

"Please." His gaze flicked to Bodey and the rest of us who were staying behind. "We don't know what resources Queen Kel has in place. We can't underestimate her."

Unease crept through me, sending a shiver down my spine. I hated that we had no idea what she was capable of. And worse, she kept exceeding my expectations. Dad had warned me all those years ago.

My eyes burned. I wondered what sort of leader I'd be if he'd been alive to guide me.

"Come on, Katelin." Jasmine looped her arm through her friend's. "Help me mend the others."

Katelin sighed. "Fine. But, Dad, be careful. With you shifting like that..." Her eyes glistened.

I understood her concern, and the loss of my adoptive father sat heavily on me. The only silver lining in this gods-forsaken situation was that my mate was back with me. The cost for me had been worth it, but I wasn't sure others felt the same way... especially Russell.

The door shut, and I went back to Bodey. His eyes were closed, and despite his current sour scent, I wanted to curl up beside him. The only thing stopping me was that he was so beat up. I didn't want to hurt him. The witch Dina was sending would be here in a few hours, so he'd have to rely on his shifter healing to mend himself until she got here.

I sat beside him and laid my head on the edge of the couch cushion. As I raised my arm, I winced, but the wounds I'd sustained were mostly healed.

"Let me see your injuries," Jasmine said as she squatted beside me.

Unable to take my eyes off Bodey, I shook my head. "I'm fine. Go tend to the others." I was certain I was the least injured because of Kel's directive. I suspected she wanted to be the one to harm me... she seemed sadistic like that.

Jasmine tensed. "But—"

"Seriously. I have a few injuries, but nothing bad." I forced myself to glance at my now-sister and smile reassuringly. "I promise, the others are worse. I'm already almost healed, and I just need to be here with Bodey."

Her face softened. "Okay, but if you need anything, you'll let me know. Right?"

"I promise." I took Bodey's hand in mine, reveling in his warm skin and the jolt thrumming between us. My wolf whimpered as I laid my head on top of his dirt-covered hand. I needed to touch him as best I could without jarring him.

For the first time, I listened to two things more comforting than song lyrics—Bodey's heartbeat and breathing. I focused on them instead of the noises of the others, and before I realized it, my eyes had closed.

A WARM JOLT caressed my cheek, and I opened my eyes. The most gorgeous set of indigo irises stared back at me, and my breath caught. The color was back to normal, like the night sky, even though there were still dark circles under his eyes.

I straightened, the world righting for the first time in days. I hadn't realized how out of sync I'd been without him, and every cell in my body buzzed as if I'd been in a slumber with him away.

"Hey," he rasped, sounding as if he needed water. "Now this right here is exactly what I needed." His hand brushed my cheek, which ached from how big I was smiling again.

Releasing his hand, I started to stand to get him some water, but his hand tightened on mine. He linked, *Where do you think you're going?*

To get you something to drink. I didn't want to think about how long he'd gone without sustenance.

No. He grasped my hand. *Don't leave.*

My heart raced. I didn't want to separate from him for a second, but I also wanted him to heal. *It'll only take a minute.* I pointed to the front door, where Michael, Jasmine, and Katelin were keeping watch, then to the back door, where Phil and Carl were guarding the back of the house in case Kel came in that way.

Fine, but don't be long. He pouted and released me.

I tiptoed across the large room and linked with Samuel, Jack, Lucas, and Miles, *Hey, is everything all right?*

We're almost back. We ran into some issues. A few wolves didn't make it, Lucas answered.

Acid crept up my throat. More lives had been lost because of me, and it made me sick.

As I stepped into the kitchen, I noticed bottled water on one corner of the counter. I grabbed three and went back to Bodey. He took one from me and drained it.

Do I even want to know how long you went without water? I cringed as I opened my bottle and drank half of it in one swig.

Probably best if you don't, and it doesn't matter. He took the second bottle and drained it as well. Then he lay back on the couch and spread his arms.

Not rushing into them was the hardest thing I'd ever done, but I hated to think about how much damage he'd taken, and I didn't want to hurt him worse.

When I didn't move toward him, he raised a brow and asked, *I will force you into my arms if you don't come willingly. I've gone too long without holding you.*

The determination wafting from him into me almost had me panting. His fierceness made me want to strip him down and have my way with him. The sweet stench of my arousal swirled between us, and he grinned victoriously.

I snorted unexpectedly and tried to keep the noise quiet. *Even though I might want to have my way with you, there are two reasons I shouldn't.* Really, there was only one, but I knew the main one was a deal breaker for me, even if it wasn't for him.

Let's hear them. He tilted his head.

I lifted one finger. *You're still injured.* With the dark circles under his eyes and the way his body was so stiff, it was apparent.

Maybe you should kiss all my boo-boos. He winked.

This leads me to reason two. I lifted a second finger. *You stink and are dirty.*

His face fell, and he flinched.

I reached over to comfort him, but he lifted a hand and linked, *Yeah, I probably am. She kept me in a cell that smelled like piss and feces.*

We should get you into a bath. If he was injured, especially with open cuts, he needed to clean up. Infection could occur even though it was rare for shifters.

Once I'm clean, we can have sex. He started to get up and grimaced, his body falling back down. His breathing became ragged, telling me everything.

I squatted beside him again and set my water on the floor. *Babe, you can't even sit up, and you want to have sex?*

He rolled onto his back, his face twisting in agony even though he tried to keep his expression neutral. He pointed to his lap. *You can be on top.*

With your dad and sister able to walk in any time, and Carl and Phil able to look inside and watch us? I leaned back on my heels. *Not happening.*

The sound of the chairs sliding sounded outside, and I looked out to see Phil and Carl talking furtively, their rifles in hand.

Russell and the others must have made it back.

Is something wrong? I linked to Jasmine and Michael. I tensed. Maybe they were going to the front to help carry the injured inside?

A car is driving up, and it isn't ours, Michael replied.

Jasmine, Katelin, and I are hiding in the bushes out front, watching them.

I glanced at my phone for the time. The witches wouldn't be here for another hour. If it wasn't them or Russell, I could think of only one option.

Kel.

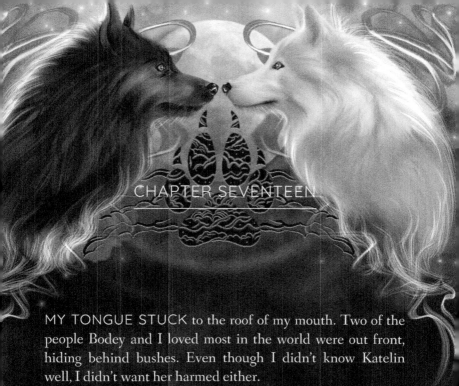

CHAPTER SEVENTEEN

MY TONGUE STUCK to the roof of my mouth. Two of the people Bodey and I loved most in the world were out front, hiding behind bushes. Even though I didn't know Katelin well, I didn't want her harmed either.

It was too late for them to move. I'd hoped they could sneak inside, but Michael had been adamant that both sides of the house needed to be watched.

This had to be the attack we were waiting for, but the lone car puzzled me. Was it a decoy?

I thought through our situation. The three former advisors and I had had time to heal, though they wouldn't be as far along as me since my injuries weren't as extensive. Bodey was still in a bad state, but he was well enough to be conscious. He might not have been that far along if I hadn't slept while touching him, allowing our bond to thrum to life even more.

Katelin and Jasmine weren't fully trained to fight. Between that and our weakened position, we were at a *clear* disadvantage. The one plus we had was our rifles, but Kel would know about those, seeing as we'd taken them from her

We'd have to do the best we could, and I was willing to die to protect my people if that's what it took.

Phil and Carl gestured toward the stairs. Their faces were grim as they attempted to communicate without words, unable to pack link.

I had to join them. I linked to the two of them to sort out the plan. *We should go down the stairs and under the house so we can see through the lattice opening from that spot underneath the porch. Heading out the front door will make us a target.*

We needed to surround whoever was here.

I'll be right back, I linked to Bodey and turned to the back door. I didn't want to tell him what was going on, fearing he'd try to join us.

His alarm rang through our bond, and my breath caught. I'd hoped he'd be distracted with his injuries, but I should've known better. Maybe I shouldn't have touched him after all. Being unconscious would have prevented him from fighting, although, if he was awake, at least he could protect himself if our enemies made it inside.

He groaned, and the couch squeaked as I reached the back door. He was sitting up, but I didn't falter, rushing outside.

The two former advisors rushed down the steps to the cutout at the bottom of the house. The house was on stilts in the back to stay level with where the front side met the earth, with a small latticed bottom that would allow us to see the front yard and driveway.

We should've gone to a new location, but in our state of recovery, our options had been limited, and none of us could have made a long drive. Besides, we couldn't leave Russell and his pack behind after everything they'd done for us.

What's going on? Bodey linked.

My stomach sank hard, but I refused to lie to him. *There's an unknown car outside.*

Phil disappeared from sight, and I raced to catch up with Carl.

I felt bad leaving Bodey, but Jasmine, Katelin, and Michael were covering the front, and the former advisors and I were watching the back. As long as we could hold off Kel's people, he'd be safest inside. I refused to let my mate be taken from me again.

Dammit, Callie, he groaned. *I'm coming. I won't sit here while you're at risk.* His anger flowed into me, along with his determination. He and I could argue later; right now, my goal was to protect him.

I reached the bottom of the steps and hurried across the concrete ground under the house, following the former advisors. The faint smell of smoke from the grill hung in the air, and my stomach rumbled.

Pain pulsed through my bond with Bodey, causing my chest to clench. I linked, *Get back on the couch. I'll let you know if we need you.*

Not happening. His suffering pulsed through me more strongly. *I need to be there with you.*

Carl had a rifle, and he jogged past the grill and the round table to Phil. The area shrank, and the three of us were soon on our hands and knees, crawling across the dirt toward the lattice so that we were at eye level with the front lawn and driveway.

I didn't hear a vehicle running, just Michael's, Jasmine's, and Katelin's heavy breathing from their spot behind the bushes in front of the house.

So far, there's only one vehicle. If you come out here injured and I have to protect you, we could both get hurt. I needed him to stay put... needed him to be safe. *If more people come or we expect an ambush, I'll let you know. I promise.*

Bodey hesitated, but the pain eased as if he wasn't moving around like before. *Fine, but as soon as it happens, you tell me. I'll be waiting.*

I couldn't blame him. If our roles had been reversed, I'd be acting the same way—begrudgingly appeasing. *Thank you.* Wanting to keep him informed, I added Jasmine and Michael to our link. *Have you spotted any more vehicles? I don't smell or hear anything out of the ordinary.* One car made me nervous. Normally, Kel used force to get what she wanted, and this didn't seem like her. What other attack might she have up her sleeve?

Just the one, Michael replied worriedly. *Four women are sitting inside.*

Phil asked, *What are they doing? And I'm surprised Kel sent only women.*

Nothing. They're just sitting there, Michael answered. *I'm about to leave my spot and head down to them.*

Something wasn't right. *If it's all women, they could be witches. We know Kel works with witches, and she could have more allies here. If their goal is to make us nervous, they've succeeded. Either they're here to distract us, or they want us to strike first.*

Dammit, I'm coming, Bodey connected. *I can't sit in here with you all out there. It's making me sick.*

A sharp wince damn near crumpled me over. Bodey was trying to stand again. I swallowed a growl. *Bodey...!* I warned.

One of the women just put a phone to her ear, Jasmine linked. *They must be ready to make their move.*

Shit. This was horrible. I wasn't sure how we could fight against witches, especially when we didn't have any here to help us. From everything I'd learned, witches' magic drained quickly, but they were super powerful until that happened.

My phone rang, startling me.

What's wrong? Bodey linked.

Lungs seizing, I snatched the phone from my back pocket. *I'm getting a phone call.* I silenced the ringer and glanced at the unfamiliar number scrolling across my screen.

I had no fucking clue who it was, but instinct screamed at me to answer. After all, Kel had a habit of calling, and even if I didn't want to play the game, I had to.

I swiped the answer button and held the phone to my ear.

"Hello?" I whispered, not wanting to speak too loudly.

"Can you please call off your hounds?" a deep, unfamiliar female voice asked. "You should be expecting us."

I swallowed. *I think I'm on the phone with a woman from the vehicle,* I informed everyone. I inched to the left and moved closer to the lattice holes so I could see the women. The one in the front passenger seat held a phone to her ear, her eyes locked on the place where I assumed Michael, Jasmine, and Katelin were hiding.

The women know where you three are, I linked to Michael and Jasmine before speaking to her. "And why would I do that? Those *hounds* are my people." Of course, they'd use a dog joke. She must have thought she was being original.

She laughed, but the lack of malice in her tone had me freezing.

"It's just a figure of speech. I didn't mean to offend, but I can see it was in poor taste." The woman sighed. "I apologize. The last thing I'd ever want to do is upset the queen."

I couldn't hide my bitterness. "You say that, but here you are, ready to attack us."

"What?" she gasped. From my spot, I watched her bright-green eyes widen and flick toward the door. Her light-brown hair fell into her face as her brows furrowed. "Dina sent us. What are you talking about?"

I stiffened. "Dina?" I pulled the phone away and looked at the time. It was nine in the morning. The coven Dina had called shouldn't be here yet.

"Yes, she said you had many wounded and to come heal them."

I blinked, and the world steadied itself again, but I didn't want to be tricked. Kel wanted to make me feel incompetent. I linked with Stevie, Stella, and Janet, hoping one of them could confirm what this woman was telling me. *Are any of you with Dina? She said she was sending witches here from a coven three hours away, but they're here early. I'm not sure I believe them.*

Janet replied, *We're not with her, but I'll get you an answer right now.*

I needed to hold off doing anything until I could confirm their story. "Dina said it would take the coven three hours to get here. How did you arrive so quickly?"

"We were in a town thirty minutes south of our lands, and we drove fast. We've heard stories of what Kel has done. We didn't want to leave you injured and unprotected. Four other witches are on their way, about thirty minutes behind us. They're coming from the pack and coven neighborhood."

That sounded reasonable, but Kel had a knack for making things sound true, like when she'd vowed she wouldn't hurt us at our parlay, but she'd meant she wouldn't hurt those in her immediate vicinity and had attacked two Oregon packs after I'd refused to submit.

What's going on? Bodey linked, his agony multiplying tenfold. *Are they out of their car?*

No, I'm verifying their story. I wanted to scold him. He

shouldn't be up and moving, but I understood why he was. Our time apart had impacted him as well.

"Well, well." The witch muttered on the other end of the line. "Dina is calling. I'll need to take this."

"Please, go ahead." I had no doubt the woman had realized what we were doing, but I couldn't blindly trust someone after everything that had happened these past few weeks.

I heard the back door to the deck open. Bodey had finally made it outside. Just when I was about to head up and stop him from falling down the stairs, the car's passenger door opened.

Phil and Carl stiffened and crawled backward, moving out of the spot under the house, readying to respond to an attack.

The woman stepped out and held out her phone, the sun hitting her face and catching the dark-red highlights in her light-brown hair. She looked to be in her forties, and she wore the standard long cotton dress that witches favored.

"Callie, I can vouch for Prue." Dina's voice came from the phone. If I hadn't been a shifter, I wouldn't have been able to hear. "She's a friend."

The tension in my shoulders released, and my head hung. "Thank gods." I then linked to everyone here, *The witches aren't a threat. They're here to heal us.*

Carl lowered his weapon and glanced at me. He smiled and patted my arm while he linked, *You did good.*

I snorted. *Not sure I'd go that far. I just wasted about ten minutes when they could've been healing Bodey and the rest of us.* I tended not to be cautious enough when there was a threat and overly cautious when we weren't at risk. Would I ever get it right?

You're learning, and you did what you felt was right. They did show up early.

He squeezed my arm, and we climbed out from beneath the deck.

Phil, Carl, and I headed back around the deck to the stairs. Bodey stood at the top with his arms crossed.

I moved to be the first to climb to him, and at the top, I noticed how tense his jaw was. He was hurting, and he was trying to keep the pain from me, but I could still sense it.

I wrapped my arms around him, giving him a hug but also supporting his body. He groaned lightly as we pivoted toward the door. I dropped one arm and helped him to the back door just as the front door opened.

As we entered, Prue's gaze landed on my mate, and when her gaze slid down to his chest, I wanted to scratch her eyes out. But she stopped at his tattoo, and then she met my eyes.

My wolf retreated, relieved that her interest was in our tattoos and not in pursuing my mate. Bodey was sexy as hell, even injured.

"I'll take the king consort. You three," she said, glancing at the other three witches, "can pick who you want to help."

Chest constricting, I inhaled. "Obviously, everyone here needs healing, but several other wolves are heading this way who might need healing too."

Bodey and I shuffled toward Prue and met her at the couch.

"How many?" she asked.

"Let me find out." I linked to Samuel, Miles, Jack, and Lucas. *How many are badly injured? The witches are here, and we need a count.*

Ten are very hurt, Lucas answered. *The rest of us have minor injuries, but Callie, five died.*

My heart ached. Five out of twenty-five was a huge-ass amount. Even one death was one too many, but five? I was going to be sick. Having Bodey here and needing me was the only thing keeping me together.

I repeated the information, and I heard Katelin sniffle. I noticed how red her eyes were, something I'd missed between caring for Bodey, sleeping, and facing the threat. I hated that her pack had lost so much, and all for my people.

Prue exhaled noisily. "Okay, mend them enough to get them near full strength. We can't heal them completely with ten other substantially injured wolves on the way."

Bodey and I sat on the couch as the three other witches went to Michael, Phil, and Carl. They sat at the kitchen table, and the ladies began their healing.

"This shouldn't hurt at all," Prue said, bringing my focus back to her.

She placed her hands on my mate's shoulders and closed her eyes. When her hands glowed white, I knew she was working her magic... literally.

The fated-mate bond between Bodey and me warmed, and a soothing sensation filtered in as her magic began to work.

His pain eased as his body repaired itself, and I enjoyed the warm buzzing sensation as my mate's injuries mended. The healing power of magic was so different from the power they'd used when prodding me for answers. Their magic seemed to blend with ours, making our bodies and wolves whole instead of trying to peel back layers.

"Thank you," Michael murmured, causing me to glance at him. His color was better, and he didn't flinch every time he took a breath.

The younger witch then moved to heal Carl.

Callie, we're here, Jack answered. *We don't want to alarm you, but we have a problem.*

The faint rumble of vehicles grew louder and stopped in

front of the house. Jasmine moved toward the door. Someone from her pack must have informed her it was them as well.

Of *course* there was a problem. When was there not?

I kept that comment to myself. *What's wrong?*

The wolves are too injured to shift back into human form, and it's daylight. Some of the neighbors are outside.

Shit. The witches would need to use more of their magic to get the injured wolves into the house.

"There," Prue said and lowered her hands from Bodey. "You should be healed enough."

Bodey rolled his shoulders and raised his arms. "Thank you so much. I'll be fully healed in a few hours." He took my hand, and the jolt between us sprang to life.

He moved with only slight winces of discomfort and not the agony I'd felt from him earlier.

"We've got a problem." I hated to ask them to do more, but our hands were tied, especially after Russell's pack had lost five of their own. I filled the witches in.

She *tsk*ed but nodded. "It'd be best if we healed them in the car. We can drive somewhere else to heal them. There are a few places up the road we could stop, or at least not cause alarm. It won't take long since we can't do much. I'll get the other four witches to meet us there."

I nodded. Taking the new arrivals somewhere else was in everyone's best interest. I doubted Kel would attack with the sun high and humans out and about, but I wouldn't put it past her.

"Please, help them." Katelin sniffed, and Jasmine pulled her into a hug. "They're not doing well. Dad and the king are beside themselves."

Standing, Prue lifted a hand. "The four of us will go out so we don't cause a bigger disturbance. I won't have enough magic to alter human memories." She waved her hands. "Let's go."

I informed Samuel, Lucas, Miles, and Jack of the plan, and when the four witches went to leave, Katelin followed them.

"You should stay with us," Jasmine yanked on Katelin's hand to keep her in the kitchen.

Katelin frowned. "I'm sorry. I can't stay."

Something about the way she said it caused me to tense.

"Of course you can—" Jasmine started.

"Dad says I have to go."

There it was. Confirmation. Something else *was* going on, and I needed to know what. "Why does he want you to leave?"

She wrung her hands and bit her lip. "Because..." Her voice broke, and she glanced at Jasmine.

That alone told me everything I needed to know.

CHAPTER EIGHTEEN

THERE WAS silence as the four witches exited the house.

Clearing her throat, Katelin wrapped her arms around her waist. "I'm sorry. I don't have time. I've got to go." She turned and rushed out the door.

That isn't a good sign, Michael linked with Bodey and me.

That was an understatement. The likely reason behind Katelin's abrupt departure had my stomach roiling.

Before Jasmine could make it past me to follow her friend, I grabbed her arm, holding her back. If she forced a confrontation, it might strain their relationship.

Her head jerked toward me, and she stiffened. "She's upset. I need to check on her." Jasmine tried to free herself from my grasp.

That was the problem. "Going after her will make it worse."

Jasmine froze and lifted a brow. "How? We're friends. We support each other."

I didn't want to explain it to her. My throat tightened.

Bodey came to me and wrapped an arm around my shoulders. *I'll take it from here.* He pulled me to his side and said out loud, "Russell wants to go home after they're healed."

I probably shouldn't have let him handle it, but his touch soothed me, and I hadn't had the heart to tell his sister. I'd seen how close she and Katelin were, and I couldn't imagine telling Stevie I couldn't help her anymore. It would be on the same level as when I'd decided to lock Stevie in the basement, almost getting her killed.

Shaking her head, Jasmine crossed her arms. "They won't leave us like that. They've seen that an entire state was ripped away from us, strengthening Kel. They'll want to stay here and fight to help us."

I damn near winced but somehow held my composure.

"Honey." Michael stood up from the table and walked toward his daughter. "They lost multiple people, and more are severely injured. Queen Kel knows the Midwest is involved. King Sutton won't risk his territory any further. It has nothing to do with Russell and Katelin not wanting to help."

"No," she scoffed, then glanced at the other two former advisors sitting at the table. Her expression became strained as the corners of her mouth tipped downward.

I followed her gaze and saw the same uncomfortable looks on their faces. Everyone agreed, but no one wanted to hurt Jasmine.

"Carl and I should head outside and keep watch," Phil said as he patted Carl's shoulder. The two of them jumped to their feet and hurried out the front door, leaving the uncomfortable situation behind. I didn't argue. With the others leaving, we needed someone to watch out for Kel's attack.

"It's not personal." I reached out to touch her again but dropped my hand. I'd just grabbed her, and I didn't want her to feel uncomfortable with me. "They did what we asked them to do, which was more than I expected." I looked at

Bodey, relieved to see that the dark circles under his eyes were gone and his complexion was almost back to its usual warm-olive tone. "They helped us save Bodey without me needing to hand myself over."

Miles linked to Bodey and me, *The witches are pulling out and waving for us to follow them. We would join you all, but the men are saying we're going somewhere else for the witches to heal us.*

That's right, I replied as I watched Jasmine scowl. *We don't want to risk any humans seeing injured wolf shifters being carried into the house. They're taking you to a remote spot to heal you all as much as they can.* It was the least we could do for the Midwest wolves, even if they planned on returning home. *We'll join you soon.* We needed to get away from this house anyway. Kel would attack us here as soon as possible; I almost expected her not to wait until nightfall.

Jasmine rubbed her arms and remained silent.

Michael glanced at me with a raised eyebrow.

He didn't need to link or say anything. I understood the message.

"We need to leave," I said.

"Or find a place to stay in Idaho." Michael ran a hand through his hair and glanced at the others.

"We need to go home." Bodey's hands tightened on my waist. "Kel will retaliate, so our priority is to get back to our packs and deal with the fallout of Oregon leaving the territory before she does."

"We've had little to no sleep," Michael said, staring at Bodey. "And we're still healing. We can't push ourselves."

This was new. Normally, Bodey and Michael were in agreement. Both had a point, but I agreed with Michael. "You're right. We're all tired."

Michael nodded, and Bodey sucked in a breath as disappointment wafted through our bond. Whatever was going on with him was strange, but I'd have to figure it out later when we weren't under threat of an attack.

"But the risk of not getting back to our people is greater," I said and swallowed, trying to figure out the best answer. "I've had a nap, so I can drive." I hated driving, but when the situation arose, I'd do it.

"I've been locked up in a dungeon and feel better than I have since I got captured." Bodey squeezed me lovingly. "So I can drive as well, even though I don't want to be separated from Callie."

So we only needed a driver for the third vehicle.

Jasmine groaned. "I can drive Dad's car. I didn't fight much, and I'm pretty well rested. As long as we stop somewhere to get coffee and some candy, I'll be good for a few hours. By then, someone else will probably be up for driving."

"If you can give me three hours to rest, I can take over then." Michael licked his lips. "We'll be safest at home, and we need to make sure Oregon doesn't try anything."

Shit. We needed to inform the other Northwest states that Oregon was no longer ours. My skin crawled as I thought about how our people already had concerns about me. This would only validate their feelings and have more of my people thinking I was an incompetent leader. Yet another thing Kel no doubt desired.

What's wrong? Bodey turned to me, examining my face.

I didn't consider Oregon trying to take over the rest of the states. Lynerd could be coordinating more attacks. My parents and childhood pack were no longer tied to me. All this time, I'd thought I'd be relieved once I was free, but now I felt a deep ache from losing my links to Theo, Mom, Stevie, and even Pearl. *What if my family gets hurt? And we need to inform all the alphas about Oregon leaving.* I'd been so consumed with Bodey and his injuries that I hadn't considered the impact of losing Oregon on the rest of our people. What kind of queen was I turning out to be?

We'll make sure that doesn't happen. I'll reach out to the alphas in the Northwest Territory to spread the word, Bodey vowed. *We'll return home and make sure we protect them.*

My heart sank, and I thought about Bodey driving after everything he'd gone through. I connected with him, *Are you sure you're up for driving? You're still healing, and I hate to put that pressure on you.*

He turned me to him and cupped my face as he leaned his forehead against mine. His irises lightened to nearly cobalt as an endearing expression softened his face. *Being with you has done wonders for me mentally and physically, and the thought of getting you back home where we can connect in a way we haven't in too long has my wolf stirring. Even if my human side gets tired, my wolf won't let it rest.*

I grinned, liking the thought of him clean, naked, and underneath me. Hell, he probably wouldn't make it out of the shower before my self-control snapped and my wolf surged. *Okay, you have a point.*

I thought that might ease your mind. He winked and kissed me.

But the uneasy feeling coursing up my spine ruined the moment. With Kel breathing down our necks, I was eager to get the hell out of here.

Pulling away from Bodey was the last thing I wanted to do, but my wolf relented at the thought of him getting captured again or worse. I stepped away and faced the group. "I'll drive the Mercedes, Bodey will drive the Navigator, and Jasmine will take Michael's car. Split up as you see fit and let's move out."

"Sounds good." Bodey winked and then linked, *And I'm*

contacting the alphas of Idaho now about what happened. Miles, Lucas, and Jack are handling their states.

Some of my worries eased. Maybe I should've handled that sooner, but I hadn't yet established those relationships. Yet another issue to address quickly.

"First, let's put the towels in the washing machine with bleach, and then we should be ready." Jasmine jogged over, gathered the dirty and bloodstained towels, and ran toward the kitchen. "The directions say to run the washing machine when we leave and strip the beds, so you all help do that so we can get out of here."

Everyone sprang into action, and within minutes, we were walking outside and getting into the vehicles. I linked with Miles for directions to wherever they were.

I pulled out, Bodey right behind me with Jasmine at the rear, and we made our way to our people.

They'd wound up in a park ten minutes away where only a few kids were playing on a playground hidden behind trees and bushes. Five cars were gathered in the lot's back corner, and a few of the more healed wolf shifters were hanging out by a car's trunk as if they were meeting up to talk. Despite the tinted windows, my wolf eyes noted the witches in the back seat, the faint glow of their hands barely noticeable even to my shifter vision.

Another vehicle was there, which had to be the second group of witches.

I pulled up beside the closest vehicle to Samuel, Miles, Jack, and Lucas. All three of them looked better than they had, despite the splotches of blood on their clothes. Luckily, we had a change of clothes in the back of the Navigator.

Bodey and I climbed out. My mate met me at the back of the Mercedes and took my hand, and the royal advisors and Samuel joined us, getting distance from Russell and his men.

Katelin rushed over to her dad with their two large suitcases.

Jack glanced over his shoulder and wrinkled his nose. *Russell's guys were murmuring. But we've picked up enough to know they're planning to head home.*

There it was. Confirmation.

Lucas tilted his head, watching my expression. He linked, *You're not shocked.*

Not with the way Katelin was acting when she left. Guilt had been written all over her face, and with Russell wanting her to go, it had been an educated guess. *We all need to go home. You can sleep in the car.*

Wait. Jack lifted a finger. *I can sleep in the car? My car? Who do you think is going to drive my baby?*

Oh, great. He was one of those guys. *Bodey.*

No one drives my car but me. Jack pointed to his chest as he yawned.

I arched a brow. *Says the guy whose yawn almost swallowed his face. What would you prefer? Letting Bodey drive and get you back to Stevie quicker, or having to pull over and sleep somewhere for several hours, knowing Kel is planning retribution?*

He scowled, and his gaze flicked from his Navigator to me. He sighed. "Well played. You're learning the art of negotiation."

I laughed. Jack cracking jokes while grumbling and Bodey almost being back to normal beside me made things feel a little less dire.

But the moment I noticed Russell heading toward me, I straightened. He grimaced.

I licked my lips. *I'll be right back.*

Bodey surprised me by walking with me.

I paused, glancing at him.

He stiffened. *Is it not okay for me to go with you? I mean—*

No, it's fine. When it came to royal duties, he usually stayed put, letting me handle it alone or with Samuel. *I'd like you to come with me.* Having him beside me felt right. Bodey viewed himself as the alpha of Idaho, and he was, but him standing beside me as my equal was what I'd been wanting all along.

Good. He smiled and moved in sync beside me.

As we met him at the witch's car that separated us from their vehicles, Russell stopped, waiting for us. When we approached, he put a hand into his pocket.

"I hate to say this, but King Sutton has requested that we come home." Russell frowned, and there was a sniffle behind us.

I glanced over my shoulder to see the passenger window of the SUV cracked open. Jasmine could hear the entire conversation.

"Thank you for your help." Even though I hated to lose their assistance, I understood. This wasn't their fight, not yet, and they'd already lost seven men. "I'm sorry for your loss, and your sacrifice won't be forgotten."

Russell's head tilted back. "You aren't mad?"

"Not at all." I smiled sadly. "I hate that we cost you so much." I reached over and squeezed his hands.

"When we can return the favor, let us know," Bodey added, shaking Russell's hand.

The witches climbed out of the vehicles and stood at the back.

Prue lifted her chin. "We're done."

Then there was no reason for us to loiter here any longer.

Katelin slammed the trunk of the car and jogged over to us, biting her bottom lip. "Can I talk to Jasmine?"

Russell gestured at the SUV. "Make it quick. We all need to get home."

Katelin hurried over to Jasmine, and I heard the car door open.

"If I could find a way to stay—" Russell started, regret on his face. Despite losing men, he didn't want to leave us stranded.

I patted his arm. "I promise. We understand. Go home and mourn the ones you lost."

"Thank you for understanding." His eyes glowed, and his men moved toward the cars. "You're a good ruler."

I wasn't so sure about that, but I smiled and thanked him.

Katelin hurried to one of the vehicles as Prue focused on me. "We'll be heading back too. But please let us know if you need anything more from us. It has been an honor."

"Thank you for your help. I won't forget it." I nodded, hating to cut our time short, but my hands were tied. We split up, got into our cars, and headed back home.

It was close to nine when we arrived home in Idaho. We had fifty wolves running the town's perimeter as we advised the other packs—especially those close to the borders—to do the same.

As soon as we arrived, the mates split apart from the others, needing time alone and time to rest before we helped keep watch.

It bothered me that Stevie didn't need me to help mourn our father and instead desired to be alone with Jack. Though I was happy that both of us had a mate, it'd been her and me against the world for so long that her turning to Jack had hurt a little. I understood. No one could comfort me like Bodey.

Another thing that both comforted and worried me was that Stevie hadn't heard from anyone from my former pack, including Theo. Although, with the way she and Jack were looking at each other, I suspected her pack alignment would change tonight.

Are you okay? Bodey asked as he stepped out of our bathroom. He'd turned on the shower and stripped off his shirt, tossing it onto the dark-mahogany floor of our bedroom.

Even stinky and with a dirt-crusted body, he appealed to my every sense. I admired the curves of his muscles and the trail of hair that led to my very happy place, which his jeans obstructed. *Very much okay with you here like that.*

He smirked and readied to unfasten his jeans. Then he paused. "I'm still sore and can't raise my arm well. I might need you to get in the shower with me and clean me off."

My body warmed. I tilted my head and bit my bottom lip. "I suppose I could help you."

"Suppose?" He unfastened the button but didn't drop his pants. "I'd hate to be a bother."

I shrugged. "Whether you're a bother depends on whether you'll make it worth my time?"

"I'm eager to please you in whatever way you like." He leaned against the black dresser close to the bathroom door, watching me earnestly.

My breath caught as I ran my fingers over our cream comforter and walked toward him. "Then... it won't be a bother."

I'd missed our flirty banter, but most of all, I'd missed connecting with him in a way that merged our souls and made us complete, if only for a short while. My body thrummed, and my wolf surged forward, needing to unite with him desperately.

He dropped his jeans, and I shed my clothes as we

entered the bathroom. He stepped into the stall and under the water. Dirt trickled to the gray tile and swirled down the drain.

Not wanting to be separated from him one second longer, I joined him, snatching the bar of soap and sudsing up his body. Heat flooded me as my hands caressed his hard muscles and I cleaned him thoroughly. As I washed his mark, I admired the tattoo. It wasn't as intricate as mine, consisting of only a paw print beneath the center of his collarbone, and it was about one-third the size, but I loved it. It was further proof that we were mated to each other.

He swiped the soap from me and quickly cleaned the rest of his body. I arched a brow and pouted.

He laughed. "You're way too slow. I need to touch you, and I want to be clean before I do."

Soon, he was rinsing off and pulling me against his chest.

Desire flared within me, and I desperately needed to taste him. I kissed him, and he responded with vigor, his tongue slipping into my mouth. His minty taste infused me, his scent making the world spin. My heart swelled as my body pulsed with need.

We couldn't go slow. I *needed* him... needed our connection. Slow could come later.

He must have felt the same because his hands slid between my legs, circling between my lower lips. I tilted my head back as he kissed his way down my chin and neck, his teeth grazing the base of my throat where he'd bitten me when he'd claimed me.

I sagged against him, and he stepped forward, pushing my back against the tile as he moved into the water.

My eyelids lowered, heavy with desire as I ogled him. His hand brushed my nipple as he quickened his pace between my legs. His mouth went to my breast, and his tongue licked the nipple. Need clenched inside me.

I moaned, unable to stop myself, and ground my hips against his hand, prompting him to slip two fingers inside me. His teeth gently grazed my sensitive flesh, and I whimpered. My muscles clenched as he moved both his fingers and tongue faster, bringing me to ecstasy. Even as I pulsed and melted, he didn't relent, continuing his torture and turning me into a mess of a puddle for him.

I reached down and stroked him, and his breathing turned ragged as his hips jerked in time with my hand. We worked each other into a frenzy.

Another orgasm consumed me, my muscles tensing as pleasure rolled through me. My body clenched around his fingers.

As the second wave of pleasure eased, I tried to pull away, more sensitive to his touch now, but he held me firmly.

"Again," he growled, his words igniting something inside me.

Somehow, my body responded, ready for more. But my wolf howled in my head, confirming what we both needed. "Not your fingers. I need *you*."

"Fuck," he gritted out, stepping between my legs and lifting me against the wall.

I wrapped my legs around his waist as he pushed in, filling me. He pressed his mouth to mine, and his tongue stroked me in rhythm with his thrusts, driving me wild.

With Bodey inside me, I adjusted my legs so he could sink deeper.

Each time he completed me, our emotions and sensations swirled together as our souls became one. *This* was the connection I'd missed and desired.

My next release was imminent, and our kisses became

messy as our pace quickened. He pushed hard inside me and stilled, reaching down to circle between my lips, and another orgasm rocked through me, filling our bond.

I love you, he linked as his body quivered with his own release. Our pleasures melded, and the world grew hazy around us.

I love you too, I responded as I tightened around him even more.

All too soon, our pleasure ebbed, and our souls separated again. The jolt of our bond and our love for each other still swirled between us.

Damn. He peppered kisses over my face as he pulled away and stepped back into the water. I followed him, not ready to give up touching him. I pressed my lips to his, and our tongues tangled again.

The water turned cold, and we rinsed again quickly.

Your Majesties, a man linked with us. *There's an unfamiliar car approaching.*

Bodey and I glanced at each other and reached for our towels. We dried off as Bodey replied, *How many people are inside?*

Just one.

That was suspicious. *Don't let your guard down. It could be a diversion.*

We'd gone into the bedroom to dress just as the doorbell rang. As I pulled on my fuchsia shirt, I heard Samuel move from the kitchen to the front door.

When the door opened, the voice that answered Samuel turned my blood to ice.

CHAPTER NINETEEN

OUT OF EVERYONE who might come here and cause problems, I hadn't expected *him*.

Theo.

I understood I'd taken Oregon away from him, which clearly had been a huge error. If I hadn't, we wouldn't be in the mess that Lynerd had put us in. Still, Theo and I had been childhood friends. I hoped that still counted for something.

"I need to see Callie," he repeated to Samuel.

Bodey's nostrils flared, and his breathing quickened, causing the white shirt that was damp from our shower to cling more tightly to his skin. He turned to the door.

I couldn't help but admire my mate's physique, but I forced my attention away and removed a knife from the top drawer of our dresser before joining him.

"Not calling first and showing up here demanding to see her isn't the best way to handle things," Samuel gritted out.

"I've been trying, but her phone's going straight to voice mail."

I hurried to my jeans, slipped them on, and removed my cell from my pocket. I hadn't realized it was dead. I linked

He's right. I didn't know. With all the chaos, I'd assumed the pack would link with me if something went awry.

Uh... Jack popped into Bodey's and my link. *Stevie's worried that something's wrong with your mom and sister. I'm forcing her to stay in our room, but she's beside herself.*

Sweat pooled in my armpits. What if Mom had tried to call? Shit, what if Theo was here because something had happened to her or Pearl? *Has Mom or Pearl contacted her?*

No.

I was rushing for the door, wanting answers, when Bodey gently clasped my wrist and linked, *What's wrong?*

What if Mom's been trying to call me? I didn't want to be reckless, but at the same time, Theo had knocked on our door instead of attacking head-on.

She would've contacted Stevie too, and neither of you have heard from her or Pearl. The corners of his eyes relaxed. *This sounds more like a trap, especially if Theo came alone.*

He was right. If Zeke had convinced Theo to strike back, this could have been his move. Stevie could link with our pack to tell me if something was amiss. But she was in the room next to us and not with the rest of the pack, and if Theo had alpha-willed Mom and Pearl not to say anything, she'd be as clueless as we were. I wished like hell I could link with my sister. I'd expected her and Jack to complete their bond by now. Stevie holding off surprised me. *Jack, has she heard anything through her pack link?*

When the transition happened, people panicked, but Theo called a meeting. She hasn't heard anything since.

Great. If I wanted answers, I'd have to go downstairs and talk to Theo, even if that was part of his plan. The only good thing was that I knew how to read him since we'd been close for the past seventeen years. Besides, I couldn't leave Samuel alone with him.

Theo huffed and then yelled, "Callie! I need to talk to you. It's about our pack and Lynerd."

That was enough to get me moving. I removed my hand from Bodey's grasp, opened our bedroom door, and marched down the hall. Bodey was right on my heels, and as I passed by the guest bedroom—the one I'd originally slept in when I'd first come to this house—the door opened.

Stevie stood there, her blonde hair a tangled mess, no doubt courtesy of Jack, and her brown eyes determined. Unlike me, she was wearing a tank top and pajama shorts, another testament to what she and Jack had been doing.

"Dammit, Stevie," Jack rasped from behind her, shuffling as if he was throwing on clothes.

Yeah, I definitely didn't want to address that.

Callie, stay up there, Samuel linked with me. *I can handle Theo. It's best if we don't give in to his demands.*

We reached the stairs, and Jack's feet padded after us. *I want to find out what's going on.* Staying up here would only drag out the situation. It wouldn't actually prevent anything.

As soon as I reached the bottom of the stairs, I locked eyes with Theo at the door.

Turning toward me, Samuel shook his head and linked to Bodey and me, *You should've stopped her from coming down here, man.*

I agree with Callie—Theo needs to be handled, Bodey replied as we paused at the threshold to the living room, staring Theo down.

Staying out of striking distance, I straightened my shoulders. "What do you want?"

Stevie and Jack came up behind us, and the four of us huddled together, facing our enemy.

"Are you serious?" Theo lifted his hands. "After what

Lynerd did today, you don't answer my calls, then you ask *that*?" He glared at me like he didn't know me.

There it was. What I'd feared.

Maybe that was what happened when you stopped viewing someone as your alpha and were no longer forced to regard them with respect. "My phone is dead. I didn't know you were trying to call me. You could've called Stevie."

"Talking to her wouldn't resolve a damn thing." Theo ran his hands through his hair as the cool March breeze swirled past him and into the house.

Even though my shifter body kept me warm, I shivered. I forced myself to believe it was from the wind and not what was going down between me and my oldest friend.

Stevie huffed as if she'd been hit, and Jack snarled.

"What the fuck does that mean, douchebag?" Jack stepped forward.

Bodey moved in front of Jack, preventing him from walking past us. I didn't have to turn around to know how angry Jack was, especially with Bodey's intervention. His anger was palpable, but I appreciated the way he stood up for my sister.

"Look, I didn't mean it like that." Theo glanced over his shoulder as if expecting someone to pull up. "Can I come in?"

I leaned back on my heels and waved toward the couch.

Samuel's mouth dropped. *You've got to be kidding me. He needs to go. There's no telling what he's planning or what information he's gathering for Lynerd.*

This is Callie's call, Bodey replied, tensing beside me. *And I agree with her. If we don't hear him out, he'll hang around and keep trying. If we want him to go away, we need to listen. Unfortunately, I learned that when he kept sniffing around Callie while she was staying here the first time.*

My chest expanded. I didn't know what had changed, but I was so happy we were on the same page and together.

Although Bodey and I hadn't known each other long, it felt like years. So much shit had happened in such a short time that it all blended together.

Nostrils flaring, Samuel stood rigidly by the door while Theo rushed inside as if we might change our minds. The fact he'd come alone gave me pause. I would have expected him to bring Charles, or at least *someone* else, to see us.

Jaw twitching, Samuel shut the door but remained next to it, tightly coiled and ready to spring.

How's everything out there? I linked with the man who was part of Bodey's pack. If things ever settled and I somehow remained in charge, I'd need to spend more time with Bodey's pack and all the wolves in the entire territory. I didn't want others to think Bodey's pack was getting preferential treatment because he was the alpha.

Another problem for another day.

The man replied, *Nothing out of the ordinary. A few more wolves have joined us since the strange visitor arrived.*

Out of the corner of my eye, I noticed Bodey smirking as if he liked that description of Theo.

Pacing between the couch and the windows, Theo wrung his hands.

His anxiety was making me more nervous. I wanted to snap at him, but instead, I took a deep breath. I didn't want him to know he was getting to me. I asked, "Theo, why are you here?"

He stilled and dropped his hands. "Is Jasmine all right?"

For a moment, I'd forgotten about their connection, but now I understood why Jasmine had been more of a mess when she'd learned that Russell and his wolves were heading back home. She'd probably realized she and Theo were enemies now.

My heart hurt. I'd assumed her anxiety was only due to her friend leaving her behind. I'd bet she felt alone. I understood that sentiment all too well.

"Jasmine is none—" Bodey started, his anger and resentment over Theo's and my complicated past taking control.

"She's fine." Maybe I shouldn't have given Theo that, but if Bodey and I had been in the same situation, I'd want someone to let me know. "Now, I need you to answer my question."

His shoulders sagged as if my answer had taken a ton of weight off them, and he nodded. "Yeah, that's fair. But she's why I'm here."

"You're not taking Jazzy or Stevie back with you." Jack took a step forward, blocking Stevie from Theo's view while wedging himself between Bodey and me. "If that's your goal, turn your weak ass back around and go home."

Blowing out a breath, Theo fisted his hands together. "I really need your two guards to shut the fuck up. They're making this harder." His eyes narrowed as he stared me down.

"I'll show you—" Jack moved forward.

"Let's hear him out." I'd laced alpha will into my voice. I hated to do it, but things were going to get chaotic if I didn't intervene. Power vibrated through the room, echoing off the walls and crashing back into me.

Jack's mouth shut almost comically, and Theo's eyes widened.

"Damn." Theo stumbled back a few feet. "I knew you were strong, but this is the first time I've experienced it like that."

I rolled my eyes as Samuel shook his head.

He's stalling, Samuel linked to Bodey and me.

I was big enough to admit he was right and glared at Theo.

"Time's ticking, and I'm out of patience," Bodey snarled beside me. "Do you know how damn hard it is having you here in our house after all the shit you pulled with her? Say what you need to say, or get the *fuck* out."

Theo looked at me as if he expected me to come to his aid again.

All I did was shrug and add, "I'm in agreement with him."

Theo straightened and lifted his chin. "Fine."

That was his tic for when he was getting ready to do something he didn't want to do. I'd sometimes seen it when he was younger and preparing himself to protect me from Zeke. After realizing it had only made things harder for me, he'd stopped.

This was the first time his preparation had been directed at me, and I braced myself for whatever he would say next.

I held my breath, not wanting to make a sound, when he dropped the final blow.

"I want to submit to you," he said quickly.

My head jerked back, and I blinked. I must have heard him wrong.

"Not happening." Bodey shook his head. "That would make you a royal advisor, and you have no territory to rule, nor do we trust you."

I snorted bitterly. I hadn't picked up on that. This was a Zeke-style move. As I suspected, the two of them were colluding.

"Fine." Theo nodded and homed in on me again. "Then who do I need to submit to? I want to be part of this pack. I don't want to be your enemy and separated from you."

Bodey stalked toward him, and I didn't intervene. Whatever game Theo was playing, I was over it, and my mate needed to know I was firmly with him. I'd never want him to feel discounted.

"She's my mate." Bodey gestured to his neck and the faint scar from when I'd claimed him, then pointed at his tattoo. "You need to get it through your thick head." He grabbed Theo by the collar of his shirt and shoved him into the wall.

"I didn't mean it like that!" Theo's Adam's apple bobbed. "I don't have those feelings for Callie, not anymore. I meant I don't want to be part of Queen Kel's territory."

I winced. I wasn't sure how to process that he'd been genuinely interested in me before.

Bodey's hand fisted, and I had no doubt a punch would be thrown.

"Look, I'll submit to you." Theo lifted his hands again to prove he wasn't trying to cause problems. "I want to belong to your pack, but when I submit, the rest of Oxbow will come with me. Do you have enough room for us?"

My. Heart. Stopped.

Never in a million years would I have dreamed that Theo would be willing to submit to Bodey. They hadn't liked each other from the start. Although one explanation made sense.

Jasmine.

"You're kidding." Bodey loosened his hold on Theo's neck as his brows furrowed.

There was no scent of a lie, which had my mate stumped.

"I'm not." Theo pointed at him, Stevie, and me. "Stevie won't be part of the pack any longer, and Julie won't want to live without both of them anyway. We can join you and help fight Queen Kel. That will give you a hundred more fighters."

The Oxbow pack was slightly under two hundred, including children. Theo's offer showed he was willing to have his strongest pack members fight alongside us. Even though it wouldn't be ideal to have Charles living nearby, he and his father were strong. We needed more numbers.

I don't like it. Samuel frowned. *They have to be up to something.*

But if Theo's pack joined ours, it would be harder for them to hide things from us. Having our potential enemies closer would be ideal, especially now. *I always wanted to escape my former pack, but I think we need to accept them.* I paused, waiting for Bodey's response.

I was ready for him to side with Samuel, but he sighed and stepped back from Theo. *I hate to agree, but Callie has a point.*

My mind went blank, causing Bodey's shoulders to shake.

You don't have to be so surprised. He turned around and smiled sadly. *I may not like it, but we do need to think strategically.*

Once again, he'd reinforced just how amazing he was. Even if he didn't like Theo and most of Theo's pack members, he'd put that aside for me and to help our people. Not many would do that, but my mate was nothing less than special.

"Dude, no." Jack shook his head hard. "You can't seriously be entertaining this. He's a fucking tool."

"Thanks," Theo deadpanned. "I'm trying to be a good leader for my pack, and I get called names."

"It'd be nice to have Mom and Pearl here permanently," Stevie said softly. "Especially if we're supposed to be enemies now."

Jack sighed, already succumbing to defeat because my sister wanted them to join us.

At one point, I'd thought the advisors were tough guys. Now I knew they were, except when it came to their mates.

"Why didn't you just call one of the royal advisors?" Samuel arched a brow. "Or pack link with Stevie?"

"For one, none of you would have trusted me over the phone since you wouldn't have been able to smell that I wasn't lying." Theo crossed his arms. "And two, I've shut down my pack link, so Lynerd can't access me easily. I don't want him to force me to do something I'll regret."

That was fair. He'd have assumed I would be the most likely to believe him—or hear him out.

"Okay, I'll bite." I wanted to call his bluff and see if this was a game. "Submit to Bodey."

"Fine," Theo scoffed and turned to Bodey, ready to avert his eyes and submit to him.

Bodey tensed and lifted a hand. "No. Wait."

Exhaling, Jack rubbed a hand down his face. "I thought we agreed to let him join."

"That's the thing." Bodey bit his bottom lip and glanced at me. "Remember when I said I've been thinking about some things?"

The conversation replayed in my mind. He'd mentioned it during our link talks while he'd been Kel's captive. "Yeah." My pulse pounded. Where was he going with this?

"I want to be at your side the way I *should* be." Bodey clasped his hands and moved in front of me. "I grew up thinking I was responsible for Idaho, and I thought that was my place even after you and I were marked. But I've realized that our bond sealed our real fates. I want to be your king consort, help you make decisions, and be by your side."

Even though I appreciated Samuel's guidance and he'd become someone I relied on, this was what I wanted too: for Bodey and me to rule together as equals. Smiling, I cupped his cheek. "I'd like that."

Samuel scowled, and I could see the hurt on his face. I hadn't meant to cause that.

"Uh... man." Jack chuckled dryly. "I hate to tell you this,

but you're Idaho's royal advisor. Someone would have to take your place, and Jasmine's in school."

"I was hoping Samuel would take my place." Bodey turned to my brother. "And if he agrees, Theo should submit to him as Samuel's first act as alpha of the pack and territory." Bodey reached out to take Samuel's hand, and I could feel his nerves. "Will you accept the position and become an official advisor to your queen?"

My heart thundered, and my chest warmed. Samuel would have an official role as advisor and some of the responsibilities he'd grown up expecting. Bodey was making things right in the best way possible under the circumstances.

Samuel froze, and his face turned pale. Something unreadable crossed his face, and he opened his mouth to respond.

CHAPTER TWENTY

THE TENSION HUNG SO heavy in the air that I could barely breathe. Having Bodey focus on the entire territory with me was something I'd wanted—not that I felt as if I couldn't rely on Samuel, but I *knew* my mate and I would be stronger if we worked together. I just hadn't wanted to ask him.

Theo fidgeted, and Bodey's arm shook slightly as he continued to hold his hand out toward Samuel. Between that and his increasing worry through our bond, I'd had enough.

I opened my mouth to say something—*anything*—but before I could speak, Samuel cleared his throat.

He straightened and homed in on me as he linked, *Is that what you want?*

The question seemed simple, but the answer wasn't. I wasn't sure how to navigate it, and Samuel's face was indifferent. I wished I could feel the other pack members the way I sensed Bodey so I'd have a better idea of how to respond in a way that would do the least amount of damage. Since I couldn't do that, I'd give Samuel the answer I would want to hear, the carefully worded truth. *Having Bodey as a royal advisor and the king consort is a conflict of interest that I fear will become a problem if we defeat Kel.*

My wolf growled at the word *if*, but I couldn't be foolish or arrogant. Kel had the upper hand, and losing Lynerd and Oregon had been a critical blow. Dancing around the truth wasn't wise, especially in a time of war. *It's not that I don't want your counsel. I do. I appreciate your insight and opinions, but you can still offer that in the royal advisor role. If you don't want the position, I completely understand. You don't have to take it.* We could put Jasmine in charge when she graduated. She might not have the strongest wolf, but I doubted this region would argue with it, especially since she'd have my backing and Bodey's.

"Uh..." Bodey began lowering his hand. "If you aren't—"

Before he lowered it completely, Samuel took it and gave it a firm shake. Samuel blew out a shaky breath and said, "It would be an honor."

Bodey's lips pressed together. "Look, if you aren't sure, it's fine. You can take time to think about it. I just—"

"No, I want it." Samuel scratched the back of his neck. "I needed to make sure Callie was okay with it before accepting, in case she had other plans."

I smiled sadly. "If I had something brewing, I would've run it past you or stopped Bodey before he offered you the position, but like he said..." I placed my head on Bodey's shoulder and interlaced our hands. "If you need time, you can have it. We don't have to make any rash decisions."

Snorting, Jack deadpanned, "Really? With Queen Kel around, I feel like we're always chasing her tail."

"Man." Bodey scoffed, glaring over his shoulder at Jack.

"What?" Jack retorted.

"Sometimes it's better to leave things unsaid," Stevie chastised.

I couldn't take my eyes off my brother. I searched for any clue that might tell me how he felt inside since he kept himself so guarded.

His forehead smoothed out, and he smiled easily at Jack's comment; he truly seemed relieved. My lungs worked easier. At least one more thing hadn't imploded.

Jack huffed. "Please."

I managed to pull my attention from Samuel to study Jack.

As expected, he was being more himself now that he was back with Stevie.

"Nothing is better left unsaid as long as you *mean* it." Jack waggled a finger. "Here are my rules. If I care for a person, I don't say anything out of anger or annoyance. That shit has to be something I've felt for a while, or I know it won't change. It's gotta come from a place of love. And unfortunately, Queen Kel is kicking our butts. That's no reflection on Callie and her role as queen. Kel had this shit planned long before Callie was ever inked as our ruler."

Now that he'd pointed that out, I realized it was true—he didn't give us hell unless it was out of fun. He liked to cause problems, but his intentions were usually innocent. And he wasn't stating anything many of us hadn't been thinking.

"You don't hold back with me." Theo placed his hands in his pockets as he stood awkwardly at the end of the couch.

Turning back to him, Jack narrowed his eyes.

"I kind of feel part of the group." Theo grinned, though it didn't completely reach his eyes.

"Don't." Jack cleared his throat. "I say shit to you all the time out of anger because I don't give a fuck about you. The way you stood back and allowed Callie and Stevie to be mistreated was cowardly. If you were meant to be an alpha, you would've challenged your dad. Instead, he's rotting in a basement because he went unchecked for too long."

Theo flinched, and I grimaced.

There wasn't much I could say to correct Jack. He hadn't said anything untrue, which was his point.

I also didn't want Theo to take back what he'd said. "You coming here and asking to join our pack shows that you're changing."

Displeasure soared through Bodey as he wrapped his arm around my waist, anchoring me to him. He linked, *I really hate this guy. If it weren't for your family, I'd kick his ass and tell him to go away.*

I didn't doubt that, but I couldn't abandon Theo even if Bodey wanted me to. *It's not an excuse, but Theo tried to do right by me and Stevie when we were younger. Zeke treated us even worse because of it, so Theo stopped. He was too young to take over the pack then.*

Yeah, but when he got older, he should've done something.

It's hard to see that when you were raised a certain way. I nuzzled into his side, making sure Bodey didn't feel threatened by my feelings of friendship for Theo. They weren't anything close to what I felt for Bodey, but I understood that Theo was a sore subject since he'd been trying to date me just a few weeks ago. *Now that his eyes are open about his dad, he's here, trying to do the right thing. He could schmooze up to Queen Kel and offer Mom and Pearl to her, but instead, he's here to ally with us, and it has nothing to do with me.* Now wasn't the time to add that it probably had a lot to do with Jasmine.

As long as we make it clear that you're mine, I'll manage. He bent down and kissed my lips gently, then pulled me against his chest, claiming me in front of Theo. I enjoyed every kiss and touch, not bothered in the least by his attention.

If allowing him to do that also made him feel more secure and safe about me, who was I to argue?

You better cut that shit out, or I'll be performing the same show with your sister, Jack linked, effectively killing the warmth spreading through me.

Thinking of Jack mauling my sister beside me made me sick.

Damn you, man, Bodey linked, but I could feel humor swirling from him. *I was trying to make a point to Theo.*

Dude, you made a point to all of us, Jack replied as I leaned back. He waved a hand in front of his nose. *We smell you both clearly. You don't need to worry.*

Samuel coughed, and his nose wrinkled. I had no doubt he felt the same way about Bodey's and my display.

Steepling his fingers, Samuel rolled his shoulders. "We need to connect Theo before Lynerd forces the pack link and alpha-wills him."

He had a point. We didn't have time to waste.

Again, my lack of knowledge surfaced. "How does that work with you being the royal advisor and him already being in your pack?" I asked my mate.

"I need to hand my pack over to Samuel." Bodey released me and cracked his neck as he moved toward my brother. He linked with us both and asked Samuel, *Are you sure? I don't want you to feel pressured.*

Since I wasn't marked, I've been a little out of sorts. My entire life, I expected to be king even though I didn't want it. Then, to have it taken away... I've been off balance, especially with Callie growing into her position. Being responsible for Idaho feels meant to be. His expression looked earnest.

I'd thought he was upset about me becoming queen, but he was unsettled because he didn't know his place in this world. My mate had finally given him the answer.

"Uh... are you two sure about this?" Jack moved to Bodey's other side and tugged on his collar. "Maybe we should—"

Something hard furled in my stomach.

"Is there a problem?" Theo asked, his gaze flicking between Bodey and Samuel. "We can do it later."

"Everything's fine." Bodey walked to the end table next to the couch and removed a small knife.

He cut his fingertip and held out the blade to Samuel. Samuel didn't hesitate to mimic the gesture. Blood welled up on each of their fingers, and Bodey held out his hand to Samuel.

Samuel touched his bloody fingertip to Bodey's, and their eyes glowed, their wolves surging forward.

"What are they doing?" Stevie whispered as she came to stand at my side.

Jack rubbed his hands together. "They're transferring the pack. Unlike witches, we can't push a lot of our magic into one another, so blood blending is the best way for one wolf's magic to enter another wolf. It's similar to a mate bite but not as intimate. Now Samuel has to submit to Bodey."

My body turned rigid. That was why Jack had been nervous. Samuel's wolf surged forward, and sweat beaded along Bodey's upper lip. Samuel's jaw tensed, but Bodey was clearly having a harder time.

If Bodey lost this battle, Samuel would become the alpha of the pack and the territory, with Bodey as his beta.

Samuel, you need to avert your gaze, I linked with him, worried about what the implications would be if Bodey was viewed as weaker in the eyes of our people. It didn't matter to me; Bodey was my mate, no matter what happened here. But whether I liked to admit it or not, Bodey being seen as a beta could make it harder for my people to get behind us.

I can't, Samuel replied. *I'm trying, but my wolf won't have it.*

He had to be feeling the same way I'd felt all those times growing up when I'd known I should cower and shut my mouth, but something inside me wouldn't allow me to do it. It wasn't Samuel's fault.

I had no idea what to do, but I had to figure something out, even if I had to sucker punch Samuel.

Maybe it wouldn't come to that.

Instinct had me reaching for the thread of our fated-mate bond. I grasped onto it. My wolf surged forward in my head, and she pushed our magic through the connection like when Bodey had been injured and sleeping. I shoved more magic through, funneling it into him.

"What the fuck?" Theo rasped.

I glanced at him as I continued to funnel my magic into my mate. Theo's eyes were locked on Bodey.

I almost faltered.

Bodey's eyes were still glowing, but their indigo color had lightened as if the Caribbean blue of my eyes had mixed with his. The indigo had become a vibrant cobalt with a faint green edge around the rim, the colors moving like a river every few seconds.

Whimpering, Samuel lowered his head as sweat sprouted along his hairline. The tables had turned, and now my mate was definitely the strongest, thanks to our mate bond.

Dina's words from days ago replayed in my mind. She'd said that fated mates could channel their magic into one another, and this had to be what she meant.

When Samuel averted his gaze to the wooden floor, I let out a breath, and my wolf began to retreat. I didn't feel different, but Samuel rubbed his chest, and I knew the warm spots of all the wolves in Idaho were flaring there. I remembered that overwhelming, comforting heat vividly from the day the ink had accepted me.

Turning to me, Bodey took my hand. His eyes were returning to their dark-indigo color, but a faint greenish blue along the edge proved that my magic was still flowing to him.

I didn't realize Samuel's wolf would fight me like that. The only reason I didn't lose my position was because of you. Bodey's gaze was like a caress. *Thank you.*

I winked. *Anytime, babe, but we need to tell the pack what's going on.*

Dad's on it. He took my hand and stepped to my other side so I was between him and my sister. *He linked when our magic merged, concerned about what was going on. We told him, and he knew that either way, Samuel would be alpha, so he's communicating it with the pack and letting them know we're taking in a lot of new pack members. There's land we can build on to expand the neighborhood, but we'll have to make do with the available houses until we have time to develop it.*

I should've thought to reach out to Michael. I hadn't considered where Theo's pack would stay. But there were several vacant houses they could use in the interim.

"Shit," Theo rasped. "I need to submit *now*." His eyes glowed, indicating that his pack link had been activated. "Lynerd is pushing through my block."

Samuel turned to him, lifted his chin, and said, "Let's do it." He wiped the tip of his finger on his pajama shorts, removing the blood.

Breathing quickly, Theo locked eyes with Samuel. His eyes were already glowing, but as they connected with Samuel's, the color intensified.

It wasn't long before Theo averted his eyes, and around two hundred pack links sprouted in my chest. Theo and the others were officially part of Idaho. "Now you need to bring the pack here—and Charles and Trevor need to learn their place."

"They're all moving now." Theo leaned his head back as if the weight of the world was gone from his shoulders. "I told the pack to be ready—they knew what I was planning. Your mom was upset since your dad—"

A deep ache throbbed in my chest. He didn't have to finish; I knew what he'd been about to say—since Dad had been buried.

Bodey's warmth flooded into me, reminding me he was there. I reached out and took Stevie's hand, knowing she and I were feeling the same thing.

"They're on their way. We just need to tell them where to go." Theo bit his lower lip.

"I can take it from here." Samuel opened the front door and glanced at us. "You four get some rest. This is my responsibility now."

Pride shone on his face, and I was so thankful Bodey had made this decision. It had made a good difference for each of us.

Jack and Stevie headed back to their room, and Bodey and I went to ours, where I promptly showed him my love and appreciation all over again.

After we pleasured our bodies once more, I fell asleep in the safety of my mate's arms.

THE NEXT DAY went by quickly as Samuel contacted all the alphas in Idaho, explaining his new role, and helped my childhood pack get acclimated. Luckily, everyone arrived without incident, and they took up the ten available houses scattered throughout the neighborhood. They'd stay in them until we could build more homes on the one hundred acres of woods the pack owned about an hour away.

Mom and Pearl chose to stay with Theo, Tina, Charles, and Trevor, which made me cringe. She didn't want to stay with Bodey, Jack, Samuel, Stevie, and me. I suspected she didn't want to see us with our mates after losing hers of thirty years.

The royal advisors spent all day contacting the alphas and coming up with plans to protect their packs. The witches reinforced their spells more often, and more wolves ran the perimeter. Weaker packs were instructed to relocate temporarily to a stronger pack so they could work together. Before we knew it, it was close to midnight, and we all crawled into bed.

After some time, a loud howl filled the air, and a pack member linked to Bodey, Samuel, and me, *There's something strange going on out here.*

I rolled away from Bodey toward the clock on the nightstand. It was two a.m.

My heart thundered, though I tried to keep calm. *What do you mean?*

There's some sort of... But he stopped, and his link cooled as if he'd lost consciousness.

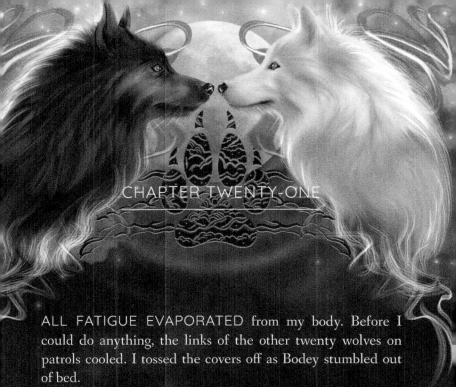

CHAPTER TWENTY-ONE

ALL FATIGUE EVAPORATED from my body. Before I could do anything, the links of the other twenty wolves on patrols cooled. I tossed the covers off as Bodey stumbled out of bed.

We frantically gathered our pajamas, which we'd scattered all over the floor as we'd unclothed each other earlier. Something we should've maybe rectified before falling asleep, but Kel and her constant threats had been the furthest thing from my mind.

Simon, get another thirty wolves and check the perimeter, Samuel commanded, keeping Bodey and me in the conversation. *Thirty of our strongest.*

We need to inform Dina of what's going on, Bodey linked to me. *She's the priestess and part of the coven assigned to protect us. She might know what to do and how we can protect ourselves. Queen Kel has made it no secret that she doesn't mind using human weapons as well as witches' magic.* He picked up his cell phone from the nightstand, readying to make the call.

Good plan. I pulled on my flannel pajama bottoms, then

yanked my fuchsia shirt on and down over the waistline. *I'll join the thirty running the perimeter.* I needed to get out there and see what was happening.

Bodey frowned and lowered the phone. *That wouldn't be wise. If this is Kel, which it likely is, you're their target. If anything, I should—*

I burst into laughter; the noise was so bitter that my throat ached. *You just got back from a three-day stint where you were beaten, starved, and tortured. The last person who should go is you. You've only just healed.*

Tossing the phone onto the bed, he stalked toward me. His irises darkened to a midnight blue as he gripped my arms.

My wolf soared inside me, upset and ready to stand our ground. The emotions swirling from him were so damn volatile that it was hard to latch on to just one.

His determination finally pulled to the forefront. *If you go out there, I'm going with you.* His fingers remained firmly on me but nowhere close to the point of hurting me. His eyes glowed faintly as our wolves communicated with each other. *She took me to get to you. Everything she does revolves around you.*

My chest tightened, and I hated that he had a point. *How many more people are going to get hurt in my name?*

As many as it fucking takes. His hand slid up my arm to my neck, supporting my head so our eyes remained locked. *If she gets you, she'll hurt far more than a handful of people. It'll be every person who defies her, including all the people you love.*

I sucked in a breath, not having expected the bluntness, but every word was pure truth. That was something Samuel would have said, while Bodey usually protected me from that kind of pain. He had a point, and it even broke through to my wolf as her anger receded from a boil to a simmer. *Don't sugarcoat it or anything.*

You wanted me to stand beside you as king consort, and that's what I'm doing, he linked as he kissed my lips softly. *And I will protect you, which, fortunately for me, isn't a conflict of interest since it also benefits our people. I'll do all I can to reinforce how important it is to keep you safe.*

Then you need to include yourself in that protection because I damn near fell apart while you were her captive. The agony of our separation still hit me so strongly that my eyes burned. *If something else happened to you...* I trailed off, not even willing to link the words to him.

That's why I'm calling Dina and we're staying put until we have a better idea of what's going on. He turned, snatched the phone off the bed, and typed out a message.

I exhaled. He was right. They probably wanted me to run out there. I hadn't been thinking logically. My entire life, the only person I'd had to depend on was myself. The thought of other people running around out there on my behalf while I stayed safe in a house didn't sit right. "It's hard standing still and doing nothing."

"Babe, it's the same for me." His expression softened. "I want to be out there too, and sometimes staying still is the hardest decision to make, even if it protects the most people. Strong wolves inherently want to be in the fight." He mashed his lips together as his irises lightened back to their normal color. "I'm willing to do anything to keep you safe because I'm selfish enough not to want to lose you either."

Any anger I felt washed away as my heart expanded almost uncomfortably. He was struggling just like me, and his love was the only thing keeping him here. If he could do it for me, I could do the same for him.

His phone dinged, and the corners of his mouth tipped downward again.

My stomach ached. "What's wrong?"

"Dina's on her way here." He grabbed my hand and led me through the bedroom doorway.

At Stevie and Jack's room, Bodey banged on the door, and Stevie yelped.

He linked with Jack, Stevie, and me, *Get your asses up. We're under attack.*

I winced, hating to bother them, but we needed all hands on deck, especially the royal advisors.

Samuel's feet scuffed the floor downstairs, and I could tell he was pacing. I didn't want him to feel he had to carry the weight of this attack on his own. Yes, he might be the alpha here now, but he had all our support.

Are Mom and Pearl okay? Stevie asked, and for a moment, I was puzzled. She could link with them just as well as I could.

I tugged on the links. Both Mom's and Pearl's were warm. More of the wolves in the pack were stirring, and all of us were on guard. *Yeah, but you can check on them yourself.* I understood she was struggling with losing Dad, but linking was as inherent to wolves as breathing.

Bodey and I were hurrying down the stairs when my sister replied, *Actually, I can't. Not anymore.*

My feet missed the last three steps, and I stumbled. Bodey moved lightning fast, caught me in his arms, and pulled me to his chest.

He grinned, examining the expression on my face. *Are you okay?*

Yeah. I shook my head as the world stilled under my feet. I wasn't surprised that Stevie and Jack had completed the bond —I knew the connection had been inevitable—but Stevie had put it off. *I'm fine. The one night I didn't expect them to complete their bond was the night they did.*

Setting me down, Bodey interlaced our hands, and we hurried down the hallway toward the den. He linked, *I'm surprised she held out this long. Jack was ready to seal the deal the day he met her.*

I flinched, not wanting to picture the image that conjured in my mind. Instead, I focused on Samuel, who was standing between the couch and the fireplace and staring out the window of the door closest to Michael and Janet's house.

We scurried past the kitchen on our left and the dining room on our right and went into the den to join him.

Let's go, Samuel grasped the door handle. *Our thirty wolves are together, and they've picked up the scent. They should reach the other wolves in five minutes. We can't catch up with them, but we won't be far behind if we move fast.*

A huge lump formed in my throat. *I don't think we should join them.*

He whipped toward me and froze. He blinked, then nodded. "It makes sense for you to stay here, but I gotta go out there with my pack."

He turned to march back to the door, but Bodey had already moved to stand in front of him.

Samuel glared at Bodey as if he had two heads. He rasped, "What the hell do you think you're doing?"

Bodey crossed his arms. "You shouldn't go out there for the same reasons Callie and I shouldn't."

"Like hell," Samuel seethed as he tried to pivot around Bodey.

Bodey pushed him in the chest, shoving him back several steps.

"Get out of my way," Samuel rasped as his shoulders heaved from how hard he was breathing. "You want to stay here, fine, but I need to be out there with those people. They need to see me standing with them."

Two sets of footsteps came down the stairs, and I sprang into action. If Jack got involved, the situation would only get worse. I had to release the tension and stop the two most important men in my life from fighting each other.

"I don't know of anyone who would attack us right now besides Kel." That was one thing I'd learned about Samuel—he responded to logic more than emotion.

Bodey pointed at me and added, "And if Kel gets you, she'll get Callie. You know Callie couldn't stand the idea of something happening to you, and Kel will know we can't be trusted again to do an exchange. This is another one of her games."

"Shit." Samuel hung his head. "You're right."

Jack breezed into the den with Stevie at his side.

Raising both eyebrows, Jack cupped his ear. "Wait. What was that? I couldn't hear you."

Taking a few steps back, Samuel huffed and bared his teeth. "You heard me loud and clear. I won't repeat it."

Jack pouted. "Dammit. I've never heard you admit that before. I wasn't certain your mouth could even form those words."

"Behave," Stevie chastised and smacked his arm. "There's an attack going on."

"Fine." Jack rolled his eyes. "But only for you."

There was a knock on the front door, followed by Dina, Miles, Stella, Lucas, the four former advisors, and their mates strolling in.

One person was missing.

"Where's Jasmine?" Bodey asked before I could.

"She's with the new pack, settling them in." Janet's face blanched, making her indigo eyes, which matched Bodey's, appear all the darker, especially when contrasted with her strawberry-blonde hair. "She's staying with Julie and Pearl at the other end of the neighborhood. We'd hate to risk her coming here."

In other words, she was staying with Theo, but Janet was smart enough to know not to say his name.

Miles's mother's dark eyes latched on to Jack's mother's, an unspoken exchange occurring between them from their spots in front of their mates. If Alicia and Destiny knew about Jasmine and Theo, Bodey wouldn't be far behind.

"What's going on?" Taylor, Lucas's mom, clutched her chest. Her long, dark hair cascaded over her blue silk nightgown. She took her mate's arm, her tan complexion a shade paler than usual.

"One second." Dina lifted a hand, her charcoal eyes scanning the place as if searching for something. Then she flicked her hands so hard that her auburn hair lifted around her, and she chanted, "Seal the house."

Out of the corner of my eye, I noticed a faint glimmer that soon faded.

Destiny walked toward her son but stopped and sniffed. Her eyes widened as she glanced from Jack to Stevie. Then a blinding smile spread across her heart-shaped face. She bounced up and down. "You completed your mate bond!"

"Yes, but now isn't the time to celebrate, Mom." Jack sighed and squeezed Stevie's hand softly. "We'll do the celebrating after we've eliminated the threat."

Alicia moved to the side of the granite island that separated the kitchen from the den. She ran her hands through her dark hair, and Phil followed her.

"What are you doing?" Stella asked, her dark-violet eyes on Dina. Flipping her dark, wavy hair, she moved to the spot between me and Miles.

"Putting a perimeter spell in place." Dina dropped her hands and turned to us. "Witch magic is pouring into our territory."

Shit. That wasn't good.

"Do you recognize the magic?" Lucas rubbed the back of his neck.

"I don't." Dina bit her bottom lip. "But they're powerful."

I was tugged into a link with Samuel, Bodey, and thirty others. A wolf shifter I wasn't familiar with linked, *It's some sort of gas. I don't know what.*

That reminded me of the day the wolves had attacked Stevie and almost killed her. A witch had come with them and cast some sort of smoke spell to block our sense of smell and our vision. *What does it smell like?*

We're going in... His words trailed off, and his link went lukewarm, just like the others. The other twenty-nine followed within the next second.

My wolf howled in my head, her frustration mixing with mine. Something was happening to my people, and I had no clue what.

Samuel snarled, "I'm going."

"Whoa." Dina lifted a hand, blocking him from leaving like Bodey had. "What happened?"

"My pack is in danger." Samuel wheezed, and I'd never seen him like this. He was like a different person.

Something's wrong with him, I connected with Bodey.

He wants to be the perfect alpha. His wolf isn't acting normally, so he seems out of character. His drive to do every-thing the way he thinks your dad did is throwing him off. He'll come around and figure it out just like you've been doing.

I wanted to laugh. Figuring it out felt like the last thing I'd done. I'd more often fucked things up, but I didn't need to dwell on that now, especially with a threat here. Instead, I answered Dina's question. "They said it's smoke. They were entering the area, and then their pack links went lukewarm, so they were probably all knocked out at the same time."

"Smoke." Dina's mouth twisted. "I bet it's lavender and they're performing a witch spell. You're supposed to do it with the herb on the ground, but to make it act quicker and more potent, some witches burn it and use it against their enemies to make them fall asleep."

"Sleep?" Jack's brows furrowed. "That doesn't sound like Kel. It might be someone else."

Miles shook his head. "That's not necessarily true. Kel wants Callie to submit, but if she can accomplish that without killing more of our wolves, that's to her benefit. She wants to rule over all the wolves—she doesn't want most of them dead."

"Then what's their plan?" If witches were putting our wolves to sleep, what would that accomplish?

Dina tapped her foot. "If I were them, I'd think, why come inside the area where we've put guards in place when they can send their strongest wolves to investigate us? I would stay in one place and have them come to me, easily wiping out my enemies."

This night kept getting worse and worse. "But if we leave the witches alone, they'll eventually come onto our land and put us all to sleep anyway." I wanted to hang my head, but I kept it held high. "What do we do? Is there a spell that can counteract theirs?"

"Hey, as long as Stevie and I are in bed together, and she's wrapped in my arms, a nap kinda sounds like heaven." Jack shrugged, like what he'd said was completely reasonable.

Lucas smacked him in the back of the head, and at the same time, Stevie punched him in the arm. She growled, "Not helping," at the same time, Lucas snarled, "Man, shut it."

Jack spun around, glancing at Stevie, then Lucas, then

back at her again. He pointed at his mate and his friend and said, "What the fuck just happened?"

Snorting, Bodey tried to hide his smile. "I think you're mated to the female version of one of your closest friends. Obviously, you like to be smacked around."

"Guys." Samuel clapped. "We need to focus and come up with a plan." A loud howl rang outside, and he tensed. "More of my wolves are heading toward the enemy."

"Tell them to abort." Dina raised a hand in front of her face. "They'll only wind up unconscious or hurt."

I clenched my hands and tried to hold on to my calm, but there was no comfort to latch on to.

Bodey's hand tightened on mine, increasing the jolt of our bond. I tried to take comfort in it, but knowing this whole pack was in danger made it hard. "We should tell everyone to get in their vehicles and leave." That probably wasn't rational, but staying here wasn't an option either. We had to try something. I hated to run, but I didn't know what choice we had. "We can find somewhere to take cover even if we need to split up temporarily."

"They'll expect that." Bodey frowned. "Kel is smart."

"He's right." Dina's expression crumpled. "Let me see what I can find out. I'll be right back."

As she opened the back door, I called out, "Wait. Someone should go with you."

"I'll be fine." Dina inhaled and winced. "I won't go near the witches—I'm going to see what I can determine from the magic without getting harmed."

After she left, everyone fell silent. Then a phone rang.

Bodey removed the phone from his pocket and flinched.

When I peered at the screen, the one name I never wanted to see ever again scrolled across.

Kel.

I didn't want to answer; I wanted to give her the middle finger. But she was vindictive. Maybe her anger would make her spill her secrets. She liked games, after all.

I had only one real option.

I took the phone, hoping like hell I didn't regret the decision.

CHAPTER TWENTY-TWO

BEFORE I COULD ANSWER IT, Bodey placed a hand over the screen, blocking me.

My head jerked up as he said, "Let it ring another time or two. We want her to think we aren't desperate and might not answer her call."

I nodded, though I wasn't sure if that proved we weren't desperate. She could easily assume we were in wolf form, heading toward the threat she had a hand in.

"While you answer, I'm contacting the pack that lives an hour away for help." Samuel's eyes glowed as his wolf surged forward, reaching out to the pack's alpha.

I allowed it to ring one more time, but I couldn't handle waiting any longer. I inhaled sharply to steady my voice and answered, "Hello?"

A dark chuckle came from the other end, followed by Kel's bored, regal voice. "For a moment, I thought you might be sleeping in the woods or too preoccupied to answer."

Kel had called to gloat. She didn't even pretend not to know what was going on. My blood boiled, adding to my

She was a sick, sadistic bitch who needed to learn a lesson.

My wolf brushed against my mind, growling. She wanted the queen to suffer, and I was fully on board. Each time I spoke with her, I hated her more, which was *really* saying something. "Well, I'm not sleeping, but I'd rather not have taken this call. Thanks for your strange concern, but I'm going to hang up." I refused to pretend to be scared. That would only make her feel more in control. I needed her to come a little unhinged and let some of her secrets slip.

"And hanging up has nothing to do with your wolves, who are supposed to be running perimeter, taking a nap? I've heard that even the backup you sent out is sleeping next to the original guards." Her voice dripped with amusement, and I could hear the smile in its tone. "If you hand yourself over, no one else needs to be harmed."

She was so damn smug, and I was thankful she wasn't here and able to smell my lies. "Ah... so this *is* your attack. Samuel suspected it, but I wasn't convinced."

What are you doing? Samuel asked. His brows furrowed as he moved beside Bodey.

I didn't have time to answer him, needing to focus on what Kel said next, but my mate smirked and replied, *Pushing her buttons.*

"That's why the ink should've chosen Samuel instead of you, but that wouldn't have mattered," Kel replied, her voice obnoxious. "He has the brains for this, but you... you have the heart. That's the only reason you've made it this far, but I'm tired of humoring you. This shit ends now."

That almost sounded like a compliment, and this was the first time she'd revealed her frustration about me. I went in for the kill. "Yeah, well, he thought this was a clear move of yours, but I thought you'd finally come along with your wolves to attack instead of staying behind. I didn't expect *this*. Not only did you not show up, but you sent witches in your stead. I guess that's what happens when you lose too many wolves and don't feel safe. You send other beings in their place. What did you do to force the witches to attack us?"

She scoffed and growled, "You haven't *weakened* me. My wolves are attending to other pressing business, and the witches want to prove their worth to me. A real leader stays behind and doesn't foolishly put themselves in harm's way. That is how I win."

I forced myself to laugh. Nothing about this situation was funny, but I had a role to play. And Kel had dropped some information, maybe without realizing by trying to prove she was smarter than me. "How are others supposed to be willing to die for your cause when you aren't willing to yourself?"

My gaze landed on Bodey, who nodded and linked to everyone in this room, *Her wolves may not be here with the witches, but we can't let our guard down. There's no telling what else she might have up her paw.*

"If I die, I don't achieve what I've been planning all these years." She paused, which had to be a tactic.

I wouldn't ask her to continue because I already knew where she was going with it. Plus, I'd hate for her to be under the impression that I cared.

"I'll be taking over your land and your reign. This is the last time I'll offer this—hand yourself over now, and your loved ones will be given grace." Her voice lowered to almost a purr. "If you don't, I'll make you watch everything I do to your packs, as well as to your mate. He *is* gorgeous, and it's been quite a while since I've had any sort of attention from a man."

I snarled, my wolf soaring so damn close to the surface that my skin tingled. Every time I thought she couldn't get any worse, she proved me wrong. I had no doubt she was evil incarnate, and I'd be damned if she ever touched my mate again. "I'll never turn myself over to you, and I look forward to the day I get to kill you." I'd never relished taking a life before, but she'd just become my exception.

"You lost Oregon, and you still think you have a shot in hell at winning against me." She snickered and cleared her throat. "I tried to be diplomatic and even gave you one last chance. I just hope Stevie isn't fatally hurt tonight. Too bad you weren't willing to protect her before."

Stevie.

Lynerd must have told Kel she was still alive. I wasn't surprised, but I wished he'd kept my sister out of it.

"Listen here," I started, but the line went dead. She'd made sure to have the final word, and I'd foolishly let her have that control.

A faint sob came from Stevie, and I tossed the phone onto the end table.

Jack pulled her into his arms and cradled her to his chest as he murmured, "They won't get anywhere near you or Callie."

"What was the point of calling you?" Stella wrinkled her nose.

"To gloat?" Lucas pursed his lips.

"I think she meant what she said about Callie's heart. She knows if she takes us over by force, she'll lose more lives and loyalty, and she was giving Callie one more chance to surrender before she orders the witches forward." Michael pinched the bridge of his nose. "The death of witches won't be as easy for her to wash away, but if she promised the witches something they want badly enough, they're more likely to overlook a few of their own casualties. She was trying to eliminate a fight."

Phil blinked. "*And* Kel got clues about where Callie's staying and who she's with. With the lack of outside noises, she'll know Callie is in a house, and from Stevie's reaction, Kel knows Callie's sister is with her."

I fisted my hands. "I shouldn't have answered."

"You had to. If you hadn't, her actions would have become more volatile. At least, this way, you were able to get information too. Her wolves are somewhere else, so there's no telling how many witches she has surrounding us." Miles tightened his arm around Stella's waist, tugging her closer. "We need to get out of here."

Leaving the neighborhood would be problematic with over four hundred wolves and Dina's coven, but I wasn't sure what other option we had. My wolf howled inside my head, opposing the idea of running from our home, but I couldn't let my pride be the reason more of my people wound up injured or dead. *Babe, we can't leave the wolves that are asleep behind.* My heart revolted at the thought alone.

We won't.

The sounds of two sets of light footsteps on our deck had me freezing. I glanced at the others, and their eyes narrowed with concern.

Stay where you are, Bodey linked and turned toward our deck as Dina came into view.

I blew out a breath as Chelsea stepped next to Dina, her dark-blonde hair tied in a low ponytail that hung over her shoulder and her aquamarine eyes serious.

The two of them opened the door and hurried to join us inside.

Though I'd been around Chelsea at the inking ceremony and when Kel's first witch had attacked alongside Kel's wolves, I didn't know her that well. The coven kept to themselves, with Dina being the main liaison between us and them, but I knew Chelsea was the second most powerful witch in the royal coven.

"Did you learn anything?"

Dina's mouth turned down further, sending goose bumps across my skin.

"At least one hundred and twenty witches have us surrounded." Dina rubbed her hands together.

Michael scowled. "That's more than our coven."

That wasn't good. *How many coven members are here?*

Eighty, and that includes the eleven in the royal coven, Bodey answered.

"Is there something we can do to stop them?" Given how isolated my childhood pack had been from witches, I didn't know what that meant.

Dina came toward me and stopped at Bodey's side. Her charcoal irises darkened. "We can gather the coven and try to hold them off, but with those numbers, we won't last long."

"Even with your power?" Bodey sounded defeated.

"They've moved so their gas and spell are upwind from us." Chelsea crossed her arms. "So they don't need to use magic to direct the smoke. All they need to do is send out magic to guide the wolves straight into the smoke."

Biting her bottom lip, Dina paced. "Our witches are fanning out in case some of theirs move into the territory. They can hold the smoke back temporarily."

Jack stepped toward the front door, his hand on Stevie. "We should get Callie and Stevie the fuck out of here."

Bodey nodded. "While a group of us stay behind to retrieve the unconscious wolves. Everyone else should leave."

"We could get a few members out, but not many more than that." Dina rubbed her forehead as if to relieve pressure. "If you want us to hold off the witches while you rescue the wolves, we won't be able to hold off the twenty or so enemy witches watching the road. We'd have to pull resources from the line to do it, which would impact the number who can escape, how long we can hold them off, and how many wolves you can retrieve."

My heart sank.

"At least Callie would be safe, right?" Carl asked from behind me. "That's what matters most."

Dan nodded, making me swallow.

"No." I shook my head so hard that the room spun. "I'm not leaving when my people are at risk. I won't race out of here and save my own ass." I clenched my teeth, hoping they knew me better than that.

"I'm with her." Stevie nodded. "You need to conserve your power to help everyone, not just Callie and me."

"Your capture or death *is* the worst outcome." Bodey spread his hands. "It's not ideal, but—"

My vision blurred as my anger soared through me. "Not *ideal*. It's worse than that. I couldn't live with myself if something happened after I left everyone behind and let's not even talk about what our people might think."

"Fuck them." Bodey's determination flowed straight into me as his nostrils flared. "At least you'd be safe."

I understood that he loved me. If I could talk him into leaving and getting out of this mess, especially after what Kel had threatened, I'd do it in a heartbeat. "There has to be another way. I'm not leaving without a solid plan to keep everyone safe. We're all in this together. Besides, Kel will use them against me. Don't act as if my leaving will prevent her from having something to hold over me!"

Samuel fisted his hands in his hair. "She's right. Kel will dangle whoever they capture in front of Callie to get her to surrender, and if she doesn't, Kel will tell people she ran to save herself, and we could lose more of our packs to Kel."

Bodey's jaw clenched so tightly that his teeth cracked. "That's still a better alternative to her capturing Callie now."

"Not necessarily, son." Michael tapped his foot against the floor. "The more people we lose, the less powerful Callie and you are."

"We need to hold off the witches until the pack arrives." Samuel swallowed and looked at Dina. "Is there anything else you can try?"

The gas is moving toward the houses, a female wolf linked to Samuel, Bodey, Michael, and me. *We're trying to clear the area and reach the neighborhood before—* Her link cooled.

Bodey snarled. "The witches are on the move. They just took down several of our shifters."

"Chelsea, gather the other witches and bring them here." Dina's face paled. "I'll stay here in case someone slips through."

Not hesitating, Chelsea ran out the back door, her blonde hair and gown flying behind her. She raced into the woods just as Dina's face twisted in agony.

My heart caught. "What's wrong?"

"The coven. We're already using a ton of magic." Dina blinked, her face strained. "The magic the other witches are using is enhanced by charms."

"Charms?" Destiny whimpered.

Dina reached the door. "They're carrying magic from other covens to make themselves stronger. I didn't realize it until our coven began fighting against them."

I had no clue what any of this meant, but it was bad. Bodey raced to me and tugged me toward the garage. "I'm getting her out of here."

"No, the witches watching the road will have charms too." Dina bit her bottom lip so hard that blood welled and trickled down her chin.

My heart raced. Kel had thought of everything again, and

we were on the losing side. I didn't know what to do, but running wasn't an option.

The thought of her capturing any of us, especially Bodey, made me want to claw the flesh from my bones.

"Fuck!" Jack heaved. "What do we do?"

"There is something I can try." Dina looked at me, face set in determination, and blew out a breath. "Stay right here." She raced to the door Destiny had exited through and stepped outside. The wind was blowing more powerfully than seemed natural for a clear night.

"Death goddess!" Dina called out as she ran down the stairs and into the yard. "I'm calling on you to help me eliminate the enemy!"

Death goddess? I parroted back to Bodey. I'd never heard anyone call out to the goddess of death before. It didn't sound safe.

I don't know what she's doing. Bodey tensed beside me.

"Dina!" Chelsea shouted from wherever she'd wound up. "No!"

"Take your chosen sacrifice from me and block our enemy's magic," Dina chanted, her hands glowing white like when she healed someone. She removed a dagger from a pocket and cut into her palm. "The witches came to harm us when we've never hurt them. I ask you to turn them to ash and to earth as nature intended."

Static filled the air, and a sandpaper-like sensation brushed over my skin again and again. Dina lifted her hands toward the sky, her magic like white lightning streaking into the atmosphere. Her auburn hair lifted as a jolt shook her body and reverberated into the air.

Something wasn't right. I could feel it in my soul.

When I tried to race to the witch, Bodey held me tight, but that wasn't what prevented me from going. Something invisible blocked me from moving more than two feet from where I stood.

I watched helplessly as Dina's body jerked and shuddered, and Chelsea ran out of the trees, her eyes wide and bloodshot.

As abruptly as the chaos had started, it ended.

Dina crumpled to the ground.

"No!" Chelsea screamed, barreling toward the fallen priestess.

CHAPTER TWENTY-THREE

THE LOOK on Chelsea's face as she dropped to her knees beside Dina shocked me back into motion.

I took a tentative step forward, expecting to meet the invisible wall, but when I didn't meet resistance, I moved faster.

Callie, wait, Bodey linked, but my feet had a mind of their own. He growled in frustration.

I ran through the door, Bodey, Samuel, and Lucas right on my heels. Tears dripped down Chelsea's face as she rolled Dina onto her back and placed her hands on her chest.

She lifted her head toward the cloudless sky and stared at the moon, crying, "Goddess, please help me save her."

I slowed as realization slammed into me, taking the oxygen from my lungs. Dina's heart was barely beating. My mouth dried.

Chelsea's hands glowed, and her breath caught as she gritted her teeth and channeled her magic into the high priestess.

The world seemed to stop. I forced my eyes away from Dina and toward the woods. Our enemy wasn't far away.

I wanted to ask what I could do to help, but Chelsea kept her face skyward as her lips chanted the same sentence over and over.

Bodey wrapped an arm around my waist and pulled my back against his chest. He linked, *We need to get you back inside. Standing out here will make it easier for Kel's witches to find you.*

I tensed but didn't fight his hold. I linked with him and Samuel, *We need to get the unconscious wolves away before the enemy witches do something worse to them.* Fighting witch magic was hard enough—the thought of so many of our people unconscious and vulnerable to witches' whims made my skin crawl.

I have a group heading to them now. Samuel came beside me, his gaze locking with mine. *I'm going with them this time.*

No. Bodey tensed. *If they take you—*

They have enough of our people. As Chelsea murmured continuously in the background, I took a step away and turned to Bodey. I needed him to understand that even though he and Samuel were two of the most important people in my life, all my people mattered to me too. The purpose of my position was to protect them, not leave them defenseless. *I'm going with him.*

Bodey's brows furrowed.

The queen sends her people out with no regard for their well-being. Bodey, we're supposed to protect them. We can't *hide. That isn't right.* Stevie and me leaving wasn't happening. I wouldn't *allow* it to happen. I'd agreed not to run out there right away because we didn't know the risks, and we'd held everyone else back too. Now we understood what we were up against.

Conflict warred in my mate's gorgeous indigo eyes. He didn't like what I was saying, but he also agreed.

I'll head out there now, Samuel linked as his bones broke and re-formed. Fur sprouted over his body as his clothes ripped away. He landed on all four paws and raced toward the woods.

Though I knew he was strong, it didn't feel right to let him go out there alone. *Lucas, can you shift and go with him?* I wanted to go, but I needed to make sure Chelsea didn't need anything first.

I'm on it. Lucas didn't hesitate. He shifted and was soon only a few paces behind my brother.

Miles and Jack joined us, with the former advisors right behind them. I knew leaving their mates behind was the last thing they wanted to do, but they had responsibilities just as Bodey and I did.

I turned to Chelsea, but she was still chanting at the sky. I wanted to stay and help, but I couldn't do anything here.

The mates stepped onto the back deck, and Jack groaned. "Stevie, if you love sex, you're going to march your hot ass right back inside that house." He crossed his arms, glowering at her.

My sister rolled her eyes. "I'm not worried about you holding out."

That was not a conversation we needed to hear, especially with Dina barely holding on to life. *Chelsea is trying to cast a spell, and we need to back up Samuel and Lucas. The former advisors can stay here and keep watch while the four of us join them.*

Everyone nodded. We knew the enemy witches were coming toward the houses, so there was no reason for me to stay put when I could help my people.

I hurried to the woods with Bodey, Jack, and Miles behind me. When I reached the first thicket of trees, my skin tingled, and my fur tried to sprout. I forced the shift back, linking with the others, *I'm going to stay in human form. We might need to talk to the witches, and it'll be easier to carry the wolves back with human legs and arms.*

I'll do the same, Bodey replied, catching up to me and running at my side.

The two of us will shift in case we run into trouble, Miles linked, and I heard his and Jack's bones crack behind me. Soon, both of them were in wolf form and flanking Bodey and me.

Have you found anyone yet? I linked to Samuel, my muscles burning from how hard I was pushing myself.

No, but Jasmine, Theo, and twenty more pack members are near the unconscious wolves, Samuel replied. *I told them to hold back. But they don't see any enemies.*

Bodey growled and bared his teeth. *Of course Jasmine is out there. She was supposed to stay at the house.*

I paused, thinking through my response. Jasmine was a strong wolf and didn't like hanging back while the people she loved were under attack. Bodey was a protector, and he struggled when the people he loved were in imminent danger. Unfortunately for him, he had a strong-willed mate and sister who weren't okay with being left behind. *Maybe you should train her to fight. That might make you feel better.*

Her staying behind is the only thing that will work! His frustration bled through our bond. *Knowing the two of you are safe would make my life a whole lot easier.*

Choosing not to respond, I kept my focus forward. I tapped into my wolf, attuning my senses to anything that seemed out of sorts and pushing myself faster. The only sounds were of wolves, and I could feel the tug to each of them in my chest, informing me they were our pack.

Lucas linked, *We've found the wolves and some of Dina's coven members. But something's weird.*

Don't get close to the smoke, Bodey reminded him. *It's gassed.*

There's no smoke, Samuel replied. *I don't know what the hell this is.*

I flinched. I'd assumed that the witches would keep directing the smoke toward our houses, but maybe that wasn't their plan. That made me nervous. *Stay back until we reach you.* I didn't need them running into trouble before we got there.

Miles and Jack huffed and spread out, and Bodey and I parted ways to dodge a tree trunk. I spotted fur through the thinning branches.

We were getting close.

I scanned the area for anything out of the ordinary. I half expected a witch to jump out and cast magic at us, but nothing happened.

The rough sandpaper sensation brushed over my skin, and my wolf whimpered. Trying to remain silent, I forced myself to keep moving forward, though everything inside me screamed to retreat.

Do you feel that? Jack linked from behind. *It feels like something is hovering over us, but I can't see a damn thing.*

It's probably witch magic, Miles replied. *We could be attacked any second.*

I glanced at the treetops and saw the gas-infused smoke, but nothing happened to us.

When we joined the others, our neighborhood witches were grouped together and glancing at one another uncomfortably. Forty of them stood at the edge of the boundary, their eyes locked on an area across from them. Many wolves lay unconscious where Kel's witches must have been located.

Our witches huddled together, their faces pale, even with

the moon shining brighter than it did on most nights. Something was off with them, so I headed to their group.

I lifted a hand, wanting to seem unthreatening, given their apparent wariness. It took me a minute to read the expression on each of their faces.

Fear.

"Do you sense the other witches?" I whispered just loud enough for the first few of them to hear me.

An older woman with silver hair shook her head. "No. Just death."

Death.

Dina had prayed to the death goddess. "We need to retrieve the wolves. We can't leave them here. Can you help us?"

"No." The older witch shook her head so hard that a stray hair smacked the side of her face. "We can't get any closer without tainting our souls. But you should be safe."

Should be safe.

That didn't sound reassuring. "Are the witches gone?" I didn't want to walk into a trap.

"They can't hurt you or your pack." The older one clasped her hands. "But we can't get any closer than here, and the sooner we leave, the sooner we'll feel safe again. The essence of evil is all around them. Bring the wolves to us, and we can wake them up."

Yeah, that wasn't creepy at all. *Everyone, let's each grab a wolf.* Between the witches' response and the friction chafing my skin, I didn't want us to stay any longer than we needed to.

Several wolves shifted back into human form, not worried about their nudity. We all spread out and chose a person to carry, either alone or with help. The witches remained on one side, watching us and not providing any aid.

The anger Bodey gave off overrode the eerie sensation. I

linked, *What's wrong? You're upset, more so than you were a few minutes ago.*

I'm fine. It's just Jasmine. We talked, and she pretty much told me that I may be her king, but I'm not her master. That she can handle herself and wants to help her fellow pack members when they're at risk.

I mashed my lips. I wasn't surprised, but Bodey was super protective of the ones he loved. *Babe, she's an adult, and she's right. And if you let your anger lead you out here, you might not notice if something's amiss.*

He huffed. *You're right on both counts, even if I don't like it. Let's hurry up and get the hell away from here.*

I went to the farthest wolf, each step raising goose bumps on my skin. Bodey, Jack, Samuel, Lucas, and I took our time. When we reached the end of the line of fallen wolves, something caught my eye.

Three piles of ash.

What the— I started but cut myself off as I took another step closer.

The sandpaper sensation morphed into intense burning. I glanced at my arms, but nothing seemed physically affected. The agonizing sensation of being burned swirled over me so hard that I stepped back.

Bodey's hands settled on my shoulders, the jolt of our connection easing my anxiety.

Is that ash? Jack asked, his gaze on the place where I'd been standing a moment ago.

Looks like it. Bodey's grip tightened. *Something feels sinister here. Let's get the wolves and go.*

I wouldn't argue with that.

More people joined us, and we moved the wolves to the witches quickly. I scooped up a female wolf, and as I lifted her over my shoulder, Bodey grabbed two shifters on his own and carried them to the witches. They began spelling the wolves awake.

When everyone was accounted for, I walked the territory boundary, searching for the enemy. There was no hint anyone had been here except for the wolves and the piles of ash. I was becoming more certain those ashes had once been the witches who'd attacked us.

Had Dina done this to them to protect us?

I'd never seen anything like it, and I was certain I didn't want to ever again.

Bodey came to my side and took my hand, his dark hair disheveled from our work. He linked, *Let's get back and check on Dina. Dad told me she was awake. They're waiting for us to talk to her.*

I nodded as I found another pile of ash a few feet away from where the wolves had been unconscious. It was the thirtieth pile I'd counted, and I hadn't gone deeper into the woods to look for more.

We split up and headed to our homes. Jasmine headed back with Theo, a scenario I'd expected Bodey to protest, but he said nothing. I suspected he was preoccupied with Dina and what waited for us back home.

My body was tired from the work, the stress, and the strange sensation that followed us back to the house.

As we reached our backyard, I looked for Dina and Chelsea, but they were no longer outside. I could see Chelsea inside the house, standing at the back door, her gaze on me.

We reached the deck, and Chelsea opened the door, stepping out. Her expression was strained, and her hair hung in loose waves down her back. She cleared her throat and nodded. "I hate to leave like this, but I must go and help the coven. We need to cleanse the area so we can spell the perimeter to prevent this from happening again."

My brows furrowed. "Shouldn't Dina go with you?"

"No. She's the last person who should be involved." Chelsea scowled. "I'll be back shortly."

As she breezed past me, I touched her arm and whispered, "Thank you for saving her."

"*Saved* isn't quite the word I'd use." Chelsea's eyes glistened, and she pressed her lips together. "What she did should've cost her life."

That sounded ominous. "What do you mean?"

"She practiced death magic." She huffed. "And she didn't have a proper sacrifice for it."

"Death magic?" I knew about blood magic, but this was new.

"It should've been blood magic, but she didn't sacrifice anyone, so the spell damn near took her life instead." Chelsea blew her long bangs out of her eyes. "If I hadn't gotten here when I did..." She exhaled. "I did, and she's *alive*. But all magic comes at a cost."

I'd heard that mantra repeated several times.

"I need to go, but Dina can tell you the rest." She smiled sadly. "There's something she needs to inform you about." With that, she headed off, leaving the five of us glancing at one another.

Something was up, and I wasn't sure I wanted to know what.

However, putting off things always had a way of biting me in the ass, so I opened the door and prepared to face the problem head-on.

CHAPTER TWENTY-FOUR

FORCING one foot in front of the other, I entered the den with Bodey at my side.

What do you think Chelsea meant? Jack linked. *She could've been less cryptic, or maybe she shouldn't have said a damn thing.*

I heard a *whack*, and I guessed it was Lucas thumping Jack on the back of the head. Confirming my suspicion, Lucas grunted and linked, *None of us know, and we're dealing with witches. Cryptic is ingrained in their blood.*

The corners of my lips tugged upward, easing some of the chill that had sunk into my bones thanks to the eerie situation. There was something comfortingly normal about Lucas and Jack bickering that grounded me.

Dina sat in the center of the couch with Michael and Phil at her sides. Carl and Dan stood between the back of the couch and the kitchen island, where Stevie was sliding a plate of scrambled eggs over to the men.

Dan reached for it just as Janet clucked her tongue and turned from her spot in front of the black stove. "Wait. She needs a fork." She got one from the center drawer and placed the utensil on the plate. "There! Now give it to her."

My stomach grumbled, but I wasn't sure I should eat. The stench of ash, which I suspected was due to the missing witches, tied me in knots.

"I'm really not hungry." Dina sighed as Dan obeyed and handed her the plate despite her protest.

She put the plate in her lap, her hand shaking. Between her skin not glowing like usual and her confident manner so subdued, she didn't resemble the priestess I'd come to know.

Still, having her sitting up and talking was much better than how I'd left her on the lawn. I went to stand against the overhang of the fireplace in front of her and met her gaze.

I gestured to the plate. "Eating should make you feel better."

Dina smiled sadly. "I'm not sure anything can do that."

"You were lit up like the fucking Fourth of July." Bodey gestured outside just as Miles shut the door. "I'm sure those lightning bolts shooting from your body will take time to heal from."

The image flashed through my mind, and I shuddered. She'd protected all of us at a great cost to herself. I'd always known she took her role as priestess seriously, but I respected her twice as much after witnessing her willingness to sacrifice herself for everyone else. "Chelsea said you almost died."

Jack strolled to Stevie and placed an arm around his mate's waist.

"I did." Dina took a bite of the eggs before placing the plate on the coffee table.

Not wanting to interrupt the conversation, I linked to Michael and Bodey, *Where are the other mates?*

Helping the packs calm down and settle in after the attack since Dina asked that the former advisors stay here until you got back. She and Chelsea were whispering before we heard all of you marching up.

A lump formed in my throat, making it hard to swallow. Dina wasn't one for theatrics, so whatever was going on had to be big for her to want to tell us all at the same time.

Dina took a sip of her water and set the glass next to her plate before leaning back and inhaling. "Honestly, Chelsea shouldn't have been able to save me, but the moon goddess blessed her wish. I almost wish she hadn't." She rubbed her arms and closed her eyes.

"What?" Bodey's shock barreled through our bond, adding to my panic. "You can't mean that. You couldn't have really wanted to die."

"You're right." Dina dropped her hands into her lap. "I didn't want to die, but I also don't want to live like this."

Moving to the other spot beside me, Samuel tilted his head and examined the priestess. "Live like what?"

Chelsea's words echoed in my head, so I asked, "Is it because you didn't have a sacrifice for the spell?"

Dina flinched, and her face was strained.

"A sacrifice?" Stevie's brow furrowed. "Like a rabbit or something?"

Jack brushed his thumb against her chin and cooed, "Aw. You're so cute."

"And who is the death goddess?" Lucas propped his arm against the door, blocking our view of the outside. "I've heard of the nature goddess and the moon goddess but never a goddess of death."

"I'm assuming it has something to do with evil magic." Miles lifted his chin as his attention locked on Dina. "Priestess River always told our packs no good comes from magic involving death."

Hanging her head, Dina blushed as everyone looked at me.

I wanted to laugh. They expected me to know how to get Dina to talk, but I didn't want to push her when she was clearly struggling with whatever had happened. I understood the pain of having everyone stare at you while you wished you could disappear. That was how I'd felt every day for the past seventeen years... until I'd found Bodey.

My eyes widened. I could tell Dina was retreating inward and that she felt very alone. She needed to know she *wasn't* alone.

I released Bodey's hand to move closer to her, but he held on tight, pulling me back. He linked, *There's something not right about her. Maybe you shouldn't get too close.*

Staying away was the worst thing you could do to someone who felt broken. Eggs and water wouldn't cut it. She needed to know that the people she was desperate to protect were just as willing to stand beside her.

Trust me, I linked, and I walked around the coffee table and squatted in front of Dina. I placed a hand on her knee and said, "After what you did out there to save us, you can tell us what's bothering you."

Her head lifted, and her eyes lasered in on my hand before flicking up to meet mine.

"Priestess River is right." Dina exhaled noisily and straightened her back. "The death goddess is vindictive and greedy. She offers up the sort of magic that the earth and moon goddesses refuse to get near. She'll kill without a moment's regret as long as she gains something from the person making the request or the witch casting the spell. Like how Zeke killed his beta to block you from accessing your wolf."

"Dear gods." Michael shook his head. "Why would you ask a deity like that to help you?"

"We were greatly outnumbered, and there would have been deaths on our side." Her gaze never left mine as she nodded at me. "Callie could have gotten caught in the cross fire. The witches came here to prove themselves to Kel, which means they were probably desperate to kidnap Callie, no matter the cost."

My limbs trembled. "You did this to protect me?"

"Not just you." Dina pressed her lips together. "All of us. I didn't want any of our coven or our wolves to die either. Queen Kel's witches would've used the unconscious wolves to get you, Bodey, and the royal advisors out there. I could see it on your faces after Queen Kel hung up, even though none of you real-ized your decision had been made. By sacrificing myself, I was protecting *all* of you. One life for, no telling how many."

"No harm, no foul." Jack tapped his free hand on the island. "Chelsea saved you, and the enemy died. We don't have a problem."

"Son." Carl pursed his lips. "Life isn't usually that cut and dried, especially when witch magic is involved."

Dan pulled out one of the barstools and sat. "It's all about balance, and Dina thought she would die. So, is something going to bite us in the ass now?"

"No, it won't," Dina said. She removed my hand from hers and stood, moving to the front side of the house, opposite the deck. She stared out the window before turning to stare at each of us. "The moon and earth goddesses decided on another fate in lieu of my death." She wrapped her arms around her waist, holding herself.

I climbed back to my feet, holding my breath. Whatever they'd decided seemed as if it might be worse than death.

"Which was?" Bodey murmured gently, going still as stone.

Her bottom lip quivered, and just when I thought she wouldn't answer, she did. "My magic." Her chest heaved as she tried to hold back a sob. "It's gone." A tear trickled down her cheek.

My brain short-circuited. Out of every possible scenario, that wasn't one I'd expected. A witch losing their magic would be like me losing my wolf.

An integral part of myself.

Even when I'd been closed off to my wolf, she'd had influence over me, and I couldn't fathom living without her. The only thing worse would be losing Bodey.

"Dina, I'm *so* sorry." I wished there was something more I could do than say those futile words.

Bodey rubbed his hands together as he moved closer, the mate bond drawing him to me because of the heartbreak I felt for our friend. He rasped, "There has to be a way to get your magic back. If the moon and earth goddesses saved you, maybe—"

"They won't give it back." Dina wiped the tears from her cheeks. "The only reason I'm alive is because I performed the spell to save my coven and your pack. The goddesses told me that before they allowed Chelsea to bring me back. Still, that sort of spell can't go unpunished, and the cost was my magic. I'll never get it back."

My throat tightened. We'd ended Kel's attack and struck the enemy dead, but Dina had lost her magic as a result. She'd been the strongest witch in this coven and this region, and she was the royal priestess assigned to protect the marked king and queen.

Even when we beat Kel, she *still* won. Our resources were

weakening, and I had no fucking idea how Bodey and I would make it out of this alive and together.

I wanted to sulk, but we had to be there for Dina. She'd lost something precious because she cared about us, not just the witches. "That hurts. I can only imagine how you feel, but it doesn't change anything. Your place is still with us and the coven."

Dina shook her head. "I can't be a priestess. Chelsea will take over that position. She's the next in line, and the earth and moon goddesses made her stronger than me when my magic was taken to make sure we go into battle prepared."

"Priestess or not, I need you." I met Bodey and placed a hand on his arm. "*We* need you."

She inhaled shakily and smiled. "Thank you. I needed to hear that."

"Just because you lost your magic doesn't mean you're less of a person," Stevie added and touched her heart. "Even though I still have my wolf magic, it's never been strong. I understand what it's like to feel worthless."

I hated that Zeke had made her feel that way—correction, made *us* feel that way—until my wolf had broken free. No one should ever feel unvalued. Both these women would do anything to protect the ones they loved, even if it went against their beliefs. I'd always live with the regret of throwing Stevie into that basement when she'd been trying to protect me, but I couldn't go back in time and change it. We had to move on, and I'd do everything I could to make it up to her in the future.

"Listen, I'm not trying to be ungracious. It means a lot that each of you is looking at me with compassion and not disgust, but I need to head home and get some rest. I need to figure out how to move on from here. Time to pray to the goddesses and come to grips with this loss on my own." Dina ran a hand down her stomach, smoothing the white priestess dress—a dress I was accustomed to seeing her in and probably would never see her wearing again.

"I need to check on Jasmine." Michael rose and yawned. "Janet should get home and rest while I help run the perimeter."

Samuel dragged a hand through his hair. "I've got it. You, Janet, and the others should get some sleep. A few of you will be on patrol tomorrow night until we can figure out a way to prevent this from happening again. I know the witches are adding more perimeter spells, so they'll be alerted before Kel's people can get to the place where they were hiding tonight, but we can't let our guard down."

I hated that Samuel was handling this alone, so I linked, *I can go with you.*

Please, let me do it. He turned to me. *I need to do this. I need to be out there tonight and have this pack see me taking charge after that threat.*

How could I say no to that? *If you need something—*

You'll be the first person I link to.

"I'm going to find Stella and see if she needs help with anything." Miles headed to the back deck door.

"I'll join you." Phil stretched and made his way to the back door.

We all said good night, and soon Jack, Stevie, Bodey, and I were alone. We went upstairs and retired to our own beds.

As Bodey shut our door, I climbed into bed, but sleep was nowhere close to taking me under. I huffed, wishing there was a way to turn off my mind. "Bodey, we're screwed. We've lost Dina's magic. Kel keeps attacking us while we're sleeping, and we have yet to understand the consequences of losing Oregon and if that means other packs or territories will join Kel."

"Right now, you need your rest. We can't make good decisions after what just happened." Bodey went to a corner of the room and grabbed his guitar, and then he slid into bed beside me.

I smiled. "You going to play me a song?"

He winked. "Nope. I just thought the guitar needed some cuddling."

I stuck out my tongue as I settled onto my side, gazing at him as he situated the guitar and strummed a chord.

"I thought a song might help you unwind." He tuned the guitar for a minute.

I watched happily as his biceps bulged and he made the sound just right. Then he grinned at me and launched into a song, one I hadn't heard him play before—"(Everything I Do) I Do It for You" by Bryan Adams.

The song spoke straight to my heart, conveying the message he intended. His eyes bored into mine, and in that moment, there was no doubt how much we loved each other and how the words he sang went both ways. There was nothing I wasn't willing to do for him, even if it meant laying down my life to save his.

After he played the last chord, he set the guitar on the floor, and I was on top of him in a second. With the shitty night, I needed to be in his arms and have him inside me.

He kissed me eagerly, matching my ardor, and I opened my mouth and let his tongue slip inside. As I straddled him, his minty taste overrode my senses, and when his hands slipped under my shirt, grazing my sides, the jolt had my body flooding with warmth.

Pulling away, I removed my shirt, and then he rolled me onto my back. I gripped his shirt and ripped it down the center. He chuckled as he discarded what little was left on his body. Then he lowered his head to my breast and sucked my nipple into his mouth.

My body quivered, and I trailed my fingers along the curves of his abs, a knot tightening in my stomach.

He tugged my pajama bottoms down and slipped his fingers between my legs. His tongue rolled across my breast as he circled the sensitive spot, and I panted, throwing my head back.

Wanting to give him the same pleasure, I slid my hands under the waist of his pants and touched his shaft. As my thumb brushed over the sensitive tip, he quivered.

We caressed each other, the friction building until it felt like we were the only two people in the world.

He moaned and circled my spot faster, and my body exploded in ecstasy, but it wasn't enough. I removed my hand from him, and he groaned in protest.

I pushed him over and kicked off my pajama pants, not worrying about being graceful. Then I grabbed his pant legs and yanked them down.

His indigo irises darkened. *I love watching you want me this bad.*

That orgasm was a tease. I stared into his eyes as I straddled him and lowered myself onto him.

His mouth opened slightly as his eyelashes fluttered, making me feel very much in control as I rode him. His attention went to my breasts, and he cupped one in his hand and raised his mouth to the other.

As his tongue stroked me and he pushed deeper inside, warmth curled within me. I moved my hips, increasing our pace. Bodey leaned back against the headboard and clutched my waist. "Oh, gods. You feel better every fucking time," he groaned as he bucked underneath me.

Bodies slick with sweat, we moved in rhythm. Sensations built inside me, and then my body clenched as the most intense orgasm ever rocked through me. I locked eyes with my mate, his irises glowing as our pleasure melded together and his body finished along with mine.

All too soon, the pleasure waned, and he tugged me against his side. Sleep was upon me in seconds, and Bodey murmured, "I love you," as I went under. Luckily, I was aware enough to link, *Love you too.*

———————

A RING STARTLED ME AWAKE. I jolted up. The clock said it was five in the morning. It wasn't much later than when Bodey and I had fallen asleep.

Samuel? I linked as I reached for my phone. *Is everything okay?*

Yeah. Did something happen there? he replied instantly.

Her phone is ringing, Bodey replied as an unknown phone number scrolled across my screen.

"Who is it?" Bodey propped himself up, glancing at the phone.

"I don't know." I didn't want to answer it, but who knew what this could be about? "But I'd better answer."

Bodey nodded, and I swiped the phone and put it to my ear. "Hello?"

"Is this Queen Caroline?" an unfamiliar, deep voice asked.

I winced, not used to that name, and pulled the covers up to my throat. "Uh, yes. Who is this?"

"King Sutton." He paused. "We need to talk."

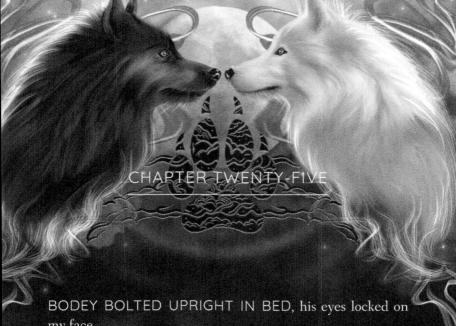

CHAPTER TWENTY-FIVE

BODEY BOLTED UPRIGHT IN BED, his eyes locked on my face.

My blood rushed through my veins, and I gripped the phone. I'd never expected to hear from Russell again, let alone his king, so this call couldn't be anything *good*. I suspected Kel was behind it, forcing King Sutton's hand since she knew Russell and his pack were from the Midwest territory, courtesy of Lynerd.

Lynerd.

That burned even more. I'd given him the position that had allowed him to cut me off at the knees by taking Oregon away.

"Are you there?" King Sutton asked, and I realized I'd been silent for several seconds. "I know it's early, but this couldn't wait."

"Yeah, sorry." I pushed my hair over my shoulders and reached for Bodey's hand. I needed his comfort, the buzz of our bond reassuring. "Before you start, I wanted to thank you for allowing Russell to help us. I know it put you in a horrible position, but—"

"Horrible doesn't begin to describe it," he interjected, his voice turning growly. "But I made the decision knowing there was a chance she would find out. Unfortunately, she did, and instead of parleying with me where I could have explained that Russell's actions hadn't been sanctioned, she decided to take immediate action."

My breath caught, and I whispered, "What happened?"

"She attacked my home tonight, and ten of my most trusted pack members were killed." King Sutton's voice deepened. "If it weren't for the royal witches on the premises, my son would've been gone alongside them."

"Wait. You were attacked *tonight?*" No wonder only witches had been here. She'd sent wolves to King Sutton's lands to punish him.

"Yes, her wolves attacked my mansion as well as the largest and strongest nearby pack." He blew out a breath. "I knew I should've taken more of a stand with Russell than I did."

He regretted helping us. I couldn't blame him. "It's my fault Kel learned about you. I trusted someone I shouldn't have. I'm sorry you got caught in the cross fire."

Babe, you only did what your parents planned to do seventeen years ago, Bodey linked and squeezed my hand.

Though his touch was comforting, the sentiment was not. I had read Lynerd all wrong.

"We've all trusted at least one person we shouldn't have. If you aren't making mistakes, you aren't learning to lead like you should. And you have nothing to apologize for. You asked —you didn't force us to help. I should have stood with you, but I was hoping Queen Kel would forget about us and leave us alone. I failed my people."

Bodey's eyebrows lifted, and his confusion mixed with mine.

"But you were attacked because of it. Maybe she would have left you alone if you had willed Russell not to come." I flinched, realizing I shouldn't have said that. Once again, my lack of royal training had reared its ugly head. I was basically asking King Sutton to blame me. Soon, I'd have Kel *and* King Sutton coming after us instead of just one enemy.

He chuckled, and my unease churned even more. "Were your memories truly wiped out? Because you sound just like Richard."

I stilled. "They aren't blocked anymore, but my father was killed when I was five, so I don't have many memories of him."

"It seems you take on the blame for everything, just like he did." He clicked his tongue. "But this isn't your fault. Kel called me just as the attack started."

I swallowed a humorless laugh, causing my throat to ache. That was exactly how Kel handled her attacks. She wanted to flaunt her power in our faces. She wanted us to know she was the person causing the havoc, needing to ensure she took *all* the credit.

"She made a point to let me know that, by helping you, I forced her to attack. She doesn't want us to help you anymore."

"I'm sorry for your loss, and I wish I could offer you aid, but Kel attacked us here tonight as well." I hated how confident she was. She had no qualms about attacking two different territories on the same night. She'd split her resources, and I suspected it was to show her power.

He hmphed. "How? How many wolf shifters does she have? We were under the impression she had three thousand in total."

"She sent a hundred witches here to attack. No wolves." At least, we'd figured out the reason behind that, though it was worse than I'd anticipated. I'd hoped that she was giving her wolves time to heal after the constant attacks on us, but I should've known she had something else planned.

"Witches attacking other territories of their own accord?" King Sutton groaned. "That alone is a problem. She's gotten them to buy into her end goal."

I leaned my head against the headboard. "Our witches took care of the problem, and fortunately, we didn't lose any lives tonight, but it came at a cost."

Don't tell him everything. Bodey kissed my shoulder. *I know we want to trust him, and I think we can, but that doesn't mean we tell him everything in one phone call.*

Nodding, I bit my lower lip. In the ideal world, I wouldn't have to worry about King Sutton backstabbing us, but if Kel had killed that many of his people, I wouldn't put it past him to try something to take the heat off his territory.

"Everything comes at a cost." The king's voice took a hard edge. "That's not applicable only to magic. Every decision has consequences, and sometimes, you don't see what they are until it's too late."

You should ask him why he called. Bodey rolled onto his side and propped himself on his elbow. *I'm sure there's a point to the conversation.*

That was easier said than done. Unsure how to ask without seeming rude, I let my mouth take over. "That's very true, which makes me wonder why you decided to call me this early in the morning. I wish I could offer assistance, but my hands are tied. All of our resources have to go toward countering Kel before she attacks us again."

Though we'd agreed to hold off until the morning to determine a battle plan, as I said the words, I *knew* that was what we had to do. We kept hoping to find a way to make her back off, but each strike of hers came faster than the previous. The time we'd spent trying to hold her off had only put her in a better position to take us down.

"You're right. You should focus all of your resources there." He cleared his throat. "And I will focus all of mine too. I called to see if you would like to unite forces and take down Kel together. Individually, we should have been strong enough to withstand her, but she's proven to have more strength than expected. If we ally and hit her hard, we'll have the best chance of taking her down."

My gaze went to Bodey, and I found him with his mouth gaping open. His shock mixed with mine, slowing my brain further. I feared this had to be a dream because every other damn thing had only set us back. "You want to fight together?"

"Like I said, Queen Kel has made her intentions clear by attacking us. Though she called it a warning, it wasn't, and she won't hesitate to hurt us again. If she overtakes the Northwest, there will be no stopping her from coming here next. Let's make her squirm for a change."

I blinked. Making Kel uncomfortable sounded like the first step toward getting my revenge and protecting my people. "But wouldn't she see our alliance coming?"

"You'd think so, but this reminds me of one of the last conversations I had with your father." King Sutton's voice deepened. "He called to congratulate me on my future heir and said he hoped our two territories could become closer. He revealed that, unfortunately, the ship had sailed with the Southwest queen because she didn't believe in befriending others."

My heart thudded against my ribs. I hadn't expected him to reference a conversation with my father, but I wanted to hear more. "I remember him mentioning to Mom over dinner one night that he hoped our families would become closer. He thought you were a good man."

"I felt the same about your family. That conversation has always stuck with me. Over the years, I saw what he'd noticed back then. No matter what happened, Kel isolated herself from the other territories. We didn't hear a damn thing from her until three years ago."

It was a whole lot of information to take in, and I wasn't sure if I was awake enough to have this conversation. I yawned and covered my mouth, trying not to let King Sutton hear. I wasn't bored, just exhausted.

Bodey snickered. *Let me go get you a cup of coffee.*

I grabbed his arm, and he stilled. *I don't want you to go. I want you to hear the entire conversation.*

He tapped my forehead gently and winked, *Then open up our connection. I'll be able to hear everything. I'll be back in a few minutes.* He kissed my nose and crawled out of our bed.

All brain cells misfired as I stared at his naked ass, and when he bent down and snatched his pajama bottoms off the floor, a bit of drool puddled in the corner of my mouth. I wasn't sure if this level of attraction was normal between mates, but I hoped it never changed.

"Caroline?" King Sutton asked.

My face flamed. Even though he had no idea what had captured my attention, he still knew I wasn't engaged. I forced my eyes away from my mate's now-covered bottom and stared up at the ceiling. "Yeah, sorry. I'm just processing everything."

Thank gods he wasn't here to smell the lie.

It didn't help that Bodey had a huge smirk on his face as he opened our bedroom door and sauntered into the hallway. He knew exactly what had distracted me.

Yanking at the tether of our bond, I opened myself more to my mate, similar to when we'd orgasm together and our souls merged. I could feel him opening up to me as well, our warmth blending.

I racked my brain to get on track. "What happened three years ago?" I wanted to pat myself on the back for remembering the last thing he'd referenced.

"She visited my territory, asking questions and wanting to see certain places. She was scoping out the area, and when I confronted her, she didn't deny it. I had Russell escort her out. We didn't need a wolf war—our human population is dense. I kept waiting for her to come back, but we learned she'd attacked your territory. I foolishly thought we were safe, knowing that seventeen years without a royal had made the Northwest vulnerable."

And he didn't think to help us? Bodey linked, his anger warming my blood.

Our connection was working, and Bodey's question was fair, so I asked it.

King Sutton sighed. "I thought about it, but I feared another royal making overtures might make the advisors and Samuel uneasy. I didn't want to give the perception that I wanted to take over your territory."

"Or give her the illusion you were trying to move in before she could." If he wanted to be allies, he needed to be honest. That was the only way things would work between us.

"That too. If war breaks out in this area—and I now fear war is imminent—there is no way even thousands of witches could control that exposure. We need to take the fight to her."

I liked the sound of that. "I don't know where she lives."

"We have that information here. It's been passed down by previous generations."

Information I no longer had access to because my father's study had been destroyed. The gifts of Zeke's betrayal just kept coming. "How do I know I can trust you?" My father had, but he had also planned to put Lynerd in charge. I'd corrected the latter, and here I was without Oregon. I didn't want to put my faith in my dad's gut based on the person King Sutton had been seventeen years ago.

"Good question," he said with approval. "And one I fear you won't have an answer to until we meet. I'm hoping you're up for a visitor or three."

My brows furrowed. "You want to come here?" Out of every scenario, I'd imagined he'd want to meet halfway or have us come there.

"I hate to ask my mate and my son to come with me, but after what happened tonight, I don't want to part with them. You could have someone pick us up from the airport."

Bodey? I didn't know the right answer. Sutton coming here would give him access to more information on us, but at least we wouldn't be going into his territory, where we could be captured far more easily. *What do you think?*

Tell him to come. We don't have to bring him to our home if we get a bad vibe. We can take him somewhere else.

Good point. "Okay. When do you want to visit?"

"There's a flight leaving within a few hours. We can be there by this evening."

Okay, he moved fast. "Today?" I squeaked.

"If we're going to attack Kel, time is of the essence. We need to be ready to strike before her wolves regroup and come up with a new plan. Twenty of my strongest wolves have already left for California. They'll scope out Kel's house while I meet with you and the king consort."

He truly was a man of action. I couldn't complain. Having experience in this arena could go a long way if we could trust him. "Okay, book the flight. Send me the text with your arrival information."

"Will do. See you soon." The line went dead.

I could only pray to the gods that Bodey and I hadn't invited another threat onto our land.

At nine that evening, Bodey and I drove Jack's Navigator up to the Lewiston, Idaho airport, over an hour away from our Grangeville neighborhood. Jack had pouted, but we needed three rows of seating, so Stevie had gotten him to relent.

The royal advisors and the former advisors agreed with our decision to have King Sutton, his mate, and his son visit us. Even though we were all weary, Jasmine vouched for King Sutton again, and the former advisors had nothing but good things to say about him. Despite all of our reservations, this was the best chance we had to double our resources and beat Kel.

I tapped my foot to let out some nervous energy. With the way my decisions had been backfiring lately, I feared having them here would make things worse for us.

We're going to be careful, Bodey assured me, reaching over the center console to take my hand. *If either one of us feels uncomfortable taking them back to the neighborhood, we won't. We have credit cards, and we can book rooms at a hotel.*

He was right. I was letting my nerves get the best of me, but Lynerd's betrayal had been a huge hit to my confidence.

With each minute we waited, more sweat pooled in my armpits. I wasn't a patient person to begin with, and this uncertainty was stressing me out even more.

When the clock struck nine thirty, a horrible thought hit me. What if King Sutton had never planned to come? What if this was all a plan to get Bodey and me to the airport alone? He'd know that either we or Jasmine would come here to greet him. Either way, it would get Bodey and me exactly where he wanted us.

That was when a tall, bulky man strolled out of the airport's double doors. His hazel eyes focused directly on me, and he smirked.

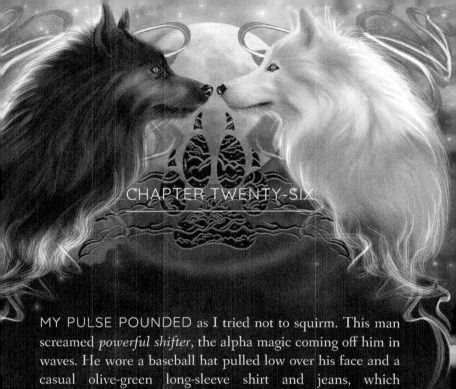

CHAPTER TWENTY-SIX

MY PULSE POUNDED as I tried not to squirm. This man screamed *powerful shifter*, the alpha magic coming off him in waves. He wore a baseball hat pulled low over his face and a casual olive-green long-sleeve shirt and jeans, which contrasted with his intense stare.

"Bodey," I murmured, holding the door handle.

"Sutty," a female voice groaned behind him. "A little help would be nice!"

The man froze and winced. The smirk vanished as he spun around and hurried to the woman behind him. He took the large rolling bag from her and pulled it to his side as the woman straightened.

Despite her jeans and stylish flowy purple shirt, she had on black stilettos. She flung her dark-burgundy hair over her shoulders and arched one perfectly sculpted eyebrow as her emerald eyes sparkled. "That's more like it."

"I'm sorry, my love," he said adoringly and kissed her crimson lips.

"Seriously, you two always gotta be doing that?" A younger man who had to be their son strolled out from behind them, rolling a carry-on. "I don't know how I haven't stabbed my eyes out." His nose wrinkled as his golden irises lightened with mirth.

As I watched the family's interaction, some of the tension melted from my body. They seemed so genuine that I couldn't believe it was an act.

Do you want us to leave? Bodey asked, his right hand settling on the gearshift.

Not budging my gaze from the king and his family, I linked, *No, but I don't want to take them far unless we're comfortable with them. I want to be able to drop them off here and tell them to get on the next plane if anything unsettles either of us.*

Of course. It's you and me against the world. He rubbed a hand along my arm. *We'll stay close to the airport until we're both comfortable.*

I really liked hearing him say that. Having him here to make decisions alongside me eased the worry inside me and my wolf. I trusted Samuel, but Bodey was my other half, and I felt stronger with him by my side. *Let's go introduce ourselves.*

He turned off the vehicle, and we climbed out. I waited by my door as he walked around the hood to my side.

As we made our way to King Sutton, his mate, and his son, the three of them grew somber and met us a few feet from our car.

Wanting to take charge since this was my territory, I extended my hand to King Sutton. "Hi, I'm Caroline." The name still didn't flow off my tongue naturally, but thankfully, I didn't hesitate. "And this is my ma—" I stopped myself since there were a few humans nearby waiting for their rides. "My —er—*husband*, Bodey." That word, unfortunately, did give me pause and made me feel unsettled. *Husband* didn't hold half the same meaning as *mate*, but that was the closest thing I could risk saying.

King Sutton chuckled and shook my hand. "You look just like your father. The resemblance is uncanny."

It wasn't the first time I'd heard that. Samuel favored our mother, while I was the female version of our father.

"Dear..." His mate patted his arm and shook her head before turning to me. "I'm Brittany, and this is our son, Edward."

Edward jerked his head to the side, flipping his light-brown bangs out of his eyes. "You two are the ones we're visiting? I thought you'd be older. You're almost my age."

Hazel eyes glowing, King Sutton turned to Edward. Edward winced due to whatever King Sutton had told him through the pack link.

Not wanting to dwell on my parents' deaths, I gestured to the trunk of the Navigator. "Let's get your things in there."

King Sutton didn't hesitate, wheeling the sizable bag toward the trunk with Edward on his tail.

Bodey opened the back for them but didn't help them get their things inside, which I knew went against his nature. I could feel his discomfort, and I pushed warmth to him.

If you want to help him, you can, I linked, brushing my arm against his.

Not if I want him to view me as his equal and worthy to be by your side. Bodey glanced at me sideways. *Which is one of the most important things in my entire world—deserving to be your king consort and stand firmly beside you.*

Brittany chuckled, and I turned to find her beaming at the two of us. She sighed dreamily. "I remember what that felt like—the newness of our relationship. I would say I miss it, but honestly, time only makes it stronger."

I hadn't realized how much I'd needed to hear that, but I had so many questions I couldn't ask right now.

The SUV dipped as King Sutton put the larger luggage inside, and Bodey's brows rose. My mate cleared his throat. "Uh... what's all in that?"

"Clothes and shoes." Brittany smiled even bigger. "Just the usual things any woman needs."

Without a struggle, Edward put his carry-on in the trunk, and the vehicle barely moved.

"For a short visit?" Bodey blinked, his suspicion getting the best of him.

"Are you telling me Caroline doesn't pack like that?" Edward shut the trunk.

"If I had to pack Bodey's stuff with mine, then maybe." I didn't have enough clothes to fill even half her suitcase, but I didn't want to let Brittany know we were wary of them.

King Sutton bellowed, startling me.

"Oh, don't give her that much credit." He strolled to his mate and slung an arm around her waist. "She wouldn't let me put my things with hers. Edward happily obliged, though, and we managed to fit all our things into one carry-on."

"A woman always needs to be prepared." Brittany lifted her chin. "There's no telling what tools I may need, so I brought something for every possible situation."

Kissing her forehead, King Sutton rolled his eyes. "And don't worry. She did just that."

Edward yawned. "I hate to rush the introduction, but I'd love to get settled in. We've been traveling nonstop."

I didn't miss Bodey's jaw tightening, and he didn't miss a beat as he opened the front passenger door and waved me inside.

As I slid into my spot, Edward opened the back seat and crawled into the back row, where he stretched out. His lackadaisical demeanor settled my nerves. If I were planning to betray someone, I might be able to sit back and relax, but I wouldn't be able to lie down and take a nap.

Brittany moved into the seat behind me as King Sutton and Bodey opened their doors at the same time.

As Bodey drove off, I took a deep breath. They'd arrived, and we'd gotten out of there with no issue. It was promising, but that could change at any time.

Merging onto the main road, Bodey glanced into the rearview mirror. "We were getting worried that something might have happened."

I faced the back so I could watch the three of them and their body language.

"Sorry about that." King Sutton buckled his seat belt and adjusted his seat backward to give his long legs more room. "I hadn't planned on checking a bag." He looked sideways at his mate. "It seems we need to take most of our closet with us when we travel, even when we're in a hurry."

"In fairness, I didn't realize I packed so much until we arrived at the airport." Brittany huffed. "Greg put everything in my bag for me, and then he took it to the car and didn't say a word."

Edward lifted his head and snickered. "Greg is our butler. Of course, he won't say anything. He gets paid to be accommodating."

"Listen here." Brittany crossed her arms. "You keep running that mouth, and we'll see if you go to college."

"Mom," he whined and lay back down in the seat.

I didn't have to see him to know he was pouting. Their relationship was genuine, and my heart ached. I bet I would've had that with my parents if Zeke hadn't killed them. Even though my adoptive parents had been decent to me, our relationship hadn't been the same as theirs with Pearl and Stevie. This was something I'd missed out on.

Bodey reached over and squeezed my leg. King Sutton gave me a sad smile as if he'd noticed and could hear my thoughts. Great, he was perceptive too. It was a good attribute for a royal, but I didn't want him to read me like I was reading them.

"I know this has to be hard for you, but thank you for allowing us to visit on such short notice." King Sutton's expression turned solemn. "Russell told me what happened, including that one of your royal advisors betrayed you. That was why I wanted us to meet in person—so you could see my face and smell that I wasn't lying."

The fact that he'd addressed the issue within minutes of getting into the vehicle with us had to be a good sign. It would help Bodey and me get a quicker read on him. "I appreciate that. It did help that you asked to visit me in my territory instead of the other way around."

"I wanted to prove that my request is genuine, and you do live closer to California." King Sutton steepled his fingers. "My men took a flight this morning, and they landed in Los Angeles about three hours ago. The queen lives two hours from the airport, so they located an Airbnb to drop off their things and are heading out as we speak. In a few hours, we should have a good idea of the layout and her numbers."

I jerked my head backward. "Oh. I thought they were driving."

"That was the plan, but when we mapped out the trip, we realized it would take them twenty-eight hours to arrive. I didn't want to wait that long. We made the decision for all of them to fly so we could coordinate an attack quicker."

Bodey missed the exit to the interstate that would lead us

home. "And you're sure you want to attack her?" he asked nonchalantly, but his Adam's apple bobbed.

"She's trying to intimidate us, which I won't tolerate." King Sutton's nostrils flared. "She's not the Midwest royal—I am. Her attention will turn to us if she takes control of your territory. If we sit back and let that happen, we will lose. I'd like to say I'm here to support you because it's the right thing to do, but that would be a lie. I'm here to create an alliance to prevent her from getting the power she needs to take over my people." He placed a hand on his heart, his forehead creasing.

Sincerity poured off him, and any reservations I had about his offer disappeared. I linked with Bodey, *Is it bad that I find his honesty comforting?* He had admitted to not caring about helping us and that, by allying with us, it was a means to protect what was his.

Not at all. Telling us up front that allying with us is about protecting his people is the only way we would trust him. Bodey's hands loosened on the steering wheel. *Otherwise, we'd know he was blowing smoke up our asses. He couldn't risk his people to help us. His getting security out of it is valid.*

Knowing that Bodey and I were on the same page, I brought the royal advisors into our connection and filled them in on everything. *Bodey and I want to bring them back to the house.*

I have no objections, Samuel replied.

Man, I just want my Navigator back, Jack deadpanned. *So yeah, come on. And I swear, if there are any scratches on it, you're getting me a new car.*

What Jack means is he also agrees, same as me, Lucas said. *He wouldn't risk Stevie.*

Miles got straight to business. *Where do you want them to stay? Stella and I can get two rooms ready.*

I hated to displace Stevie and Samuel, but the king and

his family should stay with us since all the vacant houses were filled with Theo's pack. I connected with only Bodey for a moment, *Would your dad and mom take issue with Jack, Stevie, and Samuel staying with them?*

Of course not. Bodey tapped his head. *They'll be happy to help us make room to host King Sutton. I'll connect with them while you tell Miles what to do.*

I smiled at him and nodded, linking back with the royal advisors. *Jack and Samuel, do you mind staying at Michael and Janet's for a night or two?*

Stevie and I can go back to the other house with Miles, Lucas, and our parents, Jack replied. *That way, Jasmine has a room if she comes back from Theo's.*

I was so glad that Bodey wasn't in the connection to hear that comment.

You mean the bachelor pad? Miles retorted, which was unlike him.

No! Jack emphasized way too hard. *I told Stella I'd stop calling it that, remember?*

And you didn't until Stevie.

I swallowed a laugh, but I was glad Miles was finally giving Jack a little bit of hell back. *That works too. But if you could help change the sheets in both those rooms, I'd appreciate it.*

Bodey turned onto the next entrance to the interstate.

We'll be there in an hour, I finished.

We're on it. See you soon, Miles replied.

"Does getting onto the interstate mean we're officially allies?" King Sutton asked.

I glanced over my shoulder to find that his gaze had never left me. "Yes. We're in this together."

He beamed. "Excellent."

The five of us settled in for the hour-long ride home,

sharing our history with one another, including how my heritage had been revealed and I'd become queen.

WHEN WE PULLED up to our white, modern, colonial-style house, all the lights were on. Bodey parked the Navigator in our driveway and opened the garage.

By the time the five of us climbed out of the vehicle, the four royal advisors, Stella and Stevie, had come through the garage door to meet us.

King Sutton's eyebrows rose. "How many people live with you?"

"Oh, we were just getting the place ready for you all." Stella smiled, looking welcoming in her trendy long-sleeve, belted black dress. "The royal advisors wanted to greet you before we left."

"Your dress." Brittany's mouth dropped open. "I love it."

Stella chuckled. "Finally, someone here with fashion sense. Callie'd rather go barefoot than wear heels, and Stevie mostly sticks with cotton clothing."

I huffed. "The one time I wore heels, they prevented me from fighting and getting away from Kel's wolves." I glanced at King Sutton. "And I go by Callie."

Not even listening, Brittany pointed to the Navigator. "Oh, you should see what I packed. You may want to borrow something!"

Miles stepped forward and introduced himself and the others. King Sutton reciprocated with his family, and before I knew what was happening, Jack was hurrying to the back of the Navigator.

"Let's get your luggage out so I can have my baby back." He reached for the largest piece of luggage, but when he went to pull it out, it didn't budge. He scoffed and yanked harder, causing the luggage to hit the driveway. "Holy shit. What the hell is in this? A dead body?"

I remembered the smirk King Sutton had worn when he was walking out of the airport. I'd thought it was menacing, but Brittany had called after him. He must have been messing with her, making her pull her own luggage.

King Sutton pinched the bridge of his nose. "You don't want to know."

"I have shoes, jewelry, clothes, perfume, and all my make-up." Brittany straightened her shoulders. "I brought only the necessities."

"Here, I can take it." King Sutton chuckled and grabbed the luggage from Jack.

Edward retrieved his carry-on, but King Sutton froze, and his eyes glowed. He reached out, touching the car to steady himself.

Something was wrong.

CHAPTER TWENTY-SEVEN

THE PART of me that knew better than to hope came back to the forefront. The past seventeen years had taught me not to latch on to that dangerous emotion, but since meeting Bodey, I'd started to believe it had to get better.

Fate might hate me, but dammit, I refused to allow her to take my mate away.

"Are you okay?" Bodey asked, placing his hand on the center of my back.

King Sutton lifted his head, a frown on his face. "One more man in my inner circle passed away. The witches couldn't heal him. They suspect the wolf scratch he sustained had something extra in it because it kept fighting their magic. Now eleven of the fifteen members of my personal guard have died, and if I'd listened to my gut instead of trying to appease *her*, they might be alive."

He felt guilty, a sentiment I completely understood. Trusting Lynerd would haunt me for the rest of my life. "Hey, didn't you say if you aren't making mistakes, you aren't doing it right?" I asked, tossing the words he had spoken about an hour ago back at him.

The corners of his mouth tipped upward into a sad smile. "Those sound like wise words, but sometimes, they're hard to hear."

"I won't even attempt to argue with that." When you were responsible for thousands of lives, any miscalculation could hurt the very ones you were supposed to protect. I'd let at least two thousand of my people down by choosing Lynerd to take the spot of royal advisor instead of handing it to Theo. I'd been so afraid of Zeke's influence over Theo that I hadn't considered what Lynerd might do to get even with me for my parents' choices to place Zeke in the position of the royal alpha.

Bodey intertwined our fingers and said, "I'm going to call Dina. She might have some insight into what could've prevented the witch's magic from healing the shifters."

"Is anyone else affected by their injuries from Kel's wolves?" Even though I was all for getting Dina's help, she'd had a rough day, and it was late. If no one else was in danger, it might be better to call her in the morning.

King Sutton rubbed his hands together. "No. The only wolf that was struggling with healing was Tony, and he just died. The other pack members healed like usual."

Samuel stepped out of the garage. "It has to be magic since it impacted only the wolves at your mansion. I wonder if she disguised her intention to kill you as a warning."

I hadn't thought of that. Any of the royal family could have been killed by a mere scratch, depending on how the spell worked. King Sutton had mentioned on the phone that Edward had almost been injured.

"Don't act like it was just me at risk." Edward pointed at his father. "You were right beside me. For all we know, they could've been going for you."

"Thank gods Tony was there to protect you both. I only

wish he hadn't died." Brittany's hands shook as she grasped her mate's arm, and her bottom lip trembled.

They needed time to mourn. King Sutton had called me right after the attack, and then they'd rushed here.

I squeezed Bodey's hand. "It's been a long twenty-four hours for everyone. We should all get some rest, and we can have breakfast together in the morning and strategize."

Bodey linked to me and the royal advisors, *In the meantime, I'll call Dina and see what she and the coven might know about the spell and what Kel could've done to make her wolves' claws deadly.*

Running a hand down his face, King Sutton hung his head. "That's an excellent idea. It's even later for us with the time difference, and by the morning, my men should have numbers to report back so we can plan and get moving."

"I'll help you cook breakfast in the morning," Stevie offered as she came over and kissed my cheek. *I'll get here around seven.*

Bless her. I was never one for cooking, and Janet and Bodey had spoiled me by doing most of it here.

"Please." Jack snorted. "Like Callie will be doing the work. Bodey will be down there slaving away while he lets her get more shut-eye."

"Wait." Brittany blinked. "You don't have staff to handle that?"

My brows lifted. "You do?" I'd thought Edward was being sarcastic when he'd said they had a butler. The idea of having people wait on me had never crossed my mind, but now that I thought about it, I did remember some staff in my parents' house.

"That all changed when King Richard and Queen Mila died." Bodey pressed his lips together. "When Samuel came to live with us, he took care of himself the same as the rest of us."

"Either way, we'll all have breakfast in the morning." Stella winked and took Miles's hand. "Good night, everyone. Let us know if you need us for anything. Otherwise, we'll see you in the morning."

Lucas, Miles, Stevie, Jack, and Stella headed off while Samuel lingered.

Do you want me to put extra wolves on the perimeter? he linked, his irises darkening. *I'd hate for something to happen.*

Though I trusted King Sutton, there was no harm in having more wolves on the lookout for Kel and her shenanigans. *Good idea. Kel will want to confirm what happened to the witches.*

Cold dread swirled through our bond as Bodey's hand tightened. He linked, *The coven will know that their witches died, but you're right. Eventually, they may try to determine what happened.*

I hated how everything was stacked against us. *When you reach out to Dina, let's ask if the coven will make sure the woods are spelled more thoroughly. We don't need any surprises.*

While you talk with the witches, I'll work on assigning more wolves to the watch tonight. Samuel bowed his head to King Sutton and started to leave for Michael and Janet's.

My heart ached. He was now the royal advisor of Idaho and alpha of this pack, and he didn't have his own home. I hadn't thought about it until this moment—when we'd displaced him for King Sutton. Yet another thing Bodey and I needed to fix when things with Kel settled down.

Samuel, please don't go on watch tonight. Even though Samuel and I hadn't been raised together, we had several things in common, one being that we didn't like to ask others to do something we weren't willing to do ourselves. *When we head out to the fight tomorrow, I would like you to come with us, which means I'll need you rested.*

He stopped and smiled, his irises lightening to a milky brown. *Of course. I'll make sure to keep some of our strongest back too, since we'll want to take them with us.* He hugged me then continued around the front of the house.

"That's a pleasant surprise," King Sutton murmured when Samuel was far enough away that he wouldn't hear the low words.

Unsure what he meant, I turned my attention to him. "What?"

"You and your brother." King Sutton picked up the heavy luggage. "I feared there would be animosity between you two, but your relationship doesn't seem strained at all—either that or you two are very good at pretending."

"Oh." That was a fair assessment, and I could tell by the way the three of them were studying me that they were curious. I shrugged. "He didn't want to rule. It's been an adjustment since he expected to have this role, but he's now a royal advisor and the alpha of Idaho. It works well, and Bodey and I listen to his opinions."

Edward yawned.

"Let's get some rest." I smiled, knowing we were all tired.

Bodey took a few steps toward King Sutton and offered, "I can help you get that bag into the house."

"It's heavy, but I'm used to it." King Sutton chuckled while Edward snagged the carry-on and wheeled it through our garage.

The five of us headed inside, and within a few minutes, they were situated in their rooms, and we were getting ready for bed.

As soon as I was in my pajamas, I crawled into bed while

Bodey called Dina. A few minutes later, my mate slipped in beside me and pulled me into his arms. Listening to Bodey's breathing and steady heartbeat, I soon drifted off to sleep.

WE HAD A FULL HOUSE. The former advisors, their mates, the royal advisors, Stella, Stevie, King Sutton, Edward, Queen Consort Brittany, Dina, Chelsea, Bodey, and I were at my and Bodey's house eating breakfast.

Janet, Stevie, Taylor, and Destiny had arrived at seven and taken over the kitchen, not allowing Bodey and me anywhere near the stove. For a moment, I'd worried they wouldn't let me get a cup of coffee, but Stevie had handed me one right away. She knew me well enough to know that if I didn't get my morning cup, things would get scary.

We placed two additional chairs at the table so fourteen of us could sit in the kitchen while Janet, Taylor, Destiny, and Alicia sat at the island. Stella, Stevie, and Brittany sat on the back deck, enjoying the fresh air while those of us at the table were deep in conversation.

Bodey and I sat crammed together at the end of the table nearest the wall, and King Sutton sat on my left side.

The king took a bite of his eggs and swallowed. "My men watched the guards around Kel's property all night. There was a guard outside each exit at the queen's mansion, with one additional man at each corner of her house, for a total of ten guards. There is a separate garage a few feet away, which four guards surround."

"That gets us to fourteen." Samuel, who sat directly across from me, placed his fork on his plate. "What about guards running the perimeter?"

Edward popped a piece of biscuit into his mouth from his

spot between his dad and Jack. "Twenty-five ran the perimeter the entire night, even during shift change."

At least it was a consistent number. If it had been random, that would have made things harder for us.

"How many do they think are inside?" Miles tapped a finger along the table.

King Sutton shrugged. "It's a guess, but there were five guards that swapped from inside the house, so we're assuming just five. They switched out at the same time as the others for a shift change."

"That sounds like a fair guess," Lucas said, standing between Samuel and Miles.

After taking a sip of coffee, Michael set his cup down and stared at Bodey. "It sounds like we should expect forty-four."

"We should say fifty to be safe." Dan chewed a piece of bacon as he leaned back in his chair across from his son.

Phil snarled, his arms brushing Carl and Dan. "If she thinks she's so invincible, why does she even need guards?"

"It's all about appearances." My throat ached, the few bites of breakfast I'd eaten heavy in my stomach. "A queen needs protection, and she wants to ensure no one questions her claim to the title." I hated that I was beginning to understand her.

Chelsea sat taller, the white priestess dress looking different on her, especially with Dina on the other side of her, dressed in black.

"Were there any signs of witches?" Chelsea held a cup of tea in both hands.

King Sutton winced. "We didn't send any witches with them, but they saw five women working in a garden in the backyard. They wore dresses similar to yours."

"From what I remember, Kel's royal coven consists of twenty witches." Dina held her head high, but her dull-looking skin made her appear like a different person. "I'd estimate at least twenty there with her, just to be safe."

"Seventy is what we need to account for." Bodey nodded. "Fifty shifters and twenty witches. We should bring at least double."

That sounded reasonable, but what did I know? I'd never planned a war before. We were done allowing Kel to bring the battles to us—we were bringing the whole damn war to her doorstep.

"Not trying to be negative here"—Jack lifted a hand—"because, really, that's Lucas's job, but how certain are we about these numbers?"

Carl tipped his head toward his son. "Jack's right."

"I know." Jack leaned forward, glaring at Lucas. "Lucas always smacks me or complains about my observations. I think he feels inferior to my dashing good looks and boyish charm. If I had to guess, his obsession and jealousy of me began twenty-four years ago on April eighteenth. It was a dark and stormy night until a woman went into labor and the rain rolled away."

"Oh my gods." Lucas rolled his eyes. "Are you really trying to make your birth sound as if it was a miracle?"

Jack pointed at him and rasped, "See? Right there. All that negativity. To be fair, *Lucas*, my mom said the day I was born, the whole world became brighter."

"Man, my mom says the same thing." Edward snorted. "That's what moms do."

Head snapping toward Edward, Jack scowled. "Unlike your mom, mine means it."

"Is this normal?" King Sutton tilted his head, smiling faintly. "We were having a serious conversation."

"I'm sorry." Carl rubbed his temples. "Jack is special, and what I meant—which I now regret saying—is that Jack was right about knowing numbers. Not Lucas being negative. How did your wolves get so close without alerting the queen?"

"Good question." King Sutton wiped his mouth with a napkin. "A drone. Russell had just gotten home when the attacks occurred, so he was able to grab the drone and come to California to help fight. He's been honing his drone skills for the day this situation arose. We invested in an expensive drone that can do this sort of surveying for us. The queen lives far enough away from Los Angeles that flights aren't a problem."

Maybe that was something we needed to do more heartily —embrace technology.

"Where are we gonna get a hundred shifters and forty witches?" The longer we waited to attack, the greater the chance the queen would strike at us again. And fast.

"I can bring another twenty from my area," King Sutton offered and placed his napkin on his lap. "That would provide almost half the shifters, and I could ask some of the witches from the larger pack's coven to join them."

Though more of his men would help, they were over a day away, and he'd already brought twenty of his wolf shifters here. I rubbed a finger along the rim of my coffee cup. "We should use wolves from our territory. They can get there faster. If we move quickly, maybe we can beat Kel's wolves that are returning from attacking you."

Samuel's face tensed. "We'd have to move now."

"I can send forty from Wyoming." Miles pushed his plate away. "My wolves will take about the same amount of time as us to get there, and I can ask for twenty of our witches to join them."

"Uh... I can offer some Washington wolves, but it'll take

them longer to get here." Jack scowled. "And Lucas will have the same problem I do."

My attention landed on Samuel, and I linked to him and Bodey, *Could Idaho make up the rest?* I hated to ask, but that made the most sense.

Samuel pursed his lips. *Do you think your uncle would bring half?*

I had seen Bodey's uncle, Reggie, only in passing, at the coronation dinner, but I remembered Queen Kel attacking him when I'd first stayed here.

He will. Most definitely, Bodey replied.

"I'll bring the other forty wolves." Samuel tapped his knuckles on the table.

My attention homed in on Dina and Chelsea. "Could you two come, along with eighteen others?"

"I should stay here." Dina averted her gaze to the table. "Ever since—"

"No, I need you there." Chelsea reached over and took Dina's hand. "For your guidance. I'm not ready to do this alone. Please."

Chelsea asking for help made me feel more confident. The worst thing you could have was a new leader who refused help from their predecessor.

"Well, okay." Dina stood. "But I can't do much besides offer counsel on which spells to use."

"That's exactly what I need." Chelsea exhaled like the pressure of the world had vanished from her shoulders.

We had a plan. I glanced around the table, knowing that we needed to hurry. "Everyone, get your weapons and coordinate the packs, and let's head out within the hour. If we leave now, we can attack tonight."

Everyone stood, breakfast forgotten. We had a long drive ahead of us and an even longer night.

"Wait." Dina lifted a hand. "We need to tell you what we and the Chicago coven figured out last night about what happened." Her eyes narrowed. "It's one more thing to prepare for with Kel and her tactics. She's using a resource we didn't anticipate."

My heart stopped. Once again, Kel had surprised us, and I feared whatever the hell she was using now.

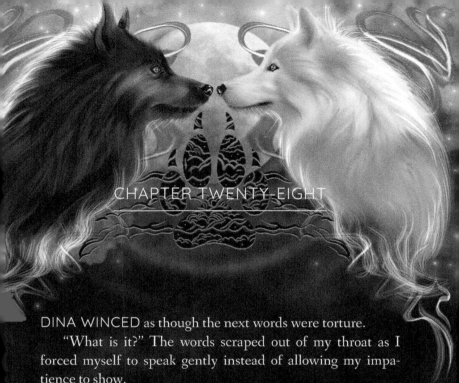

CHAPTER TWENTY-EIGHT

DINA WINCED as though the next words were torture.

"What is it?" The words scraped out of my throat as I forced myself to speak gently instead of allowing my impatience to show.

Dina turned to Chelsea and nodded.

"Oh. Right." Chelsea straightened her shoulders. "We're pretty sure the wolves had the witches coat the tips of their claws in nightshade, which is what killed the shifter."

Bodey's anger swirled into me, heating my blood. He growled, "Of course. Why not add poison to her ever-growing list of ways to harm others? The bitch wouldn't know a fair fight if it slapped her in the face."

"How the hell did they think to use that?" King Sutton rubbed his forehead.

"Witches." Dina frowned. "This coven has no trouble ignoring the whole *do no harm to others* promise. But why would they still help after losing so many of their coven members?"

The room descended into tension-filled silence, every one of us absorbing the news.

We were wasting time.

Time we didn't have.

A delay would only afford Kel more opportunities to think of creative ways to fuck us over.

"This doesn't change anything." I kept my breathing even. Showing my rage wouldn't do any good, and I needed to save my energy for later. "We'll need to be more careful when we attack, and hopefully, they won't have time to take preventive measures since we should be the ones catching her off guard."

Bodey's jaw clenched, and cold tendrils of his fear squashed his anger and turned my blood to ice. He linked, *Is there any way I can convince you to—*

Don't finish that sentence. I didn't want to argue with him even though I understood his concern. *If we're going to war, I need to be there with my people. How would you like it if I asked you to stay behind?* A selfish part of me hoped he would say that he'd stay if I asked. He was the one who'd been captured and beaten.

His silence spoke volumes and confirmed what I already knew.

He wouldn't.

"How did you figure out it was nightshade?" King Sutton clenched his hands at his sides. "And why wasn't my coven able to determine that?"

"We figured it out together." Dina lifted both hands as if in surrender. "They were focused on healing a normal shifter wound, which doesn't have herbs involved. As we discussed the wolf's struggle right before death, we were able to determine the cause." She nodded to Chelsea.

"Right." Chelsea bit her bottom lip. "Fortunately, our coven has an antidote for nightshade on hand."

Michael's brows lifted. "We do?"

She nodded. "We have the manchineel fruit preserved

just in case someone ever tries to poison our king and queen. We've never used it before, and we have several doses that we can take with us. We'll still need to be careful, though. We don't have enough for everyone."

Some of the tension eased from my body. I should've known Dina would have something like this in place. She was thorough, and that was one reason I was so thankful to have her on our side.

"If they use nightshade, they might also have an antidote in case of accidents." Samuel tugged down his cotton shirt, pulling it over the waistband of his jeans. It was strange to see him dressed so casually. "If it comes down to it, we'll force them to give us theirs."

"Agreed," Lucas said as he patted Samuel on the back.

Janet strolled into the dining room. "You all prep for war, and the rest of us can clean up."

After kissing his mate's forehead, Michael strode from the room with everyone behind him.

The time had come, and there was no point delaying anymore.

An hour after breakfast, we were ready to go. There were two points of contention with our plan—having the former advisors stay here with the pack and Theo, Charles, and Jasmine joining us.

Bodey didn't want Jasmine along. He also wasn't thrilled about Theo and Charles, but they were strong wolves, and they'd joined our pack. We needed as many capable hands as possible, and though I didn't trust Charles, I knew Theo would keep him in line, especially with Jasmine there.

Jasmine held firm and told us if we didn't bring her with

us, she'd find her own way there. Bodey and I believed her threat, and I'd seen her fight. She wasn't trained, but she was on par with me, which counted for something. Besides, given the way Theo and Jasmine looked at each other, there was no doubt they were fated mates, and I knew Theo had visited with Michael to talk about his future with Jasmine and making things right.

Secondly, the former advisors had been adamant about going with us, but Bodey and I had decided on another strategy.

If things went wrong, we needed the former advisors here to take control and protect the pack. Their magic was waning, so even though they were extremely strong wolves, it made sense for them to remain behind in case of an attack. We couldn't leave our packs vulnerable. Jack, Miles, and Lucas had strong betas who were still at home to protect their states, so their locations weren't as much at risk.

With that, the eleven witches of the royal coven and eleven shifters total—including the royal advisors, King Sutton, Edward, Theo, Jasmine, Charles, Bodey, and me— were on our way to Kel's mansion.

Bodey demanded Theo and Jasmine ride with us in his Jeep, which had finally been fixed after being damaged during our fight to leave the coronation dinner. For the entire ride to California, Bodey shot daggers at Theo any time he got too close to Jasmine.

King Sutton and Edward rode with Jack, Lucas, and Miles in the Navigator while Samuel drove Michael's SUV with Charles, Dina, Chelsea, and two other witches. The other seven witches had split up between two of their cars.

Thirty minutes from the houses Russell had rented for himself and the nineteen others, I reached over and squeezed Bodey's hand. It was approaching two in the morning, and he'd driven ten of the eighteen hours with Jasmine, Theo, and me taking driving shifts so we could take naps.

Butterflies took flight in my stomach. Miles's pack had arrived a few minutes before us, and as soon as we reached the houses, we would leave for Kel's estate. We'd be about twenty minutes from her house and planned to walk through the woods to reach it.

I won't let anything happen to you, Bodey vowed as he stroked his thumb along my hand. *You have nothing to fear.*

I turned my head toward him and frowned. *If you think I'm worried about myself, you're wrong.* The closer we got to our destination, the more my nerves frayed. I tapped my foot against the floorboard, needing to expel energy. Between bouts of increasing fear and uncertainty, Bodey's capture replayed in my head. I relived the torture of being apart from him, unable to do anything to help him while he endured beating after beating. Kel had vowed there would be a repeat, but this time, she'd do so much worse.

The edges of my vision darkened. *I can't lose you like that again.* A sob built in my chest. I would have begged him to stay behind if I hadn't known how that would make him feel weak and unworthy.

Babe, we're in this together. He glanced at me. *We stay beside each other. No matter what this time. Theo will be tied to my sister, and they've made their intentions known.*

They love each other. I tried to comfort him, thankful for the distraction. *That's a good thing. Remember what happened when people tried to get between us?*

I don't like you comparing what we have to them. Bodey scowled. *She deserves better than that jackass.*

I mashed my lips together. *What's your real issue with Theo? Is it that he was pressured by his dad into pursuing me?*

He snarled, his irises glowing. *That prick tried to keep us apart.*

That was Zeke's doing, and Theo had a rough childhood. I didn't want Bodey to think I wasn't on his side, but he was letting his grudge impact his sister's relationship. Bodey's main issue with Theo revolved around me. *He and I were friends for a long time. He tried to protect me from Zeke, but Zeke just made my punishments harsher. And Zeke was always hard on him, never happy with the way he did things. It came off like he thought Theo was incompetent.* Which had been Zeke's goal. If Zeke made it seem like Theo couldn't handle the responsibilities, he had no reason to hand off the pack and advisor position to him.

I don't like where this conversation is going. Bodey's displeasure flowed between us. *He's trying to take Jasmine from us, and you're on their side.*

I tried not to smile. He was being silly, but I wouldn't share that observation with him. Unlike a lot of men, I knew better than to tell someone who was upset to calm down. The last thing I wanted to do was gaslight him. His feelings were valid. *Actually, I'm taking your side because I know you. If you give your sister grief about being with her fated mate, you'll regret it. I was just giving you the backstory to explain why I'm no longer upset with Theo. He was as much of a victim as me for all those years, and we're trying to move beyond that. Do you realize how hard it must have been for him to come to us and ask to be part of our pack, knowing how much you dislike him?*

A bit of regret took the sting out of his reaction. *You can't just let me go on disliking him?*

There was the man I knew. He was protective as hell of me and those he loved, but he was a genuine person who wanted his sister to be happy. *I could, but then I wouldn't be a good mate to you.*

His expression softened, and his hand relaxed on the steering wheel, allowing his white knuckles to turn back to olive. *You think those two are fated mates, really?* He glanced in the rearview mirror.

I didn't have to look over my shoulder to know what I'd find. Theo'd had his arm around Jasmine earlier, ignoring Bodey's death glare, while Jasmine had cuddled into his shoulder and fallen asleep in his arms.

Do you really think they aren't? Ever since they'd met, Jasmine had been at Theo's side constantly. She'd been staying with him, Pearl, and Mom and getting my sister in line.

No. That's one reason why I've been so grumpy. He rolled his eyes. *He's an ass.*

I've become a better person with you by my side. I leaned over the center console and kissed his cheek. His faint scruff scratched my lips, and I damn near moaned. *I think she's doing the same for him. He'll get there. I have no doubt your sister will make sure it happens.*

He chuckled. *I'll give you that. She won't settle for anything less than what she deserves. And I guess I better give him a chance.*

I'm not saying don't make him earn it. We all had to be accountable for our mistakes. *But keep an open mind, and don't be biased.*

Only for her, and because you asked me to. That's how much I love you.

I didn't doubt it one bit. *And I love you even more.* And now I wanted to let him stew on everything we'd discussed.

I leaned forward and turned on the music, flipping

through the stations until I landed on "Wolves" by Selena Gomez, letting the words speak to us both.

NOT AN HOUR LATER, the former advisors, Russell, King Sutton, Edward, Theo, Jasmine, Dina, Chelsea, Bodey, and I, were standing in front of the two houses that Russell had rented.

Forty of the wolf shifters would stay in human form, including everyone in our immediate group. Russell handed each of us two rifles, a belt with two holders, and a dagger. We needed a way to protect ourselves, and a decent chunk of us needed to head indoors to find Kel. She wouldn't leave her secure position to join the fight.

As he handed King Sutton his weapons, Russell flinched. He didn't like his king being here, but I had to give it to King Sutton and Edward. They'd insisted on coming, which made me like them even more.

"Your Majesty, maybe you and Edward should stay here." Russell hung on to the dagger a little longer while King Sutton put on the belt. "You two haven't trained like the rest of us."

"I have a strong wolf." King Sutton fastened the belt. "I'll be fine. Besides, I know how to fire a weapon."

"I want to see that bitch when we take her down." Edward pumped his dagger in the air.

King Sutton glowered at his son while Jack cackled. "Fuck yeah. We'll both be there."

Even though I loved their enthusiasm, I took no pleasure in what was about to happen. Lives would be lost on both sides, and that would be a tragedy.

"We'll stay in the front with the shifters leading the way." Chelsea glanced at the sky, a thin, whimsical cloud hiding half the moon. "If we sense magic, we'll need to take the spell down before anyone passes through it."

That was the thing: none of the shifters had gotten close to the house due to the range of the drone.

It was nearing three in the morning, and we needed to move before dawn came too close. Russell had found two sizable cabins in the mountains, and with the cool air in March, no humans should be out.

I glanced around at the one hundred of us standing outside. Miles's men were next to Bodey's uncle Reggie's, and the Midwest wolves had gathered together. The witches were different, all of them mingling and talking as if they'd known each other for years. From what I had remembered, the witches got together annually, so they probably knew each other well.

"We need to take cover in the woods." Bodey took my hand, urging me forward. "If someone does stumble upon us, we'll look strange like this."

"Especially with all the guns and daggers," Samuel added, gesturing to our weapons.

"I'll lead with nine of the men who came with us," Russell said. "And our last ten will stay in the back."

Chelsea nodded. "Some witches will too, in case they attack from the rear."

She was now doing the talking, taking charge, and leading them instead of Dina.

The four advisors flanked Bodey and me. Part of me wanted to protest, but I swallowed it down. They wanted to make sure their king and queen remained unharmed, and I couldn't blame them, but I'd be prepared to attack when the time came.

Samuel stood next to me with Miles beside him, near the

edge of his pack, while Jack and Lucas took Bodey's other side.

Where do you want us? Reggie linked to Bodey and me as we spread out to begin our attack.

Stay in the center near Jasmine, please. Bodey hadn't shot Theo any more looks, but that didn't mean he fully trusted Theo yet. Trust had to be earned.

I'll watch her with my life, Reggie vowed, his sincerity palpable even without a bond.

Following Russell's men, our group headed out. Chelsea and Dina were front and center with the ten shifters, Russell at Dina's side. Dina kept her chin high and moved forward. I was grateful she'd come. Even without magic, she was an incredible resource for our side.

The Jeffrey pines didn't give us much coverage, but as we moved deeper into the woods, firs began filling in the gaps, keeping us hidden from view. The terrain was different from back home, the ground drier and desertlike instead of wet mulch, but our group powered on.

Two miles from Kel's estate, Dina let out a loud gasp and rammed into Russell, causing him to fall back into Jack.

"What the fuck?" Jack rasped, but Dina lifted a hand as she squatted close to where Russell had almost stepped.

Chelsea's eyes widened. "Is that what I think it is?"

CHAPTER TWENTY-NINE

I STARED at the spot of dirt between two sizable firs, but no matter how many times I blinked, I didn't see anything threatening.

"Their perimeter spell is intermittent." Dina shook her head, standing tall. "It's so subtle that it's barely noticeable."

Chelsea rubbed her arms. "I sensed a hint of magic, but I assumed it was because the coven comes out here periodically to practice their craft. How in the moon goddess did you sense it?"

Shrugging, Dina stood, holding the hem of her dress so it wouldn't hit the spell. "I... I don't know. It was as if the magic called to me."

"Thank gods it did." I moved so I could place a hand on her shoulder. "Or we'd have lost the element of surprise." Not that we'd get much farther without alerting the guards on the perimeter run or the witches. Our time in stealth mode was running out.

"Whoa." Jack raised his hands. "Are you telling me the witches created a minefield of perimeter magic?"

Dina bobbed her head. "That's a good metaphor. They've

spelled compact areas, hoping intruders will step through one and alert them without knowing it."

"That's badass." Jack flinched. "And I hate that I said that, but damn, that's sick."

Man, sometimes it's best not to say anything, Lucas linked with Miles, Jack, Bodey, and me.

There's that negativity I've been talking about. Jack snorted.

Not wanting to hear them bicker, I cleared my throat. Samuel was lucky that Lucas couldn't pull him into the connection. My brother hadn't forged the same unique pack link bond the other advisors had, so he couldn't be linked in.

"Dina, if you can sense the magic, you should take the lead." Two days ago, I never would've had to make that comment, but she'd been taking a back seat since losing her magic. I wasn't sure if it was a confidence issue or if she was trying not to step on Chelsea's toes. Either way, I felt the need to make the request to ensure it happened.

"Of course." She bowed her head slightly and stepped around the spelled area. "Everyone, follow me. We're getting too close for me to speak aloud, so if I point in a direction, form a tight line and follow my steps. The closer we get, the less spread out the magic will probably be."

No one said anything to counter her instruction, so she moved forward. She turned her head from side to side and raised her hands, searching for magic, but she didn't say anything.

My heart pounded. We wouldn't know when we inadvertently alerted them to our presence. I stepped closer to Bodey, using the jolt that came each time our arms brushed to steady myself.

Bodey pushed comfort into me, not saying a word. Even

mind-linking could distract us, and we couldn't lose focus on our surroundings.

The trees remained thick, and the sounds of raccoons and deer were comforting. I could almost pretend we were on a run, but the looming threat pulsed like a beacon.

Every fifty yards or so, Dina changed directions, and we all followed suit. The pattern was random, but her shifts became more frequent the closer we got to Kel's mansion.

Dina stopped, lifting a hand. She glanced over her shoulder at Chelsea, who nodded. Then the two of them turned to us, shaking their heads and spreading their arms out.

Bodey sighed beside me as his dread floated into me. *I'm assuming the whole perimeter is spelled.*

As if Fate wanted to give us the middle finger, the sound of wolf paws hitting the ground on the other side filtered through.

My breath caught. That had to be Kel's perimeter guards.

We were here. They'd know any minute, either by us walking through the perimeter or by them picking up our scent if they got close enough. The wind was blowing toward Kel's mansion, so our scent could hit them at any second.

Remember, we stay close together, Bodey linked and placed an arm around my waist, pulling me to his side.

I closed my eyes and focused on his touch. A lump formed in my throat. I hadn't allowed myself to think much about this moment, and I almost fell to my knees from the grief that damn near overwhelmed me. One thought kept circling inside my brain: This could be the last time we touched.

Bodey pulled Theo into our link and said, *I'm counting on you to take care of my sister. If that's not your plan, I need to know now.*

There's no one more important to me than her, Theo replied without hesitation. *She promised to stay by my side.*

My chest expanded. Bodey had listened to me in the car. Asking Theo to protect his sister was a huge step for him. He was giving Theo a chance to prove he was worthy, and I couldn't have been more proud of him.

I leaned my head on Bodey's shoulder, feeling the faint sizzle even through his shirt.

Jasmine tugged Bodey and me into a link, saying, *Callie, I'm counting on you to keep an eye on my brother.*

Bodey inhaled, and the rush of air into his lungs vibrated my ear.

I swallowed a snicker. He didn't like his sister asking me to protect him. I knew, without a doubt, he had every intention of making sure that if one of us got injured, it would be him, not me. But that went both ways.

I'll make sure I do that, I promised, causing his eyes to dip toward me.

He leaned down, his scruff tickling my face as he kissed my lips.

The padding of paws stopped, followed by an eerie silence.

They'd found us. I turned around. The sixty shifters in animal form all had their hackles raised.

A wolf howled on the enemy's side, the sound of battle roaring in my ears.

"Attack," King Sutton commanded to Russell and the other nine men in front, who were only a few feet back from the witches. He gave the order so everyone on both sides would know what was going on. "We have no time to lose."

He was right. We had to reach the house and eliminate Kel before backup arrived.

As I moved, the guns hit my hips. I tried not to focus on the firearms and tapped into my wolf, concentrating on the noises and scents in front of me. The enemy wolves raced toward us, and from what Russell and the others had observed, there would be only twenty.

There were more than enough of us.

As I tried to calm my breathing so I could hear over the pounding of my heart, the first wolf raced from between a fir and a pine. The moonlight glinted off his silver eyes, making him look even more menacing.

He launched at Russell, homing in on the man he thought was the bigger threat as five more wolves charged through the area outside of us. Russell removed his dagger from its sheath seconds before the wolf was on top of him.

Our wolves hurried forward, moving quicker than those of us in human form. Reggie launched an attack, sinking his teeth into the neck of our enemy. The scent of copper hit my nose. Within a minute, the fight had become bloody.

Come on, Bodey linked, taking my hand.

The nine front witches, King Sutton, Edward, the royal advisors, Bodey, and I, split from the fight and rushed toward the house as planned. We'd stay in human form so we could get inside and kill Kel.

I moved toward the back of the group, trying to keep an eye on the people behind us. Our group of nineteen moved steadily but slower than normal, needing to make sure we didn't go too fast for the witches.

With every step we took, the scent of enemy wolves picked up. Tapping into my hearing, I detected three sets of steps following our group and getting louder. They were in wolf form, so I stopped and turned to face the direction they were coming from.

I'd removed my dagger when Bodey appeared at my side. His eyes glowed as he removed his firearm. *You were going to fight without me.*

Stab. Not fight. The wolves had to be planning something.

We have incoming, Bodey linked with the royal advisors. *Three wolves heading this way.*

The wolves spread apart, the three sounds coming from different directions.

I'll stay with you, and we can catch up with the others after we've handled them, Miles replied as his footsteps slowed and he headed back to us.

The wolves were already on us.

A wolf leaped at me from the thick brush, her large green eyes wide as she opened her mouth, aiming for my neck.

I swung the knife, but she jerked her head back and countered the move. Her body slammed into mine, and I crashed onto my back with her on top.

Bodey turned as the other two wolves charged from his side and attacked him.

The wolf lurched for my neck again. I dropped the knife and gripped her throat, using all my strength to keep her jaws from reaching me. She jerked her head, trying to slash at my upper arms, but that gave me time to curl my legs underneath her and push her up. I kicked toward my head, flipping her wolf body behind me. She landed on her back.

I jumped to my feet and spun around to see the darker enemy wolf bite into Bodey's shoulder.

Miles appeared, his attention on me.

Help Bodey, I linked. *I can handle her.*

He nodded as the female enemy rolled over. Not wanting to give her time to collect herself, I kicked her in the side, and she crumpled.

My dagger had landed several feet away, and I searched for something closer to use as a silent weapon. The female enemy swiped at my leg and slashed through my jeans, cutting into my skin. I gritted my teeth at the sting, annoyed that I'd let her get the shot in, then bent down, grabbed a rock, and smashed it into her head.

The sickening crunch sent acid inching up my throat. I dropped the rock, not wanting to look at what I'd done. I had to survive, but I wondered if she'd been following Kel willingly or if she'd been forced into this position.

I spun in time to see Bodey slit the throat of one wolf while Miles gutted the other. With all three down, my vision blurred. I hated fighting and death, but we hadn't chosen this.

Kel had taken this path.

Come on, Bodey linked, placing my dagger back into my hand and taking my other hand in his. *We need to catch up.*

Your shoulder. I reached out to look at it, noting the blood coating his sleeve.

I'll heal. We need to focus. He cupped my cheek and kissed my lips.

Miles appeared beside me. *Let's hurry before they get into trouble. Or we do.*

He was right. We were separated from everyone else.

Tapping into my wolf, I took off, following the scent of our friends. A breeze picked up as we raced through the woods, the sounds of fighting echoing around us. We soon caught up with our group since they'd been running slower for the witches, and we settled back into a rhythm with them.

We were getting worried, Samuel linked. *Jack and Lucas were about to turn around.*

We're fine, I assured him, not wanting to talk long. *We dealt with the three wolves chasing us.*

Something cold tingled down my spine, and I turned to the right. The edge of a black dress caught my attention before it vanished behind a huge fir.

Someone was watching us.

A witch— I started, but then the ground underneath my

feet began to shake. I stumbled, and my teeth rattled. Pain shot up my jaw as I tried to find steady ground.

"The magic is coming from there," Dina exclaimed and gestured toward the hidden witch.

The ground cracked, and my legs parted on either side of the split.

Chelsea hurried over, lifting her hands. "Make the witch fall to her knees." A gust of wind shot from Chelsea toward the witch, but something burned my right hand, which was holding the dagger.

The throbbing pain stole my breath as the ground quaked underneath me. The urge to drop the dagger was strong, but I gritted my teeth and forced myself not to give in. I moved to one side as the crack split further.

"There!" Dina shouted to a middle-aged witch on her left. "There's another one using magic on Callie!"

I stumbled away, desperate to stop the pain. No matter where I moved, the flames followed me despite the darkness surrounding us, but soon, I found a large tree to jump behind. For a moment, I thought the fire was still hitting me, but when I glanced down, that wasn't the case.

Bodey raced to me. He took my hand and grimaced. *Babe, this is a bad burn.*

Blisters were forming. *I'm fine.* I had to be. We hadn't even reached the house, and I was already injured. Maybe coming here had been a bad idea, but it was too late to rethink the plan. Besides, this was better than doing nothing.

"More witches are coming!" Dina exclaimed from her spot.

I wanted to ask for numbers, but that wouldn't matter. I linked with the royal advisors and Bodey, *Let the witches fight their kind while we sneak toward the house.*

It wasn't like we wolves had a chance against the witches

when they were fresh and topped off with their magic. The one person we needed to reach while we were at full health was the queen, and we couldn't do that while hiding behind trees.

They seem to be arriving from the east, Samuel linked.

Bodey frowned, staring at my hand, but he interjected, *Chelsea is using her magic. More witches will sense the attack and come here. Let's move before we get caught up in the mix.*

I pushed off the tree, running to the right, away from the witches. I hated to leave our coven there, but they were strong, and I trusted their abilities.

Dammit, Callie, Bodey complained, but I didn't slow down and soon heard the royal advisors, Bodey, Edward, and King Sutton, following me.

The eight of us sprinted away from the witches, but another pair of footsteps sounded behind us. Unsure who would be following us now, I darted left and stopped in some thick brush between two trees, Bodey and the others right on my trail.

What are you doing? Bodey asked as he settled in beside me.

Seeing who's following us.

The eight of us were breathing heavily, waiting for whoever it was to stumble into view.

I took a gun in my uninjured hand and lifted the weapon, pointing it toward where the enemy would come. I kept my other hand clutched to my side, the pain intensifying.

My wolf surged forward, helping me focus and protect my friends and family.

Dark-auburn hair peeked from behind a tree, and I put my finger on the trigger. Waiting for the enemy to step out, I got ready to squeeze. Then the person came into view.

Unable to stop in time, I fired the gun to the left. The

sound rang through the trees for anyone close by to hear, but I managed not to shoot Dina.

She yelped, her hands clutching her mouth, and I stepped from my hiding spot.

I rasped, "What are you doing?" My hands were shaking, the reality of what I'd almost done rushing through my head.

"I'm sorry." Dina exhaled shakily. "I saw you all run off, and I followed. The witches are fighting Kel's, and I can't help them, but I might be able to help you not fall into any magical traps."

"Next time, maybe call out to us," Bodey muttered, rubbing my back.

We need to get going, Miles linked. *With that shot, more wolves are bound to come here, if not witches too.*

Bodey took the lead, and I kept pace close behind him. We moved slower so Dina didn't get left behind again, and I kept my ears peeled.

How's everything? I linked with Reggie and our pack members.

We're managing. We're about to head your way, Reggie answered.

That was good news.

A familiar scent hit my nose, and I stopped dead in my tracks. *Lynerd is near,* I linked with everyone here.

As if he could hear our pack link, Lynerd stepped out of the trees fifty yards away. Twenty shifters in wolf form appeared behind him, all of them glaring at me.

I felt stupid all over again. I'd given him the power to screw us over, and here he was with a huge smirk on his face, gloating as he took us in. The one silver lining was that none of the Oregon wolf shifters were with him. I didn't have to fight them and potentially kill wolves that had been forced to defect.

"I thought you might sneak up on us." Lynerd crossed his arms, his eyes hard. "It's what I'd do."

Bodey lifted his gun. "Clearly, you aren't as smart as you think you are. I'm the one aiming a gun at you."

Something wasn't adding up.

Lynerd grinned bigger, and his eyes flicked toward a tree between us. I followed his stare, tapping into my wolf, and saw a woman in the tree with a rifle, likely aiming at my mate.

Then the woman fired.

CHAPTER THIRTY

THE WORLD MOVED in slow motion, and my wolf howled as I launched into action. I crashed into Bodey. As we went down, a sharp sting pierced the back of my shoulder.

I'd been shot.

Bodey's panic flooded through me, his intensity dulling the pain.

Gunfire from our group went off behind me, and Bodey rolled me over, his body covering mine.

Dammit, Callie, he whimpered as he tried to cover every inch of my body. *That was meant for me, not you.*

Snarls sounded as yet another fight broke out, but between my chest constricting in fear and Bodey, who lay on top of me, oxygen couldn't fill my lungs.

I need you to move, I grunted, trying to push him off me.

He didn't budge. *No way in hell are you taking another bullet. You're staying right where you are.*

Pain sliced through Bodey, strangling me as more weight pressed on my body as if a wolf was standing on top of my mate. Bodey tensed, and he groaned faintly, but he remained

Bodey! A scream strangled me, but I couldn't release it since my lungs were empty.

I'm fine, he replied, but his agony rolled through me.

He wouldn't fight until the woman with the gun was killed. That wasn't how this worked. I wouldn't allow him to die protecting me... not like this.

We got the bitch in the tree, Jack linked as the scent of blood thickened around me, no doubt Bodey's.

Tapping into my wolf, I pulled strength from her and slid my legs out from under his body. I rolled to the side, forcing Bodey off me gently while removing my dagger from the sheath with my injured, throbbing hand.

A light-gray wolf tumbled off Bodey's back to the ground, and I pushed through my pain and sank the blade into the enemy's side.

The wolf whimpered, swatting at where the weapon protruded from her body, as three more wolves charged toward Bodey and me.

Bodey grunted and stood slowly, the agony of his wounds mixing with mine. I attempted to stand, but my head spun, followed by a burning sting of discomfort shooting from my shoulder where the bullet had hit. It didn't hurt as much as the burns on my hand, but it was distracting.

Maybe my body had been denied oxygen underneath Bodey.

As I pulled out a gun, two of the three wolves lunged at me. With their speed, I couldn't aim, and Lucas and Samuel were in the same direction, fighting two more wolves.

I couldn't risk shooting and hurting someone I loved.

Three wolves are racing our way, I linked with Bodey, noticing the blood soaking the back of his shirt along with three deep slashes from the enemy wolf's claws.

My heart lurched into my throat. He'd been scratched,

and so had I. What if they'd laced their claws with night-shade? But there was no time to find out. More urgently than before, we had to keep going. All I could hope for was that, since they hadn't been expecting us, they hadn't had time to take those precautions.

The darker enemy wolf charged my left side, coming between Bodey and me, while the other attacked my right side. The white wolf aimed for Bodey.

The two wolves moved in tandem, and I rolled my legs left, timing my attack so my feet hit one wolf in the chest while I hit the other wolf on the side of the head with the butt of my gun. The wolf at my feet flew back several feet, but I missed the mark on the lighter-gray wolf on my right side. I hit her neck instead of the side of her head.

Her teeth clamped down a few inches in front of my shoulder. The impact had her stumbling a few steps away, giving me a minute to get my thoughts right.

The enemy wolf hadn't gone for the kill, meaning the wolves knew who I was. There was no other reason that they wouldn't try to kill me unless Kel wanted me alive.

Bodey snarled as he fought on my left, but I couldn't take my eyes off my target to check on him or anyone else. My saving grace was that the pain hadn't intensified on Bodey's end, which meant he hadn't gotten injured again.

The lighter enemy wolf's eyes widened as she bared her teeth and countered, heading back toward me.

Her gaze had flicked to the darker wolf, proving they were timing their strikes together when the hairs on the back of my neck rose. I turned my head quickly. A third wolf was sneaking up behind me.

I was their target, and I'd bet more wolves were trying to break away and attack me.

Knowing I had to do something quickly, I grabbed one

gun with my right hand, the intense burning pain throbbing, and shot at the wolf sneaking up behind me. None of my people or allies were back there, so I fired without hesitation.

The bullet lodged between the shifter's eyes. I hadn't practiced shooting often, but I wouldn't complain about hitting my target.

Callie, I'm coming, Bodey replied.

He'd mistaken my surprise for something worse. *I'm fine. Focus on your own fight.*

Something clamped down on my hiking boot and started dragging me a few feet off the ground. I swung my arms, careful not to fire the rifle, just as the lighter wolf swiped at my side.

I turned to my left, her nails missing me by millimeters. Then I swung my arm back to the right, aimed my gun at her chest, and pulled the trigger.

A shrill whimper strangled out of her as she hunkered down, but I'd missed her heart by a good several inches. I'd managed to hit her shoulder, which was more in line with what I expected of myself.

At my feet, the darker wolf shook its head like it was trying to kill my boot or take it off. It growled, reminding me of a puppy with a stuffed animal, but this was not cute. This was my foot, and I was damn lucky he hadn't pierced through the shoe.

With my free foot, I kicked the darker wolf in the snout, and a dark-beige wolf bounded toward me. The dark wolf jerked back, releasing the boot and dodging my second blow at his nose.

Something had to give. We hadn't even made it to Kel's mansion, and Bodey and I were already injured.

More wolves are coming, Reggie linked. *Behind us.*

I tensed. Reinforcements were here. We should've known

Kel was paranoid as fuck. *Do you need us?* I sure hoped they didn't, but I refused to let my people and King Sutton's be slaughtered.

We're fine, Reggie replied. *Just wanted to let you know to watch your back.*

Another time, his choice of words might have been funny, but not with the dark-beige wolf breathing down my neck.

Holstering my gun, I tried to remove the dagger from the sheath again, but I wasn't as quick with my injured hand. The beige wolf was on me, literally. Her claws dug into my shoulders, and I whimpered.

A gunshot went off, and the wolf landed hard on my chest. For a second, I was confused until blood poured from the back of her neck and dripped all over me, soaking my black shirt. I gagged. Not being in wolf form during fights like this was hard to stomach.

Pushing the wolf off, I stood and took in the damage. Edward's shirt was torn, and blood dripped down his jeans. King Sutton was fighting off a charcoal enemy wolf with his dagger. It looked like he had a bite on his forearm. The four royal advisors had a few scratches, but they hadn't taken the brunt of torture like Bodey, King Sutton, Edward, and I had.

Dina had a dagger in her hand, and blood dripped from the end of the blade onto the dead wolf at her feet. Surprisingly, she had no wounds.

Most important, there was no sign of Lynerd.

The bastard had run off.

Bodey rushed over and scanned me as the four royal advisors helped King Sutton kill the last wolf.

Baby, you're hurt. He grimaced. *We need to get one of the witches to heal you.*

My lips tipped up. *Says the man with huge slashes on his back.* I examined his wounds. The bleeding was slowing down due to his shifter healing. If he'd been human, he'd have been in danger.

I blew out a breath. No nightshade. Thank gods.

"Did the bullet lodge in her back?" Dina asked, wiping her blade on her dress before sticking it back in its sheath.

Bodey examined my shoulder. His hand touched the bullet wound, which still stung but was nothing compared to the deep throb in my hand.

He exhaled. "It just grazed her. The wound's not that deep."

"Good." Dina came over and took a look herself. "That would've been bad."

"That bastard ran off like a fucking coward." Lucas's nose wrinkled. "I'm going to beat his face into a bloody pulp before killing him. That's what he'll get for turning on us."

Not only was Lynerd personal for me, but he was for Lucas too, since they'd fought just after Lynerd had betrayed us.

"Was that the man?" King Sutton placed a hand over his wound, putting pressure on it. "The one who informed Kel that my people aided you?"

"The one and only." Samuel rolled his eyes.

When Dina dropped her hands from my shoulder, Bodey cleared his throat. "Reggie informed us that more wolves arrived, coming in from behind them. Her guards must reside in another place close by, so we need to hurry."

I didn't want to force anyone who was injured to fight. "If anyone wants to head back or hide and heal, that's an option too. Everyone here has already done more than enough."

"We aren't pussies." Jack patted his chest. "There's no way I'm not kicking more Southwest wolf ass."

"Man, calling people pussies is sexist. Those things give birth to babies, which is the opposite of being weak or scared."

Lucas puffed out his chest. "The right saying is we aren't chickens."

Miles shook his head. "Now is not the time for this."

I had to agree. "If everyone is good moving forward, let's go." I waved my left hand, then put all my weapons back in their places and cradled my right hand. The agony had improved marginally, but the pain was still damn near debilitating.

Bodey moved beside me, the area around his eyes strained. The two of us marched forward, the others following close behind.

I tapped into my wolf to heighten my senses. I heard scurrying not too far ahead, along with the sound of doors shutting. We were close to the mansion.

Finally.

I dreaded the next part. We didn't know the layout of her house, which meant we were going in blind. The drones hadn't been able to get close enough to get an idea of the setup inside without alerting Kel's guards.

The nine of us moved efficiently. To Dina's credit, she kept up.

The woods opened up, revealing a small garden.

Bodey stopped, lifting his hand, and pointed to the left, where the mansion peeked through the thinning trees. *Let's head straight there.*

Dina shook her head and pointed at the garden. She murmured, barely louder than a breath, "That's all herbs, so it likely belongs to the coven. I can see an aloe plant, which would help your wounds. I'll get some while you all scope out the house."

The garden was fifty feet away, but there was no one close by. All sounds of movement indicated that people were outside the house or heading toward the wolves we'd left behind.

Why weren't any wolves looking for us here?

"Hurry," Bodey muttered. *We need to watch for a minute to see if we can figure out who's here.*

I moved to the edge of the tree line and hunkered down behind some brush. Queen Kel's mansion was huge and gorgeous, fronted by a rolling green lawn and a pond with stones around it. The pale-yellow house was two stories high, with a deck that spanned the entire top floor and stairs that led to a cement pathway to the pond. What was most interesting was that there was an attached garage as well as another garage separated from the house.

Every light was on, and several men ran past the top-level windows toward the left side of the house, right above the attached garage.

That had to be where the queen's bedroom was.

Six people stood in front of the house, confirming the counts from Russell and his men.

The backup guards are arriving, Bodey linked with the royal advisors and me as he squatted next to me, his arm brushing mine.

The contact was exactly what I needed. The jolt of our connection eased some of the pain and anxiety swirling within me.

That's good. Miles crouched beside me. *As long as we move before more wolves get here.*

How are things going back there? Miles linked with Bodey, me, and his men, who were in the woods with the other sixty wolves.

Some wolves have split off and are heading your way, a woman replied, confirming what we already knew.

Kel would make sure she was heavily guarded.

"What's the plan?" King Sutton muttered as the others came and sat behind us.

I hated that we couldn't pack link. We had to ensure we were all in agreement. "We pick off the guards one by one." I removed the firearm from my side. "We're hidden. They aren't. We stay here and fire until we're forced to come out."

Dina appeared again, her face twisted with concern. She broke off the tip of an aloe plant and applied it to us one by one, but her attention kept going to the unattached garage.

"What's wrong?" I asked.

"There's something strange about that building. I can't put my finger on it." She finished with my hand, the aloe soothing the throbbing. I hadn't expected it to make such a difference.

"We'll check it out after we detain Kel." I trusted Dina. If she said something strange was going on in there, it was.

The sound of more wolves approaching made the decision for us.

We had to move.

Everyone removed their firearms, and we spread out in the brush. We all lifted our guns as Dina wiped her hands on her dress. I tried not to cringe, thinking about the blood she'd wiped off her dagger.

We all took aim, and I fired the first shot. My bullet hit the ground a few inches from a guard, who snapped his head up and stared at where we were hiding. "Over there!" he yelled. "Someone is there."

All eight of us fired.

Four of the men went down, and the wolves behind us drew closer. We wouldn't make it out of here before they were on top of us.

The guards ran to the corners of the house, taking cover. Soon, we were firing at one another. They had the advantage and just needed to hold us off long enough for their backup to attack.

This would have been a good time for the witches to arrive, but Dina couldn't check in with them like we could with the other wolves.

Our two sides continued to fire at one another, with the wolves breathing down our necks.

We had to do something and fast, or we'd lose our lives for nothing.

"The magic coming from the garage," Dina said. "It's getting stronger. I've got to go."

"What do you mean?" I turned to her in time to see her sprint out from behind the brush.

My heart clenched. "Dina!" I yelled, but she kept running toward the garage, not paying attention to the gunfire all around her.

"What the hell!" Bodey growled. "Cover her."

There was no way in hell I was letting her reach the garage all by herself.

The men continued shooting, keeping the guards behind their shield, and I stood and ran after Dina. I didn't have a death wish like she did. It was as if she was drawn to the magic and not thinking.

Callie, Bodey linked. *Wait!*

I slowed down but didn't stop, my focus on Dina as she locked on the garage.

Within a minute, Bodey was at my side, and we tapped into our wolves as we raced to reach Dina.

The distance narrowed as we got close to the side of the garage. Then a bullet hit Dina in the leg.

"Dina!" I screamed, pushing myself to run faster. We were running out of the tree cover.

She stumbled but caught her balance and kept up her

pace. A few steps later, she reached the side door to the garage. A guard who had taken cover at the side of the garage jumped out and attacked Dina head-on.

My wolf howled as Bodey and I raced toward them, the gunfire picking up as our people held the guards off. This guard had his hands around Dina's throat. When we reached him, Bodey removed his dagger and stabbed the guard in the back.

The man stumbled away, eyes wide as he took us in, but Dina was already back in action. She gasped for breath as she placed her hands on the door. Blood leaked out of the guard's mouth, and he fell backward.

When Dina's hands touched the door, they glowed like when she'd performed magic. Her breathing turned ragged as the glow brightened and her arms began to shake.

I had no idea what was happening. She'd lost her magic. Whatever *this* was couldn't be normal.

Dina threw back her head and screamed, the sound of pain slicing through us.

"Dina," I said, unsure what to do. I reached out to touch her, but Bodey pushed my hand down.

You can't risk it. Bodey's jaw twitched. *She isn't using magic. This is painful for her.*

The glowing stopped, and Dina slumped against the door, which opened. Bodey caught her as she collapsed.

When I looked inside the open doorway, the sight and stench froze me.

This was a hell I'd never imagined, and again, Kel had proved she was one sick bitch.

CHAPTER THIRTY-ONE

THE SMELL of piss and feces hit my nose, and vomit lodged in my throat. It burned like hell, but I swallowed, not wanting to add to the horrendous stench.

The garage had cement walls, and two barred cells stood across from us with a solid wall between them. One was vacant, but the other one held someone. A figure crouched in the corner, hiding its face. The only evidence that it was human was the clothes I could see and the lack of hair on the arms.

Bodey gasped and gagged. "This is where they held me."

The cells' floors were covered in straw, but it was soiled and, from what I could tell, had been for a while.

White-hot rage boiled in my veins. *This* was where she'd kept Bodey the entire time he was away from me. I had a hard time believing Kel ever set foot in this place. *I'm going to kill her.*

Dina straightened and stepped back outside as she placed a shaky hand over her nose as if that would filter the air. "Witches spelled this place so tightly that no one could've

"Then how did you get us in?" I stepped inside, though my wolf whimpered. My eyes locked on the person in the cell, who I thought was a man. Kel wouldn't keep just anyone alive in here. He had to have a purpose, if only to use against her enemies.

"I... I don't *know*." Dina's voice shook. "I touched it, and the magic funneled into me."

What are you doing? Bodey linked as he snagged my arm, tugging me back toward him. *We need to find Kel.*

I know. I stared into his eyes. *But we can't leave without freeing this prisoner. If someone had stumbled onto you like this, I'd have wanted them to help you.*

His face softened. *Fine, but I have no fucking clue where the keys are.* He prowled across the room and stopped at the cell door.

The man's head lifted, and I froze. His long, dark, greasy hair clung to him, the frayed ends hitting past his butt. Dirt and blood coated the exposed part of his skin, which looked unnaturally pale. His beard hung past his stomach and had sticks, dirt, and blood stuck and crusted in it. There was no question he'd been here for a long time.

You didn't mention him before, I linked to Bodey.

I didn't know he was here. Most of the time in here, I was unconscious, and when they moved me, they put something over my head. He shivered. *And the stench—I couldn't smell anything but piss and shit.*

I'm so sorry you went through that. I tore my gaze from the man. The room held nothing beyond the two cells. No table, no keys hanging anywhere. It was like no one but this man was ever in this room, except for Bodey's small stint. *I was hoping there'd be an obvious way to let him out.*

It's not your fault. Bodey reached for the cell door and yanked on the bars. *Don't feel guilty for a second.*

The man inside hunkered down even more, his bottom lip quivering. "I haven't done anything. Please, don't take me to her." His voice was gravelly, like he hadn't spoken in forever.

My heart clenched. Whoever this poor man was, he had suffered for far too long. We had to get him out of there.

I studied the cell door and noticed something odd. "There's no lock." I pointed to the smooth place where there was merely a handle. "It has to be open."

"Magic," Dina rasped, the sound odd.

I spun around and saw the glazed look in her eyes. It wasn't as intense as when she'd run past the guards who were shooting at her, but there was a spark in her eyes, and her skin shimmered like when she'd had magic.

"I didn't realize that was possible, but it makes sense." Bodey pulled on the door again with all his strength. "I never saw anyone with a key, but they always knocked me out before unlocking the door."

Dina came to the door, her hands outstretched like before, and murmured, "I need to touch it."

Bodey's eyebrows lifted, and he took in Dina's expression. His forehead creased with concern.

"Are you sure?" I hated to ask her to do something that might cause her pain, even if it was for a good cause. She'd sacrificed so much for us. Hell, she'd lost a part of who she was to protect us.

She nodded eagerly like she needed another hit of a drug.

Callie, behind you, Bodey linked as he moved toward me, his eyes wide with fear.

I spun around to find a wolf already airborne, coming right at me. I'd been so preoccupied with the man in the cell and Dina that I hadn't noticed what was going on outside.

On instinct, I threw a punch with my right hand. I hit the wolf in the side of its head, and pain exploded in my hand again. The reprieve the aloe had given me disappeared, and a fresh wave of sharp, stabbing soreness stole my breath.

The wolf landed on the cement floor and swiped at my legs. I jumped, and its claws hit the rubber soles of my boots. When I landed, Bodey flashed past me and stabbed the wolf through the back of its head with his dagger.

There was no holding back the vomit now. I turned to my left and emptied my stomach. That was a death like I'd never seen before, and I was certain it would haunt me.

Something behind me clicked, and I knew the moment Bodey retrieved the dagger because the suctioning sound had my tummy roiling again.

I'm sorry, but I couldn't reach its heart or throat, he linked, his concern flowing through to me. *I should've gotten to you faster.*

He'd just saved me, and he was apologizing because I'd vomited. Add ungrateful to my ever-growing list. *You have nothing to apologize for. I should've been paying attention. Thank you for saving me.* I took a second to squeeze his hand.

The prison cell door swung open, and Bodey tucked me against his side with the hand not holding the bloody dagger.

I expected the prisoner to try to leave while he could, but instead, he remained in the corner of his cell.

Dina stared at her hands and murmured, "It's gone again."

The sounds of battle raged on outside, and our element of surprise was long gone. Kel's backup had arrived, and we were trapped in a pretend garage, trying to save a man who was still cowering in the corner of his cell. This decision wasn't my finest.

Yet again.

We've got to go, Bodey linked, tugging me toward the door. More wolves would be coming any minute.

Something inside me screamed that this man was important, especially if Kel had kept him in here for this long.

"Sir." I paused. I didn't know his name, but *Hey, you* didn't sound right. "We need to get you out of here."

Babe, I love that you want to help everyone, but we don't have time to convince someone to leave. Bodey's hands settled on my back, and he tried to guide me to the door.

I had to try one more time before abandoning the guy. "Go before Kel realizes you've been freed and locks you up again."

Something flickered in his cognac eyes, the first hint of a person within him. "Kel?" The tone held an odd mixture of emotions, and I couldn't determine how he felt about her.

"Yes, Kel. The queen of the Southwest territory." I bit my bottom lip. "She kept my mate prisoner in here, with you, several days ago."

A wolf howled outside the door, no doubt informing more of Kel's people where Bodey and I were. Time had run out.

I held out my hand. "We'd love for you to come with us. We're here to end her reign, but we have to go."

He nodded and stood to his full height. He was as tall as Bodey, which startled me.

"Yes, she must be stopped." The last word rasped from his throat, the sound torn between wolf and human as fur sprouted from his body. Dark fur coated him in seconds, and then he was on four legs. He threw his head back and bellowed a loud wolf cry. A howl didn't even come close to describing it. Then he took off out the door.

I didn't hesitate to follow. We needed to find Kel and, nearly as important, get away from the unspeakable smell.

Bodey and Dina were on my heels, and as soon as I ran out the door, I took a deep breath. Fresh air filled my lungs.

Looking around, I found that our people had caught up to

us. They were fighting everywhere, in the yard and woods, while the witches cast spell after spell. I didn't have to do a head count to know we were missing some people. They were no doubt dead, but now wasn't the time to mourn.

In here, Bodey linked, taking my hand and leading me across a concrete walk toward the main house.

Dina moved with us, and we tried to be as discreet as possible. Any second, someone could notice us.

There are fewer guards around the back of the house, Miles connected, the thread of our connection pulling to my right, in the direction he was telling us to go.

I turned and saw him step partially out of the shadows.

The three of us headed toward him. When we stepped around the back, I caught Jack's, Lucas's, and Samuel's scents moments before I saw them.

What the hell happened back there? Lucas frowned. *We were coming to you.*

The garage was actually a prison and encased in magic. If it hadn't been for Dina, we might not have searched it. Kel was too smart for her own good. That was likely why she'd made it look like a garage.

You sure took your sweet-ass time in there. Jack rolled his eyes. *It's not like we're outnumbered or anything.*

Bodey snarled and grabbed Jack by his shirt. *You don't talk to her that way. Ever. Do you understand? Friend or not, I'll fuck you up.*

What are you two doing? Samuel blinked, looking at Bodey and Jack.

He wasn't part of the conversation since he couldn't link with the other royal advisors, so he had no clue what was going on.

Do not *turn on one another,* I commanded without adding alpha will, but my wolf surged forward, ready to do my bidding. The last thing I wanted to do was alpha-will my mate, the king consort, into obeying me, especially when he was standing up for me. Cutting off his nuts would be less brutal than that, especially for a wolf. *Let's get inside the damn house.*

Cracking his neck, Bodey released Jack's shirt then pointed at his face. *One more snarky comment to my mate, and I'll kick your ass when this is over.*

Jack rolled back his shoulders but averted his eyes.

With me as his mate, Bodey was far stronger than Jack now.

They'll expect us to go up the front to the second floor. Hopefully, this will surprise them.

I glanced at the back of the house. The yard was flat, and the double-glass doors in the middle led into the living room, which had stairs in one corner. *Let's get in through there.*

Our group of seven moved, Dina hanging in the back. Samuel and Lucas were in front, and when they reached the double doors, Samuel tried to open them.

They didn't budge.

We can't get in, Lucas started, but Jack removed a firearm from his holster, slid between Lucas and Samuel, then hit the butt of the gun against the glass, shattering it.

Man, what the hell? Lucas glowered.

Jack shrugged as he slipped his hand through the broken glass and unlocked the door, then swung it open. *It's not like they don't know we're here.*

Maybe it hadn't been smart, but we were in. It wasn't like they were going to open the doors for us. *Let's go.*

We hurried into the house, the glass crunching under our feet.

Footsteps pounded down the stairs, heading our way.

Though we'd have to fight, that meant Kel would be less protected for the moment.

I hurried behind a gold-painted wooden couch, making room for everyone to come in. As Dina filed into the room, ten guards raced down the stairs.

We were again outnumbered.

Four of their gazes locked on me, their eyes glowing as they connected via their pack link. There was no telling how many were now rushing here to fight us.

I jumped over the couch, landed on a Tiffany-blue cushion, and launched myself toward the three in front of me. I sailed over the matching ottoman, kicked my feet out, and hit two of them in the chest.

Dammit, Bodey linked, his fear and frustration slamming through me.

The two guards gasped as they tumbled into the guards behind them.

My head was jerked back, and sharp pain radiated down my spine. I turned awkwardly to find that the third guard had fisted his hand in my hair. He dragged me toward him.

Bodey appeared at my side as the royal advisors launched their attacks. I gripped the hilt of my dagger, ignoring the way my hand still screamed from my injury.

I leaned toward the guard fisting my hair, sending him off balance since I wasn't fighting him anymore. Bodey punched him in the face, and his grip loosened. The guard's head snapped to the side as Bodey swiped his blade across his throat. Blood squirted from the cut, hitting Bodey in the face, but my mate didn't flinch.

An arm clenched around my waist and pulled me back against a hard chest. A guard with a mustache ran through the middle of the fighters, heading toward me with handcuffs. Kel still wanted to take me prisoner, but I'd rather die than allow that to happen.

I snapped myself forward, and the guard behind me grunted as I flipped him over my body into Mustache Guard.

Bodey fought two guards beside me while the others were engaged in their own battles. One smaller guard crept around the circle, and my wolf surged forward.

My skin tingled, and blonde fur sprouted from my body. My bones cracked, and I shifted into animal form. I hadn't meant to shift, but I embraced my animal. She was furious, and I felt more confident fighting in this skin than with the human weapons. My clothes ripped, and the belt that holstered the guns and dagger clanked to the floor.

Not hesitating, I lunged at the man who'd attacked me from behind as he clambered to his feet. I landed on his back, dug my claws into him, and thrashed the back of his neck with my teeth. He growled and fell again, and I leveraged his momentum to leap at Mustache Man, who was now aiming his weapon at me.

I landed on his chest, knocking him onto his back just as he fired. I expected pain to sear into me but felt nothing as I ripped out Mustache Man's throat. A pricking sensation inched down my spine, alerting me to the guard who was trying to sneak around me.

More guards came rushing down the stairs. At this moment, I hated each and every one of them. If Kel was using something against them to keep them in line, now would be the time to riot. Anyone who fought against us was a true enemy.

The small guard's hand shook as she raised her firearm at me. Sweat beaded on her forehead and rolled into her eyes.

I crouched, wanting her to know I wouldn't give up and cower, then charged.

Blinding pain exploded through my bond with Bodey, and my heart shattered. I stopped, not caring if the woman shot me, and turned toward my mate.

Lynerd had a knife to Bodey's neck, the tip of its blade cutting into his skin. Blood trickled down his neck. Worse, I could see why my mate was in severe pain. Blood from another wound had already soaked his entire shirt, and even the top of his jeans had turned crimson.

"Everyone stop, or the king consort dies," Lynerd rasped.

The royal advisors kept fighting, and I could only assume Bodey had told them not to stop and to protect me.

I had one choice.

Through the links, I alpha-willed, *Everyone, stop fighting now.*

Callie, no, Bodey linked, but the damage was done. The royal advisors stopped. Dina stood panting over a man she'd slain herself.

A maniacal laugh rang out from the stairs, and Kel descended.

We hadn't won. In fact, we were about to lose more than I'd ever thought possible.

CHAPTER THIRTY-TWO

KEL WORE BLACK SILK PAJAMAS, and she was barefoot as always. Even in bedroom attire, she'd done her makeup and hair to perfection.

I wondered if, when she'd learned we were here, she'd prepared herself for our arrival, applying makeup and pulling her hair into a French twist instead of fighting alongside her pack.

"Callie, it's so nice to see you again." Kel beamed as she stepped over the body of one of her guards, the heel of her foot landing in a puddle of his blood. She didn't flinch. Instead, she kept her eyes on me, leaving bloody heel prints on the wooden floor. "I must say, you did catch us by surprise, but rest assured, I have accommodations a few miles away where another fifty guards live, just in case something like this ever happened."

Here I'd thought we'd prepared strategically. I wanted to speak, but I was stuck in animal form.

"Being a paranoid psycho bitch has really paid off for you, hasn't it?" Jack sneered from my right side, his cobalt irises glowing. *What are we going to do?* he linked to Miles, Lucas, and me, leaving Bodey out.

Protect him however we need to. Bodey had suffered enough of her abuse, and after the threat she'd made, I refused to hand him over. I'd use alpha will to force them to obey me if necessary.

Rubbing a finger over her bottom lip, Kel walked toward Jack, smiling coyly. "You're handsome and young, and there's time to train you and mold you into someone worthy of my territory. Maybe I won't kill you. I do like them young and eager."

Jack flinched and gagged. "Please, stop. The thought alone is enough to make me want to die."

Man, you bring this shit onto yourself, Lucas replied from his spot on my other side. He glared at the guard he'd been fighting, and I noticed he had a stab wound in his right side. We'd all taken a beating.

You two shut up, Miles interjected, not acting at all like the calm person I was familiar with. He was in the corner of the room closest to the stairs, blood pouring from his nose. *This isn't the time to bicker among ourselves or with her.*

I lifted my wolfish head, giving the illusion of confidence, though my limbs were shaking from fear. This was my worst nightmare—Bodey being captured again... or killed.

"Ah, I must admire your attempt to be strong, but we both know I have you by your metaphorical balls," Kel said, moving closer to Bodey. She reached out a hand like she might cup his. "Or your mate's."

A deep, threatening growl vibrated my chest. She wanted to get a rise out of me, and I wasn't falling for it. But the thought of her touching him, especially in that way, had me wanting to kill her on the spot. No one but me touched my mate, and if they dared, then Kel and Lynerd would feel my wrath. Maybe not today, but eventually.

"Oh, mates." Kel rolled her eyes. "So predictable. I told you he'd be your downfall."

Baby, you need to run, Bodey linked, pushing his determination and fear into me. *Get out of here. If she gets you—*

I'm not going anywhere. And there wasn't a damn thing he could do about it. Using his tactic, I filled our bond with my determination and resolve. *Don't say anything like that ever again.*

His fear cooled my rage-hot blood slightly, but not enough to make a difference.

Lynerd's gaze kept flicking between me and the back door.

I wanted to laugh. Was he pretending he wanted me to leave, or did he actually want me to go so he could slit Bodey's throat right then and there? Either way, I wouldn't give Lynerd the pleasure.

"Kel, we can live as allies." Across the room from me, Samuel lifted his hands and winced. He took a step closer to me. The way he favored his right side told me he was injured, but I couldn't tell where. He pressed, "We don't have to be enemies."

"Enemies?" Kel snorted and flipped a hand. "In a moment, you'll all belong to *me.*"

My heart hammered against my ribs, and I huffed, shaking my head. It was probably best that I was in animal form. I was almost tempted to hand myself over, but my mate would pay the price.

Dina spoke up. "You won't get away with this."

"I already have." Kel's cold gaze swiveled to me, and her lips curved over her teeth. She pointed at me and said, "Submit to me, or your mate dies."

I had every intention of doing just that, but my wolf refused to lower our head. I flashed back to when I'd been separated from her and unable to submit to Zeke, Charles, and Trevor. I hadn't understood then, but now I knew that had been my wolf shining through.

Once again, she refused to listen to me.

If I didn't do something quickly, my mate would lose his life. I could feel that my wolf was desperate not to lose him either.

Realization hit me.

Kel wouldn't let Bodey go. She'd kill him as soon as I submitted, and my wolf knew it.

That was what I'd been missing during my time as queen. I'd relied on the judgment of human Callie more than my wolf. Maybe if I started listening to her and not fighting her, we'd make a great team.

I relaxed and allowed her to take over.

Our consciousnesses merged.

Attack on my command, I linked to the former advisors. I couldn't relay the message to Dina, but I counted on her to spring into action as soon as we made our move.

I had to pretend to consider submitting to get close enough for the attack.

Taking a deep breath, I prepared to argue with my wolf, keeping my head lowered slightly, but the merge we'd done had stopped her from fighting me, both sides now working together.

Kel laughed. "That's what I thought."

"No," Bodey growled. He tried to jerk away from Lynerd, and the blade cut deeper into his skin. More blood trickled down his neck. *Don't do this. You have to protect our people. I need you to be safe.*

You matter more. The words were simple and true, and he

felt the same way about me. I wanted to tell him that I planned to save us both, but I needed his reaction to be genuine. This plan might not work, but I couldn't hand myself over to Kel and risk the same outcome. We'd give this our best shot.

As I inched toward her, I heard pawsteps behind me. They weren't familiar, but when the stench of piss and feces filled my nostrils, I knew who it was.

I kept my focus on Kel, needing to face the biggest threat here. The prisoner had only himself, whereas Kel had an entire army.

Kel paled and blinked. For a moment, she seemed to forget about me. She rasped, "How is he out?"

Taking advantage of the disruption, I quickened my pace slightly, hoping to reach her before she redirected her attention to me.

"I... I don't know, ma'am," the tallest guard said. "We weren't alerted that he'd escaped."

"Impossible." Kel's chest heaved. "Get him now. Put him back."

The prisoner snarled, the sound full of hurt and malice.

Leave while you can. Bodey's face twisted in agony. *Please. She's distracted.*

I was three feet away, close enough to launch my attack. *Now.*

I leaped, and Kel's head snapped back toward me, but she wasn't my target. Lynerd's arm was—the very one with a hand holding the edge of a blade against my mate's throat.

A split second before my mouth would have met his arm, Lynerd released Bodey, shoving him out of the way and striking Kel in the arm. His knife lodged deep into her muscle, and she yelped as she stumbled back toward the stairs.

My mouth snapped closed, and I landed, digging my claws into the wooden floor.

The royal advisors moved in tandem, fighting the remaining guards as Bodey bent and retrieved a gun from a dead guard by his feet. He spun and aimed the gun at Lynerd and Kel just as the prisoner ran toward him.

I swerved and charged the prisoner, ignoring his pungent stench. His eyes were on Bodey, the very man I had to protect.

"Stay away from him!" Kel shouted as I jumped at the prisoner. I didn't want to kill the man, but I wouldn't sit back and let him hurt my mate.

The prisoner didn't notice me until I'd slammed into him and pushed him to the floor.

Fresh blood filled the air as the prisoner tried to heave me off him.

But he was too weak.

"You *bitch*," Kel roared. Then someone grabbed two fistfuls of fur on my back. She spat right in my ear, "Get off him. He's *my* prisoner."

That was more than okay with me. I flung myself backward, using the ground for leverage, and propelled Kel backward. I landed on top of her.

She grunted and wrapped her arms around me, blood dripping from the knife still lodged in her arm.

Using that to my advantage, I rolled onto her and put all my weight on the wound.

"*Ugh!*" she cried, and I kept rolling until I was on my feet.

"Don't move," Bodey commanded from where he remained focused on Lynerd.

I heard a scuffle and jerked my head that way as Lynerd struck Bodey. The two of them fought, and when Bodey lifted the gun again, Lynerd disarmed him.

I lurched forward, ready to save my mate, but something hit my stomach, the sting of pain all-encompassing.

"Dammit, Callie." Lynerd huffed, then aimed the gun at me and fired.

"No!" Bodey screamed, and I waited for my vision to go black.

Instead, a body dropped behind me.

Turning around, I saw Kel with a bullet wound between her eyes. She'd fallen backward again, but this time, she stared blankly at the ceiling.

The prisoner stood and threw his head back, whining as if in mourning.

I blinked, unsure what had happened. Lynerd had ripped Oregon away to follow Kel, but now he'd killed her to protect me. He'd stabbed Kel in the arm instead of killing Bodey. Something wasn't adding up.

Agony coursed through me, and in another second, Bodey was sitting beside me, his arms wrapped around me.

They've stopped fighting us, Reggie linked with Bodey and me. *They're standing around, looking confused.*

They felt the loss of their alpha.

Uh... did you take out Queen Kel? Jasmine's voice popped into a link with Bodey, Samuel, Theo, and me. *Some of her wolves just turned and ran back the way they came.*

One by one, more people checked in, saying the same thing.

With Kel no longer in charge, the wolves weren't sure what to do.

The world spun, and for a second, I thought it was from relief. Then my head became too heavy to hold up on my own. *So tired,* I linked to Bodey.

He tensed beside me, and as the edges of my vision darkened, he murmured, "Callie, hang on. I need to see your eyes."

Whispers hissed in my ears. My head pounded, and I slowly opened my eyes to find I was on a couch. I raised my head and grew dizzy, but nothing like before. I was still in wolf form.

"Hey, take it easy," Bodey said softly as he appeared beside me. The couch dipped where he sat, and he placed a hand on my head and scratched behind an ear. "You lost a lot of blood. Chelsea healed your wounds, but we want to make sure you stay comfortable and heal."

This time, I lifted my head slowly and saw Chelsea, King Sutton, Lynerd, and some man I didn't know sitting at a square kitchen table across from me.

Where are we? The last thing I remembered was Kel dying and the enemy running away. *And why is Lynerd here?*

We're in one of the two houses Russell rented. Bodey smiled and kissed the top of my head. *We came here so you could heal while the rest of us cleaned up. Callie, Lynerd joined Kel's pack to get close to her and help us take her down. He even made sure that none of the Oregon pack was on her property in case of an attack and that the enemy wolves didn't find us as we approached Kel's home. He's the one who killed her.*

I exhaled, trying to process what he'd told me.

I wasn't sure if I was ready to forgive Lynerd, and I could feel Bodey's conflict too. At least we weren't under threat this minute.

I sat up, remembering all the deaths. *I should help our people.*

Right now, it's more important that you shift and join the conversation. Theo, Reggie and the royal advisors are supervising the burials, along with some of the Southwest wolves. You're needed here to make a truce between all the territories.

Truce? My head fogged, and I shook it gently to clear it. *Why are the Southwest wolves involved?*

Because their new king is here and wants to make things right between us. Bodey nodded at the table and the stranger sitting there.

The very stranger who was staring at me with a neutral expression.

You were right to free him. He was Kel's mate and the rightful king of the Southwest. He tried to attack me only because of their mate bond, but he holds no ill will toward us. Even though he's grieving their lost connection, part of him is glad she's gone after the hell she put him through. Bodey mashed his lips together. *She drugged him one night and locked him in that prison. He's been there for the past fifteen years.*

My heart ached. What type of person could do that to their mate? Even in death, Kel still stunned me.

"Is she awake?" a male voice asked from a phone sitting in the center of the table.

"Just now." King Sutton smiled sadly at me. "She's still in wolf form."

"I'm surprised she's awake already," an older woman's voice said from the speaker. "I wouldn't be able to recover so quickly even with my royal coven's help."

I swallowed. *Who is that? And what happened to Kel's coven?*

King Henry from the Carolinas and Queen Mary from Alaska. Bodey reached down and lifted my fuchsia duffel bag. *Let me help you so you can shift into human form and be part of the discussions. King Adam needs to go back to Kel's mansion and take control of the Southwest territory, and he wants the agreement in place before he does. Dina and Chelsea are handling the witches. Kel had taken several husbands of the coven hostage, so they were forced to do their bidding. That's all getting resolved now.*

Tension left my body. *Thank gods they're being freed and the witches didn't want to fight alongside her.*

With my mate's help, we went to the bedroom next to the living room, and I shifted back. My head immediately felt clearer.

Once I was dressed, Bodey pulled me to his chest, pressing his forehead against mine.

Are you okay enough to go in there, or do you need a few more minutes? Bodey kissed my forehead, and I nuzzled into his arms.

For a moment, I focused on the electricity from our bond thrumming between us. *I'll be okay. I'm just ready to go home.*

Oh, believe me, so am I. He took my hand and led me out the door, and we sat down to discuss a treaty.

Four months later

I wiped my palms against my jeans for the thousandth time. Bodey took my hand as he drove the Jeep, a huge U-Haul trailer attached to the trailer hitch.

Everything is going to be fine. He squeezed my hand lovingly. *You took down a queen and got all the wolf territories to share resources and work together, and you're just nervous about us moving into our new house.*

I didn't do any of it alone. I arched a brow. *We involved everyone.*

Just like we are now. He tilted his head behind us, where the royal advisors followed us in Jack's and Lynerd's cars, along with Samuel, Katelin, Theo, Jasmine, Stevie, Stella, and Mom.

Pearl had decided to stay in Oxbow with Charles. Surprisingly, he'd stopped being as much of a dick, but the bridge between Pearl and me was too large to bridge.

Bodey was right. We weren't doing this alone either, but renovating my parents' mansion so Bodey and I could move back into it had my nerves on edge. All my memories of my parents had happened there, including their deaths, and I was nervous about what living there might do to me, even though the move had been entirely my idea.

Samuel had taken Bodey's house since he was now the alpha and needed to run his pack without the royals breathing down his neck—and for other packs to feel as if we favored Idaho. I wanted a fresh start, but I didn't want my parents' deaths to haunt me. Theo had brought over all the boxes I'd once seen in Zeke and Tina's house, which turned out to be full of photos of my mother. There were even several of her and me at the mansion, though the camera was focused on her. No wonder he hadn't wanted me to find them while I was in his house. There was no denying that little girl was me.

"I can't get over King Sutton's graciousness about Katelin mating with Lynerd." Bodey shook his head and frowned. "I had a hard enough time with Jasmine and Theo, but Lynerd killed several of Sutton's men."

That had been a point of contention and almost derailed the treaty. But Lynerd had explained that he hadn't meant for anyone to die. He'd allied with Kel to save us, not just his people, get insider knowledge, and get close to Kel so he could do what he'd done in the end—kill the bitch. He'd had to wait for the perfect time, but he hadn't hesitated to remind me again that I owed him.

Even I'd had a hard time forgiving him, but after time and

reflection and several talks, I'd gotten there. The royal advisors, Bodey, and I had agreed that, if not for Lynerd, Kel likely would've won.

Oregon had rejoined the Northwest Territory, and Lynerd had stepped down, giving the spot to Theo, whom we now trusted implicitly. That had made us more accepting of Lynerd as there was no risk of him splitting from us again, and not kicking him out of our territory fulfilled my debt to him.

"Fated mates are hard to keep apart." I leaned over the center console and laid my head on his shoulder. "You know that."

"I wouldn't change it for the world."

We turned onto the road that took us to the mansion, and when we drove up, the worry eased from my chest. We'd purposely changed the look, including adding a small prison half a mile from the house, which the royal coven had already spelled. Zeke was there, rotting away for life. Because of Theo, we didn't want to execute him, although once Zeke had realized Theo was one of us, he'd made it clear he had no interest in retaining a relationship with his son. Tina felt differently and stood beside her son, and she'd even formed a good relationship with Jasmine.

Is this how it looked when we were kids? Samuel linked to me. He didn't remember the mansion at all, except for what he'd seen in pictures. I had vague recollections of Dad's study, but that was mainly it. *The outside where we played and Dad's study are close to identical, but not the rest of the house. Bodey and I made the rest our own.*

That's fair. I'm just glad I'm getting to see what this place and land looked like when we were children.

I understood his curiosity, but unfortunately, some things couldn't be re-created. I replied, *Us being here together in this moment will make it feel like a home.*

We pulled up to the three-car garage to the right of the four-story brick house and climbed out of the car. The four vehicles pulled in behind us, and everyone got out.

"Holy shit." Jack whistled as he shut the driver's door of his Navigator. "No wonder you didn't want us to see it before now. I would've claimed a room, but man, that's still possible."

I rolled my eyes and gestured to the two smaller houses that flanked the main house. "That house there is for when you all visit, and the other one is for the royal coven."

"Yay!" Stevie smiled. "You built a house for us to stay in and visit."

Bodey wrapped an arm around my waist. "That was all Callie's idea. I wanted to make you assholes stay at a hotel in town, but she refused to hear of it."

"That's because she's good people." Theo winked, his own arm around Jasmine.

Rubbing his hands on his pants, Samuel kept glancing at the front door.

Jasmine bounced on her feet. "Let's go in and see the house!"

Our friends and family bounded inside, wanting to see what Bodey and I had done with our secret project—the first of many things the two of us would build together.

In that moment, I realized I'd been silly to be afraid. Yes, I'd always remember my parents, but with Bodey at my side, we would make the place our own, and it would truly become home.

And there wasn't anything I wanted more than that.

ABOUT THE AUTHOR

Jen L. Grey is a *USA Today* Bestselling Author who writes Paranormal Romance, Urban Fantasy, and Fantasy genres.

Jen lives in Tennessee with her husband, two daughters, and two miniature Australian Shepherds. Before she began writing, she was an avid reader and enjoyed being involved in the indie community. Her love for books eventually led her to writing. For more information, please visit her website and sign up for her newsletter.

Check out her future projects and book signing events at her website.

www.jenlgrey.com

ALSO BY JEN L. GREY

Twisted Fate Trilogy

Destined Mate

Eclipsed Heart

Chosen Destiny

The Marked Dragon Prince Trilogy

Ruthless Mate

Marked Dragon

Hidden Fate

Shadow City: Silver Wolf Trilogy

Broken Mate

Rising Darkness

Silver Moon

Shadow City: Royal Vampire Trilogy

Cursed Mate

Shadow Bitten

Demon Blood

Shadow City: Demon Wolf Trilogy

Ruined Mate

Shattered Curse

Fated Souls

Shadow City: Dark Angel Trilogy

Fallen Mate

Demon Marked

Dark Prince

Fatal Secrets

Shadow City: Silver Mate

Shattered Wolf

Fated Hearts

Ruthless Moon

The Wolf Born Trilogy

Hidden Mate

Blood Secrets

Awakened Magic

The Hidden King Trilogy

Dragon Mate

Dragon Heir

Dragon Queen

The Marked Wolf Trilogy

Moon Kissed

Chosen Wolf

Broken Curse

Wolf Moon Academy Trilogy

Shadow Mate

Blood Legacy

Rising Fate

The Royal Heir Trilogy

Wolves' Queen

Wolf Unleashed

Wolf's Claim

Bloodshed Academy Trilogy

Year One

Year Two

Year Three

The Half-Breed Prison Duology (Same World As Bloodshed Academy)

Hunted

Cursed

The Artifact Reaper Series

Reaper: The Beginning

Reaper of Earth

Reaper of Wings

Reaper of Flames

Reaper of Water

Stones of Amaria (Shared World)

Kingdom of Storms

Kingdom of Shadows

Printed in Great Britain
by Amazon